The Ryders: Jared, Royce and Stephanie

BARBARA DUNLOP

MILLS
BOON

Published in Great Britain 2015
by Mills & Boon, an imprint of Harlequin (UK) Limited,
Eton House, 18-24 Paradise Road, Richmond, Surrey, TW9 1SR

THE RYDERS: JARED, ROYCE AND STEPHANIE
© 2015 Harlequin Books S.A.

Seduction and the CEO, In Bed with the Wrangler and *His Convenient Virgin Bride* were first published in Great Britain by Harlequin (UK) Limited.

Seduction and the CEO © 2010 Barbara Dunlop
In Bed with the Wrangler © 2010 Barbara Dunlop
His Convenient Virgin Bride © 2010 Barbara Dunlop

ISBN: 978-0-263-25217-0
eBook ISBN: 978-1-474-00396-4

05-0615

Harlequin (UK) Limited ... papers that are natural, renewable and recyclable ... grown in sustainable forests. The logging ... legal environmental regulations ... the country ...

Printed and ... in Spain
by CPI, Bar...

Barbara Dunlop writes romantic stories while curled up in a log cabin in Canada's far north, where bears outnumber people and it snows six months of the year. Fortunately, she has a brawny husband and two teenage children to haul firewood and clear the driveway while she sips cocoa and muses about her upcoming chapters. Barbara loves to hear from readers. You can contact her through her website at www.barbaradunlop.com.

SEDUCTION AND THE CEO

BY
BARBARA DUNLOP

For my amazing husband—
cowboy, pilot and businessman

One

Journalist Brandon Langard's blunder was the talk of the bullpen at *Windy City Bizz*. The odds-on favorite for a promotion to feature writer, he'd struck out in his attempt to get an interview with Jared Ryder.

Melissa Warner and the rest of the sixth-floor magazine staff watched the fallout with morbid fascination. The managing editor's door was closed tight, but through the interior window, it was obvious Seth Strickland was shouting. His eyes snapped fire, and his face had turned a mottled purple. Brandon's head was bent and still, his shoulders hunched.

"They've already designed the cover," photographer Susan Alaric stage-whispered over the low barrier between her and Melissa's desks.

"That's because Brandon swore it was a done deal,"

said Melissa, remembering his swagger last week when he'd announced the plum assignment.

"Nothing wrong with that man's confidence," Susan returned with an eye roll. Brandon's habit of bragging, flirting and ogling the female staff had long since alienated them.

"I was sure he'd pull it off," Melissa had to admit. Brandon might be obnoxious, but he was also driven and hardworking. And like all the journalists at the *Bizz,* he knew an in-depth article on Chicago's most elusive entrepreneur and bachelor would clinch the promotion to feature writer.

That Jared Ryder had made a fortune in the Chicago real estate market fit *Windy City Bizz*'s mandate for business news. That he was the heartthrob of half the city's female population suited the magazine's new focus on circulation numbers.

Seth became even more animated, gesticulating with both arms as he rounded his cluttered desk to confront Brandon face-to-face. The occasional word filtered through the closed door. "…incompetent…unreliable…reckless…"

"Ouch." Susan cringed.

Melissa experienced a fleeting twinge of pity for Brandon. But then she remembered how he'd eavesdropped on her conversation with the Women in Business organization last month and presented the story idea as his own. She still owed him for that one. Or rather, he still owed her.

She paused on that thought.

It was true. He *did* owe her one. And maybe it was time to collect.

It would serve him right if she swooped in on this particular story. And why not? Seth clearly needed the Jared Ryder interview. And Melissa would kill for a chance at that promotion.

Through the window, Seth stopped talking. His breathing went deep, his nostrils flared, as he set his jaw in a grim line. Brandon bolted for the office door, and Melissa saw her chance. She quickly came to her feet.

Susan glanced up quizzically, assessing the determined expression on Melissa's face. She obviously came to the right conclusion.

"Do it," she begged with a grin. "Oh, *please* do it."

Melissa's heart upped its rhythm. She swallowed hard, trying not to think about the career-limiting consequences of failure. If she promised the interview and didn't deliver, she'd be in more trouble than Brandon.

Still, as Brandon yanked Seth's door open, she tamped down her fear and made her move.

Her colleagues' gazes hit her from all sides as she made a beeline for the editor's office. Some probably guessed her plan. Others would be simply shocked to see her approaching Seth before he had a chance to calm down. His tirades were legendary. They normally sent the staff scurrying for cover.

Brandon peeled off to the right, studiously avoiding eye contact with anyone.

Melissa rapped on the still-open door. "Seth?"

"What?" he barked, without looking up, rustling through a pile of papers on his cluttered desk.

She took a couple of steps into the office, clicking the door shut behind her.

His round face was flushed all the way to his receding hairline. There was a sheen of sweat above his bushy brows. His white shirt was rumpled, sleeves rolled up. And his tie was loose and dangling in two sections over his protruding belly.

"I can get you the interview," she stated outright, standing tall, her three-inch pumps giving her a slight height advantage.

"What interview?"

"The Jared Ryder interview."

"No. You can't."

"I can," she insisted, voice firm with the confidence she'd learned facing down five older brothers. "I will. What's the deadline?"

"Ryder left Chicago this morning."

"No problem. Where'd he go?"

Seth glared at her without answering.

"I can do it, Seth."

"He turned Langard down flat."

"I'm not Langard."

"You're not," Seth agreed in a tone that told her she'd never be as good as Brandon Langard. Then he picked up his phone and punched in a number.

"Give me a chance," Melissa insisted, closing the space between the door and his desk. "What can it hurt?"

"We're out of time."

"A week," said Melissa. "Give me a week."

"Is Everett available?" Seth asked into the phone.

Everett was publisher of the *Bizz,* the head honcho, the guy who approved the lead headlines and the cover copy.

"Can we at least talk about it?" she pressed.

"Nothing to talk about. Ryder ran off to Montana."

That information took Melissa by surprise. "What's Jared Ryder doing in Montana?" Surely he wasn't building a skyscraper in Butte.

"He's holed up at his ranch."

Melissa hadn't known he had a ranch. Sure, there were rumors he was once a cowboy. But there were also rumors he was once a spy.

Seth gauged her confused look and raised his bushy brows. "You didn't know he had a ranch."

She couldn't argue that one.

"It's the foundation of the entire Ryder conglomerate. How're you going to save my ass when you didn't even know he had a ranch?"

"Because I will," said Melissa with determination. Just because she didn't happen to know Jared was a cowboy didn't mean she couldn't get an interview. "I'll fly to Montana."

"He hates the press. He really hates the *Bizz.* He'll probably run you off his land with—" Seth's attention went to the telephone. "Everett?"

"I can do it," Melissa said, feeling her big chance slip away.

"I have a situation," Seth said to Everett.

"I'll get on the ranch," she pressed in an undertone,

her mind scrambling. "I'll go undercover. I *will* get you the story."

Seth's attention never left the telephone. "It's the Jared Ryder interview." He paused, face flushing deeper, while Everett obviously voiced his displeasure.

"Have I ever let you down?" Melissa went on. She hadn't. But then, she'd never tackled anything this big, either.

"Yes. I know I did," Seth said to Everett.

"Please," said Melissa, leaning forward. "I'll buy my own plane ticket."

Seth shoulders tensed. "Langard *was* the best I—"

While Everett obviously weighed in again, Melissa searched her mind for fresh arguments.

"I grew up with horses," she blurted out. Well, one horse, really. It had lived in a field, on the edge of suburbia, across the street from her new house. She'd nicknamed it Midnight. "I'll—"

Seth's glare warned her to shut up.

"—get a job on the ranch."

Seth smacked his palm over the mouthpiece. "Do you know who this is?"

She gave a small nod.

"Get out."

"But—"

"Now."

Melissa pursed her lips.

Seth's gaze glittered dark with warning as he went back to Everett. "The Cooper story can take the cover."

Melissa debated a split second longer. But bravery

was one thing, stupidity quite another. She'd pushed Seth as far as she dared.

She retreated, and Seth's voice followed her back to the bullpen. "I'll get a photographer on it right away."

Like Brandon had done only minutes before, she avoided eye contact as she made her way to her desk.

"Susan," Seth bellowed from behind her.

With a darting look of pity at Melissa, Susan rolled back her chair, came to her feet and headed for the editor's office.

Melissa dropped into her own chair and stared at the randomly bouncing colored balls of her screen saver. She could have gotten that interview. She knew she could have gotten that interview.

"It's Lorne Cooper on the cover," said Susan as she slipped back into her seat.

Melissa nodded with resignation. "The sports-gear king." There was a new megastore opening on Murdoch Street, and "Cruisin' Cooper" was sponsoring a bicycle race to celebrate.

"The article's written. All it needs is an update and some new art."

Melissa pulled herself closer to her computer screen and hit the space bar. "It was written by R. J. Holmes," she pointed out, voice laced with self-pity. R.J. was one of the newest journalists on staff, and he was beating her out for a cover.

"I guess Seth wasn't feeling charitable toward Brandon."

"Or toward me." Melissa's screen powered up on a search engine.

"What've you got ready?"

"Myers Corp. or the Briggs' merger."

Susan didn't answer.

"I know," Melissa conceded, randomly poking the *H* key. "They're even lamer than Cooper." Not that any old cover story would clinch the promotion. There was only one story that would catapult her into the feature writer's job.

She backspaced to erase the *H* and typed Jared Ryder into the search engine.

In a split second, it returned a list of options that included the home page of Ryder International, Jared's speech last month to the Chamber of Commerce, contact information for his new office tower and a link to the Ryder Ranch.

Curious, she clicked the ranch link.

A brilliant green panorama of trees, meadows and rolling hills appeared in front of her. The sky was crackling turquoise, while a ribbon of pale blue meandered through the meadow, nearly kissing a two-story, red-roofed house surrounded by pens and outbuildings.

So that was what Montana looked like.

A row of thumbnail pictures lined the bottom of the screen. "Natural beauty," advertised one caption. "Surrounded by wilderness," read another. "South of Glacier National Park."

Susan shut down her own computer, rising to sling three cameras over her shoulder. "Gotta get to work."

"Have fun," Melissa offered, clicking on a thumbnail

of summer wildflowers. Red, purple, yellow, white. They really were quite gorgeous.

Susan grinned as she pushed a drawer shut with her hip. "I will. Headshots today. Then there's a gala Friday night, and I'm going to hitch a ride on the channel-ten chopper for the bike race Sunday."

"Shut up," Melissa griped as Susan rounded the end of the desk.

Melissa would be sitting right here all week long, in the stuffy, hot office, combing through the minutes of various City Hall committees, looking for permits or variances or financial-policy news, anything that might lead to an interesting business story.

"What's that?" asked Susan, nodding to the computer screen.

Melissa refocused on the verdant green and bright flowers. "Montana," she answered. "Where *I'd* be if Seth had half a heart." *Or half a brain.*

She clicked on an area map. There was an airport in Missoula and everything.

"Not my cup of tea," said Susan, popping a jaunty plaid hat on her curly brown locks.

"Not mine, either," Melissa admitted, gathering her own straight, blond hair into a knot at the nape of her neck in an effort to let the building's weak air-conditioning waft over her hot skin. "But I'd fly there in a heartbeat to meet Jared Ryder."

"So do it," said Susan.

"Yeah, right."

"Why not?"

Melissa swiveled to face her coworker. "Because Seth turned me down flat."

Susan shrugged. "Tell him you're doing City Hall research from home. Then get on a plane."

Oh, now that seemed brilliant. "Lie to my boss and ignore his orders?"

"He'll forgive you if you get the story." Susan's lips curved in a conspiratorial grin. "Trust me."

Melissa let the hair slip out of her hand. The idea was preposterous.

Susan leaned in and lowered her voice. "If you don't get the story, somebody else will."

"At least it won't be Brandon."

"Result will be the same."

"Flying to Montana could get me fired," Melissa pointed out.

"It could also get you promoted." Susan straightened.

"Easy for you to say."

Susan shrugged the cameras into a more comfortable position, then adjusted her cap. "Up to you. But no risk, no reward. My biggest payday was when those vandals let the lions loose at Lincoln Park."

"That was insane," Melissa reminded her. Susan had been clinging to the branches of an oak tree with a hungry male lion pacing below when the animal-control officer had darted the thing.

Another shrug.

"Are you suggesting that if I don't put myself in mortal danger, I'm not trying hard enough?"

Susan patted Melissa's shoulder. "I'm suggesting if

you don't torpedo Brandon and go after that promotion, you're not trying hard enough."

Point made, Susan winked and sauntered away, while Melissa drummed her fingertips on the desktop.

She glanced at the pictures of the Montana ranch. Then her gaze shifted to the spacious window cubicle reserved for the new feature writer.

She pictured Seth's expression when she presented the article. She pictured Brandon's face when he learned of her coup. She pictured her byline on the cover of the *Bizz.* Then just for good measure, she pictured herself at the podium, accepting a Prentice award next January. She could wear her black-and-gold-layered gown, with the teardrop medallion she'd found last week in that funky little art gallery on Second.

Take *that,* Brandon Langard.

Her life would be perfect. All she had to do was talk her way onto the Ryder Ranch.

Body loose in the saddle, Jared Ryder held his horse Tango to a slow walk across the wooden bridge that led to his sister Stephanie's place. Her jumping-horse outfit was built on Ryder land up on the Bonaparte Plateau, about ten miles into the hills from the main spread at Spirit Lake. Tango's ears twitched and his body tensed as he took in the nearly hundred head of horses grazing in the fields and milling about in the pens clustered around the main riding arena.

Jared was feeling just as twitchy as his horse. Far from the haven he'd always known, the familiar sights and sounds of Montana brought a crush of memories. And a fresh surge of anger roiled in his belly.

His instinct had been to stay far away from the ranch this week. But his sister, Stephanie, needed him. Besides, Chicago had its own problems at the moment.

Ryder International had just signed a long-term lease to rent space to the City of Chicago in the Ryder office tower that was under construction on Washington Street. For some reason, the mayor had insisted on parading Jared from charity ball to art gallery opening. Jared had been out in public so often that the tabloids started to believe there was a reason to take his picture and stuff a microphone in his face.

It was beyond frustrating. He was a businessman, not a politician or a celebrity. And his personal life was none of their damn business. The reporter from *Windy City Bizz* camping out at the end of his driveway Monday night was the last straw. When he got back to the city, he was looking into restraining orders and disguises.

But for the moment he had no choice but to come to terms with the home front. He cleared the main equestrian barn, and a cluster of people on horseback at the riding arena came into view. His appearance caught their attention. One horse and rider immediately broke free from the group, trotting down the dirt road to meet him. Both Jared and Tango tracked the pair's progress past the pens, dotted outbuildings and sparse trees.

"The prodigal returns," sang his twenty-two-year-old sister, Stephanie, pulling her mare to a halt, raising a cloud of dust in the July sunshine. Her smiling, freckle-flecked face peeked out from her riding helmet. Her long legs were clad in tight jodhpurs and high, glossy brown boots, while a loose, tan blouse ballooned around her small frame. Her unruly auburn hair was tied back in a ponytail.

"I think you're confusing me with Royce," said Jared, watching her closely. She might not know what he knew, but they'd all been shaken by their grandfather's death three months ago.

He halted Tango, who eyed the mare with suspicion.

"At least Royce makes it to my competitions," Stephanie pointed out, shifting in her stirrups. "He was there to watch me win last week at Spruce Meadows."

"That's because he lives on his jet plane," Jared defended. His brother, Royce, routinely flew from New York to London, Rome and points east, checking out companies to add to the Ryder International empire. Royce was mobile.

"I live in a boardroom," Jared finished.

"Poor baby," Stephanie teased. She smiled, but Jared caught the veiled sadness in her silver-blue eyes. Stephanie had been only two when their parents died, and Gramps was the closest thing to a parent she'd known.

"Congratulations," he told her softly, reflexively tamping down his own anger to focus on her needs. He'd been fifteen when they lost their parents, and he liked to think he'd had a hand in raising her, too. He was immensely proud of her accomplishments as both a rider and a trainer.

"Thanks." She leaned forward to pat Rosie-Jo, her

champion gray Hanoverian, briskly on the neck, but not before Jared caught the telltale sheen in her eyes. "Want to see our trophy?"

"Of course," he answered. There would be plenty of time later to talk about their grandfather.

"We've got a few hours before the meeting." She drew a brave breath and squared her shoulders, shaking off the sadness as she turned the horse to draw alongside Jared.

Together they headed toward her two-story blue-gabled ranch house.

The annual meeting of the Genevieve Memorial Fund, a charitable trust named in memory of their mother, would take place today. Each year, it was scheduled to coincide with the anniversary of their parents' deaths. Picturing his parents, Jared felt his anger percolating once more. But he had to suck it up, be a man about it. There was absolutely no point in disillusioning his younger brother and sister.

"I saw *you* in the Chicago paper last week," Stephanie chimed in as they left the river behind them.

"That was a picture of the mayor," Jared corrected. He'd done his best to duck behind the burly man.

"They named you in the caption."

"Slow news day," he told her, remembering the flashbulbs outside the gallery and how the reporters had shouted inane questions as he'd helped Nadine into the limo.

Stephanie's expression turned calculating, her tone curious. "So who was she?"

"Who was who?" he asked, pretending he didn't

know exactly where his baby sister was headed. Raised in a male-dominated household, she'd been lobbying for *somebody* to please marry a nice woman since she was seven years old.

"The bombshell in the picture with you."

"She was my date," he offered, letting the statement dangle without elaboration.

Stephanie pasted him with a look of impatience. "And?"

He forced her to wait a beat longer. "And her name is Nadine Romsey. Sorry to disappoint you, but she's not a bombshell. She's a lawyer with Comcoe Newsome."

Stephanie's interest grew. "Looks *and* brains. This must be something serious."

"It was a business arrangement. The mayor invited me to the party, and there were people attending that Nadine wanted to meet."

Stephanie pouted. "But she's so pretty."

"And you're so hopelessly romantic."

"Will you take her out again?"

"Only if she needs to get into another party." He admired Nadine, but he didn't have any romantic interest in her.

Stephanie compressed her lips in frustration. "You've written her off after one date? You know, you're never going to meet a woman if you don't get out there and—"

"I'm 'out there' 24/7, little sister." He gestured around the spread. "That's what pays for all of this."

Stephanie pointed her nose in the air. "Ryder

Equestrian Center brought in a million dollars last year."

Jared snorted a laugh. "While you spent four million."

"We also provided dozens of marketing opportunities for the firm, and we improved your corporate image. That is priceless."

"You rehearsed that, didn't you?"

"You should get married, Jared."

"Aren't you a little old to be angling for a mother figure?"

"I'm looking for a sister now. You should find someone young and fun. Who likes horses," she added for good measure, kicking her mare into a faster walk.

Jared shook his head. Between the revelation his grandfather had spoken on his deathbed, the mayor and the media, and Ryder International's accountant's concerns that the company was expanding too fast, Jared didn't have a scrap of emotional or intellectual energy left over for romance.

As he followed Stephanie past the open door of a stable, a sudden tingle spread up his spine. He turned sharply and locked gazes with a blond-haired, green-eyed beauty who stood just inside the main doorway. She was wearing blue jeans and a crisp white shirt, and she held a manure fork in both hands.

She quickly glanced away, but his radar pinged.

What was it?

He stared at her a little longer.

It was the makeup. Her makeup was subtle, but she was definitely wearing some. And he'd bet her blond highlights were from a salon, not the sunshine. Her collared shirt was pressed, and the hands that held the manure fork were soft, bare, no gloves.

"Who's that?" he asked his sister.

Stephanie turned and followed the direction of his gaze.

"Why? You think she's pretty?"

Anyone could see the woman was gorgeous. But that wasn't the point.

"I think she's a rank greenhorn," he said.

"Her name's Melissa...something. Webster, I think. You want me to introduce you?" The calculating flare was back in Stephanie's eyes.

"Stop," Jared ordered.

His sister grinned unrepentantly.

"What I want you to do," he continued with ex-aggerated patience, "is to hire experienced staff. We're blowing enough money on this place as it is."

"She needed a job," said Stephanie. "She's from Indiana."

He wasn't sure what the hell Indiana had to do with anything. While he watched, the woman awkwardly scooped a pile of horse manure from the wooden floor and dumped it into a wheelbarrow. "If she needed a million dollars, would you give it to her?"

"She didn't ask for a million dollars. She's on her way to Seattle. She needed money for bus fare."

"You're hiring transients now?"

"She's mucking out our stalls, Jared, not signing the company checks."

"I'm not worried about embezzlement. I'm worried about labor cost efficiency."

He was also worried something wasn't quite right. Why would a woman that polished take a menial job for bus fare?

She could be running away from something, he supposed. Or she could be running from some*one*. Which seemed more likely. An ex-boyfriend? Someone's angry wife? It had better not be the FBI or the state troopers.

He considered her delicate profile, trying to decide if she was a criminal. She tackled the next pile of manure, her city-soft hands sliding up and down the wooden handle.

"She's going to get blisters," he voiced the thought out loud.

"You want to give her some gloves?" asked Stephanie.

"Somebody better," he conceded. Aimless wanderer or criminal on the run, if they were going to employ her, the least they could do was make sure she avoided injury.

"Hey, Melissa," Stephanie called.

The woman paused and glanced up.

"Grab some gloves out of the storeroom."

Melissa gave her hands a puzzled look.

"She hasn't a clue," said Jared, hit with an unexpected flash of pity. Maybe she was running from an angry ex. He quickly reined in his thoughts. None of his business.

"You *sure* you don't want me to introduce you?" Stephanie singsonged.

Jared turned Tango toward the house. "You going to show me your trophy or what?"

"Can't blame a girl for trying."

"Yes, I can." But Jared glanced over his shoulder one last time as they moved away. Manure fork balanced in the crook of her elbow, the woman named Melissa was wriggling her fingers into the pair of stiff leather gloves. The fork slipped and banged to the wooden floor. The sound startled a horse. The horse startled the woman. She tripped on the fork and landed with a thud on her backside.

Their gazes met once more, his amused, hers annoyed.

He turned away, but the flash of emerald stayed with him as he followed Stephanie to the hitching rail in front of the house.

Two

By the end of the day, the bruise on Melissa's left butt cheek had settled to a dull ache.

While she swept the last of the straw from the stable floor, a late-model Bentley rumbled its way to the front of the farmhouse. The glossy black exterior might be dusty, but it was still one impressive automobile. And the chauffeur who jumped out of the driver's seat was crisp in his uniform.

She moved into the oversize doorway, leaning on the end of the broom handle while she waited to see who would emerge from the backseat.

It was an older man, distinguished in a Savile Row suit. He was tall, with a head of thick silver hair. He nodded politely to the chauffeur, then headed up the stairs to the wraparound porch, where both Stephanie and Jared appeared to greet him and usher him inside.

The chauffeur shut the car door. He glanced curiously around the ranch yard before moving to open the trunk. Melissa peered at the house, but there was no way to guess what was going on inside. The man might be a friend, or perhaps he was a business associate.

Jared's sister's house seemed like an odd location for a business meeting. Unless, of course, somebody wanted to keep the meeting a secret.

Now *that* was an interesting possibility. Was there something clandestine in the works for Ryder International?

As the chauffeur had before her, Melissa glanced curiously around the yard. Several young riders were practicing jumps in the main ring, their grooms and trainers watching. A group of stable hands were loading hay into a pickup truck beside the biggest barn, and three cowboys were urging a small herd of horses across the river with a pair of border collies lending a hand. Nobody was paying the slightest bit of attention to the Bentley.

Then another vehicle appeared and pulled up to the house. This one was an SUV, larger but no less luxurious than the Bentley.

A thirtysomething man with dark glasses and curly dark hair stepped out of the driver's seat. He looked Mediterranean, and he was definitely not a chauffeur. He wore loafers, well-cut blue jeans, an open white dress shirt and a dark jacket. He also offered a polite greeting to the Bentley driver before striding up the stairs of the porch.

Melissa's journalistic curiosity all but ordered her to investigate. She leaned her broom up against the stable wall and started across the yard. She told herself she'd put in a good eight hours today. It was close to dinnertime, and the Bentley was at least vaguely in the direction of the cookhouse. She'd have a plausible excuse if anyone questioned her.

Ironically she'd been disappointed not to get a job down at the main ranch. The foreman there had all but sent her packing this morning when she'd told him she was a stranded traveler. Luckily Stephanie Ryder had been there at the time. The younger woman had taken pity on Melissa and offered her a job at the Ryder Equestrian Center. Melissa had been plotting ways to get back to the main ranch when Jared and his horse had wandered into the yard. Talk about good luck.

Now she was looking for more luck. She smiled brightly at the chauffeur, smudging her palms along the sides of her thighs, wishing she wasn't covered in dust and sweat, and was wearing something other than blue jeans and a grime-streaked shirt. She wasn't the greatest flirt in the world, but in the right party dress, she could usually hold a man's attention.

"Very nice car," she ventured in a friendly voice as she approached.

The man pushed the trunk closed and gazed critically at the Bentley. "I suppose dust is better than mud."

She guessed he was about her own age, maybe twenty-five or twenty-six. He was attractive, in a farmboyfresh kind of way, with blond hair, a straight nose and a narrow chin. He was clean-shaven, and his hair was neatly trimmed.

She slowed her steps, taking in the Montana license plate and committing the number to memory. "Did you have a long drive in?" she asked pleasantly.

"Couple of hours from Helena."

Helena. Good. That was a start. "So you work in Helena?"

"Three years now."

She stayed silent for a moment, hoping he'd elaborate on his job or the company. She scanned both his uniform and the car for a logo.

"Your first time at Ryder Ranch?" She tried another approach.

He nodded at that. "Heard about it, of course. Everybody in the state knows about the Ryders."

"I'm from Indiana," she supplied.

"Grew up south of Butte myself." He gave the dust on the car another critical gaze. "There a hose around here someplace?"

She had no idea. "I guess you meet interesting people in your job?" She struggled to keep the conversation focused on his employment.

"I do some." He glanced around the ranch yard while a horse whinnied in the distance, and a tractor engine roared to life. Unfortunately he didn't pick up the conversational thread.

But Melissa wasn't giving up, not by a long shot. She moved in a step closer, tossing back her hair, hoping it looked disheveled, instead of unruly.

Her actions caught his attention, and he glanced at the ground.

She lowered her voice as she gave him her brightest smile. "I'm a little embarrassed," she cooed. "But should I know the man you dropped off?"

The chauffeur looked back up. He didn't answer. Instead, he swallowed hard, and his neck flushed beneath the collar of his uniform.

"I only ask," she continued, tilting her head to one side, surprised it took so little to rattle him, "because I don't want…"

He worked his jaw.

She paused, waiting for him, but he didn't make a sound.

She suddenly realized his gaze wasn't fixed on her. He was focused on a spot behind her left shoulder. Her scalp prickled.

Uh-oh. She twisted her head and came face-to-face with Jared Ryder.

It was clear he was annoyed. He was also taller than she'd realized, and intimidating, with that strong chin and those deep blue eyes. He wore a fitted, Western-cut shirt and snug blue jeans. His shoulders were broad, his chest deep, and his sleeves were rolled halfway up his forearms, revealing a deep tan and obvious muscle definition.

"Don't want to what?" he asked Melissa, his tone a low rumbling challenge.

She didn't have a quick answer for that, and his deep blue gaze flicked to the silent chauffeur. "There's coffee in the cookhouse." He gave the man a nod in the appropriate direction.

The chauffeur immediately took his cue and hustled away.

Jared's tone turned to steel, the power of his irritation settling fully on Melissa. "I'd sure appreciate it if you could flirt on your own time."

"I…" What could she tell him? That she wasn't flirting? That, in fact, she was spying?

Better to go with flirting.

"I'm sorry," she told him, offering no excuses.

He gave a curt nod of acknowledgment, followed by a long assessing gaze that made her glad she was only pretending to be his employee.

"I don't know why Stephanie hired you," he finally stated.

Melissa wasn't sure how to answer that, or even if he expected an answer. The only thing she did know was that she was determined to take advantage of the opportunity to talk to him alone.

"You're Stephanie's brother?" she asked, pretending she hadn't been poring over his press coverage on the Internet.

"She tells me you grew up around horses," he countered, instead of answering the question.

"I did." Melissa nodded. Technically it was true. She gestured to the northern paddocks. "You obviously grew up around a lot of them."

"My qualifications aren't at issue."

"Stephanie seemed fine with mine." Melissa valiantly battled the nerves bubbling in her stomach. "I saw the main house yesterday. The one your grandparents built. Were you born on the Ryder Ranch?"

A muscle ticked in his left cheek. "Since you're obviously not busy with anything else, I need you to move my horse to the riverside pen. The one with the red gate."

"Sure." The brave word jumped out before she had a chance to censor it.

"Name's Tango." Jared pointed to a paddock on the other side of the driveway turnaround where a black horse pranced and bucked his way around the fence line. Its head was up, ears pointed, and it was tossing his mane proudly for the three horses in the neighboring pen.

Melissa's bravado instantly evaporated.

"You can tack him up if you like," Jared continued. "Or he's fine bareback."

Bareback? She swallowed. Not that a saddle would help.

"Melissa?"

Okay. New plan. Forget the interview, it was time for a quick exit.

"I…just…" she stammered. "I…uh…just remembered, I'm off shift."

His brows twitched upward. "We have shifts?"

"I mean…" She blinked up at him. What? *What?* What the hell did she say?

She rubbed the bruise on her left butt cheek, making a show of wincing. "My fall. Earlier. I'm a little stiff and sore."

"Too stiff to sit on a horse?" He clearly found the excuse preposterous.

"I'm also a little rusty." She attempted to look contrite and embarrassed. "I haven't ridden for a while."

He cocked his head, studying her all over again. "It's like riding a bike."

She was sure it was.

"Tack's on the third stand. Don't let him hold his breath when you cinch the saddle."

As far as she was concerned, Tango could do any old thing he pleased. She wasn't going to stop him from holding his breath. Quite frankly she'd rather chase lions around Lincoln Park.

"I really can't—"

"We fire people who can't get the job done," Jared flatly warned her.

The threat stopped Melissa cold. If she got fired, she'd be thrown off the property. She could kiss the article and her promotion goodbye. And if Seth found out she'd been here, she could probably kiss her job at the *Bizz* goodbye, too.

"I hope you won't," she said in all sincerity.

Jared searched her expression for a long moment. His voice went low, and the space between them grew smaller. "Give me one reason why I shouldn't."

"I've been working really hard," she told him without hesitation.

"Not at the moment," he pointed out.

"It's six o'clock."

"We're not nine to five on Ryder Ranch."

"I'm prepared for that."

He edged almost imperceptibly closer, revealing tiny laugh lines beside his eyes and a slight growth of beard along his tanned square jaw. "Are you?"

She ignored the tug of attraction to his rugged masculinity. "Yes."

"You'll pull your own weight?"

"I will."

"You can't depend on your looks around here."

Melissa drew back in surprise.

"If I catch you batting those big green eyes—"

"I never—"

He leaned closer still and she shut her mouth. "You mess with my cowboys, and your pretty little butt will be off the property in a heartbeat."

A rush of heat prickled her cheeks. "I have *no* intention of messing with your cowboys."

A cloud rolled over the setting sun, and a chill dampened the charged air between them.

Jared's nostrils flared, and his eyes darkened to indigo in the shifting light. He stared at her for a lengthening moment, then his head canted to one side.

How his kiss might feel bloomed unbidden in her mind. It would be light, then firm, then harder still as he pulled her body flush against his own. A flash of heat stirred her body as the wind gusted between them, forming tiny dust devils on the driveway and rustling the tall, summer grass.

The ranch hands still shouted to one another. Hooves still thudded against the packed dirt. And the diesel engines still rumbled in the distance.

"See that you don't," he finally murmured. "And move my damn horse."

"Fine," she ground out, quashing the stupid hormonal reaction. She'd move the damn horse or die trying.

Later that evening, in Stephanie's dining room, Jared struggled to put Melissa out of his mind. His sister had obviously hired the woman out of pity. Then Jared had kept her on for the same reason. He wasn't sure who'd made the bigger mistake.

"We've had thirty-five new requests for assistance this year," said Otto Durand, moving a manila file to the top of his pile. Otto had been a board member of the Genevieve Memorial Fund for fifteen years. He was also the CEO of Rutledge Agricultural Equipment and a lifelong friend of Jared and Melissa's parents.

"We do have the money," Anthony Salvatorc put in, flipping through a report. "Donations, they are up nearly twenty percent." Anthony was a distant relative, the son of Jared's mother's cousin. The cousin had met and fallen in love with Carmine Salvatore on a college trip to Naples, and their only son had held a special place in Genevieve's heart.

Stephanie replaced the empty bottle of merlot on the large oblong table as the housekeeper cleared away the last of the dinner dishes.

Although Royce was stuck in London until Saturday, the remaining four board members of the Genevieve Fund were empowered to make decisions on this year's projects.

"I like the school in West Africa," said Stephanie.

"Most of the kids in that region are from agricultural families."

"Mom would like that," Jared acknowledged, then caught Stephanie's fleeting wince. This year in particular, he knew his sister felt a hole in her life where her mother should have been.

Along with their grandfather, he and Royce had struggled to keep their mother's memory alive for her, showing videos, telling stories, displaying mementos. But there was a loneliness inside her that they couldn't seem to fill. It had always manifested itself in hard work and a driving need to succeed. Jared only had to look at the row of equestrian jumping trophies along the mantelpiece to know how hard she pushed herself.

"Yes to the West Africa school." Otto put a check mark on page three of his report. "And I think we can all agree on increasing the animal shelter contributions. Now, the South American clinic project?"

"I still think it's too dangerous," said Jared. He knew his brother, Royce, had advocated for the project after meeting a British university student who'd worked in the mountainous region. But there were too many unknowns, too many frightening stories coming out of the area.

"The rebel activity has been down in that area for six months now," Anthony put in. "And we will use a contractor with experience in the area."

"What about security?" Jared countered. It wasn't the first time the Genevieve Fund had worked in an unstable part of the world, but the other projects had a multiagency, multinational presence, and security had been provided by experts.

"We will hire our own security," said Anthony.

Jared wasn't going to be easily convinced. "For the cost of private security, we could take on two other projects."

"None that are as critical as this one," said Anthony, warming up to the debate. The two of them settled into a familiar rhythm of point counterpoint, each trying to convince Stephanie and Otto of the merits of their respective positions.

Jared acknowledged it was a worthwhile project, while Anthony acknowledged the security circumstances were less than ideal. Still, on balance, Jared felt the situation was far too dangerous, and he made that clear in no uncertain terms.

Finally Anthony threw up his hands in frustration. "I am going for some air."

Fine with Jared. It would give him a few minutes alone with Stephanie and Otto to solidify his case.

Stephanie stood to stretch, while Otto dropped his pen on the report in front of him, speaking before Jared had a chance. "Maybe we should go with Anthony and Royce on this one."

"And if somebody gets kidnapped or killed?" It was a worst-case scenario, but it was also a realistic one.

"They have signed a ceasefire," Otto said.

"Not worth the paper it's printed on. It's Sierra Benito, for goodness' sake. The political situation could turn on a dime." Jared's gaze caught Anthony's profile through the gauzy curtains.

"How many kidnappings last year?" asked Stephanie.

"Too many," replied Jared.

"Nothing since December," said Otto. "I don't want to go against you on—"

"And I'm not looking for risk-free," Jared stressed. "And I don't mind spending the extra money on security. But do we *really* want to take Royce's advice on what's dangerous and what's not?"

Neither Otto nor Stephanie had an answer for that.

In the sudden silence Jared caught another movement on the porch. But this time it wasn't Anthony's profile. It was...

"Excuse me for a moment." He rose from his chair, ignoring their looks of surprise as he crossed to the front door.

"We still have the family home in Naples," Anthony was saying to Melissa as Jared pushed open the screen door. "And I visit it as often as possible." Anthony had planted his butt against the log railing of the porch, one arm bracing him on each side while Melissa stood in front of him.

"I've always wanted to see Italy." She sighed. "The Colosseum, Vatican City, the Sistine Chapel."

Jared scoffed. Pretty big dreams for a woman who couldn't even make it to Seattle.

Anthony levered himself forward to standing, and Melissa didn't back off.

"I would love to show you Venice," he said in a voice that promised more than a tour of the Grand Canal.

Jared wasn't sure who he should warn—Melissa that

Anthony was a player, or Anthony that Melissa's only life skill appeared to be flirting.

"I assume you moved my horse?" he said, instead, causing her to turn her head. Once again she looked both guilty and surprised to see him. And once again he was stabbed in the solar plexus with a shot of unwelcome attraction.

He determinedly shook it off.

"Melissa and I were discussing the treasures of Italy," Anthony offered conversationally, but the set of his shoulders and the tightness around his mouth told Jared that he didn't welcome the interruption.

Too bad.

"You're supposed to be thinking about Sierra Benito," Jared reminded him, moving through the beam of the porch light, transmitting his clear intention to join the conversation.

"Business can wait," said Anthony.

Jared made a show of glancing at his watch. "It's been a long meeting already."

"Give me five minutes. I will be right in."

But Jared had absolutely no intention of leaving.

Melissa glanced back and forth between the two men. Her expression hadn't changed, but the interest in her eyes was obvious.

"Since Melissa's here—" Jared angled his body toward her "—maybe she has something to contribute. What do you think? Is Sierra Benito too dangerous for a humanitarian project?"

Anthony jumped in. "I am sure Melissa doesn't want to discuss—"

"Do you mean right in Suri City?" she asked. "Or up in the mountains?"

Her answer surprised him. Most people had never heard of Sierra Benito, never mind its capital city.

"A little village called Tappee," he told her.

Her head shook almost imperceptibly, but the small motion emphasized the bounce to her silky blond hair. "Horrible conditions up there. The villagers live in abject poverty."

Anthony chuckled and swung an arm around her shoulders. "I welcome you to the debate, Senorita Melissa."

Jared steeled himself against the urge to rip her out of Anthony's arms. It was a ridiculous reaction. The half hug was a friendly gesture, nothing more.

"Do you have any idea what the gold miners do to the villagers?" Melissa asked. She didn't react to Anthony's hug—didn't lean in, didn't shrug him off, either.

"Do you have any idea what the rebels do to the gold miners?" Jared asked around the clamor of emotion inside his head.

What the hell was the matter with him?

What did he care if Anthony hugged Melissa?

She shook her head in disgust. "I can't believe you're going to exploit them."

Jared jerked back at the accusation. "Exploit *who?*"

"The villagers."

"I'm not going to exploit the villagers." Jared's gaze caught on Anthony's hand and held.

Melissa was wearing a white cotton shirt. It was thin

fabric, hardly a barrier between Anthony's fingertips and her shoulder. Why didn't she shrug him off?

She scoffed. "Right. You'll subcontract the exploitation to Madre Gold to Tomesko Mining."

"That's a leap in logic," he pointed out.

"There's no other reason to go to Tappee."

"We are building a medical clinic," Anthony put in.

"Not necessarily," Jared countered with a warning glare.

Melissa glanced from one to the other with surprise and more than a little curiosity.

"How do you know anything about Tappee?" he couldn't help but probe, watching her closely for signs of…he wasn't even sure what.

"I read the *Chicago Daily*," she answered with a blink, and her green eyes went back to neutral. "There was a story last year about a mining engineer who was kidnapped by rebels."

"The company paid a million dollars." Jared took the story to its conclusion. "And they killed the guy, anyway."

"That was more than a year ago," said Anthony. "And we are not going there to mine."

"You think they care?" asked Jared. "Do you honestly believe they won't take any Westerner hostage?"

"I believe they do care," said Melissa.

"Yeah?" Jared challenged. "Is that conclusion based on your vast travel experience with the American national bus system?"

"Do not be rude," Anthony cut in, anger clear in his tone.

Well, Jared was angry, too. He'd had about enough of the argument, and he'd had about enough of watching Anthony maul Melissa. He grabbed his Stetson hat from a peg on the wall and crammed it on his head.

"I'm going to walk Melissa back to her cottage," he announced, linking her arm and moving her firmly out of Anthony's grasp.

"What in the hell…" Anthony began.

"*You* need to get back to the meeting," Jared ordered over his shoulder, propelling Melissa toward the stairs. It took her a second to get her feet sorted out under her, but he made sure she didn't stumble.

He could feel Anthony watching them as they crossed the darkened yard toward the driveway lights. Jared knew he was going to get an earful back in the house, but he didn't care. He could give just as good as he got.

He marched her forward at a brisk pace. He didn't know which cottage Melissa had been assigned, but single women were usually on the river side of the arena, so he took a chance and turned right.

"Why do I get the feeling this isn't about walking me back to my cabin?" asked Melissa.

Jared gritted his teeth, struggling to bring his emotions back under control. "Why do I get the feeling you're not here to earn money for a bus ticket?"

Three

Melissa ordered herself not to panic. There was no reason to assume he knew the truth. But even as she mentally reassured herself, the roots of her hair prickled in dread.

His pace was brisk, his large hand still wrapped around her upper arm. It felt strong and uncompromising as steel. She wondered if he intended to march her all the way to his property line.

"First the chauffeur." Jared's angry voice cut through the night air. "Then Anthony." He sucked in a tight breath. "And I can guess what went on with the damn horse."

The last took Melissa by surprise.

The *horse?* Why would she interview his horse?

"Ride it yourself?" Jared taunted.

Melissa struggled to make sense out of the accusation. She hadn't ridden the horse herself, but how could that possibly be relevant?

"Or did you get a little help?" he finished on a meaningful lilt.

He obviously already knew she had. There was no point in lying about that. "I got one of the cowboys to help me. Rich or Rand or Rafe...something..."

"I'll just bet you did." The contempt in Jared's voice was crystal clear.

"So what?" Her confusion was starting to turn to annoyance. Rafe had, in fact, offered to help her. The whole operation hadn't taken more than fifteen minutes of his time.

"So *what?*" Jared jerked her to a stop and rounded on her, glaring from beneath his battered tan Stetson.

Melissa caught her breath while she searched his hard expression in the shadowed light. Why was the horse such a salient detail? Shouldn't he be more upset about the way she'd pumped Anthony for information?

Unless...

It suddenly hit her that she'd jumped to the wrong conclusion. She wasn't caught. Jared was angry about her interaction with his cowboys.

"Is there a company ban on cowboys helping stable hands?" she asked.

"No, but I'm thinking about banning *fraternization.*"

His obvious euphemism was more than a little offensive. "You think I had time to *fraternize* with Rafe before dinner?"

Something flickered in his eyes. It might have been regret. "I think flirting is your only life skill."

"It's not." For starters, she had a university degree. She owned real estate. And she had a good job, soon to be a great job if she could pull off this interview.

"Do tell," he challenged.

"I'm intelligent, articulate and organized."

"You couldn't even organize a bus ticket to Seattle."

"Buying the bus ticket ahead of time wasn't the point."

"What was the point?"

"I'm experiencing America."

"By batting your eyes and swaying your hips?"

She held up her blistered palms. "By shoveling your stable for eight hours."

He reached for her wrist, moving her hands under the beam of a yard light, and his expression tightened. "You put something on this?"

"Work gloves." And she wished she'd thought to do it sooner.

"I'm serious."

She pulled her hand from his grasp. "I'm fine."

He took in her body from head to toe. "I don't think you're cut out for manual labor."

She subconsciously shifted her injured hands behind her back. "I told you I was fine."

"You know how to operate a computer? Type? File?"

Oh, no. She wasn't giving up her ranch job. "I've never worked in an office," she lied. "Besides, I only need bus fare. I'll be out of your hair in a week." At least that part was true.

"You might not last a week."

"I lasted a day."

"Maybe." He paused. "But you know those guys you're flirting with are going to eventually expect you to put out."

"No, they won't." She wasn't flirting anywhere near that seriously.

Jared grunted his disbelief.

The man was an alarmist. But he didn't have the worst idea in the world.

Instead of arguing with him, she sidled forward, tucking her hair behind her ears and lowering her voice to a sultry level. "So how far do you think I'll have to go?"

He brows quirked up. "You're flirting with *me?*"

She leaned in. "Is it working?"

He shifted, letting his crooked hip and cocked head transmit his indolence. "All depends on what you're after."

What she wanted was the story of his life. And she was definitely prepared to bat her eyes a little to get it. "An exemption from riding your horse," she said, instead. "He's scary. Where'd you get him?"

"He's a direct descendent of Renegade."

Melissa tilted her head and widened her eyes, letting the silence go on for a moment.

"My great-great-grandfather's stallion," said Jared. "The pair of them settled this valley back in 1883."

"I thought your grandparents built the original

house." She'd seen the impressive structure when she first arrived this morning.

"The house, yes." He nodded downriver. "The original cabin's been abandoned for decades."

"So you're the fifth Ryder generation to live here?" Her article wasn't going to focus on the family history, but Melissa found herself fascinated by the thought of such deep roots.

"I'm the fifth," said Jared. "Tango's somewhere in the twenties."

"You've kept records?"

"Of course we've kept records." His tone told her she should have known that.

To cover the blunder, she turned and started walking down the rutted driveway, continuing her way toward the Windy River and the little white cottage she'd been assigned this morning. "How many horses do you have now?"

Jared fell into step beside her. "Several hundred. Several thousand head of cattle."

"Is the ranch still profitable?"

He hesitated, and she could feel him looking down at her. "Why do you ask?"

She kept her focus on the quarter moon riding above the silhouetted mountain range across the river. "You went into construction."

"How did you know that?"

"I heard people talk. Around the ranch."

"Gossip?"

"No," she quickly denied. "Just chitchat. You're here. You're usually in Chicago. People commented on it over lunch." Truth was, Melissa had carefully orchestrated the conversation that had revealed that information and more, but there was no need to mention that to Jared.

"You seem to know a lot about me."

She dared to look up at him. "You're the boss. People naturally care about what you do."

"They shouldn't."

She couldn't help but smile at that. "Maybe not. But that's not the way life works."

"It's gossip," he stated. "Plain and simple."

"It's curiosity," she corrected. "And it's interest. And respect."

He ground out an inarticulate sound.

"You can't make millions of dollars and hope to stay under the radar," she told him.

"How do you know I make millions of dollars?"

"How many acres you got here?"

"Five thousand."

"I rest my case."

"Most cattle ranches lose money these days."

"Most construction companies make money these days."

Jared didn't answer. They came up on the short bridge over the froth of a narrow spot in the river. A dirt driveway jutted off to the south, winding through a grass-and-wildflower carpet dotted with aspen and oak trees, which fronted the staff cabins. It looked exactly like the picture on the ranch Web site. This morning it had taken Melissa's breath away.

"Which is yours?" Jared asked, nodding to the neat row of white cottages.

"Number six."

"I'll walk you down." He turned on the driveway, and Melissa was struck by how easily he fit into the surroundings. He had a smooth, rolling, loose-limbed stride, and his booted feet never faltered on the uneven ground. A few lights burned behind curtained windows.

"Very gentlemanly of you." She hoped to keep him talking as long as possible.

"Wouldn't want you to run into a cougar." He seemed to be teasing, but it was hard to tell.

She decided to assume the ranch staff weren't in mortal danger this close to the buildings. "I'm more afraid of rogue cattle," she returned.

"The range bulls are up in the hills right now."

"Good to know. So how long are you in Montana?"

"About as long as you."

"Something you have to get back to?" She tripped on a tree root, and he quickly grasped her arm to steady her.

"Why do you ask?"

"Just making conversation. You seem to like it here."

He gazed around. The Windy River roared its way past, while an owl hooted in a faraway tree. A pair of truck lights flashed in the distance beyond the barns, while several horses whinnied to each other on the night air.

Melissa surreptitiously slowed her steps, not wanting to arrive at her cottage while Jared was still willing to talk.

"I've always liked it here." But his jaw was tight and his voice seemed strained.

Melissa sensed an undercurrent. "Why did you leave?" she dared.

"To make money," was the quick response.

"Cowboys need millions?"

"A spread this size needs millions. The past few decades have been hard on Montana ranchers. It'll change in the future. It has to. But for now…"

Her footsteps slowed to a stop. There was no help for it, they'd arrived at her front porch. She turned to face him, scrambling for ways to prolong the inevitable. She wasn't likely to get another chance like this for the rest of the week.

"So for now you're building office towers to keep your cattle ranch and horse-jumping operation in the black."

"How did you know I was building office towers?" The man was entirely too observant for her comfort level.

"Somebody also mentioned it at lunch today," she said, bluffing.

Jared stared into her eyes for a long slow moment. Then his index finger went to her chin and he tipped her face to the starlight. "There's something about you, Melissa."

"I'm a decent flirt?" Better to feed into his misconception than to let him start thinking about other possibilities.

He gazed at her a moment longer. "That must be it."

He paused again, his expression going unexpectedly intimate. "So you going to put out now?"

His voice was smooth, his dark eyes sensual, and his lips full and soft. Melissa let herself envision delivering with a kiss. Would it be soft and sweet? Strong and sure? Sensual? Sexy? Or downright erotic?

"You really are frighteningly good at this." His gruff voice interrupted her fantasy.

She blinked. "Huh?"

His jaw tightened, and he took a step back. "I can see why you've got so many men at your beck and call."

She shook her head. "I don't—"

"Be careful, Melissa," he warned. "Not all of them will walk away."

And with that, he turned on his heel.

She thought about calling out to protest. Her flirtation was normally light and inconsequential. She'd never let herself get carried away. This was the first time she'd ever even considered taking the next step.

And she wouldn't have actually kissed him.

There was far too much at stake. All she wanted was some information on his business, his life, his background.

And she had some.

Melissa couldn't help but smile.

Jared might think she was shameless, but at least he didn't know she was a journalist, and she'd obtained more useful material for her article.

Ignoring the anger in his stride, and the stiff set of his shoulders as he made his way back down the dirt driveway, she skipped up the stairs to her cottage. She needed to make notes right away.

"What did you do to tick Anthony off last night?" Stephanie's voice startled Jared as he tightened Tango's cinch in front of her house midmorning. The meeting had ended late last night, and it had been simpler to sleep here than ride ten miles to the main house at the cattle ranch in the dark. Anthony and Otto had left immediately after breakfast.

He took one final reflexive look at Melissa cleaning tack inside a shed across the driveway. The woman was taking an inordinately long time on a basic bridle. Then he slipped the cinch buckle into place and turned to face his sister.

Stephanie was dressed in dressage clothes, obviously ready for another day of training with Rosie-Jo. They had a competition coming up, but Jared couldn't remember the details.

"I told him to stop flirting with the help," Jared answered.

"What help?"

"Melissa." He pulled the right stirrup into place. "I don't know why you hired that woman. She's completely useless."

"She needed a job," said Stephanie.

"We're not running a charitable organization."

Stephanie stuffed one hand on her hip. "Actually we are."

Jared rolled his eyes, grasping the saddle horn to

wiggle it and test the placement. "Then she can apply through the Genevieve Fund."

"Don't be such a hard-ass."

"I'm not a hard-ass. I'm a realist." He nodded toward Melissa. "She's been working on that same bridle for half an hour. And mark my words, she's going to cause trouble between the cowboys."

"The cowboys are full-grown men."

"My point exactly."

"They're responsible for their own behavior."

Jared gave his sister a meaningful glare. Men were men. And flirtatious women were trouble. "Like I said, I'm a realist."

Stephanie set her helmet on the end post of the hitching rail and gathered her auburn hair into a ponytail. "I'm not going to fire Melissa."

"Well, I'm not going to be responsible for the fallout," he warned.

"Who said you had to be responsible? Besides, aren't you going back down to the cattle ranch today?"

Jared gently positioned the bit in Tango's mouth. "Thought I'd stay at your place for a few days."

There was a moment's silence, and he braced himself.

Her tone hardened. "I'm perfectly fine, big brother."

"I know you're perfectly fine," Jared allowed. He was sure she felt that way for now.

"This is no different than any other anniversary."

Jared didn't argue the point. But they'd just lost their grandfather, and Stephanie was hurting. No matter how hard she pretended otherwise, the siblings' annual reunion and visit to the family graveyard would be particularly difficult for her this year. He usually stayed down at the main house at the cattle ranch, since it was larger. But Stephanie couldn't leave her work and her students at the equestrian center, so he'd stay here instead.

"When's Royce showing up?" he asked, instead.

"Saturday. You should get back down there and help McQuestin." Stephanie referred to their aging cattle ranch manager.

"McQuestin doesn't want my help."

She plunked her helmet on her head and set her lips in a mulish line. "I don't need a babysitter."

Jared leaned back against the hitching rail, crossing his arms over his chest while he faced his sister. "Maybe I need you."

Her pale blue eyes immediately softened. "You *do?*"

He nodded. It wasn't a lie. He needed to be with her right now. It was the only way he'd be sure she was okay.

She moved forward and placed a hand on his arm. "I know you miss Gramps. Do you still miss Mom and Dad?"

Jared nodded again. But this time, his lie was outright. He didn't miss his parents. He was angry with his parents. Furious, if the truth be known. But that was his burden, the secret passed down by his grandfather. His only choice was to preserve their memories for his siblings.

Stephanie's eyes shimmered and she blinked rapidly. "Then you should stay."

Jared covered her hand with his. "Thank you."

"You want to watch me jump?"

"Sure." He nodded. "I'm going to check the pasture land at Buttercup Pond. Clear my head a little. I'll swing by later in the morning."

Stephanie nodded. Then she swiped the back of her hand across one cheek and headed for the main arena.

Jared tugged Tango's lead rope free and swung up into the saddle. The ride to Buttercup Pond to establish his cover story would take him a couple of hours. But his real mission was across the Windy River. Since his grandfather's deathbed revelation in April, he couldn't get his great-great-grandparents' cabin out of his mind.

The walk to the Ryders' great-great-grandparents' cabin took longer than Melissa had expected. At last she came around a bend of the river to see two cabins. One, made of logs, was nearly collapsing with age. The other was obviously newer. It was larger, made from lumber, with glass windows still intact and peeling white paint on the walls and porch.

A single story, it was L-shaped, with a peaked, green shingle roof. The rails had sagged off the porch, but the three steps looked safe enough, and the front door was a few inches ajar. The buildings were surrounded by a wildflower meadow that nestled up against steep rocky cliffs, jutting into the crystal-blue sky. The river glided by through a wide spot, nearly silent compared to the rapids upstream.

Melissa pulled out her cell phone, clicking a couple of pictures, wishing Susan was along with her camera.

Then she gingerly climbed the three stairs. She pressed the front door, slowly creaking it open. A dank, dusty room was revealed in the filtered sunlight through the stained windows. It held a stone fireplace, an aging dining table and chairs, and the remnants of a sofa. The floorboards were warped and creaky. Through a doorway, yellowed linoleum lined a small kitchen. Curtains hung in shreds over two of the windows.

Melissa let herself imagine the long-ago family. Jared's great-grandfather must have grown up here. Was he an only child? Did he have brothers and sisters? Did Jared have cousins and more-distant relatives around the country?

She made a mental note to research the family's genealogy.

On the far side of the living room, next to the kitchen door, a narrow hallway led to the other side of the house. The floor groaned under her running shoe–clad feet as she made her way through. Her movement stirred up dust, and she covered her mouth and nose with her hand to breathe more easily.

The hallway revealed two bedrooms. One was stark, with plywood bunks nailed to the wall and a hollow cutout of a closet. But the second was a surprise. Intact yellow curtains hung over the window. The bed was obviously newer than the other furnishings, and a brightly colored quilt was shoved against the brass footboard, while the remnants of two pillows were strewn at the head.

"Can I help you?"

The deep voice nearly scared Melissa out of her skin. Her hand flew to her heart as she whirled around to see Jared standing in the bedroom doorway.

"You scared me half to death!" she told him.

"Shouldn't you be working?"

"It's lunchtime. I thought you were a *ghost*." Her heart was still racing, and adrenaline prickled her skin, flushing her body, then cooling it rapidly.

"Still very much alive," he drawled, expression accusing. "What are you doing here?"

"I was curious."

He waited.

"Last night. You mentioned your great-great-grandparents and, well, I like old buildings."

"So you walked two miles?"

"Yes."

"On your lunch hour?"

"I wanted to come while it was light."

He sighed in disgust and gave his head a little shake. "You're flaky, you know that? Instead of eating, you take off on a whim to see a dilapidated old building. How are you going to work all afternoon?"

"I'll manage," she offered, already hungry and quite willing to concede his point. But she didn't have a lot of time to waste.

"You'll be passing out by two."

She could have argued, but she had more important

questions. "What's with this room?" She gestured around. "It seems newer."

Jared's gaze fixed on the disheveled bed for a long beat. His eyes hardened to sapphire, and a muscle ticked next to his left eye. "Must have been a staff member sleeping here."

"You think?" She wondered why they hadn't fixed up the rest of the house.

He seemed to guess her question. "I imagine they ate at the cookhouse with everybody else."

He turned his attention fully to Melissa and held out a broad callused hand. "Come on. I'll give you a lift home."

"You drove?" Why hadn't she heard the engine?

"I rode Tango."

She instinctively shrank back.

"Don't tell me you're afraid to ride double on him."

"Of course not." She sure hoped there wasn't a trick to riding double.

"Then let's go. You need to eat something."

"I'll be fi—"

"No, you won't. Skipping lunch was a stupid decision. Honestly, I don't know how you've managed to stay alive this long." He reached out and grasped her hand, tugging her out of the bedroom and down the hall.

"Did your great-grandfather have siblings?" she dared to ask.

"He had a sister."

"That explains the bunk beds."

"Yes, it does."

Melissa blinked in the strong sunlight, her focus going immediately to where Tango was tied to the porch.

Jared mounted, then maneuvered the horse flush against the railingless platform, holding out his hand.

Melissa took a deep breath. She braced herself against his forearm, then arced her right leg high, swinging her butt to land with an unladylike thud, off-center behind the saddle on Tango's broad back.

The horse grunted and stepped sideways.

Jared swore out loud, reached back to snag her waist and shoved her into place as her arms went instinctively around his body and clung tight.

"Sorry," she muttered against his back.

"You're a klutz," he told her. "On top of everything else, you're a klutz."

"I never learned to ride properly," she admitted.

"You need to learn some life skills," he responded. "I don't even care which ones. But damn, woman, you've got to learn how to do *something*."

He urged Tango into a fast walk. The motion and play of muscles were unsettling beneath Melissa's body. She kept her arms tight around Jared, slowly becoming aware of the intimacy of their position. Her breasts were plastered against his back, his cotton shirt and her T-shirt little barrier to the heat of their bodies. Her cheek rested against him, and every time she inhaled, her lungs were filled with his subtle, woodsy musk scent.

She was quickly getting turned on. Arousal boiled in the pit of her belly and tingled along her thighs. Her nipples had grown hard, and for a mortifying moment, she wondered if he could feel them.

"Where do you live in Indiana?" he asked, voice husky.

"Gary."

"You have a job there?"

"Not yet." She'd decided claiming to have a job would raise too many questions about why she needed money, and how she had enough time off to travel across the country.

"An apartment?"

"I've been staying with friends." Not having a job meant she couldn't claim to be paying rent. Unless she had investments or family money. In which case, she wouldn't need to earn money for a bus ticket.

As embarrassing as it might be, she had to pretend to be as big a loser as Jared had decided she was in order to maintain her cover story.

He grunted his disapproval, and she felt a twinge of regret that she couldn't set the record straight. But it wasn't her job to impress Jared Ryder. And it sure wasn't her job to be attracted to him. She'd have to fight her instincts on both fronts.

Four

Near the cookhouse, Jared helped Melissa down from Tango's back. She staggered to a standing position, and he could see the pain reflected in her expression as she stretched the muscles in her thighs. If the woman had ever been on a horse before, he'd eat saddle leather.

"*There* you are," came Stephanie's accusatory voice.

Jared felt a twinge of satisfaction at the thought of Melissa getting her comeuppance. But then he realized Stephanie was talking to him. He'd obviously missed her jumping practice.

"I gave Melissa a lift," he explained.

Stephanie looked at Melissa. "Are you hurt?"

"No, I was—"

"Downriver," Jared quickly put in. "Walking."

The explanation earned him a confused look from Melissa.

Too bad. He'd worry about that one later. For now, he didn't want to plant any thoughts about the old cabin in Stephanie's head.

Stephanie looked from Jared to Melissa, then back again. "Well, you missed a no-fault round," she told him, putting her pert nose in the air.

"I guess you'll just have to do it again."

"You think it's easy?"

"No," he acknowledged. "I think it's very, very hard. But I also know you're a perfectionist."

"I wish," Stephanie retorted. But Jared knew it was true. You didn't become one of the top-ten show jumpers in the country without a strong streak of perfectionism.

He handed Tango's reins to Melissa. "He's all yours. When you're done taking off the tack, put him back in the red-gated pen."

Melissa glanced down at the leather reins. Then she looked at Jared, her eyes widening with trepidation.

Yeah, he thought so.

He gave a heavy sigh and took back the reins. "Or I could give you a hand," he offered. "Then you can grab something to eat."

He felt Stephanie's curious gaze behind him, and he twisted his head to give her an I-told-you-so stare. If she wanted him to have time to watch her jump, she shouldn't have hired such a hopeless case.

He wrapped the reins around the horn of his saddle,

clipped a lead rope onto Tango's bridle, then walked the few steps to the hitching rail in front of the stable.

"You can start with the cinch," he called over his shoulder, and Melissa quickly scrambled into action, hoofing it across the loose-packed dirt of the pen.

Stephanie watched them for a moment longer. Then he saw a small, hopeful smile quirk the corners of her mouth before she turned away.

Great. His good deed was obviously not going to go unpunished. He was helping Melissa out of pity, not out of attraction. She might be a gorgeous woman, but he liked his dates with a little more gray matter and a whole lot more ambition.

She came to a halt a few feet back from Tango's flank. Her hands curled into balls by her sides, strands of her blond hair fluttering across her flushed cheeks as she blinked at the tall black horse.

"The cinch," Jared prompted, releasing the reins and gently drawing the bit from Tango's mouth.

Melissa didn't make a move.

He flipped the stirrup up and hooked it over the saddle horn. "The big, shiny silver buckle," he offered sarcastically.

She took a half step forward, then wiped her palms down the front of her jeans.

Jared turned, planting his hands on his hips.

She pursed her lips, reaching her hand toward the buckle. But Tango shifted, and she snapped it back.

"He's not going to bite you."

"What if he kicks me?"

"Just don't do anything sudden."

"Oh, that makes me feel a whole lot better."

This was getting ridiculous. "You know, you might want to think about another line of work."

"I was perfectly happy scooping out pens."

"Nobody's happy scooping out pens."

"I was."

"Well, that's a dead-end career." He took a step forward and captured her hand.

She tried to jerk away.

"The trick is," said Jared in the most soothing voice he could muster, "to let him know what you're doing." He urged her reluctant hand toward Tango's withers. "That way, nobody is surprised."

"Is 'surprised' a euphemism?"

"I mean it literally."

Tango craned his neck to see what was going on.

"Your touch should be firm," Jared advised, keeping himself between Melissa and the horse's head. He gave Tango a warm-up pat with his free hand before placing Melissa's palm on the horse's coat. "That way, he knows you have confidence."

"I don't have confidence."

"Sure you do." He let go of her hand, and she immediately pulled it back from the horse.

Jared drew a frustrated sigh. "I've seen five-year-olds with more guts than you."

She glared at him.

"Lots of them," he affirmed.

Her glare lasted several seconds longer, but then she squared her shoulders, screwed up her face and turned to the saddle.

"Buckle first," Jared instructed as her small soft fingers tackled the leather. "Now pull the strap through the rings."

It took her a minute to get the mohair strap untangled and dangling straight down.

"You want to take the saddle and blanket off together. Grab it front and back. Lift, don't drag it. Then carry it into the stable. I'll show you where to put it."

He stepped back to give her some room.

Tango was sixteen hands, so it was a reach for Melissa to get a firm grip. But she grabbed the saddle, lifted, pulled back, stumbled in the loosely packed dirt and nearly fell over backward.

Jared quickly wrapped his arm around the small of her back, averting disaster. Her waist was small, her body and frame light. No wonder she was such a wimp when it came to physical work.

"You okay?" he asked reflexively.

"Fine." She firmed up her grip on the heavy saddle and straightened away before he could get used to the feel of her in his arms. But not before he realized how easily he could get used to the feel of her in his arms.

He wondered if she danced. Then for a second he allowed himself to imagine her in a dress. A dress would suit her, something silky and flowing, maybe a bright blue or magenta. Despite her hesitancy in the stable yard, something told him she'd have self-confidence in a different setting.

She all but staggered into the stable, and he was forced to give her points for grit.

"Third rack from the end," he instructed, following with the reins.

She plunked the saddle down.

"You can clean it after lunch," he told her.

She nodded, obviously out of breath. Then she dusted off the front of her navy tank top.

"But first we move Tango."

"Of course we do." Her tone was sarcastic as she turned to face him.

"You ticked off at me? For helping you?"

She studied his eyes. "No." But the tone told him she was.

"You can always quit."

"I'm not going to quit." Her annoyance was replaced by defiance as she started for the stable door. "Let's go."

"You want to lead him from the left," Jared called after her as he hung up the reins, positive now that she'd never been near a horse before today.

Tango wasn't intimidating. He was an incredibly well-trained, twelve-year-old saddlebred, solid as a rock and not the least bit flighty or malicious. Any horseman, groom or stable hand would recognize that in an instant.

He came through the doorway to find Melissa sizing up Tango from about five feet away.

"Talk to him," Jared advised. "Then give him a pat and undo the rope."

"Is there a trick to it?" she asked, apparently having given up any pretext of knowing what she was doing.

"Which part?"

Over her shoulder, she cut him an impatient glare, and he was forced to tamp down a smile.

"Pull the end." He demonstrated, tugging the quick-release knot. Then he handed her the rope. "Stand on this side. Make sure he can see you. Don't let the rope trail." Jared got her positioned properly. He didn't know how much she'd have to work between here and Seattle, but she stood a much better chance of avoiding starvation if she had a clue about what she was doing.

Melissa started walking, and Tango fell in easily beside her. Her face was pinched and pale, and there was clear tension across her slim shoulders as she made her way toward the ranch road, but at least she was making the effort.

A couple of Stephanie's border collies streaked toward them, obviously assuming there was work to be done. Melissa tensed, and Jared put an arm around her. "They won't hurt you."

"I know."

"You do?"

"They look…friendly." But her voice was slightly higher pitched than normal. "Will they scare Tango?"

"Tango's bomb-proof."

The dogs circled the small group a couple of times, then settled in back of Tango's heels, obviously up for whatever the job might be.

Melissa led the horse in silence down the slight slope of the dirt road, curving east toward the river and a row of horse pens. Stephanie was teaching a junior jumping class in the main arena behind them. The Ryder farrier was working on a yearling with the help of two cowboys who were trying to teach the twitchy colt the proper etiquette for hoof care. Meanwhile, stable hands moved hay, filled water troughs and repaired fences.

There was an endless cycle of work on a horse ranch. When he was in the city, Jared missed the predictable rhythm. In his corporate life, he was putting out one fire after another. He couldn't plan a single day, never mind a season.

"Did you come to an agreement about Tappee?" she asked as they approached the red-gated pen.

Jared shook his head, increasing his pace to unlatch the gate in front of the horse. "Stephanie voted with me, but Otto sided with Anthony."

"Otto?"

"Otto Durand."

Her forehead furrowed as she cautiously led Tango through the gate. "I don't understand."

Jared pulled it shut and flipped the latch. "There's a clip under his chin. Release the lead rope."

She reached cautiously under the horse's head. But she found the clip and clicked it free.

Tango instantly reacted to the familiar sound. Knowing he was free, he bolted, spraying clods of dirt at Melissa.

It was all Jared could do not to laugh at the horrified expression on her face.

She sputtered out the dirt while the horse rolled onto his back, relieved to be free of the saddle.

"What don't you understand?" he asked, instead.

She brushed away her hair and rubbed the back of

her hand over her face. "I don't understand why you had to vote. Aren't you CEO of Ryder International?"

"This isn't a Ryder International project."

"Oh. I thought…"

Jared cracked the gate open to man-size so they could exit the pen. "It's the Genevieve Fund."

Melissa raised her brow in a question.

"The Genevieve Ryder Memorial Fund," Jared explained. "It's a charitable trust named after my mother."

"Is your mother…?"

He nodded. "She was killed twenty years ago."

Her forehead creased. "I'm sorry."

Jared shrugged, brushing past the sharp stab of conflicting emotions that tightened his chest. "It's been twenty years."

Melissa's green eyes were round and soft. Her voice dropped to a husky level that somehow hit him in the solar plexus. "I'm still sorry."

They stared at each other in silence, and once again he was struck by the intelligence in her eyes. Only this time, it was laced with compassion. There was something he didn't understand about this woman, something lurking just beyond his comprehension.

"There are five members of the Genevieve Fund board," he told her, leaning an arm on a fence rail, forcing the frustrating dilemma from his head.

"Who's the fifth?" She mirrored his posture.

"My brother, Royce."

"I take it he gets to break the tie?"

"He'll be here on Saturday."

"Does he work on the ranch or with the construction company?"

"Neither. He works for Ryder International, but he's involved in acquisitions, not in the day-to-day business."

"So he was the one who found Saxena Electronics?"

And there it was again. "How do you know about Saxena?"

"I told you, Jared." She smoothed her mussed hair back from her forehead. "I read the newspapers."

"And you remember obscure facts like that?"

She shrugged. "Sometimes it's a blessing. Sometimes it's a curse."

"Ever heard of Bosoniga?"

"Little country in West Africa." She grinned, revealing flashing white teeth. "Is this a quiz?"

"We're building a school there."

Her head bobbed up and down. "Good choice. The monarchy is stable, so poverty and infrastructure will be your only problems."

He lifted his hand, then brought it down again on the rough wood of the fence, struggling to make Melissa's lifestyle add up in his head. "Why don't you have a real job?"

"Define a real job."

"An office, where'd you put that brain of yours to work from nine to five."

"I don't think they'd let me wander across the country."

"How long have you been wandering across the country?"

Her mouth tightened imperceptibly, and something flashed in the depths of her eyes. Fear? Pain? He was reminded once again that she could be running from something or someone.

But then the look was gone.

"Not long," she answered. "Do you think Royce will side with his family or with Anthony and Otto?"

"Anthony is our cousin."

"Really?"

He nodded. "Royce is a risk taker. He'll offer to fly down to Tappee himself."

"He's a pilot?"

Jared choked out a laugh. "He's definitely a pilot. I think he likes flying around the world more than he likes investigating companies."

"Can I meet him when he gets here?"

Jared tensed. A chill hit his body, and a warning sparked in his brain. "Why?"

She drew back, obviously reacting to his expression.

"You planning to flirt with him?" Jarred pressed. He shouldn't have let his guard down. He didn't know anything about this woman.

She emphatically shook her head. "He likes to travel. I like to travel." Her words came faster. "I was thinking you could be right. Maybe I should find a real job and save up some money. I mean, seeing America is fun and all, but it might be fun to see some of the rest of the world—"

"In my brother's jet?"

"No. *No.*" She smoothed her hair back again. "I'm not going to flirt with your brother. I just thought…"

Jared waited. He truly did want to know what she thought.

She let go of the fence rail and took a step forward. "I thought he might be a lot like you. Smart and interesting."

He stared down as she moved closer. "I can't believe you're doing this." But what he really couldn't believe was that it was working. She was flirting with him, using her pretty face and killer body to gain an advantage. And it was *working.*

He was pathetic.

"You misunderstood," she told him in a soft voice. "I have no designs on Royce. I don't even know Royce. And if my mission was to land myself a rich man, do you think I'd be scooping horse poop on a ranch in Montana? No offense, Jared, but Manhattan is a whole lot closer to Gary, and their per capita count of rich eligible men is pretty darn high."

Jared watched her soft lips as they formed words, took in her feathery hair lifting in the light breeze, her bottomless green eyes, almost a turquoise, like the newly melted water of a glacial lake. She was stunningly gorgeous and intriguingly intelligent.

"So how stupid do you think I am?" Her voice dropped off into silence. The thuds of Tango's footfalls echoed around them.

"I don't think you're stupid at all," Jared admitted. "That's the problem."

* * *

Melissa had overplayed her hand.

Sitting at the end of a long table in the quiet cookhouse, spooning her way through a flavorful soup, she knew she'd made Jared suspicious. She should never have asked to meet Royce. And she should have been content to let him think she was slow-witted.

Her enthusiasm for getting the story, along with her stupid ego, had both gotten in the way. She'd just *had* to show off her knowledge of Bosoniga and Tappee. Like some schoolkid trying to impress the teacher. "Bosoniga has a stable monarchy," she mocked under her breath. Why didn't she just wave her university degree under his nose and challenge him to guess why she was out on the road playing vagabond?

She dropped the spoon into her soup.

Was she trying to sabotage the story?

"Melissa?" Someone slid into the chair next to her, and Melissa looked over to see Stephanie set a white stonewear cup on the table.

At two in the afternoon, the cookhouse had grown quiet. Faint voices could be heard from the pass-through to the kitchen. Coffee, biscuits and oatmeal cookies were still available on the sideboard in case anyone needed a snack. And a helper was setting the three empty tables for dinner.

"Hello," Melissa greeted Stephanie politely.

The younger woman's auburn hair was pulled back in her signature ponytail. She'd removed her riding helmet, but still wore the white blouse, tight jodhpurs and high boots that were the uniform of a show jumper.

Stephanie grinned happily. There was a freshness about her, Melissa thought. Maybe it was the freckles or maybe it was the complete lack of cosmetics. Or it could have been the perky upturned nose. But Stephanie looked young, carefree, almost mischievous.

"I saw Jared helping you with Tango," she began, her expression friendly and open as she turned the cup handle to face the right direction.

Melissa nodded, even while her stomach tightened with guilt. She couldn't help but like Stephanie, and she was sorry the woman was caught up in her charade.

"It was very nice of him," Melissa acknowledged. Then she paused, choosing her words carefully. "My horse skills are…" She let out a sigh, feeling like a heel for lying to Stephanie in the first place. "I guess, I, uh, exaggerated my skill level when I first talked to you." She cringed, waiting for the reaction.

But to her surprise, Stephanie waved a dismissive hand. "Whatever."

Melissa gazed at her. "But—"

"It doesn't take a rocket scientist to shovel manure."

"You're not mad?"

"Nah." Stephanie lifted the stonewear mug and took a sip of the steaming coffee. "I imagine people exaggerate on their résumés all the time."

"I guess they do," Melissa agreed, relieved—yet again—that she wasn't about to get fired.

"So what do you think of him?"

"Tango?" Was Stephanie going to try to get her to ride the horse?

"No, Jared."

"Oh." Melissa caught the speculative expression in Stephanie's eyes.

Oh.

Oh, no.

This could not be good.

"He seems, well, nice enough," Melissa offered carefully. Truth was, she thought Jared was demanding and sarcastic. Okay, in an intriguing, compelling, sexy kind of way.

Stephanie nodded cheerily. "He's a great guy. Lots of women seem attracted to him. I mean, it's hard for me to tell, being his sister, but I imagine he's pretty hot."

Melissa turned her attention back to her soup. "He's a very attractive man."

"You should have seen the woman he dated last weekend. They had their picture in the paper in Chicago. She was a knockout. A lawyer."

Melissa spooned up a bit of soup. She was not going to be jealous of some smart knockout lawyer in Chicago. Who Jared dated was absolutely none of her business.

"I told him he should see her again. But he's not interested." Stephanie gave a shrug. "So, really, he's not committed in any way, shape or form."

Melissa fought a smile. Again, there was an endearing quality to Stephanie. She was probably only four or five years younger than Melissa, but she seemed so innocent and untarnished. Maybe it was from living in the protected world of rural Montana.

"Honestly, Stephanie, I think I frustrate your brother."

Stephanie shook her head. "We can change that."

"I'm only here for a few days, remember?" The last thing Melissa needed was for Stephanie to give Jared a reason to avoid her. And she sensed that was exactly what would happen if he guessed his sister's intentions.

"He thinks you're pretty."

The assertion took Melissa by surprise.

"He told me," Stephanie continued. "The first time he saw you."

"This is a bad idea, Stephanie. Jared and I are from completely different worlds." And she was spying on him. And he was going to despise her in about three weeks when the article hit the newsstands.

"So were my parents."

"Stephanie, really."

"My dad was a rancher, and my mom grew up in Boston."

Melissa knew this was exactly the point where she should press Stephanie for some information. But for some reason, she couldn't bring herself to do it.

"My mom was gorgeous and classy. Blonde, like you." Stephanie sighed. "I wish I looked more like her."

"But you're beautiful," Melissa immediately put in, meaning it completely.

Stephanie wrinkled her little nose. "I have freckles and red hair. And, you know, I haven't bought myself a dress in three years."

"Well, that's easy to fix."

"I bet you own a lot of beautiful dresses." The speculative look was back in Stephanie's eyes.

"Very few," said Melissa. She pinned Stephanie with an earnest expression. "Promise me you won't do this, Stephanie."

Stephanie reached out to grasp Melissa's forearm, taking a careful look around the room. "I can be very discreet."

Given the woman's exaggerated spy-versus-spy room check, Melissa sincerely doubted that.

"I'll chat you up a bit," Stephanie continued. "You are gorgeous, and I can—"

"Jared is not, I repeat, not interested in me. You'll only embarrass us both if you try to match us up."

Stephanie took another sip of her coffee, a dreamy faraway expression in her eyes. "I promise, Melissa. I won't do a single thing to embarrass you."

Five

Melissa had waited all morning for a chance to privately warn Jared about Stephanie's matchmaking plans. She could hardly walk up to the front door of Stephanie's house and knock. And Jared, as far as she could tell, hadn't come out of the house.

Standing over a tub of water in the tack room, she had a decent view of the front porch. Her hands were red and slippery from the glycerin soap, but at least the job was straightforward: wash the tack, dry the tack, polish the tack. She'd worked her way through a decent-size pile of leather.

When lunchtime came along without a sign of Jared, she started to worry. If Stephanie was already matchmaking, he was probably plotting his escape from the equestrian center. If she didn't do something soon, there was every possibility that he'd leave before she got anything more for her story.

She had to find a way to get hold of him.

She clicked through the possibilities in her brain until finally she came up with a viable plan. If she could somehow get her hands on his cell number, she could talk to him without Stephanie knowing.

She pulled her hands from the warm water, shook them off and dried them on a towel. Her cell phone was in her taupe canvas tote bag, and it didn't take her long to get directory assistance and the Chicago number for Ryder International. The receptionist put her through to Jared's assistant.

"Jared Ryder's office," said a friendly female voice.

"I need to speak to Jared Ryder," Melissa opened, hoping the office would give her his cell phone number.

"I'm afraid Mr. Ryder is not in the office today." The voice remained friendly and professional. "Can I help you with something?"

"Do you happen to have his cell phone number?" Melissa mentally crossed her fingers that the woman would be willing to give it out.

"I'm afraid I can't provide that information. Is there someone else who can—"

"Would you be able to get a message to him?" Melissa moved to plan B.

Some of the patience leached out of the woman's voice. "Can I get your name, please?"

"So you can get him a message?" Melissa's hope rose.

"He may not get it until next week."

"I need him to get it today. Right away if possible."

"If I could just have your name."

"It's Melissa. Melissa Webster." She used the alias she'd used on her résumé.

"And what is the message regarding?"

Good question. Melissa racked her brain. She sure couldn't say she was a reporter, but if the subject didn't seem important, the secretary might not send it to Jared right away. "Saxena Electronics," she offered impulsively.

"You're from Saxena?" The skepticism was clear.

Melissa could only assume most Saxena employees had East Indian accents. "I'm affiliated with them," she lied. "The message is that Melissa Webster needs to talk about Saxena right away. In private," she added, ending with her cell phone number.

"I'm not sure—"

"Please believe me that it's important," Melissa put in quickly.

The woman hesitated on the other end of the line.

"There's no risk," Melissa pointed out. "If it's not important, he'll just ignore it, right?"

"I'll see what I can do."

"Maybe a quick text or an e-mail?"

"I'll see what I can do." The voice had turned stony.

It was definitely time to back off. "Thank you," said Melissa with as much gratitude as she could muster. "I really do appreciate this."

The professionalism and the formality came back. "Thank you for calling Ryder International."

"Thanks for your help," Melissa offered once more before hanging up.

Then she plunked her phone back in her bag, readjusted the clip that was holding her hair back and pulled her damp tank top away from her chest. She hated to go to lunch looking like this, but it was a long walk back to her cottage, and there was no way she could skip the meal.

As the days went by, her respect for cowboys and stable hands had risen. They worked extremely hard. A salad or a protein shake might cut it in an office, but out here, calories were essential.

She dried the last of the washed tack, laying it out on the bench to be polished later. Then she slung her canvas bag over her shoulder and headed for the cookhouse while she waited to see if Jared would call.

A couple of steps out the stable door, Jared startled her, blocking her way. She stopped short.

"What the hell?" he demanded.

She glanced around. "Is Stephanie with you?"

"What was this about seeing me in private?"

She didn't see Stephanie anywhere. "I'll explain in a minute. Is there somewhere we can talk?"

Jared hesitated. Then he nodded at the stable. "There's an office up those stairs."

"Great." Melissa turned, and he followed her in.

They tapped their way, single file, up the narrow staircase. It opened to a short hallway with three doors.

"Far end," Jared rumbled. "And this better be good. My secretary was scrambling the Saxena team for damage control. She thought you were warning me of a hostile takeover."

Melissa cringed. "Sorry. Did you call them off?"

"Of course I called them off." His boots were heavy on the wood floor behind her. "This better not be some flirting thing."

"It's not flirting." Melissa stopped at the closed door.

Jared reached around her and pushed it open to reveal a small desk, a couple of filing cabinets. Three open, curtained windows showed a cloud-laden sky, and a comfortably furnished corner with armchairs, low tables and lamps. Through the window, Melissa could see a crowd of people at the arena. She assumed it was a jumping class and that Stephanie was there.

"Take a seat." Jared gestured to a worn, brown leather armchair.

Melissa sat down, and he took the chair next to it. They were separated by a polished pine table, decorated with three small, framed horse portraits.

He leaned back, crossing one ankle over the opposite knee and folding his arms over his chest. "What's going on?" he asked directly.

Melissa took a deep breath, giving herself a second to compose her message. "It's Stephanie."

"What did you do?"

"I didn't do anything."

"She lost patience with you? Fired you?"

"*No.*" Melissa sat forward. "Will you let me finish?"

He waited.

"Your sister, for some reason, has decided I'm…well, a good match for you."

Jared planted his feet and sat forward. "What did you say to her?"

"*Nothing.* This is about her, not me. I was minding my own business. She saw you helping me yesterday. Apparently the first time you saw me you said I was pretty."

"I never—"

"Well, Stephanie thinks you did. And she's a determined and romantic young lady, and she thinks she can subtly throw us together without you noticing. I was guessing you'd catch on, and I thought you'd appreciate a heads-up."

Jared's mouth thinned into a grim line. His hands moved to the arms of the chair, and he gave his head a subtle shake. "It's worse than I thought."

Melissa waited for him to elaborate.

He fixed his gaze on her. "If she's targeting *you,* things are really getting out of hand."

"Excuse me?" Melissa couldn't help the defensive tone in her voice. "I'm the bottom of the barrel?"

"No, you're not the bottom of the barrel." He paused. "But you're definitely from the unlikely half of the barrel."

"Is that supposed to make me feel better?"

"The last person she targeted was a lawyer."

Melissa nodded. "She told me."

"Just how long was this conversation?"

"Not long." Melissa shifted back in her chair. "For the record, I tried to talk her out of it."

Jared's expression turned thoughtful, and he glanced toward the window and out to the arena. "Did she seem…upset?"

Melissa shook her head. Stephanie hadn't seemed remotely upset. "I'd call it enthusiastic, even excited."

He stood up and walked toward the closest window, looking through the opening to the crowd in the distance. "It's about Sunday."

Melissa stood with him. The clouds were thickening in the sky and the wind was picking up.

"It's got to be," he continued.

"What about Sunday?" she dared to ask.

Jared kept his gaze glued outside. "The twentieth anniversary of our parents' deaths. And the first time my grandfather won't be here to commemorate it with us."

Melissa took a few steps toward him. "Your grandfather died?"

Jared nodded. "In April. It hit Stephanie pretty hard."

"I can imagine," Melissa said softly, her sympathy going out to the whole family.

"Look at her jump." Jared nodded toward the arena, and Melissa shifted closer to where she could watch Stephanie on her big gray horse.

"Perfect form," he continued as the two sailed over a high, white jump rail. "She's talented, driven, unbelievably hardworking. Only twenty-two, and she'll be a champion before we know it."

"Then she was only two when your parents died?" Melissa ventured.

"Only two," Jared confirmed with a nod, and his voice turned introspective. "And despite her success, all these years all she ever wanted was a mother."

Melissa didn't know what to say to that. Her own parents had moved to Florida only a couple of years ago. She saw them every few months, but she still missed her mother.

"I don't blame her," she offered.

"I understand the desire," Jared allowed. "But ever since she was old enough to understand, she's pestered the three of us to get married. Poor Gramps. And poor Royce. He was afraid to bring a date home in high school for fear of how Stephanie would embarrass him. She goes into matchmaking mode at the drop of a hat."

"You could get married, you know," Melissa offered reasonably, only half joking. "You're what, early thirties?"

"Thirty-five."

"So what's the holdup? I bet you meet eligible women every day of the week."

Jared frowned at her. "I'm not getting married for the sake of my sister."

"Get married for yourself. Hey, if you get proactive, you'll have your choice of women. If Stephanie gets her way, you're stuck with me."

It obviously took Jared a stunned minute to realize Melissa was joking. But then he visibly relaxed.

"What about you?" he asked. "Would you get married to keep your siblings happy?"

Melissa coughed out a laugh. "I have five older brothers. Trust me, no husband in the world will be good enough."

"Would they scare a guy off?"

Melissa smiled at that. "They range from six-one to six-four. All tough as nails. Adam's a roofer, Ben and Caleb are framers, Dan's an electrician and Eddy's a pipe fitter."

A calculating look came into Jared's eyes. "You think they'd be interested in jobs with Ryder International?"

"I'm afraid they're all gainfully employed."

His eyes squinted down as he stared at her, and she braced herself for sarcasm about her own dismal career status. It was going to be hard not to defend herself from his criticism.

"Might be worth marrying you for the union connections alone."

The words surprised a laugh out of her. She played along. "Plus, Stephanie would have a mother." She played along. "Well, more like a sister, really. I'm only four or five years older than she is, you know."

"Not a bad plan." Jared nodded and pretended to give it serious consideration. "Stephanie's pretty convinced the family would benefit from a few more females in the mix."

"Smart girl," said Melissa.

"Can't argue with the logic," Jared agreed. "It's her methods that cause the trouble."

As they spoke, Stephanie sailed over her final jump, completing a clean round.

"She really is good," said Melissa.

"You don't know the half of it." Jared turned from the window.

He paused, and they came face-to-face, closer than she'd realized. Sunlight streamed in, highlighting his gorgeous eyes, his strong chin, his straight nose and the short shock of brown hair that curled across his forehead.

The force of his raw magnetism drew her in, arousing and frightening her at the same time. He was all man. He had power, looks and intelligence, and she suddenly felt inadequate. She wasn't ready to work at his ranch or write an article about him. The phrase *out of my league* planted itself firmly in her brain.

For a second she let herself fear his reaction to the article. But then she banished the fear. It was her job to get the story, and she'd be far away from Montana by the time it ran in the *Bizz.*

The world outside darkened, and his eyes turned to midnight, sensuality radiating from their depths. The humidity jumped up, only to be overtaken by a freshening breeze.

There were shouts from outside as the wind swirled and a storm threatened. Doors banged, horses whinnied, and plastic tarps rattled against their ropes.

Meanwhile, gazes locked, Jared and Melissa didn't move.

The wild clamor outside matched the cacophony inside her head. This attraction felt so right, but it was so incredibly wrong. Jared was her article subject, her employer, one of the most powerful entrepreneurs in Chicago. She had absolutely no business being attracted to him.

He reached out to brush a stray lock of hair from her temple. His touch was electric, arousing, light as a feather but shocking as a lightning bolt.

Thunder rumbled in the distance, and the first fat raindrops clattered on the roof.

"I'm going to kiss you," he told her.

She drew a breath. "You think that's a good idea?"

He moved slightly closer. "It's not the smartest thing I've ever done." He stroked his thumb along her jaw, tipped her chin. "But probably not the stupidest, either. Might not even make the top three."

"What were they?" she asked.

"The stupidest things?"

She gave a slight nod.

"I don't think I'll be telling you that right now."

"Maybe later?"

"I doubt it." Done talking, he leaned in and pressed his warm lips to hers.

It was a gentle kiss, a tentative kiss. There was a wealth of respect and more than a couple of questions contained in the kiss.

She answered by softening her lips. One of her hands went to his shoulder, steadying herself, she lied. Truth was, she wanted to hang on, press closer, turn his inquiry into a genuine kiss.

He easily complied, stepping forward, parting his lips, one hand going to the small of her back, the other tunneling into the hair behind her ear. He tipped his head, deepened the kiss; she plastered herself flush against him, feeling the hard heat of his body, counterpoint to the wind and rain that rushed in through the open window.

Warning sirens clanged inside her head.

It wasn't supposed to happen like this.

She was supposed to maintain a journalistic detachment. Plus, hadn't she come up here to warn him about Stephanie? Not to flirt. Or worse, seduce. What on earth was she *thinking?*

He broke the kiss, but moved instantly into another. Melissa didn't have time to decide if she was relieved or upset before she was dragged away on another tidal wave of desire.

The world disappeared—the horses, the people, the wind and rain. Nothing existed except Jared's kiss, the rough texture of his hands, the heat of his hard body and the fresh, earthy, male scent that surrounded her and drew her into an alternative universe.

His thumb found the strip of skin between her tank top and blue jeans. He stroked up her spine, sending shivers of reaction skittering both ways. His hand slipped under her shirt, warm palm caressing the sensitized skin, working higher, closing in on the scrap of her bra.

His tongue touched hers, tentatively at first, but then bolder as she responded, opening to him, tipping her head to give him better access to her mouth. His hand caressed the back of her head. Her arms tightened around his neck. She went up on her toes, struggling to get closer.

A clap of thunder boomed through the sky, rumbling the building, lightning dancing in the clouds rapidly engulfed the ranch. The rain grew steady, blurring the world, cooling the air and clattering like a freight train against the cedar shakes above them.

Jared pulled her tighter still, leaving her in no doubt about the effect the kiss was having on him. It was having the same effect on her. It was wild, untamed, sexy and all but unstoppable.

He shifted, moving her away from the open window and the driving rain that was dampening their clothes. He backed her into the wall, and his leg slipped between hers. The friction sent a shot of desire through her body, and a moan found its way past her mouth.

Jared whispered her name, his kisses moving from her mouth to her cheek, her temple and neck. He moved aside the strap of her tank top, the thinner strap of her bra, kissing his way to her shoulder, where his warm tongue lingered, laving the sensitive skin.

Her legs grew weak, and she braced herself against the wall, clinging to Jared's strong shoulders, even as she kissed his chest through the damp cotton of his shirt. He'd crooked his knee, and she rested the core of her body against his strong thigh. A pulse throbbed through her veins, and there was no mistaking where she wanted this to lead.

"We have to stop," she forced herself to gasp.

His lips paused mid-kiss on her bare shoulder. "I'm not sure why," he breathed. He straightened, bracing his hands against the wall, arms on either side of her, gazing down with passion-clouded eyes.

"Did I do something wrong?" he asked.

She was all but shaking with reaction, afraid to move for fear she'd throw caution to the wind and lose herself in his arms. "This is nuts," she told him, struggling to bring her voice back to normal, forcing herself to drag her hands from his shoulders.

His thigh was still braced between hers, still pressed intimately against her body, still drawing a completely inappropriate reaction from her.

"Why?" he asked.

"I don't know," she nearly wailed. What had happened? Why had they combusted like that? They barely knew each other.

"I mean, why is it nuts?"

"Because…" She struggled over the question, not finding a satisfactory answer. At least, not one that she could share with him. "It's you, and it's me. And we're…" She couldn't find the words.

"Attracted to each other?" he finished for her.

"Apparently," she responded dryly.

He let his thigh fall away, and she nearly groaned with the sensation.

"Stephanie would be pleased," he pointed out.

Melissa's gaze darted to the window, suddenly wondering who had seen what before they moved away. What if Stephanie had seen them?

"Nobody saw a thing," said Jared, guessing her concern. "They were too busy running from the storm."

The rain had turned to a steady drum, while thunder and lightning punctuated the darkened sky. The yard was empty, everyone having taken shelter in one of the buildings. Horses were huddled in small groups, most of them under run-in shelters, some in the larger pens moving into the shelter of the trees. Tarps still billowed, cracking and snapping in the wind.

Jared gently stroked his thumb across her swollen bottom lip, making her desire flare all over again. "Our secret is safe."

She gazed into his eyes, unable to hide her renewed longing. And try as she might, she couldn't bring herself to walk away.

His eyes darkened further and his voice went husky. "You want to make it an even bigger secret?"

Six

Before Melissa could even open her mouth, Jared knew to retract the question.

"I'm sorry," he quickly told her. "That was way out of line."

He was her boss. Just yesterday he'd threatened to fire her, more than once, if memory served. He had absolutely no business propositioning her. It was unprincipled, immoral, probably illegal in most states.

"It wasn't—"

"It *was*." He forced himself back, hands tightening by his sides as he put some distance between them. The torrential rain was still dripping through the open windows, and he slammed one window shut, then the next and finally the third, taking some of his frustration out on the inanimate objects. He'd never felt this way before, never desired a woman so quickly and thoroughly. Yet he was wrong to feel this way, and he had to make it stop.

"Jared?" Her voice was tentative, and he felt like a complete jerk.

He latched the final window, then turned back to face her. Her hair was wet, messy from his hands. The damp blue tank top clung to her breasts, highlighting her nipples. Her eyes were round, sea-foam green and confused.

"I'm mad at myself," he assured her. "Not at you."

She took a step forward. "It was my fault, too. How about we forget it happened?"

"Can *you* forget it happened?" He'd give it a shot, but he wasn't holding out much hope.

"Sure." She nodded, offering a small smile. "Easy."

She seemed sincere, and he tried not to be offended. Maybe he'd imagined their explosive passion. Maybe to her it had been a simple ordinary kiss. He gave himself a split second to ponder exactly who the hell else she'd been kissing like that, but then he acknowledged that it was none of his business.

He took a deep breath, forcing himself to relax. "Sure," he forced out, adjusting his damp shirt and raking his fingers through his hair. "We'll just forget it ever happened."

Melissa glanced down and plucked at her own wet shirt. Then she quickly folded her arms across her breasts. Just as well, Jared told himself. Her clinging clothes were turning him on. So were her swollen lips and messy hair.

"You have a comb?" he asked.

She shook her head. "It's in my bag downstairs."

He realized they couldn't risk leaving the room with her looking like this, so he steeled himself against the inevitable reaction and moved toward her.

Her arms stayed protectively crossed over her breasts, so he reached for the hair clip. "I'll just..." He raked spread fingers through the mess, straightening out the worst of it, wondering how he'd ever manage to get the clip back in.

A voice called from the hallway. *"Jared?"* The door burst open, and Stephanie instantly appeared.

He and Melissa both jumped guiltily back, her covering her breasts, him holding her hair clip.

Stephanie stopped abruptly. "I'm sorry." But she didn't look sorry in the least. A broad grin grew on her face and her eyes sparkled in delight.

Barry Salmon and Hal Norris halted behind her. All three of them stared at the incriminating scene.

Jared inwardly groaned. Why the hell hadn't he kept his hands to himself? Melissa's reputation was about to tumble over the falls and be washed down the Windy River. Why the hell hadn't he kept his hands to himself?

She was the first to speak. "It's not what you—"

But he cut her off. "I was inviting Melissa to join us for dinner," he told Stephanie, giving the two cowboys a warning glare.

"I knew it!" Stephanie beamed.

"The rain blew right in the windows," he went on, to

explain their appearance. Then he handed Melissa the hair clip. "Thanks for your help."

She gave him a puzzled expression. "There's no need—"

He stopped her with a stare. There was every need to protect her reputation, not to mention his own. She'd be gone in a week. In the meantime, he'd rather have the ranch staff think they were dating than carrying on a clandestine affair in the stable office.

He turned to his sister. "Did you need me for something?"

"Royce just called," said Stephanie. "He's at the airport."

"A day early?" That surprised Jared. He hoped nothing was wrong.

"And McQuestin called," Hal put in. "Some of the herd's still in the south canyon, and there's a risk of flooding down there."

"Hal and Barry are going to take half a dozen men," said Stephanie, but her goofy gaze was still on Melissa.

Jared knew he'd have to deal with his sister's let-down later. But at the moment, seeing the pure joy on Stephanie's face, he was inclined to wait until they got through the graveside visit on Sunday. He wondered if Melissa would be willing to go along with the charade. It would definitely distract Stephanie from missing their grandfather.

"Do you need me?" Jared asked Hal. He hadn't played cowboy in a few years, but he was ready and able if they needed an extra hand.

Hal shook his graying head. "Should be done by dark."

Jared gave the man a nod of acknowledgment. Then he looked at Stephanie. "I'll be right down."

She all but winked in return as she pulled the door shut.

"What are you *thinking?*" Melissa demanded as the footsteps receded down the hall.

"That you cared about your reputation." He stated the obvious.

"This isn't 1950."

"It's also not Vegas. It's Montana."

"People don't kiss in Montana?"

"They didn't know we were just kissing."

"But…" Melissa took a step back.

"Your lips," he told her softly. "Your hair, your clothes. You look like you just tumbled out of a haystack."

"But we didn't do anything."

"We thought about it," he told her gruffly. "And it shows."

Her glance went down to her chest. "Oh."

"Yeah. Oh."

Melissa swiftly pulled her hair to the base of her neck and fastened it with the clip. "What about Stephanie? You know what she's going to think."

Jared nodded. "I wanted to talk to you about that."

Melissa raised her brows.

"Would you mind playing along for a few days? Have dinner with us, pretend you like me, just enough to make Stephanie think there's a possibility we'll fall for each other."

Melissa seemed genuinely astonished. "Why? Why would you do that to your own sister?"

"You saw how excited she was," Jared pointed out.

"Yes. And I know how disappointed she's going to be when she finds out the truth. Not to mention how ticked off she's going to be at you."

"Who says she has to find out?"

"I'm leaving in a few days."

"That's perfect," he said. "It'll get us through Sunday. Then we'll act like it didn't work out. She'll be disappointed, sure. But she'll also be past the hard part of commemorating our parents' deaths and remembering how much she misses her grandfather."

"I don't think you can postpone grieving."

"Sure, you can." You could postpone it. You could ignore it. And you could replace it. With, for example, anger.

Melissa shook her head. "I'm not comfortable with this."

Then, he'd simply have to make her comfortable with it. "How much are we paying you?"

"Minimum wage, why?"

"I'll double it."

"You want me to ignore my principles and fake being your girlfriend for two times minimum wage?"

"Triple."

"Jared."

"Name your price."

"It's not about money. It's about integrity." For some reason her voice trailed away on the final word. Her gaze focused on the window as she watched the rain streak down the pane of glass. "Do you really think it's best for her?"

"I do." He moved up behind her. He couldn't help but admire Melissa's decision-making process. "Do you think you could pretend to like me?"

He saw her smile in the blurry reflection of the window. "I'm a pretty good liar."

"Good to know." He restrained himself from resting his hands on her shoulders, even though he longed to touch her again.

She turned, and his desire ramped up. "What do you want me to do?"

Jared bit his tongue over the loaded question, but his expression obviously gave him away.

"You." She poked him squarely in the chest. "Have to promise to behave yourself."

"I will. If you tell me what that means."

Her eyes narrowed. "It means…" She seemed to stumble. "It means not looking at me like you're the big bad wolf and I'm carrying a basket of goodies."

"It'll probably help the charade," he reasoned.

"It'll make me jumpy."

"It should," was his blunt answer.

"Jared," she warned.

"I'll behave myself," he promised. "But it'll help if you do a couple of things for me."

"What?"

"Wear a gunnysack, and a veil, don't talk in that

sexy voice and, for the love of God, quit smelling so decadently delicious."

Back inside her cottage, Melissa was all but shaking with reaction to Jared's words. And to his kisses. And to the overwhelming opportunity he'd unknowingly handed to her.

She was having dinner with his family. Dinner with the Ryders—a private meal where she could ask as many questions as she liked, about growing up, their ranch, their charity trust, their businesses.

She already knew the article would show them in a positive light. Both Jared and Stephanie were hardworking, successful people. The fact that they commemorated their parents' deaths was admirable, and their grandfather's recent death would add a poignancy that readers would lap up like kittens with fresh cream.

She lowered herself into the armchair beside the cottage window, struggling to frame her thoughts. It was Friday today. She'd planned to give herself one more day, maybe two at the most, to gather facts at the ranch. Then she'd have to rush back to Chicago and write the article in time to have it sitting on Seth Strickland's desk for Monday morning.

But that timetable was out the window now. Her greatest interview opportunities would be in the next couple of days. Which meant there was no way to be ready Monday morning. Which meant she'd have to call Seth and confess.

She drew a breath, squeezing the fabric-covered arms

of the chair as she tried to still her racing heart. She could only hope her editor's excitement over the article would overrule his anger that she'd lied to him.

She glanced at her watch. Two o'clock. That made it three in Chicago. No time to lose. She pulled her cell phone out of her bag, pressing the buttons for his number. It rang three times, but then jumped to voice mail, giving her no choice but to leave a quick, vague message.

She replaced the phone in her bag when, over the sound of the continuing rain, she heard footsteps on the front porch. She glanced through the window to see Stephanie, a dripping white Stetson pulled low on her head, waving cheerily through the pane.

Melissa sighed inwardly. She wasn't ready for this. Being undercover to get a story was one thing, but leading Stephanie on was another thing entirely.

But Stephanie had seen her, and Melissa had no choice but to open the door. She crossed to the little foyer.

"Hi," said Stephanie, beaming as she entered the cottage.

Melissa couldn't help but smile in return. The young woman's grin was infectious.

"I told you so," Stephanie sang, hanging her hat on one of a long row of pegs on the wooden wall.

The entry area of the cottage was practically laid out. There were pegs for coats and hats. A small bench beneath, with room for footwear under it, and a bright, woven Navajo rug decorating the wooden floor.

The foyer took up one corner of the small living

room. The rest of the room boasted a simple burgundy couch, a leather armchair, a small television and two low tables with ivory lamps.

There was a compact kitchen beside the living room, a table and two kitchen chairs under the front window, and a door to a bedroom/bathroom combination on the far side. Melissa had to admit, she adored the brass bed and the claw-foot tub. And the oak tree outside the bedroom window rustled in the night breeze, while the muted roar of the river outside filled in the background.

Melissa took a step back to stay out of the way of Stephanie's wet raincoat. Not that she wouldn't have to change clothes, anyway. Standing in front of the open window with Jared had been…well, it had been amazing, of course. But mostly it had been foolish. And not just because she'd ended up with wet clothes.

Stephanie kicked off her boots. "Do you know how long it's been since Jared invited a woman home for dinner?"

Melissa knew she needed to dial Stephanie's excitement level way down. "He didn't exactly—"

"Never," sang Stephanie. "He's never invited a woman home for dinner."

"Your equestrian center is not his actual home," cautioned Melissa. "And I was already here."

Stephanie waved a dismissive hand. "Technicalities."

"No. Facts."

Stephanie pouted.

"Seriously, Stephanie. You can't get carried away with this. Jared and I barely know each other."

Stephanie heaved an exaggerated sigh, dropping down onto the couch. "Are you always this much of a downer?"

Melissa took the armchair again. "I'm always this much of a realist."

"Where's the fun in that?"

"It saves a lot of heartache in the long run."

"Disappointment, I can handle. It's never leaving the starting gate that would kill me."

Inwardly, Melissa conceded there was some logic to the argument. "It's only dinner," she said to Stephanie. "And I'm still planning to leave in a couple of days."

"But you're here now," said Stephanie with a sly wink. "What are you going to wear?"

Melissa's cell phone jangled from her bag on the floor.

"I hadn't thought about it," she said, knowing in her heart the call was from Seth. There was no way in the world she could answer it in front of Stephanie.

It rang again.

"Do you want to get that?"

Melissa shook her head. "It can go to voice mail."

"You sure? I don't mind."

Another shrill ring.

"I'm sure. What do you think I should wear?" Truth was, Melissa hadn't seen anyone wear anything but blue jeans and riding clothes since she'd arrived. Her own wardrobe was plain and meager, since she was pretending to be on a bus trip.

The damn phone rang again.

"You sure you don't want to—"

"Completely sure." Melissa reached for the slim phone. A quick glance told her it was, indeed, her boss. She sent the call to voice mail. "There."

Stephanie paused for a moment. Then her expression grew animated once again as she sat forward. "I was thinking, since it's Royce's first night back, we should dress up a little."

Melissa's attention went automatically to the downpour and the rivulets of mud streaking the narrow cottage road. Even if she had brought anything dressy, it was a virtual mud bog between the cottage and Stephanie's house.

"We'll do it up at the house," Stephanie went on. "We're about the same size. You can take a shower up there. We'll play around with your hair. Put on a little makeup, and you can borrow one of my dresses. I have a bunch I've never even worn."

"I'm not Cinderella," Melissa admonished.

"Oh—" Stephanie all but jumped up from the sofa "—that makes me the fairy godmother."

"Did you miss the word *not?*" Melissa struggled to keep a grip on the conversation.

"This is going to be great."

Still in Melissa's hand, the phone rang again. It was Seth. She hit the voice mail button one more time. She was going to have one heck of a lot of explaining to do. Good thing she would have a kick-ass story to offer up.

"Girl talk while we get ready." Stephanie laughed.

Melissa paused.

Girl talk? *Girl talk.*

Why was she trying to get out of this? Girl talk was exactly what she needed for research.

"I'll meet you up there," she agreed. A quick call to Seth, and she'd be ready for all the girl talk in the world.

"Don't be silly." This time Stephanie did jump up. "You'd drown. I'll drive you over in the truck."

Stephanie's house was rustic but undeniably gracious. A large, practical foyer led into a massive great room with polished floors, a high, hewn-beam ceiling, and overstuffed leather furniture decorated with colorful pillows and woven throws. There was a huge stone fireplace at one end of the rectangular room, and a row of glass doors down the side opened onto a deck that overlooked evergreens and snowy mountain peaks. A wide passageway opposite revealed a gourmet kitchen with a long, polished-wood breakfast bar and padded stools and a formal dining room that seated twelve, with a wood-and-brass chandelier and an impressive woven carpet under the cherry table and wine-colored armchairs.

As they made their way up a wide staircase to the second floor, Melissa wished once again for Susan and her camera. Stephanie's bedroom was at the front of the house. It had its own small balcony, a walk-in closet, an en suite bath and a small sitting area set in a bay-window alcove.

"Dresses are way in the back," said Stephanie, flicking on the closet light and gesturing into the long room. "Pick anything you want. I'll hunt through the bathroom and see what I can find for makeup."

"What are you planning to wear?" Melissa gazed through the open door at rows of blazers and blouses, situated above open shelves that held blue jeans and jodhpurs. She stepped over several pairs of polished boots as she made her way across the carpeted floor.

Stephanie hadn't been exaggerating. There were at least two dozen dresses, most with the tags still on. They were black, gold, red, sleeveless, gauzy, and one gorgeous printed silk that shimmered gold and peach, with a jeweled scoop neckline that looked like something off a Paris runway.

"Try that one," came Stephanie's voice from the doorway.

Melissa shook her head. "I couldn't."

"Why not? Royce brought it back from Europe last year. The straps are too narrow for me. It makes me look like I have linebacker shoulders."

"It does not." Melissa laughed. Stephanie had a wonderful figure.

"I'm okay with sleeveless, even strapless, but there's something about those spaghetti straps that don't work. You want to hop in the shower? I put out fresh towels and a robe."

"I feel bad invading your privacy," Melissa said.

"Are you kidding? I can't wait to dress you up and wow my brother."

Melissa placed the dress back on the rack and turned. "I don't want you to get hurt," she told Stephanie honestly. "Jared and I barely know each other."

"You have to start somewhere," Stephanie replied, obviously undaunted by reality.

"The odds against he and I clicking are about a million to one."

"The odds against me winning Spruce Meadows last week were about a million to one."

"But you practiced. You worked hard for years and years to win that competition."

"I'm not expecting you to marry him next weekend."

Melissa took a step closer to Stephanie. "I'm not going to marry him at all. You have to understand that. He's a nice man. And maybe he thinks I'm pretty—"

"He's going to think you're a knockout in that silk dress."

Melissa sighed. "You're killing me here, Stephanie. I need to know *you* know this isn't going anywhere."

Some of the optimism went out of Stephanie's blue eyes. "But you're going to try, right?"

"It doesn't matter whether I try or not, the odds are still stacked way against it." And those odds were a whole lot higher than Melissa could admit.

"I'm not afraid of the odds," said Stephanie, a new equilibrium coming into her eyes. "I'm just leading a horse to water. He drinks or not will be up to him."

"I take it Jared's the horse?"

"And you're the water."

Relief poured through Melissa. Stephanie understood just fine. She wasn't some flighty young girl with impossible dreams. She was simply trying to match up her brother and bring some balance to the family's gender numbers.

The plan didn't have a hope in hell of working with Melissa, but she could respect the effort.

"Robe's on the door hook," said Stephanie. She nodded to the en suite. "Towels are stacked on the counter."

"Okay," Melissa agreed. She could play dress-up and ply Jared with questions. Maybe they'd have wine with dinner. Even better. She'd sip slowly and let his tongue loosen up.

She followed Stephanie's directions, enjoying the marble tub and the luxurious bath products. The towels were big and plush, and Stephanie's hair dryer gave Melissa's straight, blond hair some body and bounce.

She exited the room to find Stephanie sitting in front of her vanity in a white robe, her auburn hair damp around her ears.

Stephanie swiveled on the small stool. "What do you think?"

Melissa blinked at the unexpected sight. Stephanie's delicate features had been all but obliterated by glaringly bright makeup. With spiked lashes, bright blue shadow, dark blush and a fire engine–red lipstick shade, she looked ready for the lead in a 1980s disco flick.

"Uh...I..." Melissa struggled to find words.

Stephanie's face fell. "It's that bad?" She glanced back to the mirror.

Melissa rushed forward, reflexively putting her hands on Stephanie's shoulders. "The look's a little dated. That's all."

Stephanie hardened her jaw, glaring at her features. "Is it me? Do I just not have a feminine face?"

Melissa's jaw dropped open. "Are you kidding me?"

"I can never quite seem to pull it off." She gestured vaguely toward the closet. "It's not that I don't have the ingredients. I've got plenty of clothes, shoes, beauty products. But I can never figure out what to do with them. I bought a makeover magazine once. I ended up looking like a clown."

"You're beautiful." Melissa recovered her voice. "Beyond beautiful. You're stunning."

"I have a little-girl nose, ugly freckles and funny-color eyes." She leaned forward, screwing up her face in the mirror.

"Most women would kill for your nose," said Melissa honestly. "The freckles are pretty, and you just need a new shade of shadow." She turned the stool, looking critically at Stephanie's skin tone and features. "Go wash your face. Let's start over."

Stephanie perked up. "You'll help?"

"You bet I'll help."

Stephanie jumped up and headed for the bathroom, turning on the taps in the sink. "Did you have a mom and sisters and stuff?" she called.

"A mom, yes," said Melissa. "But I have five older brothers."

Stephanie popped her head back into the room. "Five?"

Melissa nodded. "Adam, Ben, Caleb, Dan and Eddy."

"So probably no makeup tips from them."

"Nah. But I can frame up a cabin, change a car's oil and whistle."

Stephanie laughed as she rubbed cleanser over her face. "And I can rope a calf in under thirty seconds."

"You never know when these skills might come in handy."

Stephanie rinsed and dried, walking back into the bedroom, clad in her terry robe. "Where did you learn about makeup?"

"Girlfriends at school, cable TV, demos at the mall." Melissa glanced around the room and realized the wide sill on the bay window was a good height.

"My friends were in the 4H club. And we didn't get many channels out here while I was growing up."

"Can you hop up there?" Melissa gestured. "That way I won't have to bend over."

"Sure." Stephanie held her robe as she got settled, her bare feet dangling.

Melissa selected some lotion and a few cosmetics and piled them on a small table in the alcove. "It's all about subtlety now," she explained, tipping Stephanie's chin toward the light. "Women want to look natural, just a little more beautiful than nature intended. Earth tones will bring out the subtle silver in your eyes, instead of clashing with it."

"Can you cover up my freckles?"

Personally Melissa liked the freckles. "I'll tone them down a bit. They'll be less noticeable. You have amazing skin."

"Fresh air and healthy living."

"It works. I'm in an office all day, air-conditioning and recycled smog."

Stephanie's forehead wrinkled. "You have a job?"

"I used to have a job." Melissa cursed inwardly at her stupidity, struggling to recover from the gaff. "I delivered office mail for a while. Very boring."

"You seem so smart."

"I'm not that smart."

"Jared said you knew about Sierra Benito."

"That was a stroke of luck." Melissa found a thin brush and some powdered, charcoal eyeliner. "I happened to read an article in the newspaper."

"But you remembered it."

"I suppose. Close your eyes."

"You must have a good memory."

"Decent." Memory was a critical attribute for a journalist—names, dates, faces, events. Melissa gently stroked on the liner, chose silver, blue and pale purple for shadow, added a subtle blush and finished off with a neutral lip gloss.

Then she found a comb and piled Stephanie's thick, wavy hair in a loose twist at the top of her head, freeing a few locks to frame her face and trail at the back of her neck.

Melissa stood back. "Go take a look."

Obviously self-conscious and nervous, Stephanie hopped down from the ledge. She gingerly crossed the floor to the mirror, squinted, opened her eyes, then stared in silence.

"Wow," she finally breathed, turning her head from side to side. "I'm gorgeous."

"You certainly are."

Stephanie raised her brows to Melissa, mischief lurking in her silver-blue eyes. "Let's do you."

Seven

It wasn't often Jared saw his little sister dressed to accentuate her femininity. Not that he ever forgot she was feminine, but she'd run around the ranch yard like a tomboy ever since he could remember. So tonight when she waltzed into the great room in an ultra-flirty dress, he was momentarily stunned. It was white on top, with bows at the shoulders and a full black skirt that billowed around her knees. She'd done something with her hair, too. And her face looked—

Melissa appeared from behind Stephanie, and the jolt took his breath away. Where Stephanie was feminine, Melissa was sultry. She wore a shimmering thin silk sheath of a dress that clung to her figure like a second skin. Spaghetti straps adorned her smooth shoulders, while the gold and peach shimmered under the warm light. Her hair was upswept, her face flawless, and her long, tanned legs and spiked heels were going to invade his dreams for at least the next year.

He swallowed.

"Is Royce here yet?" asked Stephanie.

When Jared finally dragged his gaze from Melissa, he saw the twinkle in Stephanie's eyes. He had to hand it to his sister, she knew how to matchmake. Nothing would happen between him and Melissa, but it sure wouldn't be from a lack of desire. Given his own way, he'd drag her off to his bed right now.

"Sunset Hill flooded out," he answered. He'd talked to Royce a few minutes ago, and his brother had decided to wait the storm out at the main house with McQuestin.

Fine with Jared.

He didn't particularly want Royce laying eyes on Melissa, anyway.

Stephanie's lips pursed in a pout. "Why doesn't he ride up?"

"Probably because he'd be soaked to the ass in the first half mile." Jared gave a quick glance at Melissa to see if his coarse language had offended her.

Her little grin was the last thing he saw before the room went black.

Forks of lightning streaked through the thick sky, while thunder cracked and raindrops smashed against the roof and the wooden deck outside.

"Uh-oh," came Stephanie's disembodied voice.

"What happened?" asked Melissa.

"Could have been anything," Jared answered as he made his way toward the mantelpiece. He found a box of matches by feel, struck one and lit a couple of candles. Power outages were common in ranch country, doubly so during storms.

Stephanie crossed to the front window. "I don't see the cookhouse," she said.

"Give it a minute," Jared suggested, flipping open his cell phone. He punched in Royce's number.

Melissa joined Stephanie at the window, and Jared let himself enjoy the view of her back.

"Why would you see the cookhouse?" asked Melissa.

"They have an emergency generator," said Stephanie.

"Hey, bro," came Royce's voice on the phone.

"Lights out down there?" asked Jared.

"Just now."

"Us, too. Any problems?"

"The boys aren't back from the canyon yet," said Royce.

"McQuestin worried?"

"Won't be for a couple more hours."

"Keep me posted?"

Melissa turned, and Jared quickly averted his lecherous gaze.

"Sure," said Royce.

Flickering lights came on in the distance.

"Cookhouse is up," said Jared, and Melissa turned back to the window.

"We're striking up the gas barbecue," said Royce.

"Don't let McQuestin talk you into poker."

Royce laughed as he signed off.

Stephanie had moved into the dining room. She was on her own cell phone, checking to make sure the employees were all accounted for.

Jared tucked his phone in his pocket.

"What now?" asked Melissa.

He checked to make sure Stephanie was out of earshot as he moved toward Melissa and the window. He kept his voice low. "Now I tell you you're gorgeous."

"Stephanie's idea."

"My sister's not stupid."

"Your sister is Machiavellian."

He moved his hand forward and brushed Melissa's fingertips. "Seems a shame to let her down."

"Seems a shame to lead her on."

"Hey, she's the one playing us, remember?"

"Mrs. Belmont left lasagna in the oven," came Stephanie's voice.

Jared reflexively backed off.

"Salad's in the fridge," Stephanie finished.

"I guess we're dining by candlelight," said Melissa.

"Romantic," Stephanie put in, scooping one of the lighted candles and heading for the dining room.

Melissa followed.

Jared allowed himself a lingering glance at Melissa as she walked away. "Better than poker with McQuestin," he said out loud.

They settled at one end of the big table, Jared at the head, flanked by the two women. Lasagna, salad, rolls and a bottle of merlot were spread out in front of them. He'd lit a candelabra for the middle of the table, and kerosene lamps flickered against the rain-streaked windows.

Melissa's soft blond hair shimmered in the yellow light. Her lips were dark. Her eyes sparkled. And the silk shifted softly against her body as she moved her hands.

"Do you have political aspirations?" she asked him.

The question took him by surprise. "Why the heck would you think that?"

"You've got it all," she responded, taking another sip of the merlot, which he couldn't help but note was exactly the same shade as her lips. "Money, success, community standing, charitable work, and now you're palling around with the mayor of Chicago."

"How did you know about the mayor?"

She concentrated on setting down her glass. "One of the cowboys mentioned something about your building and the city."

Jared turned to glare at Stephanie. "How does anybody get any work done around here?" he demanded. "Melissa's been here three days, and she knows everything but my birth weight and shoe size."

"Don't be such a bear," said Stephanie.

"You're exaggerating," said Melissa.

"Not by much."

"Eight pounds nine ounces," Stephanie put in with a giggle.

"Ouch," said Melissa.

"Don't let that put you off," Stephanie came back. "It's not necessarily hereditary."

Both Jared and Melissa stared at her, dumb-founded.

"What?" Stephanie glanced back and forth between them. "You guys don't want kids?"

"Several," said Jared, deciding his sister deserved everything she got from here on in.

He took Melissa's hand and raised it to his lips. "How does four sound to you?"

"Are you going to hire me a nanny?" she asked, surprising him by playing along.

"You bet. A nanny, a chauffeur and a housekeeper."

"Okay, then." Melissa gave a nod. "Four it is. But we'd better get started—I'm not getting any younger." She reached for her wineglass. "Better enjoy this while I can. Once I'm pregnant, it's off the alcohol. And this wine is fantastic."

"I know you're messing with me," Stephanie put in. "But I don't care. I have hope, anyway."

"We have a very good wine cellar," said Jared. "It was a hobby of Gramps."

"Why don't you show it to Melissa?" Stephanie quickly suggested.

"You hoping I'll get her pregnant on the tasting table?"

Melissa sputtered and coughed over a drink.

He squeezed her hand by way of apology.

"I think Stephanie's overestimating the power of this dress," she wheezed.

Jared hesitated. Then he stepped into the breach. "No, she's not."

Stephanie clapped her hands together in triumph.

* * *

It was ten o'clock when Stephanie succeeded in getting Jared and Melissa alone together. They were in the truck, and Melissa peered in pitch-darkness and driving rain as they rounded the bend to the row of cottages by the river, the headlights bouncing off the oak trees and the dark porches.

She had to admit, she wouldn't have wanted to walk all the way back. And she wouldn't have asked Stephanie to slog through the mud to get to the truck. And that left Jared.

Then he had insisted on carrying her from the ranch house porch to the truck—which was an experience all on its own.

Now they pulled up to the front of her cottage and he killed the lights and turned off the engine.

"Stay put," he told her as he opened the driver's door and a puff of cool wind burst in. "I'll be right around."

Part of her wanted to insist on walking, but her shoes were impractical, the mud was slick, and she knew the black road would be a patchwork of deep puddles. So she waited, her heart rate increasing, her skin prickling in anticipation and her brain fumbling through sexy projections of being in Jared's arms again.

Her door swung open, and she shifted from the seat into his arms, wrapping her own arms around his neck. She'd put a windbreaker over the dress, but her legs were still bare and his strong hand clasped around the back of her thigh.

"Ready?" he asked, husky voice puffing against her cheek.

"Ready," she confirmed with a nod, and he pulled her against his chest, his body protecting her from the worst of the rain. He kicked the truck door shut and strode over the mud and up the porch stairs, stopping under the tiny roof in front of the door.

He didn't bother putting her down. Instead, he swung the door open and carried her into the warm cottage.

It was completely dark, not a single frame of reference.

He slowly lowered her to the floor. "Don't move."

"Do you have matches?" she asked as he stepped away from her.

"There'll be some on the mantel." Something banged, and he cursed.

"You okay?" she called.

"I'm fine."

Then she heard a crackle, and a small flame appeared across the living room. She could just make out Jared's face as he lit three candles on the stone mantel. There was a mirror on the wall behind, and the light reflected back into the room.

"Thanks," she told him.

He shook out the match and tossed it into the fireplace. "You want a fire?"

"It's not that cold." She hung the damp windbreaker on a wall hook. Then she wiped her face, pulled the clip from her hair and finger-combed out the rainwater.

It was late enough that she planned to snuggle into bed with her laptop and record notes from the evening.

Stephanie had predicted the power would be back on by morning. If not, the staff would gather at the cookhouse for breakfast, and they'd set priorities for animal care.

Jared crumpled up a newspaper, threw it into the fireplace and added a handful of kindling. "It's not that warm, either." He crouched down and struck another match, lighting a corner of the newspaper.

The orange flame quickly grew, reflecting off the planes and angles of his face. There was something about the actions that warmed Melissa's heart. He hadn't exactly saved her life, but he'd shown a tender, caring side that surprised her.

She automatically moved closer to the fire. "I wish I could offer you coffee or something."

He rose to his feet in the flickering light. His short hair was damp, and his cotton shirt was plastered to his chest. Power and masculinity seemed to ooze from every pore.

He eased closer, and she was instantly awash in desire.

"Coffee's not what I want."

She was dying to ask, but she didn't dare. She opened her mouth, then closed it again, warning herself that the slightest encouragement was going to bring his lips crashing down on hers, and they'd be trapped all over again in the tangle of desire.

His lips came down on hers, anyway.

And she might have stretched up slightly to meet him.

Okay, she'd definitely stretched up. And she'd tilted her head to accommodate him. And now she was opening her mouth, meeting his tongue, snaking her arms around his neck and pressing her body tightly against his own.

His clothes were damp, but she didn't care. His hands were roaming, and she loved it. His mouth was sure and strong, but still tender, and oh, so hot.

Passion quickly obliterated reason. She clung tightly as his nimble hands pulled down the zipper of her dress. He eased it over her head and discarded it on a chair. He worked at the buttons of his shirt, alternating between kissing her and staring deeply into her eyes. His were nearly black with passion, while desire pulsed through every fiber of her body.

Her hands went to his jeans, popping the button, sliding the zipper.

He groaned, tossed his shirt and pulled her back into his arms. His kisses roamed her cheeks, her neck and down to where he pushed her bra out of the way. His hot mouth surrounded a nipple, and she threw her head back, her hands grasping his shoulders for support.

He wrapped a strong arm firmly around the small of her back, holding her steady, his mouth sending sparks of desire from her breasts to the base of her belly. He released her bra, dropping it to the floor. Then he scooped her into his arms and carried her to the small bedroom.

The sheets were cool against her bare back. She could barely make out his outline as he discarded the remainder of his clothes. Then his warm, hard, musk-scented body was sliding next to her, and she was enveloped in kisses and caresses that seared heat over every inch of her skin.

She kissed his chest, tasting his salty skin, her hands roaming down his back, over his buttocks, along his strong thighs.

He groaned his approval, kissing her deeply. "You are gorgeous," he breathed. He kissed her again. His fingers found their way into her flimsy panties.

She gasped at his touch, flexing her hips, transmitting an unmistakable invitation.

He peeled off her panties, produced a condom from somewhere, and covered her body with his own. Their bodies were flush together, tight at the apex, and her legs were wrapped around his waist.

He kissed her deeply, sliding his hands to her bottom, adjusting the angle of their bodies as he eased inside. Driving rain splattered against the bedroom window. Lightning chased across the sky while thunder vibrated the cottage walls.

Then the world around Melissa disappeared. Nothing existed beyond Jared, and every sensation was magnified a thousand times, his touch, his scent, the taste of his skin, the sound of his voice as he recited her name, calling her beautiful, urging her on.

Their tempo increased. The hot and cold and electric sensations heightening to unbearable. As thunder crashed around them, her body stiffened. Her toes curled. Her hoarse voice cried out Jared's name as she tumbled from the pinnacle down into the exquisite arms of release.

As she floated to earth, Jared tucked a quilt around

them. He turned slightly to the side, keeping them locked together, but taking his weight from her body.

Their deep breaths rose in unison, both of them sucking the moisture-laden oxygen from the dark room, recovering, reframing, realizing the magnitude of what they'd just done.

"I'm not sure that was such a good idea," she ventured on a gasp.

He didn't let her go. Didn't back off a single inch. "Because you work for me?" he mumbled against her neck.

Because I'm writing an article on you. Because you don't know who I am. Because I lied to you. The reasons were endless, and she couldn't admit to any of them.

"At least for tonight," she ventured, instead, "do you think we could be clear that I work for Stephanie?"

Jared's chuckle rumbled through his frame. "So what's the problem?"

"I'm leaving in a few days."

He smoothed her hair from her forehead. "Just because something's short, doesn't mean it can't be fantastic."

"I suppose." If you took away her deception, a one-night stand certainly wasn't the end of the world. But eventually he was going to find out her true identity.

She couldn't do anything to change the past hour, but she did need to control herself going forward. Not that she'd *ever* divulge any intimate details. Every single thing that happened in the cottage tonight was off the record.

But she did need to back off. She couldn't let their circumstances get even more complicated.

She eased away from his warmth. "Stephanie's probably counting the minutes you've been down here."

"Are you asking me to leave?"

"I think that would be best."

He stilled, and she assumed he was staring at her in the dark.

A lightning bolt lit up the room, and his stark expression of disappointment tugged at her heart.

"I think it would be best," she repeated, wanting nothing more than to burrow down under the covers and sleep in Jared's warm arms for the rest of the night. But she had to be strong.

He rolled from the bed. "Of course." There was a tightness to his voice that bordered on anger.

She closed her ears to it and clung to the passion they'd shared.

His jeans rustled. Then he padded into the living room.

She held her breath while he dressed. Would he come back? Say something more? Kiss her goodbye?

Suddenly his silhouette appeared in the doorway. "Good night," he offered without coming back inside.

"Good night," she echoed, struggling to keep the hollowness from her voice. She'd asked him to leave. She was silly to feel hurt.

He waited a moment more, then turned away, heading out into the storm.

The truck engine rumbled to life. The headlights

flared up. Then the big treaded tires churned their way over the muddy road.

Melissa dragged herself from the bed. She wrapped a robe around her body, retrieved her laptop, powered it up and forced her thoughts back to the discussion at dinner. The fling with Jared might be over, but she still had her job to save.

"Seth Strickland," came the terse answer at the other end of the phone.

It was morning. The rain had stopped, and the lights were back on as Stephanie had predicted. Melissa was dressed in blue jeans and a simple tank top again, trying to push the insanity that had become her life back into perspective.

"Seth?" she said into the phone, thanking her lucky stars that he was in the office on a Saturday. "It's Melissa."

"Where the hell have you been?" he shouted without preamble.

She wasn't ready to answer that question yet. "If I could *guarantee* the Jared Ryder story, can you buy me a little time?"

"No! And what the hell are you talking about? Why didn't you call me back yesterday?"

"I'm in Montana."

"You said you were working from home."

"I'm at the Ryder Ranch. Right now. I had dinner with Jared Ryder last night."

Seth went silent.

"I need a few more days, Seth."

"You had dinner with Ryder?"

"And his sister. And his brother's just arrived."

"How the hell did you—"

"They think I'm a stable hand."

"You're undercover?" There was a note of respect in Seth's voice. "It's an exposé?"

"Yes, I'm undercover."

"What've you got?"

"A bunch of stuff. His family. His childhood. Their charitable foundation."

"Ryder has a charitable foundation?"

"Yes. But I need a few more days. Can you give it to me?"

"You're in a position to guarantee the story?"

"Yes."

There was a long silence. "If I go to Everett and you don't deliver, you know both our asses will be out the door."

"I understand."

"And you can still make the guarantee?"

"I can." She didn't have enough on the construction business yet. But she'd let Stephanie matchmake some more, and she'd find a way to meet Royce. She'd get what Seth needed or die trying.

"I have to have it Wednesday. Five o'clock. And the copy better be bloody clean. We're not going to have time for much editing."

"Five o'clock Wednesday," Melissa confirmed.

"And, Melissa?" Seth's voice was gruff.

"Yes?"

"Lie to me again, and you're fired."

"Yes, sir."

Seth hung up the phone, and she realized she was shaking. The stakes couldn't be higher, and she barely had four days to pull it off.

"Have a good time with Melissa last night?" Stephanie asked as Royce's pickup appeared in the distance on the ranch road.

"It was fine," Jared answered, keeping his voice neutral. He fully expected Melissa to make herself scarce for the rest of the week.

He wasn't sure what had gone wrong at the end of the evening, but he'd obviously made some kind of misstep. A woman didn't go from crying out a man's name to kicking him out of her bed in the space of two minutes if the guy hadn't screwed up somehow.

He started down the stairs to meet Royce at the driveway.

"You going to see her again?" asked Stephanie, keeping pace.

"I expect I will. Since she's living here." Odds were that he'd run into her eventually.

"That's not what I meant. Are you going to ask her out? I noticed you stayed down there for a while."

"I bet you did."

The sound of the truck's engine grew louder. Mud sprayed out from the tires as Royce took a corner far too fast.

"Did you sleep with her?" asked Stephanie.

Jared shot his sister a glare of irritation. "What is the matter with you?"

She shrugged. "You were only gone an hour. Not a lot of time, but then maybe you weren't very—"

"Young lady, you shut your mouth before you get yourself into a world of trouble. Where did you learn to talk like that, anyway?" Maybe he'd stayed away too long. Maybe leaving Stephanie here on her own was a mistake. Or maybe Gramps's death had affected her more than Jared and Royce had realized.

"I'm just asking a question."

"You're out of line, little sister."

Stephanie pursed her lips in a pout. "So are you going to ask her out again?"

Jared frowned.

"That can't be out of line. I'm not asking about sex."

The truck skidded to a halt, and Jared walked forward. "Let's just get through the weekend, all right?"

"I know I have to get through the weekend," Stephanie muttered as they walked down the front pathway. "I was only hoping for something to look forward to at the end of it."

Jared felt a pang of guilt. The whole reason he'd started the charade with Melissa was to keep Stephanie's mind occupied. Sure, it had run way off the rails last night. But that wasn't Stephanie's fault.

He slung an arm around his sister's shoulders, moderating his voice. "Fine. I'll ask her out again. But I can't guarantee she'll say yes."

Stephanie turned in to give him a tight squeeze. "I know she'll say yes. I saw the way she looked at you."

The words caused a sudden tightening in Jared's

chest. How she'd looked at him? What did that mean? He wanted to probe for more information. But Royce appeared across the hood of the truck, and Stephanie broke free to hug her other brother.

"Baby sister!" cried Royce, dragging Stephanie into his arms, lifting her off the ground and twirling her around.

Jared caught a glimpse of Melissa across the yard, and their gazes met. She was shoveling manure again, and for some reason, that made him angry. She was capable of so much more. She was intelligent, full of insightful opinions and thought-provoking questions.

It occurred to him that he could offer her a job in Chicago. She could work for Ryder International or even the Genevieve Fund. There had to be any number of things a woman with her intellect and curiosity could handle.

In a split second he realized what he was doing. He was working out ways to keep her close, ways that he could see her again, maybe sleep with her again. Though, judging by the expression on her face, the latter was unlikely. But what did it say about him? Was he buying into Stephanie's fantasy?

He could almost feel a debate going on inside Melissa's brain. She'd seen him, and she knew he knew. Did she duck her head and go back to work? Did she avoid him, or get the first, awkward moment over with?

While he waited, she squared her shoulders, leaned the manure fork against the fence and determinedly marched toward him. Good for her. He couldn't help a surge of admiration, and he moved to meet her in the driveway.

"Melissa!" Stephanie's voice surprised him. "Come and meet Royce." Hand in Royce's, Stephanie tugged him to intersect Melissa's pathway. The four of them met up off the hood of the truck.

"Royce, this is Melissa," said Stephanie. "She's dating Jared."

Melissa's eyes widened slightly, but she held her composure.

Royce turned to stare at Jared.

Jared gave his brother an almost imperceptible shake, and Royce immediately held out his hand to Melissa. "Great to meet you. I'm the black sheep of the family."

Stephanie laughed, while Melissa accepted Royce's handshake. "Melissa Webster. I'm the black sheep in mine."

"She has five older brothers," Stephanie put in.

"Worse off than you," Royce teased, arching a brow at his sister.

"I'd better get back to work," said Melissa. Her gaze darted to Jared just long enough to let him know she wished they'd been able to talk. Well, so did he. He felt like he owed her an apology of some kind. At the very least, he wanted to make sure things were okay between them.

"Can you come and help me with Rosie-Jo?" Stephanie asked Melissa.

Since Rosie-Jo had half a dozen grooms, Jared recognized the ruse for what it was. Stephanie wanted to pump Melissa for information. But from what he'd seen of Melissa so far, she'd be up to the task of sidestepping anything too personal.

"Dating?" Royce asked as the two women walked away.

"More like flirting," said Jared. "But I didn't have the heart to disillusion Stephanie this weekend."

"Are you going to disillusion poor Melissa?"

Jared shook his head. "She knows the score. She's leaving in a few days, anyway."

Royce reached into the back of the pickup truck and retrieved his duffel bag. "How's Stephanie holding up?"

"Too cheerful," said Jared. "You just know she's going to crack."

"Maybe going up to the cemetery isn't such a good idea this year. Gramps's grave is awfully fresh."

"Go ahead and suggest we skip," said Jared as the two men headed for the house. Quite frankly, Jared would rather avoid the cemetery. He wanted to pay tribute to his grandfather, but the anger at his parents hadn't abated one bit. His whole life, he'd admired and respected them both, never doubting their morals and integrity. But he couldn't have been more wrong. He wanted to yell at them, not lay flowers beside their headstones.

But he couldn't let on. Bad enough that he knew the truth. He couldn't drag Royce, and certainly not Stephanie, into the nightmare. At the moment, he wished his grandfather had taken the knowledge to his grave.

"She'd never go for it," said Royce, yanking Jared back to the present.

"Of course not," Jared agreed as they crossed the porch. Stephanie considered herself tough. She'd never admit how much visiting the cemetery hurt her.

"I hear there's a debate over Sierra Benito." Royce tossed his duffel on a low bench in Stephanie's foyer.

"There is. You're the deciding vote."

"You going to try talking me out of the project?"

"I am. I don't want another death on my conscience." An image of Jared's father sprang to his mind. There was no excuse. No excuse in the world for what his father had done.

Royce paused and peered at his brother. "*Another* death?"

"Slip of the tongue," said Jared, turning away to move into the great room. "I don't want anyone to die on a Ryder project."

He also didn't want to keep lying to his brother, about his parents, about Melissa, about *anything*.

Eight

Under the small light above the cottage's kitchen table, Melissa typed furiously on her laptop. She'd composed and discarded at least five openings to her article. She knew if she could get the beginning right, the rest would flow. It was always that way.

But she needed to capture Jared's essence. No small feat. Every time she thought she had him pegged he'd show her another side of himself, and she'd have to rethink the package.

Maybe it would be easier if they hadn't made love. Maybe if she hadn't seen him naked, or gazed into the depths of his eyes, or felt the strength and tenderness of his caress.

She drew a frustrated sigh as the words on the screen blurred in front of her. Unless she wanted to sell the article to a tabloid, she was going to have to nix that train of thought.

Someone tapped lightly on her front door.

The sigh turned into a frown. It was Sunday night, and the two young women staying next door had invited her over for drinks. The two had seemed very friendly, but Melissa had begged off. Between her ranch chores and allowing for time to fly back to Chicago, she only had two more evenings to pull the article together. There wasn't any time for socializing.

The knock came again.

With the light on, there was no sense in pretending she was asleep. Besides, they would have seen her through the window on their way up the stairs.

She pushed back from the table and crossed to the door.

"I'm sorry," she began as she tugged it open. "But I really can't—"

"Sorry to bother you," came Jared's voice.

His broad shoulders filled the doorway. His head was bare, and he still wore his business suit from the cemetery visit earlier. He wore a crisp, white shirt and a dark, red-striped tie. There was a frown on his face and worry in his eyes.

"Jared."

"I was out walking and I saw your light," he apologized.

Even if she had been inclined to give up a chance to get more information, his expression would have melted the hardest heart. She knew he'd been up to the cemetery with his sister and brother this afternoon, and it had obviously been tough.

"How did it go?" she asked, stepping back to invite him in.

He shrugged as he walked inside. "About how I'd expected." His voice was hollow. "We all miss Gramps."

Melissa nodded, closing the door behind him. "This is probably the worst year," she ventured.

"I suppose." His gaze focused on something, and she realized he was staring at her laptop. "You travel with a computer?"

Panic spurred her forward. She closed the lid, hoping she'd saved recently. "It's compact," she answered. "Very light."

"I guess. Did I interrupt—" he paused "—work?"

"I'm writing a letter," she quickly improvised. "Can I offer you something? Coffee?" She gestured to the small living-room grouping, taking his attention away from the table and her computer. "Or there's a bottle of wine…"

"I'm fine." He eased down into the worn armchair.

Melissa curled into one corner of the sofa, sitting at right angles to him. "How's Stephanie doing?"

"She's asleep now."

Melissa nodded. She was starting to feel close to Stephanie. The woman was fun-loving and generous. She wasn't exactly worldly wise, but she was perfectly intelligent and worked harder than anyone Melissa had ever met.

"I wish there was something I could do to help."

Jared gazed at her without speaking, an indefinable expression on his face. It was guarded, yet intimate, aloof, yet intense.

"Tell me what you were writing," he finally said.

Melissa could feel the blood drain from her face. The air suddenly left the room, and an oppressive heat wafted over her entire body.

"A letter," she rasped.

"To who?" he asked.

"My brother," she improvised, dreading what Jared must know, hoping against hope for a miracle.

"Which one?"

She waited for his eyes to flare with anger, but they stayed frighteningly calm.

"Adam." She swallowed. "I promised...I promised him...that I'd, uh, be careful."

Jared nodded. "And have you? Been careful."

"Yes."

He raked both hands through his short hair. "Oh, God, Melissa. I don't want to do this."

She jumped up from her chair, too nervous to sit still, sweat popping out of her pores. "Do what?"

"It's so unfair to you."

What was he talking about? What was he planning to do to her? She found herself inching toward the door, wondering if the women next door were still awake. Would they hear her if she screamed?

"I didn't know where else to go." His voice was suddenly thick with emotion.

The tone made Melissa pause. "What do you mean?"

Was he going to yell at her? Toss her out of the cottage? Throw her off the property?

She was starting to wish he'd just get it over with. Should she try to grab the laptop?

He shook his head. "Never mind."

Never mind?

He came to his feet, and she struggled not to shrink away.

"Did you say something about wine?" he asked.

She gave herself a mental shake, struggling to clear her brain.

"Melissa?"

"Are you angry with me?"

"Why would I be angry with you? I'm the one invading your privacy." A beat went by. "And attempting to drink your wine."

She forced herself to move. "Right. It's on the counter." What had she missed? What had just happened?

She heard him moving behind her as she opened a wooden drawer. "I think I saw a corkscrew in here."

"It's a screw top."

"Oh." Classy. She was willing to bet he didn't often drink wine from a screw-top bottle. "One of the cowboys picked it up in town," she explained.

"Did you have to flirt with him?"

"For screw-top wine? Please."

Jared grinned. "I forgot. I'm talking to the master."

"I gave him ten bucks and told him to do the best he could." She hunted through the cupboard, but gave up on wineglasses. "These do?" At least they weren't plastic.

"You sure you should be spending your hard-earned money on wine?" he asked. He poured while she held the glasses.

"You tripled my wages, remember?"

"Did we agree on that?"

"We sure did."

He set down the bottle, taking one of the short water glasses from her hand. "Get it in writing?"

"Didn't have to." She gave him a mock toast. "I know your secret."

"No, you don't," he responded dryly, downing a good measure of the wine.

She watched his stark expression with a whole lot of curiosity. Jared had a secret? Something other than playacting for his sister?

Okay, it couldn't be as big as Melissa's secret. But it might be interesting. And it could be exactly the hook she was looking for to get the story started.

Jared hadn't meant his words to sound like a challenge. But he realized they did. And if the expression on Melissa's face was anything to go by, she'd reacted the same way.

"So?" She sidled up to him, green eyes dancing with mischief.

"None of your business."

"Then why'd you bring it up?"

Fair question. Better question, why was he even here? It had been one roller coaster of an emotional day. He'd been half blind with anger at the cemetery, holding on to his temper by a thread, knowing he couldn't let Stephanie or Royce catch on.

He could tell Royce was suspicious. So when Stephanie went upstairs to bed, Jared had escaped from the house. Then he'd seen Melissa's light, and his feet had carried him to her door.

He thought he knew why. He needed to spend time with someone completely separate from his family. Melissa didn't know any of the players in their little drama. She knew nothing about his family but what he'd told her. She might annoy him or argue with him or frustrate the hell out of him with her approach to life, but she wouldn't threaten his composure.

She grazed her knuckles along his biceps. "You said you had a secret?" she prompted.

Here was another reason to darken her doorway. Her musical voice soothed him. Her scent enticed him. And when he gazed at her lips, all he could think about was capturing them with his own, tasting her all over again and letting the softness of her body pull him, once more, into oblivion.

And maybe it was as simple as that. He'd come to her because he needed to forget for a while.

He captured her hand, holding it tight against his sleeve, the warmth of her palm seeping through to his skin.

"I want you," he told her honestly.

Her voice went husky, stoking his desire. "That's not exactly a secret."

He smiled at her open acceptance of his declaration.

He liked it that she wasn't coy. She was confident and feisty. She flouted convention, ignored advice. There was something to be said for a woman who marched to her own drummer.

"I was expecting something more interesting," she said.

"Like what?"

"I don't know. A secret takeover of a multinational corporation. News that Ryder International was sending a manned mission to Mars. Maybe that you were really a CIA agent masquerading as a businessman."

Jared couldn't help but laugh at the last one. The knot of tension in his gut broke free. "The CIA?"

"Didn't you read the article?"

"What article?"

"In the *Chicago Daily*. Two years ago. Well, they outed you as a spy in the lifestyle section. Though, I suppose if they'd had any real evidence, it would have made the front page."

"You remember what you read in the *Chicago Daily* two years ago, yet you can't remember how to tie a quick-release knot?"

"Are we still talking about sex?"

"You're amazing." He'd never met anyone remotely like Melissa. She was smart, sassy and stunningly gorgeous. How had the men of Gary, Indiana, let her get away?

"So you're not in the CIA?" she pressed with a pretty pout.

He slipped an arm around her waist, settling her close and letting the balm of her company soothe him.

A breeze wafted in over the river, fluttering the plaid curtains above the small sink. The lights were low, the evening cool, the woman beautiful.

"You caught me," he said, setting his glass on the countertop and sliding hers from her fingers. "Ever slept with a spy?"

"You'd lie to get me into bed?"

"Is it working?"

"I'm not that impressed by a spy. I'd rather you were an astronaut going to Mars."

He settled his other arm around her waist, squaring her in front of him. "I can be anything you want."

He kissed her, gently, savoring her essence, forcing himself to keep it short. It was a struggle. If he let his hormones have their way, he'd be scooping her into his arms and tossing her on the bed all over again. But he pulled back.

"Is this why you came here?" Her cheeks were flushed, her lips parted and soft, but her eyes were slightly wary.

He felt like a heel. "No pressure," he quickly told her.

"Is it because I'm leaving?"

"Yes," he answered honestly. Then he realized how that sounded. "No. That's not it." He cursed himself for stumbling. "Well, it's partly…"

What was the matter with him? "I like that you don't know me, don't know my family." He wrapped his hand around the back of a kitchen chair, giving it a squeeze. "It's been a rough day."

She moved forward. "I understand."

She didn't, but it didn't matter. What mattered was that the wariness was out of her eyes. What mattered was that she was touching him, drawing forward, stretching up to kiss his lips.

There was something unfair about the situation, something unbalanced, unequal, but he couldn't put his finger on it. A split second later, he didn't even want to try.

His arms went firmly around her. He wanted to pull her inside him, keep her there, cradle her while the world moved on without them.

Her arms snaked around his neck. She tipped her head, and he deepened the kiss. Her tongue was sweet nectar, the inside of her mouth hot and decadent. She smelled like wildflowers and tasted like honey.

His hands slipped down, cupping the softness of her bottom, kneading and pressing her against his driving arousal.

She moaned his name, and he felt her breasts burning into his chest, like a brand that would mark him forever.

He lifted her, shoving the chair out of the way, perching her on the table, tugging the curtain shut behind her, before his hands went to the buttons on her shirt.

She reciprocated, her breath coming fast, head down to concentrate as she worked on his long row of buttons.

He freed her shirt, slipping it off her shoulders, kissing the velvet softness, letting his tongue explore the taste and texture of her skin. He snapped open her bra, and it fell to the floor, revealing firm, pert breasts, capped with pink nipples.

She pushed his shirt down his arms, and they were skin to skin. She was impossibly soft, impossibly warm, silken and sweet and everything a man could possibly dream.

Their lips came together, open, full on. He led her through a tumultuous kiss that left them both panting and needy for more. He kissed her again while he slid his palm up her rib cage to cover her breast, testing the hardened nipple, drawing a gasp from the back of her throat.

He caressed her body, leisurely, thoroughly; while her own hands splayed on his back, her lips found his flat nipples, and her silken hair teased his skin with an erotic brush. He scooted her forward, forcing her thighs farther apart. His fingers went to her blue jeans, releasing the button, sliding down the zipper. His knuckles grazed her silken panties, and his mind fixated on the treasures beneath.

A gust of wind cooled his back. The crisp scent of the river and the sweet aroma of the fields swirled through the room. The moon rode high above the mountains, while layers of stars twinkled across the endless sky. Horses whinnied in the distance, while leaves rustled in the oak and aspen trees.

There was perfection in the world tonight. He was home and she was in his arms, and nothing else mattered for the moment. Tomorrow would have to take care of itself.

He tugged off her jeans, then slipped off her panties,

drawing her exquisite, naked body against him for a long lingering kiss.

He finally drew back, gazing down at her ivory skin, unblemished against the scarred wood of the kitchen table.

"You are stunning," he whispered with reverence.

"You're overdressed," she said back, her hand going to his waistband.

He closed his eyes, tipped his head back and let his body drink in the erotic sensations as she slowly dragged down his zipper, her smooth warm hands removing his pants, releasing his body, highjacking every molecule of his senses.

"You're stunning, too," she whispered, body wriggling, hand moving, sliding, squeezing.

He sucked in a tight breath, holding on to his control as he feathered his hand along her thighs. He stared into her bottomless eyes. She stared back as his fingertips climbed higher, and her hands roamed further, each of them daring the other to crack.

Her beautiful mouth parted. Her eyes glazed. Her hand convulsed, and he pulled her to him, slipping slowly, surely, solidly inside.

She gripped his shoulders and leaned in for his kiss. He melded his mouth to hers, slipped his hands beneath her and settled the angle, settled the rhythm, let the roar in his ears and the pounding in his brain obliterate everything but the incredible sensation of Melissa.

He wanted it to go on forever. He was determined to make it last. She finally cried out, body pulsating before going limp. But he kept on kissing her, muttering words of need and affection.

And then she was with him. All over again, building toward a second crescendo. And he held back until the very last second before allowing himself to tumble over the cliff with her, his body drenched with sweat, his mind filled with amazement.

He carried her spent body to the bed, climbing in beside her, settling the quilt around them as he drew her into the cradle of his arms.

"You okay?" he whispered as his head found the indent on her pillow.

She drew two deep breaths while he kissed her hairline, then her temple, then her ear. He burrowed into the crook of her neck, inhaling deeply. How could a woman possibly smell so good?

"Define okay," she whispered back.

"Still breathing?"

She nodded.

"Nothing strained or broken?"

"Nothing."

"Want to do it again?"

An hour later Melissa could barely lift a finger. But she could see why Jared was the fantasy of half the women in Chicago. Word had obviously gotten around.

She was lying on her back, eyes closed. The covers were a tangle at their feet, and a cool breeze relieved her heated skin. Jared was beside her, propped up on one elbow, his fingertips feathering a small zigzag pattern over her stomach. She was amazed he could move anything.

"You still breathing?" he rumbled.

"Barely."

He chuckled at that.

"I don't think I've ever been this exhausted," she said.

"Never?" There was a hint of pride in his voice.

"Well, maybe once," she couldn't help teasing. "The day my brothers decided to build a tree fort. I was eight and insisted on helping. They nearly killed me."

"You're saying I'm a close second to your brothers?" The pride was gone.

She opened her eyes and managed a grin.

"Still feisty," he said.

"Even when I'm beat."

"Tell me about these burly construction-worker brothers of yours."

"What do you want to know?"

"If they'll have my name on a hit list when I get back to Chicago."

"If I was eighteen you might be in trouble."

"If you were eighteen, I wouldn't be in this bed."

She chuckled. "But they've mellowed over the years. Caleb wouldn't hurt a fly. Eddy's head over heels for a kindergarten teacher right now. He doesn't even call anymore. Adam, Ben and Dan are married with little kids and more important things to worry about than their sister's virtue."

"It's strange to hear all that," said Jared. "I keep picturing you as an orphan. How does such a big family let you wander off on the bus system without money? It doesn't make sense."

"It's my pride. I don't talk to them about money."

"Still, if it was Stephanie—"

"What about you?" Naked in Jared's arms, Melissa really wasn't in the mood to have to lie to him. "Extended family? Niece and nephew prospects?"

"No niece and nephew prospects. Stephanie's too young, and Royce…well, you haven't had a lot of time to spend with Royce. It's hard to picture him with a wife and a white picket fence."

"And you? Do you really want four kids?"

"I like kids," said Jared. "But I wonder…"

"It's not like you can't afford them," she put in. And he'd certainly have his pick of women. She could give him a list right now if he was interested.

His hand stilled on her stomach. "Money isn't everything."

"Said like a man who has plenty."

"There's love, affection, fidelity."

"Fidelity?" she questioned.

He didn't respond.

"Aren't you getting a little ahead of yourself?" she asked. He might want to marry the lucky woman before he planned the divorce.

Jared shifted. "It's not a given."

She tipped her head so that she was looking at his face. "Maybe. But you don't go into something planning for failure, either."

He was gazing through the open window at the near-full moon. "You can love each other, or appear to love each other, and your marriage can still crumble."

"You're a cynic."

"I'm a realist."

A sudden unease came over her. "Jared? Have you been divorced?"

He shook his head. "No."

But she could tell there was more. She waited as long minutes ticked by.

"What's wrong?" she finally asked.

Tension radiated in waves from his body.

"Jared?"

"My mother was unfaithful."

The admission hit Melissa with the subtlety of a brick wall. She was too shocked to speak.

"The old cabin," Jared rasped. "That bedroom." His hand raked through his messy hair. "Until I saw it, I'd hoped Gramps's memory had somehow..."

Melissa's stomach clenched around nothing. "Oh, Jared."

He met her gaze, his irises dark with the depth of his pain. "My whole life, I thought their deaths were an accident."

"They weren't?" Melissa struggled to understand what he was saying.

"My grandfather told me. Before he died. I guess he thought..." Jared drew a ragged breath. "I don't know what he thought. I wish he hadn't told me at all."

"Somebody killed your parents?"

"My mother's affair started a chain reaction, and three people ended up dead."

"Three?" Melissa squeaked.

Jared's tone turned warning. "Stephanie and Royce don't know. I have to pretend everything is normal."

Melissa nodded her understanding. "You went to the graveyard to keep the secret."

"Yes."

And he'd come to her afterward. She had no idea how she should feel about that.

He suddenly pulled her close, his face getting lost in the length of her hair, his arms and legs imprisoning her against his body.

"It's stupid," he told her. "I barely know you. But when I think of another man…" Jared drew another breath. "For a second tonight, I understood why my father shot him."

Melissa reflexively stiffened. "Your father shot your mother's lover?"

"Yes."

She swallowed a sickening feeling. "And the man died?"

"Yes. And that same night my parents' truck went off the cliff. But my grandfather didn't know that. So he threw the gun in the river. Two accidental deaths and a homicide with no clues. Nobody ever made the connection. *I* never made the connection."

Melissa's heart went out to Jared. What an incredible burden. And he was bearing it all alone.

"You should tell Stephanie and Royce," she advised.

Jared scoffed out a cold laugh. "Why?"

"They could help you cope."

"I'll be fine." His voice grew stronger. "Today was the worst. It'll get easier now." He gave a sharp nod. "I'll be fine."

Melissa wasn't so sure. "Do you think maybe they deserve to know?"

"Nobody deserves to know this."

She wasn't going to argue further. She barely knew the family. Who was she to give them advice?

"I wish I could stay here," he said.

"Me, too." She'd like nothing better than to sleep in Jared's arms. The morning might be awkward, but at the moment she was willing to risk it.

His hug loosened. "I leave for Chicago tomorrow afternoon."

"Oh." She thought he was talking about staying the night. But he meant he was leaving the ranch. She backed off, slightly embarrassed by her presumption. She forcibly lightened her tone. "Of course. I know you have a big company to run."

"Come with me."

"Huh?"

"Come to Chicago. I have a Genevieve Fund event Tuesday night. We could go together. Spend a couple of nights in the city. Afterward, I'll buy you a plane ticket to Seattle. You'll be right back on schedule with your trip, and you won't have to worry about the bus."

Nine

There were a dozen reasons Melissa should have said no. Not the least of which was Stephanie's resultant excitement and Royce's knowing grin. There was also Melissa's deception and the article and, though she hated to admit it, the very real possibility she was falling for Jared.

She glanced at his profile across the aisle in the compact private jet. Royce was in the pilot's seat, while the two cream-colored, leather seats facing Melissa and Jared were empty. Four others behind them remained empty, as well.

Jared had offered her a drink and snacks after takeoff, but her stomach was too jumpy for either. Was she crazy? What if there were press at the charitable event? What if somebody recognized her?

As the jet began its descent, Jared reached across the aisle for her hand. "The ball's at the Ritz-Carlton, so I booked us a suite. Royce is staying in my apartment."

Melissa nodded. She'd have loved to see Jared's apartment, but she understood he wanted them to be alone. And so did she. She wanted a night with him to herself—no Stephanie up the hill, no ranch hands next door and definitely no Royce in the neighboring bedroom.

Maybe heartache would hit her afterward. And she might be weeks recovering. But she knew a stolen fling with Jared would be worth it.

"You have a spa appointment tomorrow," he continued. "And we can wander down North Michigan Avenue and find you a dress."

"You do know how to spoil a girl." She had several perfectly acceptable dresses at home, but she couldn't admit that to Jared.

She felt another twinge of guilt over the deception. But it would end soon. And Jared might never read the article. Even if he did, he'd have to be pleased with it, she told herself. She intended to show him in a very good light.

His gaze was warm. "I'll spoil you for as long as you want."

"You don't need to spoil me at all." She brought his broad hand to her lips. "What I want from you is free."

"I'd rather give it to you at the Ritz-Carlton."

She affected a deep sassy drawl. "You can give it to me anywhere you like, cowboy."

He pursed his lips and hissed a drawn-out exclamation. "I sure hope Royce plans to entertain himself after we land."

"What are you doing now?" Stephanie's voice came through Jared's cell phone while he sat in a comfortable armchair by the window in St. Jacques boutique overlooking the lake.

"Watching Melissa try on dresses." He'd made three overseas calls and consulted with his finance department while Melissa had paraded past in about a dozen dresses. She looked great in them all.

"I bet she looks gorgeous."

"She does."

Melissa walked out of the changing room in a short gold sheath with spaghetti straps and a diaphanous scarf. He wasn't crazy about the scarf, but he liked the dress.

He held up four fingers. He'd been giving rankings out of five, since he'd been holding his PDA to his ear through the entire fashion show.

Melissa leaned forward and pointed to a looped gold-and-diamond necklace the salesclerk had fastened around her neck. He simply gave a thumbs-up to that.

"Did you have fun last night?" Stephanie asked.

"None of your business."

"It's quiet here. I miss you and Royce."

"We miss you, too. Come to the party. Royce will pick you up."

"I can't." She sighed. "We've got our first junior elite

rider starting tomorrow. He's been blowing them away on the young rider circuit."

"That's a good thing, right?"

"It's a great thing."

"Then quit your whining."

Melissa pranced back into the changing room, and he wished he'd thought to comment on the shoes. Black, sleek and high, with flashing rhinestones around the ankles. He definitely wanted her to keep the shoes.

"Is this tough love?" Stephanie asked.

"Absolutely."

"What's going on with Melissa?"

"She's going to blow them away tonight."

"Will she blow you away?"

"Don't get your hopes up, Steph."

"You have to fall in love sometime."

"Not necessarily."

But then Melissa appeared again. This time she was wearing an emerald-green strapless party dress. The bodice was tight satin, stretched snugly over her breasts, while the skirt puffed out around her thighs, showing off her toned calves and sexy ankles. It was perfect for a late-night club. It was also dress number thirteen, and he realized he wanted to take her out in all of them.

"Gotta go," he said to Stephanie, needing to end the conversation.

"Keep an open mind," she called into the phone.

"Don't worry." No point in Stephanie worrying. Jared was the one who needed to worry.

He was starting to think about jobs for Melissa again, jobs at Ryder International. Or better still, jobs at affiliated companies in the city, so she wouldn't work directly for him. But she'd still be around to date him.

He was starting to think about her skill set and who owed him favors. They had one more night together, then maybe half of tomorrow. But he knew that wasn't going to do it for him. And that was a very worrisome development.

"She's a knockout," came Royce's voice as he dropped into the armchair beside Jared.

"No kidding."

Melissa gave Royce a welcoming smile and a little wave.

Royce's long lecherous look at her legs irritated Jared, worrying him all over again. Just how deep had he let himself fall?

"You serious about her?" Royce asked.

"Why?" Jared demanded, wondering what might have given him away.

Royce gave a smug grin. "Guess that answers my question."

"She leaves for Seattle tomorrow." And that was the disappointing truth. He'd suggested she stay longer, but she'd insisted she had to get back on her trip. Whatever feelings might be building inside Jared, this was the time to shut them down.

"You want me to fly her out?"

"No." Jared did *not*. He might not be pursuing anything with Melissa himself, but that didn't mean the field was open to his brother.

Royce's grin widened. "This is fun."

"Back off."

"Not a chance."

Melissa floated out in a calf-length ivory gown. It had snug, three-quarter-length, flat lace sleeves and a sweetheart neckline gathered with a line of jewels at mid-bust. There was a wide ribbon waist band and a two-layered, flowing skirt that flirted with her legs. She grinned and gave a twirl. Her diamond earrings twinkled under the bright lights.

Jared felt a tightening in his chest. A small bouquet of flowers, and she'd be the perfect bride. Her open smile told him she was oblivious to the image, but he wasn't, and he drank in the sight for several long minutes.

He gave the dress a five, and she turned to walk away.

"Do I need to say it?" asked Royce.

"No." Jared kept his focus on Melissa until she disappeared again.

"So how're you going to keep her here?"

Jared gave up lying both to himself and to Royce. "I haven't decided yet."

They'd chosen a black silk dress with spaghetti straps and a metallic gold thread that made it shimmer under the ballroom lights. The skirt of the dress was full enough to make Melissa feel like a princess as she whirled around the dance floor in Jared's arms to the music of a five-piece string band. Her rhinestone sandals were light on her feet. Her hair was upswept, and Jared had insisted on buying her the looped gold necklace and a set of matching earrings.

He looked roguishly sexy in his tuxedo. Having seen

him in blue jeans, chaps and dust, she realized the formal clothes barely disguised the rugged man inside.

Champagne flowed, and the crystal chandeliers glittered around them as they moved past marble pillars, magnificent floral arrangements and the kaleidoscope of designer gowns. At one point, the mayor paused to chat. And everyone in the room knew and obviously respected Jared.

Though Melissa had promised herself the night was off the record, she'd decided to use a few of her impressions in the article. Jared was an intelligent, insightful man, with an amazing grasp of local issues and Chicago economic trends. There was no way she could leave that side of him out of the article.

Though she'd spent the first hour with an eagle eye out for press and anybody else who might recognize her, it turned out to be a private party. No press, and Jared's social circle was far from hers. While she might recognize the notable figures from their pictures and television appearances, she knew they'd never recognize her.

She felt like Cinderella when they finally made their way out of the ballroom and into the promenade. Her arm was linked with Jared's, and Royce was by their side.

"Barry left them at the front desk," Royce was saying, thumbing a button on his PDA before he tucked it back into his breast pocket.

"I don't want to work tonight," said Jared, and he raised Melissa's hand to his lips, giving her knuckles a tender kiss.

Royce sent Melissa a mock frown. "See what you've done? *I'm* usually the irresponsible brother."

"Not tonight," said Jared.

"Apparently not," Royce growled.

"Is it important?" asked Melissa. She was anxious to get Jared alone in their suite, but his conversations at the ball had taught her his time was valuable. His business interests were even more significant and far-reaching than she'd realized.

"Yes," said Royce.

"No," Jared put in over top of his brother.

"Do you want to get up early, instead?" asked Royce.

"No," Melissa quickly put in. She'd have to pretend to get on a plane to Seattle sometime tomorrow, but she'd been entertaining a glorious vision. One that featured a leisurely breakfast in bed with Jared, maybe a dip in their whirlpool tub and a long goodbye before they went their separate ways at, say, noon.

"Just sign them," said Royce. "I'll go over them with Barry before I countersign."

"Who's Barry?" asked Melissa.

"Ryder's financial VP," said Jared, and she could feel his hesitation.

"I don't mind waiting," she quickly put in as they stepped into an open elevator.

Royce quirked his brows at Jared, and Jared gave a nod. He pressed the button for the lobby. The door closed, and the car *whooshed* smoothly down twelve floors.

"I won't be long," Jared assured her, hand resting

lightly on the small of her back as they stepped into the opulent lobby.

She gestured toward the far side of the huge room. "I'll check out the paintings while I wait."

He nodded, and left with Royce for the front desk.

It wasn't much of a hardship to wander through the lobby. Marble walkways, elegant, French-provincial furnishings, magnificent sculpture and glorious flowers combined with the soft lighting to create a serene ambiance. It wasn't the kind of hotel where Melissa normally stayed. Then again, this wasn't exactly the kind of week she usually experienced, either.

Her heels clicked as she rounded the fountain, moving toward the main glass doors. There were a couple of furniture groupings that looked inviting. Her new shoes were comfortable, but the heels were high, and her calves were beginning to tighten up. A gold armchair beckoned. It would give her a nice view of the front desk. She could people-watch, while keeping an eye out for Jared.

But then she spotted a man on the sidewalk and halted in her tracks. He was in profile, smoking a cigarette in the muted light outside, but it was definitely Brandon Langard.

Melissa gasped, then whirled around before he could spot her. The rest of a lobby blurred in front of her panicked eyes.

"Melissa?" Her coworker Susan Alaric suddenly appeared in front of her. "*Melissa?* Oh, my God. You're back. How'd it go?"

Melissa opened her mouth to speak, but only a squeak emerged.

Susan's face nearly split with an excited grin. "Seth said you got on the ranch. Did you get the interview? Did Ryder figure out who you were?" She tipped her head back in glee. "Oh, man, Brandon is going to have a cow."

Melissa grasped Susan's arm. "Susan…" she rasped, but then her gaze caught Jared's face over Susan's shoulder, and her stomach roiled.

"The *Bizz* is going to have the scoop of the year," Susan finished.

"The *Bizz?*" Jared's voice and eyes both darkened to thunder.

Susan heard his voice and took in Melissa's stricken expression. She twisted around to look at Jared. Then she swallowed. She opened her mouth, but gave up before she could find any words.

Royce appeared, taking in the trio. He noted Susan's camera, then paused on his brother's expression. "What the hell?"

"Jared…" Melissa began, mind scrambling with panic.

She'd explain it was a good article. It would focus on the most complimentary things. He was successful, hardworking and kind. And his family was wonderful. It wasn't like they had any skeletons in their closets.

Okay, so there *was* the thing with his grandfather, but that wasn't relevant, and she sure wasn't going to write about that. And everything that had happened between them was way off the record. This wasn't a tabloid tell-all. It was a serious journalistic piece.

But before she could pull her thoughts together, his hand closed over her arm and he pulled her away from Susan and Royce.

"You *lied* to me." His graveled voice was harsh in her ear.

She didn't answer.

"You're a reporter?" he demanded.

She closed her eyes, but then forced herself to nod the admission.

"And *I'm* your subject."

"Yes, but—"

"You are going to walk out that door." He stopped, jerking her to face him. His words were measured, but she was subjected to the full glare of his anger. "You are going to walk out that door. You are going to do it quickly and quietly, and I *never* want to see you again."

"But—"

"Do you understand me?"

"I'm not going—"

"Do you understand me?"

She closed her mouth and nodded, chest tight, throat closing in. She told herself he'd read the article. Eventually he'd know she hadn't betrayed him.

"Good." He flicked his hand from her arm, his eyes filled with contempt.

She had to try one more time. "Jared, please let me explain."

"You already have. I know who you are. And I know what you've got."

"I'm not going to—"

"Know this," he cut her off, leaning in, lowering his voice to steel. "If you do *anything* to harm my family, I will destroy you."

Then he turned away, sharply and with an absolute finality to his posture.

Before she could get another word out, he was past the fountain and heading for the elevators.

"Melissa?" Susan's voice was hushed as she pressed against her shoulder.

"That was Jared Ryder." Melissa's voice was hollow. Her body was hollow. Her life was hollow.

"No kidding."

Melissa knew it didn't matter what she wrote in the article, what secrets she kept or what she revealed, Jared was never going to forgive her. She'd never see him again, never be held in those strong arms, hear his voice, smell his skin, taste his passionate kisses. She realized now how very much she'd been counting on their last night together.

"You okay?" asked Susan.

Melissa forced herself to nod. Her eyes were burning, but she blinked the sting away.

"Wow," Susan continued. "I hope your research was finished."

Melissa didn't know whether to laugh or cry. Just then, she couldn't have cared less about the article. "It is," she told Susan.

"What are you doing here?" Susan glanced around

the hotel lobby. "Brandon and I were hoping to catch the mayor."

Melissa coughed a hollow laugh. "I chatted with the mayor upstairs."

"Really?" Susan took in the dress. "You were at the Genevieve Memorial Fund ball?"

"Jared and, uh, his brother invited me along." The last thing in the world she wanted to do was invite questions about her relationship with Jared.

"Wow," said Susan, gaze going to the elevator where the two men had disappeared. "I am in awe."

Where Melissa was exhausted, both emotionally and physically. It had been a week of hard work and long nights. She'd labored over the article every spare minute. Well, every spare minute that she hadn't been falling—

She froze for a second, drew a stunned breath and closed her eyes.

Every spare minute that she hadn't been *falling in love with Jared*.

Her hands curled into fists, and she fought against the knowledge that had just exploded in her brain.

"Your article is going to kick butt," Susan was saying.

How could Melissa have been so stupid? Why hadn't she seen it coming? She should have done something to stop it. But no, she'd hung around him like an eager little puppy dog, throwing herself into his arms, into his bed, pretending she somehow belonged in his life.

Susan squeezed Melissa's shoulder. "You are *so* going to get that promotion. Seth might even smile." She paused. "Hey, Brandon's outside. You think we should go tell him?"

"*No.*" The word jumped out with more force than she'd intended. But Melissa didn't want to talk to Brandon or anyone else. She wanted to go home and hole up alone in her apartment. Some way, somehow, she had to get over Jared and get words on the page in the next twenty-four hours.

"You slept with a reporter?" Royce confirmed the obvious as the hotel-suite door swung shut behind them.

The fact that Jared had slept with Melissa was the least of his worries. Sure, maybe she could write about seeing him naked or detail his kisses and pillow talk. But it wasn't like he was into handcuffs or women in French-maid outfits.

"You didn't suspect?" Royce went straight for the bar, snagging a bottle of single malt from the mirrored top shelf.

He flipped two crystal glasses over, ignored the ice bucket and filled the tumblers to halfway.

"Yeah," said Jared. "I suspected. But I figured, what the hell? She's got a great ass. Why not sleep with somebody who'll splash it all over the front page?"

Royce rounded the bar again. "Sarcasm's not going to help."

"Neither are stupid questions." Jared took one of the glasses and downed a hefty swallow.

"Nothing gave her away?"

Jared dropped into an armchair. "She was a stable

hand. We have dozens of them. Yeah, she didn't know much about horses. And maybe her background was vague. And maybe she seemed too smart for a drifter. Which was what attracted me in the first place. She was…"

Royce cocked his head meaningfully.

"Son of a bitch," said Jared and polished off the scotch.

He'd let his sex drive override his logic. It was a clichéd, blatant, pathetic scenario. And he'd bought it hook, line and sinker. "She slept with me to get a story."

"That surprises you?"

Yes. It surprised him. He knew there were women in the world who used sex as a bargaining chip. He met them all the time. But Melissa sure hadn't struck him as one of those. She was down-to-earth, honest, classy.

"She told me she had brothers." Jared coughed out a flat chuckle. "I was afraid they might come after me."

"For defiling their sister?"

"I think about Stephanie sometimes…"

Royce stood and picked up the empty glasses. "Someday, some guy's going to sleep with Stephanie."

"He better be in love with her."

"He'd better be married to her." Royce poured a refill for each of them. This time, he added ice, then he wandered back to the opposite armchair.

"So what does she know?" he asked.

Jared slouched back, loosening his tie and flicking his top shirt button open. "The ranch, Stephanie's jumping, you, Anthony, the Genevieve Fund."

"What you look like naked," Royce put in.

Jared waved a dismissive hand. "It's not like we took pictures."

"Good to know."

Jared gazed out the wide window, letting his vision go soft on the city lights. He'd expected the night to turn out very differently. Even now, even knowing Melissa was a traitor, on some level he wished she was lying in the king-size bed, sexy, naked, waiting for him to join her.

"What's she got?" Royce asked quietly.

Jared blinked his attention back to his brother.

He had to tell him. There was no way around it.

He'd been colossally stupid to share it with a perfect stranger.

"Gramps," he said. Then he tugged off his tie, tossing it on the table.

Royce's eyes narrowed.

"He told me something. Right before he died." Jared drew a breath. "He told me Dad killed Frank Stanton."

The room went completely silent.

Jared dared to flick a glance at Royce.

His brother was still, eyes unblinking, hands loose on the padded arms of the chair. "I know."

Jared drew back. "What?"

Royce took a sip of his drink. "I've always known."

Jared took a second to process the information. Royce knew? He'd kept silent all these years?

"I don't understand," said Jared.

Royce came to his feet, then carried his drink across

the room, turning when he came to the window. "The day it happened. The day they died. I found a letter Mom had written to Dad. It was half-finished. It said she loved Frank. It said she was leaving Dad. She was leaving us." He took another sip.

"You didn't *tell* me?"

His brother was silent for a long moment. "You know, sometimes, when you *have* to keep a secret? The only person who can know is you. The second—" he snapped his fingers "—the second you let that knowledge out of your brain, you put it at risk. I knew that. Even at thirteen years old."

Jared couldn't believe his brother hadn't trusted him. "I would never have—"

"Our father was a murderer. Our mother was unfaithful. And Stephanie was two years old."

"You should have—"

"No. I shouldn't have. I didn't. And I was right." Royce paused. "I didn't know Gramps knew."

"He threw the gun in the river," said Jared.

Royce gave a half smile. "Good for him."

"He got rid of the gun before they found Mom and Dad. He thought Dad would go on trial for murder."

"Yeah." Royce returned to his chair. "Well, what do you do? He protected his son. Who are we to decide how far a man goes?"

"Do you kill your wife's lover?" The question had been nagging at Jared for weeks now. He couldn't help picturing Melissa. And he couldn't stop the cold rage that boiled up inside him at the thought of another man.

"I don't have a wife," said Royce. "I don't have to make that decision."

Jared nodded. "Simpler that way."

"It is," Royce agreed. He sat back down. "Do we tell Stephanie?"

Jared hated the thought of hurting his sister. But if the story came out in the article, she needed to be prepared. He hoped it wouldn't come to that, but he feared it might.

"Not yet," he answered Royce.

The *Bizz* was a monthly magazine. He'd have at least a few days to think about solutions.

So far, all he'd come up with was a plan to kidnap Melissa and lock her up in a tower in Tasmania or Madagascar with no telephone or Internet. Unfortunately his mind kept putting himself in the tower with her, in a big bed, where they'd make love until he tired of her. Which, if his wayward imagination was anything to go by, would take a very, very long time.

Ten

From the moment Melissa clicked the send button, she feared she'd made a mistake. While she certainly had the legal right to file her story on Jared, she wasn't so sure she had the moral right to do it.

Then she'd tossed and turned all night long, imagining his anger, his reaction, Stephanie's thoughts and feelings when she found out Melissa had been a fraud. Melissa was going to get a promotion out of this, no doubt about it. Seth was nearly beside himself with glee. Brandon was surly and sulking. And Everett himself had sent her an e-mail congratulating her on the coup.

Susan had guessed she was feeling guilty. But in her usual pragmatic style, she'd advised Melissa to put it behind her and focus on her future. Jared was a big boy, and he'd get over the inroad on his precious privacy.

It was a positive article. The quotes Melissa had used were accurate. She hadn't made anybody look foolish or mean-spirited. She'd mentioned Stephanie's jumping trophies, Jared's hardworking ancestors, his move from cattle ranching to construction to save the family's land. And she'd made Royce look like a fun-loving maverick. He'd probably get a dozen marriage proposals out of the coverage.

She hadn't used a single thing she'd learned from sleeping with Jared. Still, she couldn't shake the feeling she was wrong.

It lasted through her morning shower, through the breakfast she couldn't bring herself to eat, during the train ride to the office in the morning, up the elevator to her floor and then all the way to her desk.

Jared was an intensely private man. She'd invaded his privacy on false pretenses. And even though she hadn't used their pillow talk in her article, she'd crossed a line. She'd befriended him. She'd gained his trust. She'd let him think he could let his guard down, and he had.

Plus, and here was the crux of the matter, she'd fallen in love with him. And you didn't betray the person you loved. You were loyal, no matter what the circumstances, no matter what was to be gained or lost. You were loyal.

That was why Jared's grandfather hid the gun. An extreme example, perhaps. But his loyalty was to his son, and he'd risked his freedom to protect him. Melissa wouldn't even give up a promotion.

She dropped her purse on her desk, her gaze going to Seth's office. His head was bent over his desk—no doubt he was working his way through her article. It would go upstairs by lunchtime, be typeset by the end of the day and move along the pipe to the printing press.

At that point, nothing could stop it from hitting the streets. She had one chance and one chance only to make things right. Jared might not love her, and he might never speak to her again. But she loved him, and she had to live with herself after today.

She crossed the floor to Seth's office, opening the door without knocking.

He jerked his head up. "What?"

"I've changed my mind," she said without preamble, striding to his desk.

His mouth dropped open in confusion.

"The article," she clarified. "You can't run it."

Seth's mouth worked for a second before it warmed up to actual words. "Is this a joke? It's not funny. Now get the hell out of my office. I have work to do."

"I'm not joking."

"Neither am I. Get out."

"Jared Ryder does not want us to print it."

"Jared Ryder can stuff it. We need the numbers."

Melissa began to panic. "You can't run it."

"Yes, I can."

She scrambled for a solution. "I lied, Seth," she lied baldly. "I made it up. The quotes are bogus, and I was never on the Ryder Ranch."

Seth's complexion went ruddy, and a vein popped out in his forehead. "Have you gone insane?"

"I'll swear to it, Seth. I'll tell the whole world I made up the story."

"And I'll fire your ass."

"I don't care!" she shouted. She had to stop him. She couldn't let her work see the light of day.

Seth's gaze shifted to a point over her left shoulder and his eyes went wide.

Fear churned in her stomach, but she carried on, anyway. It was her last chance to make things right. "If you run it, I'll swear I made the whole piece up. The *Bizz* will get sued, and *you'll* lose *your* job."

Seth's mouth worked, but no sound came out.

"Don't test me on this, Seth," she vowed. "Pull the article. I'll quit. I'll go away quietly. You can make up whatever you want to tell Everett."

"Noble of you," came a voice behind her.

Everett. The publisher had heard her threats.

Not that she'd expected to keep her job, anyway, but it was humiliating to have an additional witness. She clamped her jaw, squared her shoulders and headed for the door.

Her stomach instantly turned to a block of ice.

In the doorway next to Everett stood Jared. They both stared at her, faces devoid of expression.

Neither of them said a word as she forced one foot in front of the other. She prayed they'd step aside and give her room to get out the door.

They did, but inches before freedom, Jared put a hand on her arm. Neither of them looked at the other, and his voice was gruff. "Why'd you pull the story?"

She struggled with the cascade of conflicting emotions that swamped her body. She was proud of herself.

She was brokenhearted. She was frightened and unemployed and exhausted.

She decided she owed him her honesty. So she glanced up and forced the words out. "The same reason your grandfather did what he did."

Love. Plain and simple. When you loved someone, you protected them, even at a risk to yourself.

Then she jerked away, grabbed her purse from her desk and kept right on going to the elevator.

Jared's first impression of Seth Strickland was hardly positive, so he didn't much care now that the man looked like he was going to wet his pants. Seth had shouted at Melissa. And while he was shouting, it was all Jared could do not to wring his pudgy little neck.

Jared might be angry with her, but that didn't give anyone else license to hurt her. Sure, she'd betrayed him. But she was fundamentally a decent person. Even now, he was battling the urge to chase after her. Not that he knew what he'd say. Not that he even understood what had just happened.

She'd behaved in a completely incomprehensible manner. Of course, she'd baffled him from the moment they met.

While Jared struggled to put her in context, Everett stepped into the office, moved to one side, then gestured for Jared to enter.

Everett shut the door firmly behind them and focused on the sweating Seth Strickland. "Mr. Ryder, this is Seth Strickland, *Windy City Bizz*'s managing editor. For now.

Seth, this is Mr. Jared Ryder, the new owner of *Windy City Bizz.*"

Seth's jaw dropped a notch further.

Jared didn't bother with pleasantries. It seemed a little ridiculous after what they'd just witnessed.

"Is this a copy of the article?" He advanced on Seth's desk and pointed to the papers piled in front of him.

Seth nodded.

"We won't be running it," said Jared, lifting the pages from under Seth's nose.

He gave Everett a polite smile. "Thank you for your time. One of Ryder International's vice presidents will be in touch next week."

Then he turned and exited the office. He couldn't care less if Everett fired Seth or kept him on. Melissa wasn't fired, that was for sure. And she could write for Seth or for anyone else in the company.

He took the elevator to the first floor, crossed the lobby, trotted down the outside stairs and slid into the Aston Martin idling at the curb.

"How'd it go?" asked Royce, pushing the car into gear and flipping on his signal.

"It's taken care of," said Jared.

"Good." Royce gave a nod. Hard rock was blaring on the stereo, while the air conditioner battled the heat from the sunshine.

"Did you see Melissa come out the door?"

Royce zipped into the steady stream of traffic. "You saw Melissa?"

"She was inside." Jared shoved his sunglasses onto the bridge of his nose.

"And?"

"And." Jared drummed his fingers on the dashboard. "She was trying to get her editor to kill the article."

Royce glanced at him for a split second before turning his attention to the busy intersection. "What? Why?"

"Beats the hell out of me. The guy fired her."

"She lost her job?"

"No. Of course she didn't lose her job. She works for us now, remember?"

"And you don't think *we* should fire her?"

Jared killed the clanging music. He needed to think.

"Jared?" Royce prompted.

"Why would she kill the article?" Her cryptic remark about his grandfather didn't make sense.

"Maybe she's afraid of getting sued."

Jared glanced down at the papers in his hand. He scanned one page, then another, then another. The story was innocuous. It was lightweight to the point of being boring.

"Anything about Gramps?" asked Royce as they turned to parallel the lakeshore. Skyscrapers loomed to one side, blocking the sun.

"Nothing. It's crap."

"She's a bad writer?"

"No. She's a fine writer. But she held back. She had a ton of stuff on me." He flipped through the pages again. "She didn't use any of it."

"Then why did she try to pull it?"

"I asked her," Jared admitted, flashing back to that moment, remembering her expression, remembering the emotional body slam of seeing her again, his desire to attack Seth and to chase after Melissa.

"Bro?" Royce prompted.

Jared cleared his throat. "She said it was the same reason Gramps did what he did."

Royce's hand came down on the steering wheel. "All this, and the woman's talking in riddles?"

Jared rolled it over in his mind. "Why did Gramps do what he did?"

"To protect Dad."

"Why?"

"Because he was his son."

"And…"

The brothers looked at each other, sharing an instant of comprehension. Gramps had protected Jared's father because he loved him.

"Holy crap," said Royce.

"*Not* what I needed to know," said Jared.

"Do you care?" Royce pressed.

Jared swore out loud. "She lied to me. She duped me. She invaded the hell out of my privacy." He slammed the pages onto his lap.

"Yet you love her, anyway," Royce guessed.

Jared clamped his jaw shut. Did he love Melissa? How could he love an illusion? He didn't even know which parts were her and which were the lie.

"And she loves you," Royce continued. He slowed for a stoplight, gearing the car down.

"I need a drink."

The woman was a damn fine illusion. If even half

of what he'd seen of her was real, it might be enough.
Hell, it would be enough.

"What are you going to do?"

"Drink," said Jared.

Royce laughed. "Since you're not denying it and since
you're even *considering* her, I'd say you absolutely need
a drink. You've got it very bad, big brother."

"Why *her?*"

"It doesn't matter why her. It's done."

"Nothing's done." Jared certainly hadn't made any
decisions. He was barely wrapping his head around
falling for Melissa.

"You forget, I watched you watch her," said Royce.
"You were never letting her go to Seattle."

"She never *was* going to Seattle. It was all a lie."

Royce shook his head and laughed. He glanced in
the rearview mirror. Then he spun the steering wheel,
yanked the hand brake and pivoted the car in a sharp
u-turn.

"What are you doing?" Jared stabilized himself with
the armrest.

"You *do* need a drink." Royce screeched to a stop in
front of the Hilliard House tavern's valet parking. "If
only to come to terms with the rest of your life."

Melissa should have realized her brother Caleb would
call in reinforcements. She'd found herself at his house
Saturday morning, looking for emotional support. Caleb
was the most sympathetic of her brothers, and she'd
really needed a shoulder to cry on.

Within an hour, Ben and Sheila had arrived, their

baby and two-year-old in tow. Then Eddy showed up, without the new girlfriend, demonstrating how seriously he was taking the situation. He was quick to envelop Melissa in a protective hug, and she had to battle a fresh round of tears.

Soon all her siblings and her nieces and nephews filled Caleb's big house with love and support. The jumble of their conversations and chaos of the children provided a buffer between Melissa and her raw emotions.

She'd told herself she couldn't be in love with Jared. Maybe it was infatuation. Maybe it was lust. She hadn't known him long enough for it to be real love.

But then she'd remember his voice, his smile, his jokes, his passion and the way she'd felt in his arms. What if it *was* real love? How was she going to get over it?

She swallowed, smiling as one of her nephews handed her a sticky wooden block, forcing her thoughts to the present.

The doors and windows of Caleb's house were wide open to the afternoon breeze. Some of her brothers were shooting hoops in the driveway while Adam cranked up the grill on the back deck and distributed bottles of imported beer. His wife, Renee, was calling out orders from the kitchen.

Melissa and her sister-in-law Sheila were corralling toddlers on the living-room floor, amid a jumble of blocks, action figures and miniature cars.

"Mellie?" Caleb's voice interrupted the game.

Melissa glanced up.

Her brother's brow was furrowed with concern, and she quickly saw the reason why.

Jared stood in the foyer, his suit and tie contrasting with the casual T-shirt and jeans Caleb wore.

She scrambled to her feet, drinking in his appearance, wishing she wasn't so pathetically glad to see him as she crammed her messy hair behind her ears. She hoped her eyes weren't red. She hoped he couldn't read how lonely she'd been the past few days. She'd fallen asleep each night with his image in her mind, longing to feel his strong arms wrapped around her.

She'd second-guessed herself a million times. What if she'd come clean right off? What if she'd told him who she was? Maybe he'd have thrown her off the ranch. But maybe he'd have given her an interview. And maybe, just maybe, they'd have had a chance to get to know each other without a lie between them.

She'd tried not to love him. She really had. But it was a hopeless proposition. And seeing him again told her that she'd be weeks, months, maybe even years getting over her feelings.

She heard a rustle from the kitchen and turned to see the rest of her brothers file in. They moved behind her, and Caleb joined them. As if it was choreographed, their muscular arms crossed over their chests and they pinned their gazes on Jared.

To his credit, Jared looked levelly back. "I see you didn't lie about your brothers."

The five Warner men straightened their spines and squared their shoulders. The toddlers' coos and burbles were at odds with the tension in the room.

"How did you find me?" Melissa managed to ask, searching Jared's expression, trying to figure out what reason he could possibly have for tracking her down. Had he somehow read an advance copy of the article? Had he hated it? Did he want her to change it?

"Your personnel file," Jared surprised her by answering. "Caleb is your emergency contact."

"How did you—"

"You're not fired, Melissa." He took a step forward. "I want you to know that up front."

She felt her brothers close ranks behind her.

"Oh, yes, I am," she responded, struggling to keep her voice from shaking. Seth had been crystal clear on that point.

Jared shook his head. "Ryder International bought *Windy City Bizz*. Nobody is firing you for anything."

Melissa peered at him, trying to make sense of his words.

"It was the best way I could think of to kill the story," he explained.

The babies played on in the background, while Renee and Sheila moved in beside their husbands.

Melissa subconsciously moved closer to Jared. "You bought the *Bizz?*"

"Yes."

That was insane.

"You paid, what? Thousands? Hundreds of thousands of dollars to keep my story out of the press?"

"I hadn't read the story when I bought the magazine." He offered a wry half smile. "Had I known it was so innocuous…"

"I did try to tell you," she pointed out.

"I know." His expression softened, and he moved closer still. "But you knew…" He glanced around at her family members, then peered at her to make sure she understood his code. "You know?"

She did, and she nodded. "I never would have used it."

"You lied. And I couldn't tell—"

"I am so sorry." She wished she could start over. If there was one minute in her life she could do over, it would be the first time they met. She'd tell Jared she was a reporter up front and let him do whatever he would do.

"Mellie." Caleb's arm went around her. "You don't have to apologize again."

"Agreed," said Jared, meeting Caleb's eyes, squaring his own shoulders. "It's my turn to apologize. I lied to her, too."

Caleb tensed, but Jared stepped forward, anyway, clasping his hands over Melissa's. His hands were warm and strong, sending sensory memories tingling along her spine.

His expression softened again, and his voice went lower. "I lied to you when I said I never wanted to see you again."

Melissa felt a faint flicker of hope. But she instantly squelched it. She was going down a dangerous road, erasing any gains she'd made since that horrible night at the Ritz-Carlton.

"I do want to see you again," Jared continued, and

she was forced to redouble her effort at dampening her hope. "All the time. Every day from here on in."

Melissa wanted to run. She wanted to hide. Her brain couldn't comprehend that he might be serious.

"Excuse me?" Sheila popped out from behind the men. "What are you saying to Melissa?"

Jared flicked an annoyed glance at Sheila, and Melissa could feel her brother Ben bristle.

"I'm saying," said Jared, a thread of steel coming into his voice, "I can propose to her here under, well, rather stressful circumstances."

His gaze went back to Melissa while her heart thudded powerfully in her chest. "Or we can go somewhere private, where I can do it properly."

Her mind scrambled in a freefall.

"I have a limo out front," Jared continued. "A table on the deck at the Bayside, a florist and photographer on standby, also—" he tapped the breast of his suit "—a ring. I also have a ring."

"Can we see it?" chirped Sheila.

Jared's attention never left Melissa. "Only if she says yes."

Melissa couldn't do anything but blink. Emotions that had been close to the surface for days threatened to erupt. This couldn't be happening. It must be some fevered hallucination.

She looked back at her family.

They were watching expectantly.

Could this be happening? Could it be real? If she'd had a free hand, she'd have pinched himself.

"Melissa?" Jared prompted.

"I think—" she nodded "—the restaurant is a good idea."

"Yeah?" A grin split his face.

"And the photographer." She assured herself it was all real. Jared had found her. And he wanted to be with her. "I have a feeling Stephanie will expect pictures."

Jared's grin widened.

Sheila spoke out. "But can we see the—"

Ben clapped a hand over her mouth.

It took her all of three seconds to escape. "Good grief. It's obvious she's going to say yes. They can reenact it later for the photographer."

Everyone stared openmouthed at Sheila.

"What?" she asked. "Come on, Renee. Back me up. We want to see the ring."

Adam's wife stepped forward. "I have to say, I'm with Sheila on this."

Melissa started to laugh. "Go ahead," she told Jared. She *was* planning to say yes.

"In a minute," he told her, stepping back to pull Melissa into the foyer, around the corner, beyond the view of her family.

He held her hand firmly, staring into her eyes. "I love you."

The world disappeared around them, and Melissa's chest filled with a warm shimmering glow. The worries lifted off her shoulders and the vestiges of pain evaporated from inside her.

"I love you, too," she breathed, touching his face, letting his essence seep through her fingertips and into her soul.

Jared sobered as he leaned in for a kiss. His lips touched hers and magic seem to saturate the atmosphere around them. It was a very long minute before he pulled back.

"We can reenact this part later for the camera," he whispered, reaching to his inside jacket pocket. "But will you marry me?" He flipped open the jewel case to reveal a stunning solitaire.

Melissa nodded. "Yes. Oh, yes." She couldn't imagine a more amazing future than one with Jared.

He slipped the ring onto her finger. Then he kissed her hand and whispered, "Go ahead and show it off."

Though her family was waiting, Jared was her world. She went up on tiptoe, hugging him tight, and he lifted her off the floor to spin her around.

Sheila squealed in the background, and suddenly the entire family was pouring into the foyer, admiring Melissa's engagement ring and welcoming Jared into the family.

IN BED WITH THE WRANGLER

BY
BARBARA DUNLOP

For my husband

One

Strains from the jazz band followed Royce Ryder as he strode across the carpeted promenade between the ballroom and the lobby lounge of the Chicago Ritz-Carlton Hotel. He tugged his bow tie loose, popping the top button on his white tuxedo shirt while inhaling a breath of relief. His brother, Jared, and his new sister-in-law, Melissa, were still dancing up a storm in the ballroom, goofy smiles beaming on their faces as they savored every single moment of their wedding reception.

But it had been a long night for Royce. He'd stood up for his brother, joked his way through an endless receiving line, then toasted the bride and the bridesmaids. He'd socialized, danced, eaten cake and even caught the garter—a reflexive action that had everything to do with his years as a first baseman in high school and college, and nothing whatsoever to do with his future matrimony prospects.

Now his duty was done, and it was time for a final night in the civilized surroundings of downtown Chicago before his sentence began in Montana. Okay, so managing the family ranch wasn't exactly hard labor in Alcatraz, but for a man who'd been piloting a jet plane around the world for the past three years, it was going to be a very long month.

It wasn't that he begrudged Jared his honeymoon. Quite the contrary, he was thrilled that his brother had fallen in love and married. And the better he got to know Melissa, the more he liked her. She was smart and sassy, and clearly devoted to both Jared and their younger sister, Stephanie. Royce wished the couple a fantastic, well-deserved trip to the South Pacific.

It was just bad luck that McQuestin, the family's Montana cattle ranch manager, had broken his leg in three places last week. McQuestin was down for the count. Stephanie was busy training her students for an important horse jumping competition. So Royce was it.

He slipped onto a padded bar stool, the majority of his focus on the selection of single malts on the mirrored, backlit shelf as he gave the woman next to him a passing glance. But he quickly did a double take, disregarding the liquor bottles and focusing on her. She was stunningly gorgeous: blond hair, dark-fringed blue eyes, flushed cheeks, wearing a shimmering, skintight, red-trimmed, gold dress that clung to every delectable curve. Her lips were bold red, and her perfectly manicured fingers were wrapped around a sculpted martini glass.

"What can I get for you?" asked the bartender,

dropping a coaster on the polished mahogany bar in front of Royce.

"Whatever she's having," said Royce without taking his gaze from the woman.

She turned to paste him with a back-off stare, her look of disdain making him wish he'd at least kept his tie done up. But a split second later, her expression mellowed.

"Vodka martini?" the waiter confirmed.

"Sure," said Royce.

"You were the best man," the woman stated, her voice husky-sexy in the quiet of the lounge.

"That I was," Royce agreed easily, more than willing to use tonight's official position to his advantage. "Royce Ryder. Brother of the groom. And you are?"

"Amber Hutton." She held out a feminine hand.

He took it in his. It was small, smooth, with delicate fingers and soft skin. His mind immediately turned to the things she could do to him with a hand like that.

"Tired of dancing?" he asked as the waiter set the martini in front of him. He assumed she would have had plenty of partners in the crowded ballroom.

"Not in the mood." Her fingers moved to the small plastic spear that held a trio of olives in her glass. She shot a brief glance behind her toward the promenade that led to the sparkling ballroom. Then she leaned closer to Royce. He met her halfway.

"Hiding out," she confided.

"From?" he prompted.

She hesitated. Then she shook her head. "Nothing important."

Royce didn't press. "Any way I can be of assistance?"

She arched a perfectly sculpted brow. "Don't hit on me."

"Ouch," he said, feigning a wounded ego.

That prompted a smile. "You did ask."

"I was expecting a different answer."

"I'll understand if you want to take off."

Royce gazed into her eyes for a long moment. Past her smile, he could see trouble lurking. Though women with trouble usually sent him running for the hills, he gave a mental shrug, breaking one of his own rules. "I don't want to take off."

"You one of those nice guys, Royce Ryder?"

"I am," he lied. "Good friend. Confidant. A regular boy next door."

"Funny, I wouldn't have guessed that about you."

"Ouch, again," he said softly, even though she was dead right. He'd never been any woman's good friend or confidant.

"You strike me as more of a playboy."

"Shows you how wrong you can be." He glanced away, taking a sip of the martini. Not a lot of taste to it.

"And you left the party because…"

"I wasn't in the mood for dancing, either," he admitted.

"Oh…" She let her tone turn the word into a question.

He swiveled on the stool so he was facing her. "I'm a jet pilot," he told her instead of explaining his mood. Time had proven it one of his more successful pickup lines. Sure, she'd asked him not to hit on her, but if, in the course of their conversation, she decided she was interested, well, he had no control over that, did he?

"For an airline?" she asked.

"For Ryder International. A corporate jet."

Her glass was empty, so he drained his own and signaled the bartender for another round.

"Getting me drunk won't work," she told him.

"Who says I'm getting you drunk? I'm drowning my own sorrows. I'm only including you to be polite."

She smiled again and seemed to relax. "You don't strike me as a man with sorrows, Mr. 'I'm a Jet Pilot' Best Man."

"Shows you how wrong you can be," he repeated. "I'm here celebrating my last night of freedom." He raised his skewer of olives to his mouth, sliding one off the end.

"Are you getting married, too?"

He nearly choked on the olive. "No."

"Going to jail?" she tried.

He resisted the temptation to nod. "Going to Montana."

She smiled at his answer. "There's something wrong with Montana?"

"There is when you were planning to be in Dubai and Monaco."

Her voice turned melodic, and she shook her head in mock sympathy. "You poor, poor man."

He grunted his agreement. "I'll be babysitting the family ranch. Our manager broke his leg, and Jared's off on his honeymoon."

Her smile stayed in place, but something in her eyes softened. "So, you really are a nice guy?"

"A regular knight in shining armor."

"I like that," she said. Then she was silent for a moment, tracing a swirl in the condensation on the full glass in front of her. "There are definitely times when a girl could use a knight in shining armor."

Royce heard the catch in her voice and saw the tightness in her profile. The trouble was back in her expression.

"This one of those times?" he found himself asking, even though he knew better.

She propped an elbow on the polished bar and leaned her head against her hand, facing him. "Have you ever been in love, Royce Ryder?"

"I have not," he stated without hesitation. And he didn't ever intend to go there. Love guaranteed nothing and complicated everything.

"Don't you think Melissa looked happy today?"

"I'm guessing most brides are happy."

"They are," Amber agreed. Then she lifted her head and moved her left hand, and he realized he'd missed the three carats sparkling on the third finger.

Rookie mistake. What the hell was the matter with him tonight?

Amber should have had more sense than to attend a wedding in her current mood. She should have made up an obligation or faked a headache. Her mother was in New York for the weekend, but it wasn't as if her father needed moral support at a social function.

"You're engaged." Royce Ryder's voice pierced her thoughts, his gaze focused on her ring.

"I am," she admitted, reflexively twisting the diamond in a circle around her finger.

"Don't I feel stupid," Royce muttered.

She cocked her head, and their gazes met and held.

"Why?" she asked.

He gave a dry chuckle and raised his martini glass to

his lips. "Because I may be subtle, but I *am* hitting on you."

She fought a grin at his bald honesty. "Sorry to disappoint you."

"Not your fault."

True. She had been up-front with him. Still, she couldn't help wondering if there was something in her expression, her tone of voice, or maybe her body language that had transmitted more than a passing interest. Not that she'd cheat on Hargrove. Even if…

She shut those thoughts down.

She'd never cheat on Hargrove. But there was no denying that Royce was an incredibly attractive man. He seemed smart. He had a good sense of humor. If she was the type to get picked up, and if he was the one doing the picking, and if she wasn't engaged, she might just be interested.

"What?" he prompted, scanning her expression.

"Nothing." She turned back to her drink. "I'll understand if you leave."

He shifted, and his tone went low. "I'll understand if you ask me to go."

Her brain told her mouth to form the words, but somehow they didn't come out. A few beats went by while the bartender served another couple at the end of the bar, a smoky tune vibrated from the ballroom and a group of young women laughed and chatted as they pulled two tables together in the center of the lounge.

"He here?" asked Royce, cutting a glance to the ballroom. "Did you have a fight?"

Amber shook her head. "He's in Switzerland."

Royce straightened. "Ahh."

"What ahh?"

His deep, blue-eyed gaze turned cocky and speculative. "You're lonely."

Amber's mouth worked in silence for an outraged second. "I am *not* lonely. At least not that way. I'm here with my father."

"What way, then?"

"What way what?" She stabbed the row of olives up and down in her drink.

"In what way are you lonely?"

Why on earth had she put it that way? What was wrong with her? "I am not lonely at all."

"Okay."

"I'm..." She struggled to sort out her feelings.

In a very real way, she *was* lonely. She couldn't talk to her parents. She sure as heck couldn't talk to Hargrove. She couldn't even talk to her best friend, Katie.

Katie was going to be the maid of honor at Amber's wedding next month. They'd bought the bridesmaid dress in Paris. Oriental silk. Flaming orange, which sounded ridiculous, but was interspersed with gold and midnight plum, and looked fabulous on Katie's delicate frame.

Hargrove Alston was the catch of the city. And it wasn't as if there was anything wrong with him. At thirty-three, he was already a partner in one of Chicago's most prestigious law firms. He had a venerated family, impeccable community and political connections. If everything went according to plan, he'd be running for the U.S. Senate next year.

She really had no cause for complaint.

It wasn't as if the sex was bad. It was perfectly, well, pleasant. So was Hargrove. He was a decent and pleasant man. Not every woman could say that about her future husband.

She downed the rest of her martini, hoping it would ease the knot of tension that had stubbornly cramped her stomach for the past month.

Royce signaled the bartender for another round, and she let him.

He polished off his own drink while the bartender shook a mixture of ice and Gray Goose that clattered against the frosted silver shaker. Then the man produced two fresh glasses and strained the martinis.

"His name is Hargrove Alston," she found herself telling Royce.

Royce gave a nod of thanks to the man and lifted both glasses. "Shall we find a table?"

The suggestion startled Amber. She gave a guilty glance around the lounge, feeling like an unfaithful barfly. But nobody was paying the slightest bit of attention to them.

She'd started dating Hargrove when she was eighteen, so she'd never taken up with a stranger in a bar. Not that Royce was a stranger. He was the best man, brother of her father's business associate. It was a completely different thing than encouraging a stranger.

She slipped off the bar stool. "Sure."

At a quiet, corner table, Royce set their drinks down. He pulled one of the padded armchairs out for her, and she eased into the smooth, burgundy leather, crossing her legs and tugging her gold dress to midthigh.

"Hargrove Alston?" he asked as he took the seat opposite, moving the tiny table lamp to one side so their view of each other was unobstructed.

"He's going to run for the U.S. Senate."

"You're marrying a politician?"

"Not necessarily—" She cut herself short. Wow. How

had *that* turned into real words? "I mean, he hasn't been elected yet," she quickly qualified.

"And what do you do?" asked Royce.

Amber pursed her lips and lifted the fresh drink. "Nothing."

"Nothing?"

She shook her head. It was, sadly, the truth. "I graduated University of Chicago," she offered.

"Fine Arts?" he asked.

"Public Administration. An honors degree." It had seemed like a good idea, given Hargrove's political aspirations. At least she'd be in a position to understand the complexities of his work.

"You've got my attention," said Royce, with a look of admiration.

"Only just now?" she joked. But the moment the words were out, she realized what she'd done. She was flirting with Royce.

His blue eyes twinkled with awareness. Then they darkened and simmered. He eased forward. "Amber, you had my attention the second I laid eyes on you."

She stilled, savoring the sound of her name, wrapping her mind around his words as a dangerous warmth sizzled up inside her. The rest of the room disappeared as seconds ticked by, while he waited for her response.

Then his smiled softened, and the predatory gleam went out of his eyes. "I take it that was an accident?"

"I'm not sure," she admitted.

"Well, let me know when you decide."

If flirting with him wasn't an accident, it was definitely a mistake. She needed to get herself back under control. "Tell me about Montana," she tried. "I've never been there."

He drew back, tilting his head to one side for a second, then obviously deciding to let her off the hook. "What do you want to know?"

"Your ranch," she rushed on. "Tell me about your ranch."

"We have cattle."

A cocktail waitress set a small bowl of mixed nuts on the table and took note of their drink levels as Royce thanked her.

"How many?" asked Amber as the woman strode away.

"Around fifty thousand head."

"That's a lot of cows to babysit."

"Tell me about it."

"Horses?" she prompted, determined to keep the conversation innocuous.

"Hundreds."

She plucked an almond from the clear bowl. "I took dressage lessons when I was eleven."

His wide smile revealed straight, white teeth. "In Chicago?"

"Birmingham Stables." She nibbled on the end of the nut. "I didn't last long. I wasn't crazy about sweat and manure."

"You'd hate Montana."

"Maybe not. Tell me something else about it."

"My sister has a horse ranch up in the hills. It has huge meadows with millions of wildflowers."

"Wildflowers are nice." Amber was pretty sure she'd like fields of wildflowers. "What else?"

"She jumps Hanoverians."

"Really? Is she good?"

"We expect her to make the next Olympic team."

"I bet she loves it." Amber tried to imagine what it would be like to be so passionate about something that you were one of the best in the world.

Royce nodded. "Ever since she was five." The glow in his eyes showed his pride in his sister.

Amber sighed and took a second almond. "I wish I loved something."

He considered her words for a few seconds. "Everybody loves something."

She dared to meet his eyes and rest there. "What do you love?"

He didn't hesitate. "Going Mach 1 in a Gulfstream. On a clear night. Over the Nevada desert."

"Get to do it often?"

"Not often enough."

Amber couldn't help but smile. "Are you good?"

His gaze flicked to the low neckline of her dress as his voice turned to a rumble. "I am very, very good."

"You are very, very bad," she countered, with a waggle of her finger.

He grinned unrepentantly, and the warmth sizzled up inside her all over again.

"Your turn," he told her.

She didn't understand.

"What do you love?"

Now, there was a question.

She bought herself some time by taking a sip of her drink.

"Designer shoes," she decided, setting the long-stemmed glass back down on the table.

He leaned sideways to peer under the table. "Liar."

"What do you mean?" She stretched out a leg to show off her black, stiletto sandals.

"I've dated women with a shoe fetish."

"I never said I had a fetish."

"Yours are unpretentious." Before she knew it, he'd scooped her foot onto his knee. "And there's a frayed spot on the strap." His thumb brushed her ankle as he gestured. "You've worn them more than twice."

"I didn't say I was extravagant about it." She desperately tried to ignore the warmth of his hand, but her pulse had jumped, and she could feel moisture forming at her hairline.

"Try again," he told her.

"Birthday cake." She was more honest this time. "Three layers with sickly, sugary buttercream icing and bright pink rosebuds."

He laughed and set her foot back on the floor.

Thank goodness.

"How old are you?" he asked, scooping a handful of nuts.

"Twenty-two. You?"

"Thirty-three."

"Seriously?"

"Yeah. Why?"

She shrugged, hesitated, then plunged in. "Hargrove is thirty-three, and he seems a lot older than you."

"That's because I'm a pilot—daring and carefree. He's a politician—staid and uptight. No comparison, really."

"You've never even met him." Yet the analysis was frighteningly accurate.

Royce's expression turned serious. "Why are you hiding out?"

"What?"

"When I first saw you over at the bar, you said you were hiding out. From what?"

What, indeed.

Amber took a deep breath, smoothing both palms in parallel over her hair. She scrunched her eyes shut for a long moment.

She was hiding out from the glowing bride, the happy guests and the pervasive joy of happily-ever-after.

But even as she rolled the explanation around, she knew it wasn't right. She didn't begrudge Melissa her happiness.

Truth was, she was hiding out from herself, from the notion that she was living a lie, from the realization that she'd wrapped her life around a man she didn't love.

The truth was both frightening and exhausting, and she needed time to figure it all out. More than an evening. More than a day. Even more than a weekend.

She needed to come to terms with the colossal mess she'd made of her life and decide where to go next. Ironic, really. Where Royce dreaded his ranch in Montana, she'd give anything—

Her eyes popped open, and she blinked him into focus. "Take me with you."

His brow furrowed. "What?"

"Take me with you to Montana." Nobody would look for her in Montana. She'd be free of dress fittings and florists and calligraphers. No more gift registries or parties or travel agents.

No more Hargrove.

The thought took a weight off her shoulders, and the knot in her stomach broke free. Not good.

"Are you joking?" asked Royce.

"No."

"Are you crazy?"

"Maybe." Was she crazy? This certainly felt insane. Unfortunately, it also felt frighteningly right.

"I'm not taking an engaged woman with me to Montana."

"Why not?"

He held out his palms, gesturing in the general vicinity of her neckline and the rest of her dress. "Because… Because… Well, because your fiancé would kill me, for one."

"I won't tell him."

"Right. That plan always ends well."

"I'm serious. He'll never know."

"Forget it."

No. She wouldn't forget it. This was the first idea in weeks that had felt right to her.

She pulled off her diamond ring, setting it on the table between them. "There. No more fiancé. No more problem."

"It doesn't have to be on your finger to count."

"Yeah?" she challenged.

"Yeah," he confirmed.

"What if I wasn't engaged?" Her words cut to absolute silence between them. The other sounds in the room muted, and time slowed down.

His gaze took a methodical trip from her cleavage to her waist, then backtracked to her eyes. "Sweetheart, if you weren't engaged, I'd say fasten your seat belt."

She snapped open her handbag. "Then how about this?" Retrieving her slim, silver cell phone, she typed a quick message and handed it over to Royce.

He squinted in the dim light, brows going up as he read the typed words.

I'm so sorry. I can't marry you. I need some time to think.

"Press Send," she told him. "Press Send, and take me to Montana."

"*There you are,* pumpkin." Amber's father stepped up behind her, and his broad hand came down on her shoulder.

Shock rushed straight from her brain all the way to her toes. She whipped her head around to look up. "Daddy?"

"The limo's at the curb." Her father's glance went to Royce.

Royce placed the cell phone facedown on the table and stood up to hold out his hand. "Royce Ryder. Jared's brother."

Her father shook. "David Hutton. We met briefly in the receiving line."

"Good to see you again, sir."

"You've been entertaining my daughter?"

"The other way around," said Royce, his gaze going to Amber. "She's an interesting woman. You must be proud."

Her father gave her shoulder a squeeze. "We certainly are. But it's getting late, honey. We need to get home."

No, Amber wanted to yell. She didn't want to go home. She wanted to stay here with Royce and completely change her life. She wanted to break it off with Hargrove and escape to Montana. She truly did.

Royce picked up the phone and slipped it back into her purse, clicking the purse shut with finality then handing it to her. "It was fun meeting you."

Amber opened her mouth, but no words came out.

Her father scooped a hand under her elbow and gently urged her to her feet.

She stared at Royce, trying to convey her desperation, hoping he'd understand the look in her eyes and do something to help her. But he didn't. And her father took a step, and she took a step. And another, and another.

"Amber?" Royce called, and relief shot though her. He knew. He understood. He was coming to her rescue.

But when she turned, he was holding out her engagement ring.

"Amber," her father admonished, shock clear in his tone.

"My hands were swelling," she answered lamely.

Royce didn't bother making eye contact as he dropped the diamond into the palm of her hand.

Two

"Who was that?" Stephanie's voice startled Royce as he watched Amber exit the lounge on her father's arm.

Tearing his eyes from the supple figure beneath the gold-and-red dress, he turned to face his sister. Stephanie looked young and unusually feminine in her ice-pink, strapless, satin bridesmaid dress. It had a full, flowing, knee-length skirt and a wide, white sash that matched her dangling, satin-bead earrings.

"Are all women crazy?" he asked, trying to recall the last time he'd seen Stephanie in anything other than riding clothes.

"Yes, we are," she answered without hesitation, linking her arm with his. "So you probably don't want to upset us. Like, for example, turning down our perfectly reasonable requests."

Royce sighed, steering her back to the table as he

pushed the bizarre conversation with Amber out of his mind. "What do you want, Steph?"

"A million dollars."

"No."

"Hey," she said, sliding into Amber's vacated seat as the cocktail waitress removed the empty martini glass. She kicked off one sandal and tucked her ankle under the opposite thigh on the roomy chair. "I'm a woman on the edge here."

"On the edge of what?" He pushed his half-full drink away. Had Amber's text message been an elaborate joke? If so, how warped was her sense of humor?

"Sanity," said Stephanie. "There's this stallion in London."

"Talk to Jared." Royce wasn't getting caught up in his sister's insatiable demands for her jumping stable.

"It's Jared's wedding night. He already went upstairs. You're in charge now."

Royce glanced at his watch. "And you think I'm a soft touch?"

"You always have been in the past."

"Forget it."

"His name's Blanchard's Run."

"I said forget it." He had time for maybe four hours of sleep before he had to get to the airport and preflight the jet.

"But—" Stephanie suddenly stopped, blinking in surprise as she glanced above his head.

"I sent it," came a breathless voice that Royce already easily recognized.

He jerked his head around to confirm it was Amber.

"Sent what?" asked Stephanie.

Amber's jewel-blue eyes were shining with a mixture of trepidation and excitement.

She hadn't.

She wouldn't.

"Where's your father?" asked Royce. Was this another warped joke?

"He left. I told him to send the limo back for me later."

Royce shook his head, refusing to believe any woman would do something that impulsive. "You did not send it."

But Amber nodded, then she glanced furtively around the lounge. "I figure I have about ten minutes to get out of here."

"What did you send?" Stephanie demanded. "To *who?*"

Amber slipped into the vacant third seat between them and leaned forward, lowering her voice. "I broke off my engagement."

Stephanie looked both shocked and excited. She reached for Amber's hand and squeezed it. "With *who?*"

"Hargrove Alston."

"The guy who's going to run for the Senate?"

Royce stared at his sister in astonishment.

"I read it in *People,*" she told him with a dismissive wave of her hand. Then she turned her attention back to Amber. "Is he mad? Is he after you now?"

"He's in Switzerland."

"Then you're safe."

"Not for long. As soon as Hargrove reads my text, he'll call my dad, and my dad will turn the limo around."

Stephanie's lips pursed into an O of concern, and her breath whooshed out.

Amber nodded her agreement, and both women turned expectantly to Royce.

"What?"

"We have to go," said Stephanie, her expression hinting that he was a little slow on the uptake.

"To Montana," Amber elaborated.

"Now," said Stephanie with a nod of urgency.

"They'll never think to look for me in Montana," Amber elaborated.

"I'm not taking you to—"

But Stephanie jumped up from her chair. "To the airport," she declared in a ridiculously dramatic tone.

"Right." Amber nodded, rising, as well, smoothing her sexy dress over her hips as she stood on her high heels.

"Stop," Royce demanded, and even the laughing women at the table next to them stopped talking and glanced over.

"Shh," Stephanie hissed.

Royce lowered his voice. "We are *not* rushing off to the airport like a bunch of criminals."

Stephanie planted both hands on the tabletop. "And why not?"

"Six minutes," Amber helpfully informed them.

He shot her a look of frustration. "Don't be such a wimp. If he yells at you, he yells at you."

Amber's brows rose. "I'm not afraid he'll yell at me."

"Then, what's the problem?"

"I'm afraid he'll talk me out of it."

"That's ridiculous. You're a grown woman. It's your life."

"It is," Amber agreed. "And I want to come to Montana."

The look she gave him was frank and very adult. Perhaps his first instinct had been right. Maybe there was something between them. Maybe he was the reason she'd made the decision to finally dump the loser fiancé and move on.

He felt a rush of pride, a hit of testosterone and, quite frankly, the throb of arousal. Having Amber around would definitely make Montana more palatable. Only a fool would put barriers in her way.

He stood and tossed a couple of twenties on the table. "The airport, then."

Since he'd had the martinis, it would be a few hours before he could fly. But there was plenty to do in preparation.

By the time they arrived at the Ryder Ranch, Amber had had second, third, even fourth thoughts. Both her father and Hargrove were powerful men. Neither of them took kindly to opposition, and she'd never done anything remotely rebellious in her life.

Hargrove was probably on a plane right now, heading back to Chicago, intending to find her and demand to know what she was *thinking.* And her father was likely out interrogating her friends this morning, determined to find out what had happened and where she'd gone.

Katie would be flabbergasted.

Amber had been questioning her feelings for Hargrove for a couple of months now, but she hadn't shared those fears with Katie. Because, although Katie was a logical and grounded lawyer, she was saddled with an emotional case of hero worship when it came to Hargrove. She thought the sun rose and set on the man. She'd never understand.

Amber had sent her father a final text last night from the airport, assuring him that he didn't need to worry, that she needed some time alone and that she'd be in contact soon. Then she'd turned off her cell phone. She'd seen enough crime dramas to know there were ways to trace the signal. And Hargrove had friends in both high and low places. Where the police couldn't accommodate him, private investigators on the South Side would be happy to wade in.

The sun was emerging from behind the eastern mountains as Amber, Royce and Stephanie crossed the wide porch of the Ryder ranch house. She was dead tired but determined to keep anyone from seeing her mounting worry.

In the rising light of day, she admitted to herself that this had been a colossally stupid plan. Her father and Hargrove weren't going to sit quietly and wait while she worked through her emotions. Plus, she had nothing with her but a pair of high heels, her cocktail dress and a ruby-and-diamond, drop necklace with a set of matching earrings.

And of all the nights to go with a tiny pair of high-cut, sheer panties—sure, they smoothed the line of her dress, but that was their only virtue.

"You heading home?" Royce asked his sister as he tossed a small duffel bag onto the polished hardwood floor, against the wall of a spacious foyer.

"Home," Stephanie echoed, clicking the wide double

doors shut behind her. "I can grab a couple hours' sleep before class starts."

Amber turned to glance quizzically at Stephanie. "Home?" She'd assumed they were already there. The sign on the gate two miles back had clearly stated Ryder Ranch.

"Up to my place." Stephanie pointed. "I've got students arriving this afternoon."

"You don't live here?" Amber kept her voice even, but the thought was unsettling. Sure, Royce was the brother of her father's business associate, but he was still a stranger, and there was safety in numbers.

Stephanie was shaking her head. "They kicked me out years ago."

"When your horses took over the entire yard." Royce loosened his tie and moved out of the foyer. He'd changed out of his tux at the airport in favor of a short-sleeved, white uniform shirt and a pair of navy slacks.

Stephanie made to follow him into a massive, rectangular living room with a two-story, open, timber-beamed ceiling and a bank of glass doors at the far end, flanking a stone fireplace. Amber moved with her, taking in a large, patterned red rug, cream and gold, overstuffed furniture groupings and a huge, round, Western-style chandelier suspended in the center of the room.

"You want me to show Amber a bedroom?" asked Stephanie. She was still wearing her bridesmaid dress.

"She's probably hungry," Royce pointed out, and both looked expectantly at Amber.

"I'm...uh..." The magnitude of her actions suddenly hit Amber. She was standing in a stranger's house, completely dependent on him for food, shelter, even clothes. She was many miles from the nearest town, and every normal support system—her cell phone, credit card and chauffeur—were unavailable to her, since they could be traced.

"Exhausted," Stephanie finished for her, linking an arm with Amber's. "Let's get you upstairs." She gently propelled Amber toward a wide, wooden staircase.

"Good night, then," Royce called from behind them.

"You look shell-shocked," Stephanie whispered in her ear as they mounted the staircase.

"I'm questioning my sanity," Amber admitted as the stairs turned right and walls closed in around them.

Stephanie hit a light switch, revealing a half-octagonal landing, with four doors leading off in separate directions.

"You're not insane," said Stephanie, opening one of the middle doors.

"I just abandoned my fiancé and flew off in the middle of the night with strangers."

"We're not that strange." Stephanie led the way into an airy room that fanned out to a slightly triangular shape.

It had a queen-size, four-poster brass bed, with a blue-and-white-checked comforter that looked decadently soft. Two royal blue armchairs were arranged next to a paned-glass balcony door. White doors led to a walk-in closet and an ensuite bath, while a ceiling fan spun lazily overhead and a cream-colored carpet cushioned Amber's feet.

Stephanie clicked on one of two ceramic bedside lamps. "Or do you think you're insane to leave the fiancé?"

"He's not going to be happy," Amber admitted.

"Does he, like, turn all purple and yell and stuff?" Stephanie looked intrigued and rather excited by the prospect.

Amber couldn't help but smile. "No. He gets all stuffy and logical and superior."

Hargrove would never yell. He'd make Amber feel as though she was a fool, as though her opinions and emotions weren't valid, as though she was behaving like a spoiled child. And maybe she was. But at least she was out of his reach for a little while.

"I hear you." Stephanie opened the double doors of a tall, cherrywood armoire, revealing a set of shelves. "My brothers are like that."

"Royce?" Amber found herself asking. In their admittedly short conversation Royce hadn't seemed at all like Hargrove.

"And Jared," said Stephanie. "They think I'm still ten years old. I'm a full partner in Ryder International, but I have to come to them for every little decision."

"That must be frustrating." Amber sympathized. She had some autonomy with her own credit cards and signing authority on her trust fund. She'd never really thought about independence beyond that.

Well, until now.

"There's this stallion," said Stephanie, selecting something in white cotton from the shelves. "Blanchard's Run, out of Westmont Stables in London. He's perfect for my breeding program. His dam was Ogilvie and his sire Danny Day." She shook her head. "All I need is a million dollars." She handed Amber what turned out to be a cotton nightgown.

"For one horse?" The price sounded pretty high.

"That's mine," said Stephanie, nodding to the gown.

"You should help yourself to anything else in the dresser. There's jeans, shirts, a bunch of stuff that should fit you."

"If it's any consolation," said Amber, putting her hand on Stephanie's arm, "I can't see Hargrove ever letting me spend a million dollars, either."

"And *that's* why you should leave him."

"I'm leaving him—" Amber paused a beat, debating saying the words out loud for the first time "—because I don't love him."

Stephanie's lips formed another silent O. She nodded slowly for a long moment. "Good reason."

Amber agreed.

But she knew her parents would never accept it. And it wasn't because they had some old-fashioned idea about the value of arranged marriages or about love being less important than a person's pedigree. It was because they didn't trust Amber to recognize love one way or the other.

And that was why Amber couldn't go home yet. Nobody would listen to her. They'd all gang up, and she'd find herself railroaded down the aisle.

As usual, it was frighteningly easy for Royce to slip back into the cowboy life. He'd stretched out on his bed for a couple of hours, then dressed in blue jeans, a cotton shirt and his favorite worn cowboy boots. Sasha had quick-fried him a steak, and produced a big stack of hotcakes with maple syrup. After drinking about a gallon of coffee, he'd hunted down the three foremen who reported directly to McQuestin.

He'd learned the vet had recommended moving the Bowler Valley herd because seasonal flies were impacting the calves. A well had broken down at the north camp and the ponds were drying up. And a lumber shipment was stuck at the railhead in Idaho because of a snafu with the letter of credit. But before he'd had a chance to wade in on any of the issues, an SOS had come over his cell phone from Barry Brewster, Ryder International's Vice President of Finance, for a letter from China's Ministry of Trade Development. The original had gone missing in the Chicago office, but they thought Jared might have left a copy at the ranch.

So Royce was wading through the jumble of papers on the messy desk in the front office of the ranch house, looking for a letter from Foreign Investment Director Cheng Li. Without Cheng Li's approval, a deal between Ryder International and Shanxi Electrical would be canceled, costing a fortune, and putting several Ryder construction projects at risk.

Giving up on the desk, and cursing out his older brother for falling in love and getting married at such an inconvenient time, Royce moved to the file cabinet, pulling open the top drawer. His blunt fingers were awkward against the flimsy paper, and the complex numbering system made no sense to him. What the hell was wrong with using the alphabet?

"The outfit seems at odds with the job duties," a female voice ventured from the office doorway.

He turned to see Amber in a pair of snug jeans and a maroon, sleeveless blouse. Her feet were bare, and her blond hair was damp, framing her face in lush waves. There was an amused smile on her fresh, pretty face.

"You think this is funny?" he asked in exasperation.

"Unexpected," she clarified.

"Well, don't just stand there."

"Should I be doing something?"

He directed her to the desktop. "We're looking for a letter from the Chinese Ministry of Trade and Development."

She immediately moved forward.

"Do you know what it looks like?" she asked, picking up the closest pile of papers.

He grunted. "It's on paper."

"Long letter? Short letter? In an envelope? Attached to a report?"

"I don't know. It's from Cheng Li, Foreign Investment Director. I need his phone number."

She moved on to the next pile, while Royce went back to the filing cabinet.

"Have you tried Google?" she asked.

"This isn't the kind of number you find on the Internet."

She continued sorting. "I take it this is important?"

"If I don't get hold of him today, we're going to blow a deal."

"What time is it in China?"

"Sometime Monday morning. Barry says if the approval's not filed in Beijing by the end of business today, we're toast."

"Their time?" Amber asked.

"Their time," Royce confirmed. "What the hell happened to the alphabet?"

She moved closer, brushing against him. "You want me to—"

"No," he snapped, and she quickly halted.

He clamped his jaw and forced himself to take a breath. It wasn't her fault the letter was lost. And it wasn't her fault that his body had a hair-trigger reaction to her touch. "Sorry. Can you keep looking over there? On the desk?"

"Sure." Her features were schooled, and he couldn't tell if she was upset.

"I didn't mean to shout."

"Not a problem." She turned back.

He opened his mouth again, but then decided the conversation could wait. If she was upset, he'd deal with it later. For now, he had three more drawers to search.

"Something to do with Shanxi Electrical?" she asked.

Royce's head jerked up. "You found it?"

She handed him a single sheet of paper.

He scanned his way down to the signature line and found the number for Cheng Li's office. "This is it." He heaved a sigh, resisting the urge to hug her in gratitude.

Then he took in her rosy cheeks, her jewel-blue eyes, her soft hair and smooth skin. The deep colored blouse molded to her feminine curves, while the skintight blue jeans highlighted a killer figure. There was something completely sexy about her bare feet, and he had to fight hard against the urge to hug her.

"Thanks," he offered gruffly, reaching for the phone.

He punched in the international and area codes, then made his way through the rest of the numbers.

After several rings, a voice answered in Chinese at the other end.

"May I speak with Mr. Cheng Li?" he tried.

The voice spoke Chinese again.

"Cheng Li? Is there someone there who speaks English?"

The next words were incomprehensible. He might have heard the name Cheng Li, but he wasn't sure.

"English?" he asked again.

Amber held out her hand and motioned for him to give her the phone.

He gave her a look of incomprehension while the woman on the other end tried once more to communicate with him.

"I'm sorry," he said into the phone, but then it was summarily whisked from his hand.

"Hey!" But before he could protest further, Amber spoke. The words were distinctly non-English.

Royce drew back in astonishment. "No way."

She spoke again. Then she waited. Then she covered the receiver. "Your phone number?" she whispered.

He quickly flipped open his cell to the display, and she rattled something into the phone. Then she finished the call and hung up. "Cheng Li will call you in an hour with an interpreter."

"You speak *Chinese?*" was all Royce could manage.

She gave a self-deprecating eye roll. "I can make myself understood. But for them, it's kind of like talking to a two-year-old."

"You speak Chinese?" he repeated.

"Mandarin, actually." She paused. "I have a knack." When he didn't say anything, she bridged the silence. "My mother taught me Swedish. And I learned Spanish in school." She shrugged. "So, well, considering the potential political impact of the rising Asian economies, I decided Mandarin and Punjabi were the two I should study at college. I'm really not that good at either of them."

He peered at her. "You're like a politician's dream wife, aren't you?"

Her lips pursed for a moment, and discomfort flickered in her eyes. "Are you saying I have no life?"

"I'm saying he's going to come after you." Royce put a warning in his tone. "I sure as hell wouldn't let you get away."

She blinked, and humor came back into her blue eyes. "I doubt I'd make it very far from here. After all, there is only one road out of the ranch."

Royce wasn't in the mood to joke. "He *is* going to come after you, isn't he?"

She sobered. "I don't think he'll find me."

"And if he does?"

She didn't answer.

"What's the guy got on you?"

From what Royce could see, Amber was an intelligent, capable woman. There was no reason in the world for her to let herself get saddled with a man she didn't want.

"Same thing Jared has on you," she answered softly. "Duty, obligation, guilt."

"Jared needs me for a month," said Royce, not buying into the parallel. "What's-his-name—"

"Hargrove."

"Hargrove wants you forever." Royce felt a sudden spurt of anger. "And where the hell are your parents in all this? Have you told them?"

"They think he's perfect for me."

"He's not."

Amber smiled. "You've never even met him."

"I don't have to. You're here. He's there." Royce ran

his brain through the circumstances one more time. "Your cell's turned off, right?"

She nodded.

"Don't use your credit cards."

"I didn't bring them."

"Good."

"Not really." She hesitated. "Royce, I have no money whatsoever."

"You don't need money."

"And I have no clothes, not even underwear."

Okay, that gave him an unwanted visual. "We have everything you need right here."

"I can't live off your charity."

"You're our guest."

"I forced you to bring me here."

Royce set the letter back down on the desktop and tucked his phone back into his shirt pocket. "Ask anybody, Amber. I don't do anything I don't want to do." He let his gaze shade the meaning of the words. He'd brought her home with him because she was a beautiful and interesting woman. It was absolutely no hardship having her around.

"I need to earn my keep."

Royce resisted the temptation to make a joke about paying her way by sleeping with him. It was in poor taste, and the last thing he wanted to do was insult her. Besides, the two were completely unrelated.

He hoped she was attracted to him. What red-blooded man wouldn't? And last night he had been fairly certain she was attracted to him. But whatever was between them would take its own course.

Her gaze strayed to the messy desk. "I could..."

He followed the look.

"…maybe straighten things up a little? I've taken business management courses, some accounting—"

"No argument from me." Royce held up his palms in surrender. "McQuestin's niece, Maddy, usually helps out in the office, but she's gone back to Texas with him while he recovers." He spread his arms in welcome. "Make yourself at home."

Three

Several hours later, eyes grainy from reading ranch paperwork, Amber wandered out of the office. The office door opened into a short hallway that connected to the front foyer and then to the rest of the ranch house. It had grown dark while she worked, and soft lamplight greeted her in the empty living room. The August night was cool, with pale curtains billowing in the side windows, while screen doors separated the room from the veranda beyond.

Muted noise came from the direction of the kitchen, and she caught a movement on the veranda. Moving closer, she realized it was a plump puff ball of a black-and-white puppy. Amber smiled in reaction as another pup appeared, and then a third and a fourth.

They hadn't seen her yet, and the screen door kept them locked outside. Just as well. They were cute, but

Amber was a little intimidated by animals. She'd never had a pet before. Her mother didn't like the noise, the mess or the smell.

Truth was, she dropped out of dressage riding lessons because one of the horses had bit her on the shoulder. She hadn't told the grooms, or her parents, or anybody else about the incident. She was embarrassed, convinced that she'd done something to annoy the horse but not sure of what it might have been. When a creature couldn't talk or communicate, how did you know what they wanted or needed?

The pups disappeared from view, and she moved closer to the door, peeking at an angle to see them milling in a small herd around Royce's feet while he sat in a deep, wooden Adirondack chair, reading some kind of report under the half-dozen outdoor lamps that shone around the veranda.

Then the pups spotted her and made a roly-poly beeline for the door, sixteen paws thumping awkwardly on the wooden slats of the deck. She took an automatic step back as they piled up against the screen.

Royce glanced up from the papers. "Hey, Amber." Then his attention went to the puppies. He gave a low whistle, and they scampered back to him.

"It's safe to come out now," he said with a warm smile.

"I'm not…" She eased the door open. "I'm not scared to come out."

Royce laughed. "Didn't think you were. Shut the screen behind you, though, or these guys will be in the kitchen in a heartbeat."

She closed the screen door behind her. "Your puppies?"

He reached down to scratch between the ears of the full-grown border collie sprawled between the chair and the railing. "They belong to Molly. Care to take one home when you leave?"

"My mother won't have pets in the house." The puppies rushed back to Amber again.

Royce gestured for her to take the chair across from his. "Is she allergic?"

"Not exactly." Warm, fuzzy bodies pressed against her leg; cool, wet noses investigated her bare feet and she felt a mushy tongue across the top of her toes. She struggled not to cringe at the slimy sensation. "She doesn't want any accidents on the Persian rug."

"The price you pay," said Royce.

Amber settled into the chair. One of the pups put its paws on her knee, lifting up to sniff along her jeans.

"Most people pet them." Royce's tone was wry.

"I'm a little…" She gingerly scratched the puppy between its floppy, little ears. Its fur was soft, skin warm, and its dark eyes were adorable.

"It's okay," he said. "Not everybody likes animals."

"I don't dislike them."

"I can tell."

"They make me a little nervous, okay?"

"They're puppies, not mountain lions."

"They—" Another warm tongue swiped across her bare toes, and she jerked her feet under the chair. "Tickle," she finished.

"Princess," he mocked her.

"I was once bitten by a horse," she defended. Her interactions with animals hadn't been particularly positive so far.

"I was once gored by a bull," he countered with a challenging look.

"Is this going to be a contest?"

"Kicked in the head." He leaned forward and parted his short, dark hair.

She couldn't see a scar, but she trusted it was there.

"By a bronc," he finished. "In a local rodeo at fourteen."

Amber lifted her elbow to show a small scar. "Fell off a top bunk. At camp. I was *thirteen*."

"Did you break it?"

"Sprained."

"What kind of camp?"

"Violin."

His grin went wide. "Oh, my. Such a dangerous life. Did you ever break a nail? Get a bad wax job?"

"Hey, buddy." She jabbed her finger in the direction of his chest. "*After* your first wax job, we can talk."

Devilment glowed in his deep blue eyes. "You can wax anything I've got," he drawled. "Any ol' time you want."

Her stomach contracted, and a wave of unexpected heat prickled her skin. How had the conversation taken that particular turn? She sat up straight and folded her hands primly in her lap. "That's not what I meant."

He paused, gaze going soft. "That's too bad."

The puppies had grown bored with her feet, and one by one, they'd wandered back to Royce. They were now curled in a sleeping heap around his chair. The dog, Molly, yawned while insects made dancing shadows in the veranda lights.

"You hungry?" asked Royce.

Amber nodded. She was starving, and she was more than happy to let their discussion die.

He flipped the report closed, and she was reminded of their earlier office work.

"Did you talk to Cheng Li?"

"I did," said Royce. "He promised to fax the paperwork to the Ryder financial office."

"In Chicago."

"Yes." He rose cautiously to his feet, stepping around the sleeping puppies. "Disaster averted. Sasha'll have soup on the stove."

"Soup sounds great." It was nearly nine, and Amber hadn't eaten anything since their light snack on the plane around 5:00 a.m. Any kind of food sounded terrific to her right now.

They left the border collies asleep on the deck and filed through the living room, down a hallway to the kitchen on the south side of the house.

"Have you talked to your parents?" asked Royce as he set a pair of blue-glazed, stoneware bowls out on the breakfast bar.

The counters were granite, the cabinets dark cherry. There were stainless steel appliances with cheery, yellow walls and ceiling reflecting off the polished beams and natural wood floor. A trio of spotlights was suspended above the bar, complementing the glow of the pot lights around the perimeter of the ceiling.

"I texted them both before I got on the plane."

"Nothing since then?" He set a basket of grainy buns on the breakfast bar, and she slipped onto one of the high, padded, hunter-green leather chairs.

She shook her head. "I don't know how this GPS and triangulating-the-cell-towers thing works."

Royce's brows went up, and he paused in his work.

"Crime dramas," she explained. "I don't know how much of all that is fiction. My dad, and Hargrove for sure, will pull out all the stops."

Royce held out his hand. "Let me see your phone."

She pulled back on the stool and dug the little phone out of the pocket of her blue jeans.

He slid it open and pressed the on button.

"Are you sure—"

"I won't leave it on long." He peered at the tiny screen. "Nope. No GPS function." He shut it off and tossed it back to her. "Though they could, theoretically, triangulate while you're talking, but you're probably safe to text."

"Really?" That was good news. She'd like to send another message to her mother. And Katie deserved an explanation.

He set out two small plates and spoons while she tucked the phone back into her pocket. She'd have to think about how to phrase her explanation.

Royce ladled the steaming soup into the bowls and set them back on the bar, taking the stool at the end.

"Thanks," she breathed, inhaling the delectable aroma.

Royce lifted his spoon. "So, how long have you known?"

She followed suit, dipping into the rich broth. "Known what?"

"That you didn't love him?"

Royce knew his question was blunt to the point of rudeness, but if he was going to make a play for Amber, he needed to know the lay of the land. He knew he'd be a temporary, rebound fling, which was not even remotely a problem for him. In fact, he'd gone into the situation *planning* to be her temporary, rebound fling. She wasn't going to stay the whole month. She probably wouldn't even last a week. But he was up for it, however long it lasted.

Last night, he'd known Amber was beautiful. Today, he'd learned she was positively fascinating. She was intelligent, poised and personable, and she could actually speak Chinese. Her reaction to the puppies was cute and endearing. While her fiancé's and family's ability to intimidate her made him curious.

Why would such an accomplished woman give a rat's hind end what anybody thought of her decisions?

She stirred her spoon thoughtfully through the bowl of soup. "It's not so much…" she began.

He waited.

She looked up. "It's not that I knew I didn't love him. It's more that I didn't know that I did. You know?"

Royce hadn't the slightest idea what she meant, and he shook his head.

"It seems to me," she said, cocking her head sideways, teeth raking momentarily over her full bottom lip, "if you're going to say 'till death do us part' you'd better be damn sure."

Royce couldn't disagree with that. His parents obviously hadn't been damn sure. At least his mother wasn't. His father, on the other hand, had to have been devastated by her betrayal.

Amber was right to break it off. She had absolutely no business marrying a man she didn't love unreservedly.

"You'd better be damn sure," Royce echoed, fighting a feeling of annoyance with her for even considering marrying a man she didn't love. This Hargrove person might be a jerk. So far, he sounded like a jerk. But no man deserved a disloyal wife.

Amber nodded as she swallowed a spoonful of the soup. "Melissa looked sure."

"Melissa *was* sure."

Amber blinked at the edge to Royce's tone. "What?"

"Nothing." He tore a bun in half.

"You annoyed?"

He shook his head.

"Melissa and Jared seem really good together."

"You do know it's kinder to break it off up front with a guy." Royce set down his spoon.

"I—"

"Because, if you don't, the next thing you know, you'll have two or three kids, the PTA and carpool duty. You'll get bored. You'll start looking around. And you'll end up at the No-Tell Motel on Route 55, in bed with some young drifter. And Hargrove, whoever-he-is, will be going for his gun."

"Whoa." Amber's eyes were wide in the stark kitchen light. "You just did my whole life in thirty seconds."

"I didn't necessarily mean you."

"What? Are we talking about Melissa?"

"No." Royce gave himself a mental shake. "We are absolutely not talking about Melissa."

"Then who—"

"Nobody. Forget it." He drew a breath. So much for making a play for her. It wouldn't be tonight. That was for sure. "I just don't understand why you're feeling guilty," he continued. "You are absolutely doing the right thing."

"I believe that," she agreed.

He held her gaze with a frank stare. "And anybody who tries to talk you out of it is shortsighted and just plain stupid."

"You know you're talking about my father."

"I know."

"He's Chairman of the City Accountants Association, and he owns a multimillion-dollar financial consortium."

"Pure blind luck, obviously."

A small smile crept out, though she clearly fought against it. "The No-Tell Motel?"

"Metaphorically speaking. I'm sure you'd pick the Ritz."

"I've never been unfaithful."

Royce knew he should apologize.

"I've dated Hargrove since I was eighteen, and even though he's not the greatest—" She snapped her mouth shut, and a flush rose in her cheeks as she reached for one of the homemade buns.

Okay, this was interesting. "Not the greatest what?"

"Nothing."

"You're blushing."

"No, I'm not." She tore into the bun.

Royce grinned. "Were you going to say *lover?*"

"No." But everything in her body language told him she was lying.

He gazed at her profile for a long minute.

Eighteen. She was eighteen when she took up with Hargrove. Royce could be wrong, but he didn't think he was. Amber hadn't had any other lovers. She was dissatisfied with Hargrove, but she had no comparison.

Interesting. He chewed a hunk of his own bun.

A woman deserved at least one comparison.

"What did you find?" Royce's voice from the office doorway interrupted Amber's long day of office work.

The sun was descending toward the rugged mountains, while neat piles of bills and correspondence had slowly grown out of the chaos on the desktop in front of her.

Now she stretched her arm out to place a letter on the farthest pile. It was another advertisement for horse tack. She was fairly sure the junk mail could be tossed out, but she wasn't about to make that decision on her own.

"You've got some overdue bills," she answered Royce, twisting her head to see him lounging in the doorway, one broad shoulder propped against the doorjamb, his hair mussed and sweaty across his forehead and a streak of dirt marring his roughened chin. She met his deep blue gaze, and a surge of longing clenched her chest.

"Pay them," he suggested in a sexy rumble, crossing his arms over his chest.

"You going to hand over your platinum card?"

His lips parted in a grin. "Sure."

"Then you better have a high limit. Some of them are six figures." Feed, lumber, vet bills. The list went on and on.

He eased away from the door frame and ambled toward her. "There must be a checkbook around here somewhere."

"I didn't see one." Not that she'd combed through the desk drawers. There was plenty to do sorting through what was piled on top. "How long did you say McQuestin had been off?"

"Three weeks. Why?"

"Some of these bills are two months old. That's hell on your credit rating, you know."

He moved closer, and she forced herself to drag her gaze from his rangy body.

To distract herself, she lifted the closest unopened envelope and sliced through the seam with the ivory-handled opener, extracting another folded invoice. The distraction didn't help. Her nostrils picked up his fresh, outdoorsy scent, and his arm brushed her shoulder, sending an electric current over her skin as he slid open a top desk drawer.

Lifting several items out of the way, he quickly produced a narrow, leather-bound booklet and tossed it on the desk. "Here you go. Start protecting my credit rating."

"Like the bank would honor my signature." She knew she should shift away, but something magnetic kept her sitting right where she was, next to his narrow hip and strong thigh. She didn't even care that his jeans were dusty.

Not that it would matter if anything rubbed off. She was dressed in a plain, khaki T-shirt and a pair of faded jeans she'd borrowed from Stephanie's cache in the upstairs bedroom. She could press herself against Royce from head to toe, and simply clean up later with soap and water.

The idea was far too appealing. She felt heat flare in the pit of her stomach as an image bloomed in her mind.

"I'll sign a bunch for you." His voice interrupted her burgeoning fantasy as he flipped open the checkbook.

She blinked herself back to reality. "I assume you're joking."

"Why would I be joking?" He leaned over, hunting through the drawer again, bringing himself into even closer contact with her.

She shifted imperceptibly in his direction, and his cotton-clad arm brushed her bare one. She sucked in a tight breath.

He retrieved a pen.

She suddenly realized he was serious, and placed her hand over the top check. "You can't do that."

He turned, pen poised, bringing their faces into close proximity. "Why not?"

"Because I could write myself a check, a *very big* check, and then cash it."

He rolled his eyes

"Don't give me that 'shucks ma'am' expression—"

"'Shucks, ma'am'?"

"You didn't just wander in off the back forty. You know I could drain your account."

"Would you?"

"I *could*," she stressed. Theoretically, of course.

He twirled the pen over two fingers until it settled into his palm. "And then what?"

"And then I disappear. Tahiti, Grand Cayman."

"I'd find you."

"So what?" She shrugged. "What could you do? The money would already be in a Swiss bank account."

He braced one hand against the desk and moved the other to the back of her chair, bending slightly over. "Then I'd ask you, politely, for the number."

She was blocked by the V of his arms. It was

unnerving, but also exciting. He emanated strength, power and raw virility.

"And if I refuse to tell you?" she challenged, voice growing breathy.

"I'd stop being polite."

"What? You'd threaten to break my legs?"

He smiled and leaned closer. Self-preservation told her to shrink away, but the chair back kept her in place. His sweet breath puffed against her skin. "Violence? I don't think so. But there are other ways to be persuasive."

She struggled for a tone of disbelief. "What? You kiss me and I swoon?"

His grin widened. "Maybe. Let's try it."

And before she could react, he'd swooped in toward her. She gasped as his smooth lips settled on hers. They were warm and firm, and incredibly hot, as the contact instantly escalated to a serious kiss.

It took her only seconds to realize how much she'd longed for his taste. His scent filled her, and his hands settled on her sides, surrounding her rib cage as he deepened the kiss. Her head tipped back, and her mouth responded to his pressure by opening, allowing him access, drinking in the sensation of his intimate touch.

She clutched his upper arms, steadying herself against his hard, taut muscles. He flexed under her touch, and she imagined she could feel the blood coursing through his body. She could definitely feel the blood coursing through her own. It heated her core, flushed her skin and made her tingle from the roots of her hair to the tips of her toes.

His hands convulsed against her body, thumbs tightening beneath her breasts. Her nipples hardened almost painfully as arousal thumped its way to the apex of her thighs. She gave him her tongue, answering his own erotic invitation. A river of sound roared in her ears as he drew her to her feet, engulfing her, pressing her against his hard body.

His touch was unique, yet achingly familiar, as if she'd been waiting for this moment her entire life. Her palms slid across his shoulders, around his neck, stroking the slick sweat of his hairline as their kiss pulsed endlessly between them.

His hands slipped to her buttocks, pulling her against the cradle of his thighs, demonstrating the depth of his arousal and shocking her back to her senses.

She jerked away, hands pressing against his chest, putting a barrier between them. He leaned in, trying to capture her mouth.

"I can't," she gasped.

He froze.

"I'm…uh…" She wasn't exactly sorry. That had definitely been the best kiss of her life. But she couldn't take things any further. They barely knew each other. She'd only just left Hargrove. And she hadn't come to Montana for casual sex.

"Something wrong?" he asked.

She tried to take a step back, but the damn chair still blocked her way. "This is too fast," she explained, struggling to bring both her breathing and her pulse rate back under control.

He heaved an exasperated sigh. "It was a kiss, Amber."

But they both knew it was more than a kiss. Then, to her mortification, her gaze reflexively flicked below his waistline.

He gave a knowing chuckle, and she wished the floor would swallow her whole.

"Are you blushing?" he asked.

"No." But she couldn't look him in the eyes.

"You seemed a whole lot more sophisticated when we met in the lounge," he ventured.

She couldn't interpret his flat tone, so she braved a glance at his expression. Was he annoyed?

He looked annoyed.

She hadn't intended to lead him on. Nor had she meant for the kiss to spiral out of control.

Surely he could understand that.

Or was he always so quick to leap to expectations?

Then, an unsettling thought hit her. What if Royce hadn't leaped to expectations in the past two minutes? What if his expectations had been there since their meeting in the lounge?

Had she been hopelessly naive? Did he consider her a one- or two-night stand?

"Is *that* why you brought me here?" she asked, watching closely, giving him the chance to deny it.

"Depends," he said, cocking his head and giving her a considering look. "On what you mean by *that*."

"Because you thought I'd sleep with you?"

"It had crossed my mind," he admitted.

Her embarrassment turned to anger. "Seriously?"

He sighed. "Amber—"

"You are the most egotistical, opportunistic—"

"Hey, you were the one who was dressed to kill and insisted on 'taking a ride in my jet plane.'"

"That *wasn't* a euphemism for sex."

"Really?" He looked genuinely surprised. "It usually is."

Amber compressed her lips. How had she been so naive? How could she have been so incredibly foolish? Royce wasn't some knight in shining armor. He was a charming, wealthy, well-groomed pickup artist.

Her distaste was replaced again by embarrassment. She'd proposed paying her way here by doing office work. He'd had a completely different line of work in mind.

She pushed the wheeled chair aside and moved to go around him. "I think I'd better leave."

She'd have to call her parents to rescue her, head back to Chicago with her tail between her legs, maybe even reconsider her relationship with Hargrove, since, as the three of them so often told her, she was naive in the ways of the real world.

At least with Hargrove, she knew where she stood.

"Why?" Royce asked, putting a hand on her arm to stop her.

She glanced at his hand, and he immediately let go.

"There's obviously been a misunderstanding." She'd hang out in the upstairs bedroom until a car could come for her. Then she'd head back to the airport, home to her parents' mansion and back to her real life.

This had been a crazy idea from beginning to end.

"Clearly," said Royce, his jaw tight.

She moved toward the door.

Royce's voice followed her. "Running back to Mommy and Daddy?"

Her spine straightened. "None of your business."

"What's changed?" he challenged.

She reached for the doorknob.

"What's changed, Amber?" he repeated.

She paused. Then she turned to confront him. No

point in beating around the bush. "I thought I was a houseguest. You thought I was a call girl."

A grin quirked one corner of his mouth, and her anger flared anew.

"Are you always this melodramatic?" he asked.

"Shut up."

He shook his head and took a couple of steps toward her. "I meant what's changed on your home front?"

"Nothing," she admitted, except it had occurred to her that her parents might be right. She had been protected from the real world for most of her life. Maybe she wasn't in a position to judge human nature. They'd always insisted Hargrove was the perfect man for her, and they could very well be right.

"So, why go back?" Royce pressed.

"Where else would I go?" She could sneak off to some other part of the country, but her father would track her down as soon as she accessed her bank account. Besides, the longer she stayed away, the more awkward the reunion.

Royce took another step forward. "You don't have to leave."

She scoffed out a dry laugh.

"I never thought you were a call girl."

"You thought I was a barroom pickup."

"True enough," he agreed. "But only because it's happened so many times before."

"You're *bragging?*"

"Just stating the facts."

She scoffed at his colossal ego.

"You're welcome to stay as a houseguest." He sounded sincere.

"Are you kidding?" She couldn't imagine anything

more uncomfortable. He'd been planning to sleep with her. And for a few seconds there, well, sleeping with Royce hadn't seemed like such a bad idea. And he must have known it. She was sure he'd known it.

Their gazes held.

"I can control myself if you can," he told her.

"There's nothing for me to control," she insisted.

He let her lie slide. "Good. Then it's settled."

"Nothing is—"

He nodded toward the desk. "You organize my office and pay my bills, and I'll keep my hands to myself." He paused. "Unless, of course, you change your mind about my hands."

"I'm not going to—"

He held up a hand to silence her. "Let's not make any promises we're going to regret."

She let her glare do the talking, but a little voice inside her acknowledged he was right. She didn't plan to change her mind. But for a few minutes there, it had been easy enough to imagine his hands all over her body.

Four

Royce felt the burn in his shoulder muscles as he hefted another stack of two-by-fours from the flatbed to a waiting pickup truck. The two ranch hands assigned to the task had greeted him with obvious curiosity when he joined the work crew. Hauling lumber in the dark, with the smell of rain in the air, was hardly a choice assignment.

But Royce needed to work the frustration out of his system somehow. How had he so completely misjudged Amber's signals? He could have sworn she was as into him as he was her.

He slid the heavy stack across the dropped tailgate and shifted it to the front of the box, admitting that he'd deluded himself the past few months in the hotel fitness rooms. High-tech exercise equipment was no match for the sweat of real work.

"Something wrong?" came Stephanie's voice as she appeared beside him in the pool of the yard light. She tugged a pair of leather work gloves from the back pocket of her jeans. "You looked ticked off."

"Nothing's wrong," Royce denied, turning on the dirt track to retrace his steps to the flatbed, passing the two hands who were on the opposite cycle. "Where'd you come from?"

Stephanie slipped her hands into the gloves, lifting two boards to Royce's five, balancing them on her right shoulder. "I drove down to join you for dinner. I wanted to see how Amber was doing."

"She's fine.

"She inside?"

He shrugged. "I assume so."

"You have a fight?"

"No. We didn't have a fight." An argument, maybe. In fact, it was more of a misunderstanding. And it was none of his sister's damn business.

"Something wrong with Bar—"

"No!" Royce practically shouted. Wait a minute. His sister might have changed topics. He forced himself to calm down. "What?"

"With Barry Brewster," she enunciated. "Our VP of finance? I talked to him earlier, and he sounded weird."

Royce slid his load into the pickup then lifted the boards from Stephanie's shoulder and placed them in the box. "Weird how?"

It was Stephanie's turn to shrug. "He yelled at me."

Royce's brow went up. "He *what?*"

They stepped out of the way of the two hands each carrying a load of lumber.

Stephanie lowered her voice. "With Jared gone. Well, Blanchard's Sun, an offspring of Blanchard's Run, took silver at Dannyville Downs, and—"

"*S-o-n* son?" Royce asked.

"*S-u-n*. It's a mare."

"You don't think that will get confusing?"

Stephanie frowned at him. "I didn't name her."

"Still—"

"Try to stay on topic."

"Right."

The temperature dropped a few degrees. The wind picked up, and ozone snapped in the air. Royce went back to work, knowing the rain wasn't far off.

Stephanie followed. "Blanchard's Run is proving to be an incredible sire. With every week that passes, his price will go up. So I called Barry to talk about moving some funds to the stable account."

"Did you really expect him to hand over a million?"

"Sure." She paused, sucking in a breath as she hefted some more lumber. "Maybe. Okay, it was a long shot. But that's not my point."

"What is your point?"

The first, fat raindrops clanked on the truck's roof, and one of the hands retrieved an orange tarp from the shed. Royce increased his pace to settle the last of the lumber on the pickup, then accepted the large square of plastic.

"You two get the flatbed," he instructed, motioning for Stephanie to move to the other side of the pickup box.

"My point," Stephanie called over the clatter from

the tarp under the increasing rain, "is Barry's reaction. He went off on me about cash flow and interest rates."

"Over a million dollars?" Royce threaded a nylon rope through the corner grommet of the tarp and looped it around the tie-down on the running board. It was a lot to pay for a horse, sure. But there weren't enough zeros in the equation to raise Barry's blood pressure.

"I felt like a ten-year-old asking for her allowance."

"That's because you behave like a ten-year-old." Royce tossed the rope over the load to his sister.

"It's a great deal," she insisted as lightning cracked the sky above them. "If we don't move now, it'll be gone forever."

"Isn't that what you said about Nare-Do-Elle?"

"That was three years ago."

"He cost us a bundle."

"This is a completely different circumstance. I'm right this time." She tossed the rope back. "You don't think I've learned anything in three years?"

Royce cinched down the tarp. He wasn't touching that question with a ten-foot cattle prod. "What exactly do you want me to do?" he asked instead.

"Talk to Barry."

"And say what?"

"Tell him to give me the money."

Royce grinned.

"I'm serious." The rain had soaked into her curly auburn hair, dampening her cheeks, streaking down her freckled nose.

"You're always serious. You always need money. And half the time you're wrong."

She waggled her leather gloved finger at him. "And half the time I'm *right*."

"So I'll get you half a million."

"And you'll lose out on generations of champion jumpers."

Royce walked the rope around the back of the pickup, tying it off on the fourth corner. "Sorry, Steph."

Her hands went to her hips. "I own a third of this company."

"And I have Jared's power of attorney."

"You two have *always* ganged up on me."

"Now you're sounding like a child."

"I'm—"

"I'm not giving a million dollars to a child."

Her chin tipped up. "You weren't giving it to me anyway."

"True," Royce admitted. He couldn't resist chucking her under that defiant chin. "You've got a perfectly adequate operating budget. Live within your means."

"This is an extraordinary opportunity. I can't begin to tell you—"

"There'll be another one tomorrow. Or next week. Or next month." He'd known his sister far too long to fall for her impassioned plea.

"That's not fair."

"Life never is."

Thunder clapped above them, and the heavens opened up, the deluge soaking everything in sight. The ranch hands ran for the cook shed, and Royce grabbed Stephanie's hand, tugging her over the muddy ground toward the lights of the house.

Amber stood in the vast Ryder living room, rain pounding on the ceiling and clattering against the windows in the waning daylight as she stared at the cell phone in her hand. Royce had been a gentleman about it, but that didn't change the fact that she'd put herself in a predicament and behaved less responsibly than she'd admitted to herself.

She really needed to let someone know where she was staying. She also needed to make sure her parents weren't worrying about her. Her father tended to blow things out of proportion, and there was a real chance he was freeing up cash, waiting for a ransom note.

She pressed the on button with her thumb, deciding she'd keep it short and simple.

"Calling in the cavalry?" came Royce's dry voice.

Amber glanced up to see him and Stephanie in the archway leading from the front foyer.

"Did you hear the thunder?" Stephanie grinned as she stepped forward, stripping off a pair of leather gloves and running spread fingers through her unruly, wet hair.

Amber nodded. The storm had heightened her sense of isolation and disquiet.

"I love storms," Stephanie continued, dropping the gloves on an end table. "As long as I'm inside." She frowned, glancing down at her wet clothes. "I'm going upstairs to find something dry. Is that lasagna I smell?" Her pert nose wrinkled.

Amber inhaled the aromas wafting from the kitchen. "I think so."

"My fav." Stephanie smiled. "See you in a few." She skipped up the stairs.

As he stood there in the doorway, the planes and angles of Royce's face were emphasized by the yellow lamplight reflecting off the wood grain walls.

An hour ago, she'd come to the conclusion that she couldn't really blame him for thinking she was attracted to him. She imagined most women who requested a ride in his plane were coming on to him. Not that she blamed them. His shoulders were broad in his work clothes. His dark, wet hair glimmered, and those deep blue eyes seemed to stare right down into a woman's soul.

"Did you decide to leave after all?" he asked, his deep voice reverberating through her body, igniting a fresh wave of desire.

She shook her head. "I'm just reassuring my parents."

Royce moved into the room with an easy, rolling gait. He struck her as different than the man in the hotel lobby lounge. In just a couple of days, the wilds of Montana had somehow seeped into him.

"Not worried they'll track you down?" His steps slowed as he stopped in front of her, slightly closer than socially acceptable, just a few inches into her personal space, and she felt her heartbeat deepen.

"I'm worried they might be raising the ransom."

Royce quirked a brow. "Seriously?"

"I've never done anything like this before."

"No kidding."

"Royce." She wasn't sure what she was going to say to him, or how she should say it.

But before she could formulate the words, his voice and expression went soft. "I'm sorry."

She shook her head. "No. I'm the one who's sorry. I gave you the wrong impression. It wasn't on purpose, but I realize now that—"

"It was wishful thinking on my part."

"You flat out told me you were hitting on me."

"I was."

She fought a reflexive smile. "And I'm honored." She found herself joking.

"I don't want you to be honored." His expression said the rest.

"I know exactly what you want."

He eased almost imperceptibly closer. "Yes, you do."

They both went silent, sobering. Thunder rumbled overhead, and the moisture-laden air hung heavily in the room.

Stephanie's light footsteps sounded on the landing above.

"You should make that call," said Royce, stepping back.

Amber nodded, struggling to get her hormones under control. She'd never been pursued by such a rawly masculine man. Come to think of it, she'd never been pursued by any man.

Oh, she received her fair share of flirtatious overtures on a girls' night at the clubs, but a flash of her engagement ring easily shut the guys down. Plus, usually she was out with Hargrove. And they generally attended functions where he was known. Nobody was about to hit on Hargrove Alston's fiancée.

While Stephanie skipped down the stairs, Amber pressed the speed-dial button for her mother. It rang only once.

"Sweetheart!" came her mother's voice. "What happened? Are you okay? Are you having a breakdown?"

Amber turned away from Royce, crossing the few steps to an alcove where she'd have a little privacy.

"I'm fine," she answered, ignoring the part about a breakdown.

"Your father is beside himself."

Royce's and Stephanie's footfalls faded toward the kitchen.

"And Hargrove," her mother continued. "He came home a day early. Then he nearly missed the Chamber dinner tonight worrying about you. He was the keynote, you know."

"He *nearly* missed it?" asked Amber, finding a hard tone in her voice. Hargrove hadn't, in fact, missed his big speech while his beloved fiancée was missing, perhaps kidnapped, maybe dead.

As soon as the thoughts formed in her mind, she realized she was being unfair. She'd sent a text saying she was fine, and she had expected them to believe her. She wanted Hargrove to carry on with his life.

"The Governor was there," her mother defended.

"I'm glad he went to the dinner," said Amber.

"Where are you? I'll send a car."

"I'm not coming back yet."

"Why not?"

"Didn't Dad tell you?"

"That nonsense about not marrying Hargrove? That's crazy talk, darling. He wowed them last night."

"He didn't wow me." As soon as the words slipped out, Amber clamped her lips shut.

"You weren't there." Her mother either missed or ignored the double entendre.

"I wanted to let you know I'm fine." Amber got back on point.

"Where are you?"

"It doesn't matter."

"Of *course* it matters. We need to get you—"

"Not yet."

"Amber—"

"I'll call again soon." Amber didn't know how long it took to trace a cell phone call, but she suspected she should hurry and hang up.

"What do you expect me to tell your father?"

"Tell him not to worry. I love you both, and I'll call again. Bye, Mom." She quickly disconnected.

A slightly plump, fiftyish woman, who Amber had earlier learned was Sasha, was pulling a large pan of lasagna from the stainless steel oven when Amber entered the kitchen. Stephanie was tossing a salad in a carved wooden bowl on the breakfast bar, while Royce transferred warm rolls into a linen-napkin-lined basket.

For the second time, she was struck by his domesticity. The men she knew didn't help out in the kitchen. Come to think of it, the women she knew didn't, either. And though Amber herself had taken French cooking lessons at her private school, the lessons had centered more on choosing a caterer than hands-on cooking.

"There's a wine cooler around the corner." Stephanie was looking to Amber as she indicated the direction with a toss of her auburn head. "Italian wines are on the third tier, left-hand side."

Royce didn't turn as Amber made her way to a small alcove between the kitchen and the back entryway. The cooler was set in a stone wall, reds in one glass-fronted compartment, whites in the other.

"See if there's a Redigaffi." Royce's voice was so close behind her that it gave her a start.

She took a bracing breath and opened the glass door, turning a couple of bottles on the third shelf so that she could see their labels.

"How'd the call go?" he asked.

"Fine."

There was a silence.

"That's it?" he asked. "Fine?"

"I talked to my mother. She wants me to come home." Amber found the right bottle of wine and slid it out of the holder, straightening and turning to discover Royce was closer than she'd expected. She pushed the glass door closed behind her.

"And?" he asked.

"And what?" She reflexively clutched the bottle.

"Are you going home?"

Though they'd agreed she'd merely be a houseguest, the question seemed loaded with meaning as his eyes thoroughly searched her expression.

"Not yet," she answered.

"Good."

She felt the need to clarify. "It doesn't mean—"

"I meant it's good because you don't love Hargrove, so it would be stupid to go back."

She gave him a short nod.

"Not that the other's gone away," he clarified.

Amber didn't know how to respond to that.

His gaze moved to the bottle. "Did you find one?"

She raised it, and he lifted it from her hands.

"Perfect," he said.

"Move your butts," called Stephanie from the kitchen, and Amber suddenly realized that her world had contracted to the tiny alcove, Royce and her wayward longings.

She gave herself a mental shake, while he took a step back and gestured for her to lead the way into the kitchen.

Stephanie was setting wineglasses at three places at the breakfast bar, while Sasha had disappeared. The Ryder family was a curious mix of informality and luxury. The glasses were fine, blown crystal. The wine was from an exquisite vineyard that Amber recognized. But they were hopping up on high chairs at the breakfast bar to a plain, white casserole pan of simple, beef lasagna.

"Did you talk to your mom?" asked Stephanie as she took the end seat.

Amber took the one around the corner, and Royce settled next to her. He was both too close and too far away. She could almost detect the heat of his body, felt the change in air currents while he moved, and she was overcome with a potent desire to touch him. Of course, touching him was out of the question.

"I talked to her," she told Stephanie.

"What did she say?"

"She wants me to come home and, well, reconcile with Hargrove, of course."

"And?" Stephanie pressed. "What did you tell her?"

"That I wasn't ready." Amber found herself deliberately not looking in Royce's direction as she spoke.

"Good for you," said Stephanie with a vigorous nod. "We girls, we have to stick to our guns. There are too many people in our lives trying to interfere with our decisions." She cast a pointed gaze at her brother.

"Give it a rest," Royce growled at his sister, twisting the corkscrew into the top of the wine. "You're not getting a million dollars."

"You're such a hard-ass."

"And you're a spoiled brat."

"You *are* spending an awful lot for vet supplies and lumber," Amber put in. "Those are the bills I found stacked up on the office desk."

Stephanie blinked at her. "Oh."

Royce popped the cork and reached for Amber's wineglass. "Amber has some questions about the accounts. Who does McQuestin deal with at head office?"

"I think he talks to Norma Braddock sometimes."

Royce handed the wine bottle to his sister then whisked his cell phone from his pocket. "I'll go straight to Barry."

"I'd watch out for him," Stephanie advised, forehead wrinkling.

Royce rolled his eyes at the warning.

Amber decided to stay quiet.

"Barry?" said Royce, while Stephanie handed the salad bowl to Amber.

Amber served herself some of the freshest-looking lettuce and tomatoes she'd ever seen.

"Royce, here."

Then she leaned toward Stephanie and whispered, "From your garden?"

Stephanie nodded, whispering in return. "You'll want to get out of here before canning season."

Amber grinned at the dire intonation.

"Sorry to bother you this late," Royce continued. "We've hired someone on to take care of the office while Jared and McQuestin are away." He gave Amber a wink, and something fluttered in her chest. She quickly picked up her wineglass to cover.

"She has some questions about the bank account. There have been a number of unpaid bills lately." He paused for a moment. "Why don't I let you talk to her directly?"

Amber hadn't expected that. She quickly swallowed and set down the glass. Good thing her questions were straightforward. She tucked her hair out of the way behind her ears, accepting the phone from Royce, ignoring the tingle when his fingers brushed hers.

"Hello?" she opened.

"Who am I speaking to?" asked Barry from the other end of the line.

"This is Amber, I'm—"

"And you're an employee at Ryder Ranch?" he asked directly.

She paused. "Uh, yes. That's right."

"Administrator? Bookkeeper?" There was an unexpected edge to the man's tone.

"Something like that." She gave Royce a confused look, and his eyes narrowed, crinkling slightly at the corners.

"Do you have a pen?" Barry asked, voice going even sharper.

"I—"

"Because you'd better write this down."

Amber glanced around at the countertops. "Just—"

"Sally Nettleton."

"Excuse me?"

"Sally Nettleton is the accounts supervisor. You can speak to her in the morning."

"Sure. Do you happen to have her—"

"And a warning, young lady. Don't you *ever* go above my head to Royce Ryder again."

Amber froze, voice going hollow. "What?"

"Share this conversation with him at your own peril. I don't tolerate insubordination, and he won't always be there to protect you."

Amber's mouth worked but sounds weren't coming out. Nobody had dared speak to her that way in her life.

"You're not the first, and you won't be the last. Don't fool yourself into thinking anything different." He stopped speaking, and the line fairly vibrated with tension.

She didn't know what to say. She had absolutely no idea what to tell this obnoxious man. Imagine if she really was an employee, dependent on her job. It would be horrible.

She heard a click and knew he'd signed off.

"Goodbye," she said weakly for the benefit of Royce and Stephanie.

"Told you he was feeling snarky today," said Stephanie.

"What did he say?" asked Royce. "You okay?"

"She looks a little pale," Stephanie put in.

"I'm fine," said Amber, debating with herself about what to tell Royce as she shut down the phone and handed it back.

"You didn't ask many questions," Royce ventured.

"He gave me a name. Sally Nettleton." She took a breath, framing her words carefully. "He was, well, annoyed that you'd put me in direct touch with him."

Royce frowned.

"He seems to think I broke the chain of command."

"So what?"

"I tell you, something's wrong with that man,"

Stephanie put in, dishing some of the crisp salad onto her plate.

Amber made up her mind, seeing little point in protecting Barry. In fact, she probably owed it to the rest of his staff to tell Royce the truth. "He seems to think I'm your lover."

It was Royce's turn to freeze. "He *said* that?"

"He said he didn't tolerate insubordination, and you won't always be around to protect me. That you'd lose interest."

A ruddy flush crept up Royce's neck, and he reached for his phone.

Amber put her hand over his. "Don't," she advised.

"Why the hell not?"

"Because he'll think you *are* protecting your lover."

"I don't give a rat's ass what—"

"Did I miss something?" asked Stephanie, glancing from one to the other, her tone laced with obvious anticipation and excitement. "Lovers?"

"No," they both shouted simultaneously.

"Too bad." She went back to her salad. "That would be cool."

Amber turned to Stephanie. "That would be tacky. You can't sleep with a man you've barely met." She silently commanded herself to pay close attention to those words.

"Sure you can," Stephanie chirped with a grin.

"No," Royce boomed at her. "You can't."

Stephanie giggled. "Good grief, you're an easy mark. There's nobody around here for me to sleep with anyway."

Some of the fight went out of Royce's posture, but his hand still gripped his phone.

Amber rubbed the tense hand. "Let it go."

"It's a firing offence."

"No, it's not."

"Yes, it is."

"At least give it some thought first." Barry had been a jerk, but she didn't want anyone getting fired on her account. "Maybe ask around. See if this was an isolated incident."

"He was rude to me this morning," said Stephanie.

"You're not helping," Amber warned.

Royce folded his arms across his chest. "It was *my* decision to call him directly. He doesn't get to second-guess me."

"Did you explain the circumstances?"

"I don't have to."

"So, he made an assumption. You can't fire a man for making an assumption."

He pasted her with a sharp look. "You like being spoken to that way."

"Of course not." But she'd like being Royce's lover. Heaven help her, she was pretty sure she'd like being Royce's lover.

Their gazes locked and held for a long moment, and she could have sworn he was reading her mind.

"The lasagna's getting cold," Stephanie pointed out conversationally.

Royce ended the moment with a sharp nod. "We'll talk about it later."

"Sure," Amber agreed, wondering if they were going to talk about Barry or about the energy that crackled between them like lightning.

Five

In Royce's mind, the issue was far from settled.

The storm had passed, leaving a bright moon behind. He closed the office door behind him for privacy, leaving Amber and Stephanie chatting out on the veranda, puppies scampering around them. He, on the other hand, flipped on the bright overhead light and crossed to the leather desk chair, snagging the desk phone and punching in Barry's home number.

It was nearly midnight in Chicago, but he didn't give a damn. Let the man wake up.

"Hello?" came a groggy, masculine voice.

"Barry?"

"Yes."

"It's Royce Ryder."

"Yes?" A shot of energy snapped into Barry's voice. "Anything wrong, Royce?"

There was plenty wrong. "Were you able to give Amber the information she needed?"

A pause. "I believe I did. Sally can cover anything else in the morning."

Royce waited a beat. "When I called you earlier, it wasn't because I wanted her to talk to Sally in the morning." Full stop. More silence.

"Oh. Well... I assumed—"

"Did you or did you not answer Amber's questions?" Royce repeated. And he could almost hear the wheels spinning inside Barry's head.

"I don't think you did," Royce said into the silence. "And the reason I don't think you did is because I was sitting right next to her during the call, and she didn't get a chance to ask you any questions." Once again, he stopped, giving Barry an opportunity to either contribute or sweat.

Hesitation was evident in the man's voice. "Did she... Mmm. Is she there?"

"No. She's not *here*. It's eleven o'clock. The woman's not working at eleven o'clock."

Silence.

"Here's my suggestion," said Royce. "To solve the problem. You hop on a plane in the morning. The corporate jet is unavailable, so you'll have to fly commercial. I'm thinking coach." He picked up an unopened envelope from the desktop and tapped it against the polished oak surface, dropping all pretence of geniality. "You get your ass to the ranch, and you apologize to Ms. Hutton. Then you answer any and all of her questions."

"I... But... Did you say Hutton?"

"David Hutton's daughter. But that couldn't matter less."

"Royce. I'm sorry. I didn't realize—"

"Apologize to *her*."

"Of course."

"You'll be here tomorrow?"

"As soon as I can get there."

Satisfied, Royce disconnected. Amber only needed to be sure funds would be available in the account. But that wasn't the point anymore.

He gazed at the envelope in his hand. It was windowed. From North Pass Feed. Typical bill.

Curious after Amber's concern about his credit rating, he slit it open. Then he glanced through the other piles she'd made, arming himself with some basic information on the ranch expenses.

Half an hour later, he thought he had a picture of the accounts payable situation, so he headed back down the hallway to find Amber and Stephanie in the front foyer.

Stephanie was on her way out the door, and she gave him a quick kiss and a wave before piling into a pickup truck to head for home. As he closed the door behind her, the empty house seemed to hold its breath with anticipation.

Amber looked about as twitchy as he felt.

"You want to talk about Barry?" she asked, moving from the foyer into the great room.

"Taken care of," he answered, following a few paces behind her, letting his gaze trickle from her shoulders to her narrow waist, to her sexy rear end and the shapely thighs that were emphasized by her snug-fitting blue jeans.

She twisted her head. "What do you mean?"

"He'll be here in the morning."

She turned fully then. "I don't understand."

"He's coming by to apologize. And to answer your questions in person."

Her eyes widened in shock, red lips coming open in a way that was past sexy. "You didn't."

"He insisted."

"He did not."

Royce moved closer. "I suspect he understood the stakes."

She tipped her chin. "I don't need somebody to travel a thousand miles to offer me an insincere apology."

"But I do."

She didn't appear to have a comeback for that, and it was all he could do not to lean in for a kiss. She looked as if she wanted one. Her lips were full, eyes wide, body tipped slightly forward. If this was any other woman, at any other time...

But she'd made her position clear.

And he'd respect that.

Unless and until she told him otherwise.

Midday sun streaming through the ranch office window, Amber clicked through the headlines of a national news station on the office computer, reflecting with curiosity that she didn't feel out of touch with the rest of the world. She'd become a bit of a news junkie while finishing her degree, always on the lookout for emerging issues that might impact on her research. Having gone cold turkey in Montana, she should have missed watching world events unfold.

Of course, she had been a little distracted—okay, a

lot distracted by a sexy cowboy who was quickly making her forget there was a world outside the Ryder Ranch.

She'd half expected him to kiss her last night.

He'd stared down at her with those intense blue eyes, nostrils slightly flared, hands bunched into fists, and the muscles in his neck bulging in relief against his skin. She'd imagined him leaning down, planting his lips against hers, wrapping his arms around her and pulling her into paradise all over again.

But then he'd backed off, and she hadn't been brave enough to protest.

Now she sighed with regret as she clicked the mouse, bringing up a live news broadcast from a Chicago network. The buffer loaded, and the announcer carried on with a story about a local bridge repair.

She turned back to the desk, lifting the stack that was the day's mail. Barry Brewster hadn't arrived to confirm the bank balance yet, so she couldn't make any progress paying the backlog of bills.

Truth was, she was dreading the man's arrival. No matter what he said or did, it was going to be embarrassing all around. Royce might think she needed an apology, but Amber had spent most of her life with people being polite to her because they either admired or were afraid of her father or Hargrove. She didn't need the same thing from Barry today.

"The Governor's Office can no longer get away with dodging the issue of Chicago's competitiveness." The familiar voice startled Amber. She whirled to stare at the computer screen, where a news clip showed Hargrove posed in front of the Greenwood Financial Tower with several microphones picking up his words.

"His performance at the conference was shameful,"

Hargrove continued. "If our own governor won't stand up for the citizens of Chicago, I'd like to know who will."

Guilt percolated through Amber, and she quickly shut off the sound. She watched his face a few seconds longer, telling herself her actions had been defensible. If she'd stayed, she'd probably be standing right next him, holding his hand, the stalwart little fiancée struggling to come to terms with her role in his life.

He looked good on camera. Then, he'd always had a way with reporters, dodging their pointed questions without appearing rude, making a little information sound like a detailed dissertation. It was the reason the party was grooming him for the election.

A child shouted from outside the window, and Amber concentrated on the sound, forcing her mind from the worry about Hargrove to the seclusion of the ranch. Then another child shouted, and a chorus of cheers went up. Curious, she wandered to the window to look out.

Off to the left, on a flat expanse of lawn, a baseball game was underway. It was mostly kids of the ranch staff, but there were a few adults in the field. And there in the center, pitching the baseball, was Royce. She smiled when he took a few paces forward, lobbing a soft one to a girl who couldn't have been more than eight.

The girl swung and missed, but then she screwed her face up in defiance and positioned herself at the plate, tapping the bat on the white square in front of her. Royce took another step forward.

Amber smiled, then she glanced one more time at Hargrove on the computer screen—her old life.

As the days and hours had slipped by, she'd become more convinced that her decision was right. She had no intention of going back to her old life. And she owed it to Hargrove to make that clear.

She searched for her cell phone on the desktop, powered it up and dialed his number.

"Hargrove Alston," he answered.

"Hargrove? It's Amber."

Silence.

"I wanted to make sure you weren't worried about me," she began.

"I wasn't worried." His tone was crisp.

"Oh. Well, that's good. I'm glad."

"Your parents told me you were fine, and that you'd taken the trouble to contact them."

Amber clearly heard the "while you didn't bother to contact me" message underlying his words.

"Are you over your tantrum, then?" he asked.

She couldn't help but bristle. "Is that what you think I'm doing?"

"I think you're behaving like a child."

She gritted her teeth.

"You missed the Chamber of Commerce speech," he accused.

"I hear you didn't," she snarked in return.

Another silence. "And what is that supposed to mean?"

"Nothing."

"Honestly, Amber."

"Forget it. Of course you gave the speech. It was an important speech."

Her words seemed to mollify him. "Will you be ready in time for dinner, then? Flannigan's at eight with the Myers."

Amber blinked in amazement at the question.

She'd been gone for three days. She'd broken off their engagement.

"I'm not coming to dinner," she told him carefully.

He gave a heavy sigh on the other end of the phone. "Is this about the Switzerland trip?"

"Of course not."

"I explained why I had to go alone."

"This is about a fundamental concern with our compatibility as a couple."

"You sound like a self-help book."

Amber closed her eyes and counted to three. "I'm breaking our engagement, Hargrove. I'm truly sorry if I hurt you."

A flare of anger crept into his tone. "I wish you'd get over this mood."

"This isn't something I'm going to get over."

"Do you have any idea how embarrassing this could get?"

"I'm sorry about that, too. But we can't get married to keep from being embarrassed." She flicked a gaze to the baseball game, watching two colorful young figures dash around the bases.

"Are you trying to punish me?" asked Hargrove, frustration mounting in his tone. "Do you want me to apologize for…" He paused. "I don't know. Tell me what you think I've done?"

"You haven't done anything."

"Then get ready for dinner," he practically shouted.

"I'm not in Chicago."

He paused. "Where are you?"

"It doesn't—"

"Seriously, Amber. This is getting out of hand. I don't have time to play—"

"Goodbye, Hargrove."

"Don't you dare—"

She quickly tapped the end button then shut down the power on her phone. Talking around in circles wasn't going to get them anywhere.

She defiantly stuffed the phone into her pocket and drew a deep breath. After the tense conversation, the carefree baseball game was like a siren's call. Besides, it was nearly lunchtime, and she was tired of looking at numbers.

Determinedly shaking off her emotional reaction to the fight with Hargrove, she headed outside to watch.

Stephanie was standing at the sidelines.

"Looks like fun," said Amber, drawing alongside and opening the conversation. She inhaled the fresh air and let the cheerfulness of the crowd seep into her psyche.

"Usually it's just the kids," Stephanie told her. "But a lot of the hands are down from the range today, and Royce can't resist a game. And once he joined in, well…" She shrugged at the mixed-age crowd playing and watching.

A little girl made it to first, and a cocky, teenage boy swaggered up to the plate, reversing his baseball cap and pointing far out to right field with the tip of his bat.

Royce gave the kid an amused shake of his head, walked back to the mound and smacked the ball into the pocket of his worn glove. Then he shook his head in response to the catcher's hand signals. Royce waited, then smiled, and nodded his agreement to the next signal.

He drew back, bent his leg and delivered a sizzling fastball waist high and over the plate. The batter swung hard but missed. Royce chuckled, and the kid stepped out of the batter's box, adjusting his cap then scuffing his runners over the dirt at home plate.

"That's Robbie Nome," Stephanie informed her. "He's at that age, constantly challenging the hands."

"How old?" asked Amber, guessing sixteen or seventeen.

"Seventeen," Stephanie confirmed. "They usually settle down around eighteen. But there's a hellish year there in between while their brain catches up to their size and their testosterone level." She shook her head as Robbie swung and missed a second time.

"Royce seems pretty good," Amber observed, watching him line up for another pitch. She knew she was staring way too intently at him, but she couldn't help herself.

He was dressed in faded jeans, a steel-gray T-shirt and worn running shoes. His bare arms were deeply tanned, and his straight, white teeth shone with an infectious grin.

"He played in the College World Series."

"Pitcher?" asked Amber, impressed.

"First base."

Royce rocketed in a third pitch, and the batter struck out.

The outfielders let out a whoop and ran for the sidelines. The shoulders of the girl on first base slumped in dejection. Royce obviously noticed. He cut to her path, whispered something in her ear and ruffled her short, brown hair. She smiled, and he gave her a playful high five.

Then he spotted Amber and Stephanie, and made a beeline for them. Amber's chest contracted, and her heart lifted at the thought that his long strides were meant to bring him closer to her.

His gaze flicked to Stephanie but then settled back on Amber.

"Impressive," she complimented as he drew near.

He shrugged. "They're kids."

Stephanie held out her hand, and Royce smacked the glove into her palm. "You want to play?" she asked Amber.

Amber shook her head. "I need to get back to work." Then, as Stephanie trotted toward the outfield, she confided in Royce. "I've never been much of an athlete."

His gaze traveled her body. "Could've fooled me."

"Pilates and a StairMaster."

"I bet you'd be a natural at sports."

"We're not about to find out." She'd never swung a bat in her life. There were eight-year-olds out there who would probably show her up.

"I'd lob you a soft one," Royce offered, beneath the cheers and calls from the teams.

"Think I'll stick to bookkeeping."

He sobered. "You worked all morning?"

She nodded.

"Anything interesting?"

She shook her head. Actually, she'd found a couple of strange-looking payments in the computerized accounting system. But they were probably nothing, so she didn't want to bother Royce with that. And she sure wasn't about to tell him about her conversation with Hargrove.

"You surprise me," he said in an intimate tone.

"How so?"

"I had you pegged for a party girl."

"No kidding," she scoffed, rolling her eyes at his understatement.

"I didn't mean it that way."

She looked him straight on. "Yeah, you did."

He raked a hand through his sweat-damp hair, giving a sheepish smile. "Okay, I did for a while. But I got over it."

She paused, debating for a few silent seconds, but then deciding she was going to quit censoring herself. "So," she dared, with a toss of her hair. "What do you think of me now?"

His eyes danced, reflecting the color of the endless summer sky. "It could go one of two ways."

"Which are?"

"Royce!" someone called. "You're on deck."

He twisted his head to shout over his shoulder. "Be right there." Then he turned back, slowly contemplating her.

"Well?" she prompted, ridiculously apprehensive.

His hand came up to cup her chin, his thumb and forefinger warm against her skin. "You're either shockingly ingenuous or frighteningly cunning." But his tone took the sting out of the labels.

"Neither of those are complimentary," she pointed out, absorbing the sparks from his touch.

His tone went low. "But both are very sexy."

Then his hand dropped away, and he turned to the game, trotting toward the batter's box as a player took a base hit.

Amber skipped down the staircase, recalling Royce smacking a three-base hit, bringing ten-year-old Colby

Jones home to win the game by one run. She and Stephanie had decided to dress up for dinner, and she wore a white, spaghetti-strap cocktail dress and high-heeled sandals. She rounded the corner at the bottom of the stairs and caught sight of him in a pressed business suit. He was even sexier now than he'd been this afternoon in his T-shirt and jeans.

And he didn't look out of place in the rustic setting. She was glad she'd gone with the dress.

His gaze caught hers, dark and brooding, and she faltered on her high heels. This afternoon, he'd been almost playful. Had she done something to annoy him?

And then she caught sight of the second man, nearly as tall as Royce, somewhat thinner, his suit slightly wrinkled at the elbows and knees. The man turned at the sound of her footsteps, and she knew it had to be Barry Brewster. His jaw was tight, and beads of sweat had formed on his brow.

"Ms. Hutton," Royce intoned. "This is Barry Brewster. You spoke to him on the phone last night."

Amber fought an urge to laugh. The whole charade suddenly struck her as ridiculous. "Mr. Brewster," she said instead, keeping her face straight as she came to a stop and held out her hand.

"Barry, please."

"You can call me Amber."

"No, he can't."

"Royce, please."

But Royce didn't waver, shoulders square, expression stern.

"Ms. Hutton," Barry began, obviously not about to run afoul of his boss. "Please accept my apology. I was rude and insulting last night. I am, of course, available for anything you might need."

The irritation in his eyes belied the geniality of his tone. But then she hadn't expected him to be sincere about this.

"Thank you," she said simply. "I do have a couple of questions." She looked to Royce. "Should we sit down?"

"Unnecessary. Barry won't be staying."

"This is ridicul—"

Royce's hard expression shut her up, and she silently warned herself not to get on his bad side.

"I was hoping you could tell me the balance in the ranch bank account," she said to Barry. "There are a number of unpaid bills, so I wondered—"

"You don't need a reason to ask for the bank balance," Royce cut in.

"I'd need to look it up," said Barry, shifting from one black loafer to the other. He flexed his neck to one side and straightened the sleeves of his suit.

"So, look it up," said Royce.

"I don't have access to the server."

"Call someone who does."

Barry hesitated. "It's pretty late."

"Your point?"

"I guess I could try to catch Sally." With a final pause, Barry reached into his pocket for his phone.

While he dialed, Amber moved closer to Royce, turning her back on Barry.

"Is this completely necessary?" she hissed.

"I thought you wanted the bank balance."

"I do."

"Then it's completely necessary."

"You know that's not what I'm talking about."

"Let me handle this."

She took in the determined slant to Royce's chin while Barry's voice droned on in the background.

"Do I have a choice?" she asked.

"No."

"You can be a real hard-ass, you know that?"

"He insulted you."

"I'm a big girl. I'm over it."

"That's not the point."

She fought against a sudden grin at his need to get in the last word. "Do you ever give up?"

"No."

Barry cleared his throat, and Amber smoothly turned back to face him.

"Sally is looking into the overdraft and the line of credit to see where—"

"The balance," said Royce.

Barry's neck took on a ruddy hue, and he tugged at the white collar of his shirt. "It's, uh, complicated."

"I'm an intelligent man, and Amber has an honors degree."

Barry's gaze flicked to Amber, and she could have sworn she saw panic in its depths.

"I'd really rather discuss—"

"The balance," said Royce.

Barry drew a terse breath. "At the moment, the account is overdrawn."

There were ten full seconds of frozen silence.

Stephanie entered the room from the kitchen, stopping short as she took in the trio.

"Say again?" Royce widened his stance.

"There's been… That is…" This time when Barry

glanced at Amber, he seemed to be pleading for help. There was no help she could give him. She didn't have a clue what was going on.

Royce's voice went dangerously low. "Why didn't you transfer something from corporate?"

Barry tugged at his collar again. "The China deal."

"What about the China deal?" Royce asked carefully. "Was the transfer held up?"

Barry swallowed, his Adam's apple bobbing, voice turning to a raspy squeak. "The paperwork. From Cheng Li. It didn't make the deadline."

Stephanie's eyes went wide, while Royce cocked his head, brows creasing. "They assured me the fax would go through."

"It did. But...well..."

Royce crossed his arms over his chest.

"Our acknowledgment," said Barry. "The time zone difference."

"You didn't send the acknowledgment?"

"End of day. Chicago time."

"You missed the deadline?" Royce's voice was harsh with disbelief.

"I've been trying to fix it for thirty-six hours."

Royce took a step forward. "You *missed* a fifty-million-dollar deadline?"

Barry's mouth opened, but nothing came out.

"And you didn't call me?" Royce's voice was incredulous now.

"I was trying to fix—"

"Yesterday," Royce all but shouted, index finger jabbing in Barry's direction. "*Yesterday,* I could have called Jared at his hotel. Today, he's on a sailboat somewhere in the South Pacific. You have..." Royce raked a hand through his hair. "I don't even know how much money you've lost."

"I—"

"What in the *hell* happened?"

"It was the time zones. Technology. The language barrier."

"You are *so* fired."

Amber's gaze caught Stephanie's. She felt desperate for an exit. She didn't want to witness Royce's anger, Barry's humiliation. She wanted to be far, far away from this disturbing situation.

"You're done, Barry," Royce confirmed to the silent man.

Barry hesitated a beat longer. Then his shoulders dropped. The fight went out of him, and he turned for the door.

The room seemed to boom with silence as Barry's footsteps receded and the car pulled away outside.

Stephanie took a few hesitant steps toward her brother. "Royce?"

"Cancel his credit cards," Royce commanded. "Wake up someone from IT and change the computer passwords. And have security reset the codes on the building."

"What are we going to do?" Stephanie asked in a whisper.

Royce's hands curled into fists at his sides. He looked to Amber. "I have to call Beijing. If we don't fix this, the domino effect could be catastrophic."

Amber nodded. "Just tell me what you need."

"Can we talk to Jared?" asked Stephanie.

Royce shook his head. "Not a chance. Not for a week at least."

Six

Amber hung up the phone after their fifth call to China, her expression somber as Royce's mood.

"That's it." He voiced his defeat out loud.

"Are you sure?"

"Can you think of anything else?"

She shook her head.

He slipped the phone from her hands, setting it on the end table next to the sofa in the living room. The deadline was the deadline, and they hadn't been able to penetrate the Chinese bureaucracy to make their case to Cheng Li. The deal was canceled.

It was nearly 3:00 a.m. Only a few lights burned in the house, and Stephanie had headed to her own ranch an hour ago. Amber tipped her head back on the gold sofa cushion, closing her eyes. She'd struggled through translations for hours on end, and the strain was showing in her pale complexion.

Royce gave in to the temptation to smooth a lock of hair from her cheek. "You okay?"

"Just sorry I couldn't help."

He dropped his hand back down. "You did help."

She opened her eyes. "How so?"

"I understand now what is and isn't possible."

"Nothing's possible."

"Apparently not."

She blinked her dark lashes, and her hand covered his. "How bad is it?"

He rested his own head against the sofa back. "It'll play havoc with our cash flow. We may have to sell off some of our companies. But, to start off, I'm going to have to call the division heads to keep them from panicking. Firing Barry was a significant move."

"Will they be angry?"

He shrugged. "That's the least of my worries."

Amber didn't answer, and Royce was content to sit in silence. He turned his hand, palm up, wrapping it around her smaller one. For some reason, it gave him comfort. Simply sitting here quietly, with her by his side, made the problems seem less daunting.

Her hand went limp in his, and he turned to gaze at her closed eyes and even breathing. She was astonishingly beautiful—smooth skin, delicate nose, high cheekbones and lustrous, golden hair that made a man want to bury his face against it.

He felt a shot of pity for the hapless Hargrove. Imagine having Amber in your grasp then having her disappear? Not that the man wasn't better off. Royce glanced at the portrait of his parents on their wedding day. He usually put it away while he was at the ranch, unable to bear the look of unbridled adoration on his father's face.

And that's the way it would have been with Amber, too. Her husband would have gone completely stupid and helpless with longing, only to have her change her mind and move on. Poor, pathetic Hargrove. He wouldn't have known what hit him.

Royce extricated his hand from hers, shifting to the edge of the couch, positioning himself to lift her into his arms.

"Amber?" he whispered softly, sliding one arm around her back and the other beneath her knees.

She mumbled something unintelligible, but her head tipped to rest against his shoulder. He lifted her up, and she stayed sleeping, even as he adjusted her slight body in his arms.

She weighed less than nothing. She was also soft and her scent appealing. There was something completely right about the scent of a beautiful woman, particularly this beautiful woman, fresh, like wildflowers, he supposed, but sweeter, more compelling.

He moved his nose toward her hair, guessing it was her shampoo. Hard to tell, really. He mounted the staircase, taking his time, reluctant to arrive at her room where he'd have to put her down.

His imagination wandered to that moment. Should he help her undress? Slip her between the sheets in her underwear? Would a gentleman wake her up or leave her in her clothes? Never having been a gentleman, Royce wasn't sure.

This had to be the first time he'd put a woman to bed without immediate plans to join her. He couldn't help a self-deprecating smile. It figured. He also couldn't remember a moment in his life when he'd been more eager to join a woman in bed.

He pushed open her door, carefully easing her through the opening. Then he crossed to the queen-size, brass bed and leaned down, laying her gently on top of the comforter.

She moaned her contentment, and his longing ratcheted up a notch. Their faces were only inches apart, his arm around her back, the other cradling her bare legs. He knew he had to leave her, but try as he might, he couldn't get his body to cooperate.

"Amber," he whispered again, knowing that if she woke he'd have no choice but to walk away.

"Mmm," she moaned. Then she sighed and wriggled in his arms.

His muscles tensed to iron. His gaze took in her pouty lips and, before he knew it, his head was dipping toward hers. Then he was kissing her sweet lips.

Just to say good-night, he promised himself. Just a chaste—

But then she was kissing back.

Her arms twined around his neck, and her head tipped sideways, lips parting, accommodating his ravenous kiss. Her back arched, and her fingertips curled into his short hair, even as her delicate tongue flicked into his mouth.

He leaned into her soft breasts, stroking the length of her bare legs, teasing the delicate skin behind her knees, tracing the outline of her shapely calves and daring the heat of her smooth thighs.

He wanted her, more than he'd ever wanted a woman in his life. Passion was quickly clouding reason, and his hormones warred with intelligence. Another minute, another second, and his logic would switch completely off.

He dragged his mouth from hers. "Amber?" he forced himself to ask. "Are you sure you're ready for this?"

Her eyes popped open, and she took a sudden jerk back against the pillow. She blinked in confusion at Royce's face, and in a split and horrible second, he realized what had happened.

The woman had been dreaming.

And Royce wasn't the man she'd been dreaming about.

In the morning, Amber was grateful to find Stephanie in the kitchen at breakfast. She needed a buffer between her and Royce while she got over her embarrassment.

She'd hesitated a moment too long last night. When she'd realized it wasn't a dream, she should have kept right on kissing him. She should have pressed her body tightly against his and sent the signal that she was completely attracted to him, nearly breathless with passion for him, and that making love was exactly what she wanted.

Instead, all he'd seen was her shock and hesitation. He'd been offended and abruptly left the room. She didn't blame him. And she wasn't brave enough to try to explain.

"Morning, Amber." Stephanie was her usual bright self as she bit into a strip of bacon, legs swinging from the high chair at the breakfast bar.

"Morning," Amber replied, daring a fleeting glance at Royce.

He gave her a cool nod then turned his attention

back to Stephanie. "Two days at the most," he told Stephanie.

"I'll definitely get you something," she responded and blew out a sigh. "This is the worst possible time."

"I can't imagine there being a best possible time." Royce stood from the breakfast bar and carried his plate and coffee mug over to the sink. He downed the last of the coffee before setting everything on the counter.

Amber helped herself to a clean plate from the cupboard and took a slice of toast from the platter.

"Royce has to call a division heads meeting," Stephanie told her. "We need to ask for financial reports from everybody. But he's worried about panic."

"Who would panic?" Amber addressed her question first to Royce, but when he didn't meet her eyes, she turned back to Stephanie.

"I need a pretext for the meeting," said Royce. "Barry Brewster's firing is bad enough. Add to that a sudden meeting and financial reports, and the gossip will swirl.

"We have over two thousand employees," he continued. "Some very big contracts, and some very twitchy clients." His gaze finally went to Amber, but his face remained impassive, his tone flat. "If you don't mind, we'll start a rumor you were the cause."

"You mean the cause of Barry Brewster being fired, not the money problems?"

Royce didn't react to her joke. "Yes."

"Are you leaving today?" asked Stephanie.

At first Amber thought Stephanie meant her, and the idea made her clench her stomach in regret. But then she realized Stephanie was talking to her brother.

Royce nodded.

"Where—" Amber clamped her jaw to slow herself down. It was jarring to think of him leaving with this tension between them. "Where are you going?" she finished, feigning only a mild interest.

"Chicago."

"You don't think that will bring on the gossip?"

She assured herself her caution was sincere. It wasn't merely an attempt to keep Royce here at the ranch.

His eyes narrowed.

"If you come rolling into the office, people are sure to think something's up."

"She's right," Stephanie put in.

"I don't see an alternative. I have to talk to the division VPs."

"Bring them here," suggested Amber.

Both Royce and Stephanie stared at her.

"There's your pretext. Come up with a reason to bring them here. Something fun, something frivolous, then take them aside and have whatever discreet conversation you need to have." She paused, but neither of them jumped in.

"A barbecue." She offered the first thing that popped into her mind.

Royce's voice turned incredulous, but at least there was an emotion in it. "You want me to fly the Ryder senior managers to Montana for a barbecue?"

"They'd never suspect," she told him.

"A barn dance," Stephanie cried, coming erect on the seat. "We'll throw a dance to christen the new barn."

"You're both insane," Royce grumbled.

"Like a fox," said Stephanie. "Invite the spouses. Hire a band. Nobody throws a dance and barbecue when the company's in financial trouble."

Amber waited. So did Stephanie.

Royce's brows went up, and his mouth thinned out. "I find I can't disagree with that statement."

Finished with her own breakfast, Stephanie hopped up and transferred her dishes to the sink. She gave Royce a quick peck on the cheek. "See you guys in a while. I have to get the students started."

As she left the room, Amber screwed up her courage. She definitely needed to clear the air. "Royce—"

"If you have time today," he interrupted, "could you give me as much information as possible on the cattle ranch finances?" His voice was detached, professional, and his gaze seemed to focus on her hairline.

Amber hated the cold wall between them. "I..."

"Stephanie's going to pull something together for the horse operation, and I'll be busy—"

"Of course," Amber quickly put in, swallowing, telling herself she had no right to feel hurt. "Whatever you need."

He gave a sharp nod. "Thanks. Appreciate you helping out." Then he turned and strode out of the kitchen, boot heels echoing on the tile floor.

Amber was curled up on the webbed cushions of an outdoor love seat on the ranch house deck, clouds slipping over the distant mountains, making mottled shade on the nearby aspen groves. She flipped her way through a hundred-page printout from the ranch's financial system, highlighting entries along the way.

Gopher, one of Molly's young pups, had curled up against her bare feet. At first, she'd been wary of his wet nose and slurpy tongue. But then he'd fallen asleep, and she found his rhythmic breathing and steady heartbeat rather comforting.

She hadn't seen Royce since breakfast, and Stephanie was obviously busy getting her own financial records together. Amber's thoughts had vacillated from heading straight for home, to confronting Royce about last night, to seducing Royce, to helping him sort out his business problems and earning his gratitude.

She sighed and let her vision blur against the page. For the hundredth time, she contemplated her mistake. Why had she panicked last night? Why hadn't she kissed him harder, hugged him tighter and waited to see where it would all lead?

She was wildly attracted to him. She was truly free from Hargrove now, and there was no reason in the world she couldn't follow her desires. So what if she'd only known him a few days? They were both adults, and this was hardly the 1950s.

Gopher shifted his warm little body, reminding her of where she was and that, 1950s or not, she'd blown her chance with Royce. The choices left were to leave him, seduce him or impress him. Since she was completely intimidated by the thought of seducing a man she'd already rebuffed, she decided to go with impressing him.

She forced herself to focus on the column of numbers in her lap.

There it was again.

She stroked the highlighter across the page.

Yet another payment to Sagittarius Eclipse Incorporated. It was for one hundred thousand dollars, just like the last one, and the one before that

She skipped back on the pages, counting the payments

and pinpointing the dates of the transactions. They fell on the first day of every month. Where other payments in the financial report were for obvious things like feed, lumber, tools or veterinary services, the Sagittarius Eclipse payments were notated only as "services."

Amber's curiosity was piqued. She flipped to the back page. Scanning through the total columns, she discovered one-point-two million dollars had been paid out to Sagittarius Eclipse in the current year, the same amount the year before.

She pulled her feet from the love seat cushion. Gopher whimpered and quickly scooted up next to her thigh, flopping against her.

She smiled at the little puff ball, set the financial report aside and scooped him into her arms. He wiggled for a moment, but then settled in next to her like a fuzzy baby.

"I suppose if I hold on to you, you can't do any harm," she whispered to him, checking Molly and the other pups as she rose to her feet. They were curled together at the far end of the deck. Nobody seemed to notice as she carried Gopher through the doorway.

There was a computer close by in the living room, and she sat down in front of it, moving the mouse to bring the screen back to life. She hadn't graduated in Public Administration without knowing how to search a company. Using her free hand, she called up a favorite corporate registry search program.

An hour later, she knew nothing, absolutely nothing about Sagittarius Eclipse Incorporated. They had to be an offshore company, and a hard-to-trace one at that. She could hear her father's voice inside her head, warning her that when something didn't seem right, something definitely wasn't right. But since she wasn't nearly as suspicious as her father, she refused to jump to any conclusions.

Shifting the sleeping puppy, she dug into her pocket to retrieve her cell phone, dialing Stephanie's number.

"Yo!" came the young woman's voice.

"It's Amber."

"I know. What's going on?"

"You ever heard of a company called Sagittarius Eclipse?"

"Who?"

Amber repeated the name.

"What are they, astrologers or something?"

"I hope not." Amber nearly chuckled. If Ryder Ranch was paying for a hundred grand a month of astrology services, they'd better be accurately predicting the stock market.

"Never heard of them," said Stephanie. "How are things looking at your end?"

"Best I can come up with is to stop work on the new barn," said Amber. And maybe quit paying for unidentified "services." But something stopped her from mentioning the strange payments to Stephanie.

"I hate to say it," Stephanie returned, "but I'd better not buy Blanchard's Run."

"I thought that was a foregone conclusion."

"A girl can hope."

This time, Amber did laugh at the forlorn little sigh in Stephanie's voice. "Suck it up, princess."

"Easy for you to say. It's not your business being compromised."

Amber couldn't deny it. What's more, she couldn't ignore the fact that she didn't have a business to compromise. Nor did she have a career to compromise. The only thing she'd ever been able to call a vocation was her role as Hargrove's loyal fiancée and future wife. And she'd completely blown that job yesterday.

"What else have you got?" she asked, shoving the disagreeable thoughts to the back of her mind.

"Let me see." Stephanie shuffled some papers in the background. "I can delay a tack order, struggle through with our existing jumps. Man, I hate to do that. But the horses have to eat, the employees need paychecks, and we don't dare cut back on the competition schedule."

Royce's deep voice broke in from behind Amber. "I see you've changed your mind."

She jerked around to face him in his Western shirt and faded jeans. A flush heated her face. Yes, she'd changed her mind. She'd changed her mind the second he left her bedroom last night.

But he was staring at the puppy in her lap, and she realized he was referring to a completely different subject.

"Royce is here," she said into the mouthpiece.

"Tell him I'll be down there before dinner."

"Sure." She signed off and hung up the phone, adjusting Gopher's little body when she realized her arm was beginning to tingle from lack of circulation. "He's very friendly," she told Royce.

"Are you taking him home?"

"Have you ever heard of a company called Sagittarius Eclipse?" she countered, not wanting to open the subject of her going home. She'd pretend she didn't notice he was anxious for her to leave.

"Never," he answered, watching her closely, the

distance and detachment still there in his expression and stance.

She debated her next move, unable to shake the instinct that told her the payments were suspicious.

"Why do you ask?" he prompted.

"The ranch is making payments to them."

"For what?"

"That's just it. I can't tell."

"Tools? Supplies? Insurance?"

"Insurance, maybe." She hadn't thought of that. "The entries only say 'services.'" She reached behind her for the report, and Gopher wriggled in her lap.

"Better put him back outside," Royce suggested.

Amber moved to the screen door, deposited the puppy on the deck and returned to point out the entries to Royce.

"I searched for the company on the Internet," she offered while he glanced through the pages she'd noted. "I can't find anything on them, not domestically, not offshore."

He raised a questioning brow.

"I learned corporate research at U of C."

Royce's jaw tightened, and she could feel the wheels turning inside his head.

She dared voice the suspicion that was planted inside her brain. "Do you think McQuestin could be—"

"No."

"His niece?"

"Not a chance. Not for these amounts."

"McQuestin had to know, right?" The man worked with the business accounts on a daily basis. Whatever was going on with Sagittarius Eclipse, McQuestin had to be aware.

"It's legit," Royce said out loud, but his spine was stiff, and he was frowning.

"What do you want to do?" she asked. Maybe this was the tip of the iceberg. Maybe Sagittarius Eclipse would help them solve some kind of embezzlement scheme. Maybe she could even help alleviate the company's cash flow problems.

He reached into the breast pocket of his blue-and-gray plaid shirt, retrieving his cell phone and searching for a number. His hair was damp with sweat, face streaked with dust, sleeves rolled up to reveal his tanned, muscular forearms. Amber's gaze went on a wayward tour down his body, her hormones reaching with predictability to his sex appeal.

He pressed a button on the phone, and the ringing tone became audible through the small speaker.

Amber pointed to the screen door. "Do you want me to—"

Royce shook his head. "You're the one that found it. Let's hear what McQuestin has to say."

A woman's voice bid them hello.

"Maddy? It's Royce."

"Oh, hey, Royce. He's doing okay today. They think they got the last of the bone fragments, and the infection's calming down."

"Good to hear," said Royce. "Can I talk to him for a minute?"

Maddy hesitated. "He's pretty doped up. Can I help with something?"

"It's important," said Royce, an apology in his voice.

"Well. Okay." The sounds went muffled for a few moments.

"Yeah?" came a gravelly voice.

"It's Royce, Mac. How're you feeling?"

"Like the bronc won," McQuestin grumbled.

Amber couldn't help but smile.

"You married yet?" McQuestin's voice was slightly slurred.

"That was Jared," Royce corrected.

"Mighty pretty girl," McQuestin mused. "Should have married her yourself."

"Jared might have had an objection to that."

"He's too busy... Hey! Did you wash the ears?"

Royce and Amber glanced at each other in amusement.

"Mac," Royce tried.

"What now?" MacQuestin grumbled.

"You know anything about Sagittarius Eclipse?"

There was a silence, during which their amusement turned to concern.

"I paid 'em," said McQuestin, obviously angry. "What else would a man do?"

"What exactly did you pay them for?"

McQuestin snorted. "You tell Benteen..." Then his voice turned to a growl. "Somebody should have shot the damn dog yesterday."

Maddy's voice came back. "Can this wait, Royce? You're really upsetting him."

"I'm sorry, Maddy. Of course it can wait. Keep me posted, okay?"

"Will do." McQuestin's voice still ebbed and flowed in the background. "Better go."

Royce signed off.

"Who's Benteen?" asked Amber.

Royce's voice was thoughtful, and he placed the phone

back in his pocket. "My grandfather. He died earlier this year. You think you could dig a little deeper into this?"

Amber nodded. Her curiosity was piqued. She'd like nothing better than to sleuth around Sagittarius Eclipse and figure out its relationship to the Ryder Ranch.

Seven

"Royce?"

Royce's body reacted to the sound of Amber's voice. He hefted a hay bale onto the stack, positioning it correctly before acknowledging her presence.

"Yeah?" He didn't turn to look at her. It was easier for him to cope if only one of his senses was engaged with her at a time. He only hoped she'd keep her sweet scent on the far side of the barn.

Her footsteps echoed. So much for that plan.

"I didn't find any more information," she said. "I'm going to have to try again tomorrow."

He nodded, moving to the truckload of hay bales, keeping his gaze fixed on his objective.

"It's getting late," she ventured, and there was a vulnerability in her voice that made his predicament even worse. Though he didn't look at her now, an image of her this afternoon, in that short denim skirt, a peach tank top, her blond hair cascading softly around her bare shoulders, was stuck deep in the base of his brain. It was going to take dynamite to blast it out.

"I know." He gave the short answer.

"What are you doing?"

He grabbed the next bale, binder twine pressing against the reinforced palms of his leather work gloves. "Moving hay bales."

He retraced his steps. Extreme physical work was his only hope of getting any sleep tonight. If he wasn't dead-dog exhausted, he'd do nothing but lie awake and think about Amber sleeping across the hall.

"Is it that important?" she pressed.

"Horses have to eat."

"But do you—"

"Is there something you need?" he asked brusquely.

Her silence echoed between them, and he felt like a heel.

"No," she finally answered in a soft voice. "It's just…"

He didn't prompt her, hoping she'd take the hint and leave. He'd never found himself so intensely attracted to a woman, and it was physically painful to fight it.

"I'm surprised is all," she continued.

He mentally rolled his eyes. Couldn't the woman take a hint? Did she like that she was making him crazy? Was she one of those teases that got her jollies out of tempting a man then turning up her prissy little nose at his advances?

"When you said you had to babysit the ranch—"

How the hell long was she going to keep this up?

"—I thought you meant in a more managerial sense. I mean, can't somebody else move the hay?"

He turned to look at her then. Damn it, she was still wearing that sexy outfit. Only it was worse now, because the cool evening air had hardened her nipples, and they were highlighted against the soft cotton where she stood in the pool of overhead light.

The air whooshed right out of his lungs, and he almost dropped the bale.

"I'd rather do it myself," he finally ground out.

"I see." She held his gaze. There was something soft in the depths of her eyes, something warm and welcoming.

At this very second, he could swear she was attracted to him. But he'd been down that road before. Down that road was a long night in a very lonely bed.

He went back to work.

"Royce?" Her footsteps echoed again as she moved closer.

He heaved the bale into place, gritted his teeth and turned. "What?" he barked.

"I'm…" She glanced at the scuffed floor. "Uh… sorry."

He swiped his forearm across his sweaty brow. "Not as sorry as I am."

She glanced up in confusion. "For what? What did you do?"

"I didn't *do* anything."

"Then, what do you have to be sorry about?"

"You want to know why I'm sorry?" He'd reached the breaking point, and he was ready to give it to her with both barrels. "You really want to know why I'm sorry?"

She gave a tentative nod.

"I'm sorry I walked into the Ritz-Carlton lounge."

Her eyes widened as he stripped off his gloves.

"And I'm sorry I brought you home with me." He tossed the gloves on the nearest hay bale. "And I'm sorry you're so beautiful and desirable and sexy. But mostly, *mostly* I'm sorry my family's future is falling down around my ears, and all I can think of is how much I want you."

Their eyes locked.

For a split second, it looked as though she smiled.

"You think this is *funny?*"

She shook her head. Then she took a step forward. "I think it's ironic."

"You might not want to get too close," he warned, drinking in the sight, sound and scent of her all in one shot, wondering how many seconds he could hold out before he dragged her into his arms.

"Yeah?" She stepped closer still.

"Did you not hear me?"

She placed her flat palm against his chest. "I heard you just fine." Her defiant blue eyes held one of the most blatant invitations he'd ever seen.

He hoped she knew what she was doing.

Hell, who was he kidding? He couldn't care less if she knew or not. Just so long as she didn't back off this time.

His arms went around her and jerked her flush against him, all but daring her to protest.

Then he bent his head; his desire and frustration transmitted themselves into a powerful kiss. He all but devoured her mouth, reveling in the feel of her thighs, belly and breasts, all plastered against his aching flesh.

He encircled her waist, pulling in at the small of her back, bending her backward, kissing deeper as his free hand strummed from hip to waist over her rib cage to capture the soft mound of her breast.

She groaned against his mouth, lips parting farther, her tongue answering the impassioned thrusts of his own. Her nipple swelled under his caress, fueling his desire and obliterating everything else from his brain. He bent his knee, shifting his thigh between hers, pushing up on her short skirt, settling against the silk of her panties.

Her hands gripped his upper arms, nails scraping erotically against his thin shirt, transmitting her passion to the nerves of his skin. He lifted her, spreading her legs, hands cupping her bottom, shoving the skirt out of the way and pressing her heat against him.

Her arms went around his neck, legs tightening, her lips hot on his, her silky hair flowing out in all directions around her shoulders. She braced her arms on his shoulders, fingers delving into his short hair. Her kisses moved from his mouth to his cheek, his chin and his neck. She tugged at the buttons of his shirt, loosening them, before dipping her head and trailing her kisses across his chest.

He tipped back his head, drinking in the heat and moisture of her amazing lips. Then he took a few steps sideways, behind the bale stack, screening them from the rest of the cavernous room. He shrugged out of his loose shirt, dropping it on a bale before settling her on top. He braced his arms on either side of her and pulled back to look.

Her eyes were closed, lips swollen red. Her chest

heaved with labored breaths, and his gaze settled on the outline of her breasts against the peach top.

"Royce?"

His name on her lips tightened his chest and sent a fresh wave of desire cascading through his veins. He swiftly stripped her top off over her head, revealing two perfect breasts peeking from a lacy, white bra that dipped low in the center and barely camouflaged her dusky nipples.

"Gorgeous," he breathed, popping the clasp and letting the wisp of fabric fall away. "Perfection."

Her lash-fringed lids came up, revealing blue eyes clouded with passion.

They stared at each other for a long suspended breath. Then he reached out, his tanned hand dark against her creamy breast. He stroked the pad of his thumb across her nipple.

She gasped, and he smiled in pure satisfaction.

He repeated the motion, and she grabbed for his waist, tugging him toward her. But he stood his ground, his gaze flicking to the shadow of her sheer, high-cut panties, the skirt pulled high to reveal her hips.

He traced the line of elastic, knuckle grazing the moist silk. She moaned, head tipping back against the golden hay, her arms falling to her sides, clenching her fists tightly.

He could feel his anticipation, his own blood singing insistently through his system, hormones revving up, his passion making demands on his brain. But he wasn't ready. He wasn't ready to let the roar toward completion hijack his senses.

While his fingertips roamed, he leaned forward,

taking one plump nipple into his mouth, curling his tongue around the exquisite texture.

A deep sound burbled in Amber's throat, and her hands went for his belt buckle, the snap of his jeans, his zipper, his boxers, and then he was in her hand, and he knew time was running out.

He hooked his thumbs over the sides of her panties, stripping them down, letting them drop to the floor. Then his body moved unerringly to hers.

Her legs wrapped around his waist, and he raised his head, gazing into her eyes as he flexed his hips, easing slowly as he could to her center and into her core. Her eyes widened with every inch, she clenched her hands on his hips, and her sweet mouth fell open in a pout of awe.

Unable to resist, he bent his head, her features blurred as he grew close. Then her mouth opened against his, and his tongue thrust in, mimicking the motions of his hips as nature took over and he let the primal rhythm throb free between them.

He cupped her face, caressed her hair, kissed her neck, her temple, her eyelids. His hands roamed free, stroking her thighs, her bottom, her belly and breasts. Her panting breaths were music to his ears, her nails crescenting into his back transmitted her fervor.

Then she cried his name, urging him on, playing havoc with his self-control. But she was with him, and the small tremors contracting her body catapulted him over the edge into oblivion.

Amber blinked open her eyes.

She was vaguely aware of hay strands tickling her bare back. But she was much more aware of Royce's hard, hot body engulfing her own. Her lungs were struggling to get enough oxygen, and every fiber of her muscles danced with the aftershocks of lovemaking.

Royce's palm stroked over her hair, and he kissed her eyelids. Despite her exhaustion, her lips curled into a smile. But she was a long way from being able to speak.

Her skirt was in a bunch around her waist, her other clothes scattered. Her hair was wild and disheveled, tangled with hay, while her lips tingled with the heat of his kisses.

"I don't know what to say," Royce whispered in her ear.

She struggled through a few more breaths. "Well, I'm definitely not sorry," she managed, and she heard him chuckle.

"Definitely not sorry," he echoed.

He eased back, taking in her appearance.

"Bad?" she asked.

He pulled some straw from her hair. "Telltale."

She raked spread fingers through her hair in an attempt to tame it while he refastened his jeans.

He bent and picked up her bra from the floor, frowned at the dirt streaks on it and tucked it into his back pocket. He located her tank top, gave her breasts one last, lingering look, then pulled her top back over her head. The peach color was blotted with dust. And Royce's attempts to brush it off made things worse.

"We'll probably want to sneak you in the back way," he joked as she tugged down her skirt. He watched her movements closely.

She slipped his wrinkled shirt from beneath her butt

and held it out to him. "You're not looking so sharp yourself, cowboy."

"I've been working hard." As he shrugged into his shirt, his gaze strayed from the top of her head to the tips of her toes, and his tone went soft and intimate. "What's your excuse?"

"Someone stole my underwear."

He reached for the wisp of silk caught on the side of a bale and tucked it into his pocket with her bra.

"That's my only pair."

"Yeah?" He gave her body another long look. "Lucky me."

He fastened his buttons then helped her down, tucking her hand in his as they headed across the barn. "I hope you know you're sleeping in my bed tonight."

"Only if you give my underwear back."

"Maybe."

"Maybe?"

He turned to gaze at her. "Talk me into it."

Her footsteps slowed, and so did his. With their joined hands, he reeled her in, then he smoothed her hair back once more, moving closer still, voice intimate. "You know, you are stunningly gorgeous."

A smile tickled the corners of her mouth. "Is that why you're sneaking me in the back way?"

"I'm keeping you all to myself," he whispered, lips coming down on hers.

The kiss nearly exploded between them. For all that they'd just made love, Amber's arousal was strong as ever. She wrapped her arms around his neck, came up on her toes, welcomed his tongue and reveled in the feel of his warm hands as they stroked over her back, across her buttocks, down her thighs, then back up beneath her skirt.

She pressed her body against his as the kiss went on and on. A groan slipped from her lips.

"Again?" he asked, voice husky.

She nodded.

"Here or in bed."

"I don't care." She truly didn't. Royce could make her body sing, and propriety didn't appear to have a lot to do with it.

He backed off slightly on the kiss and smoothed her skirt back down. "In bed."

"Really?"

He grinned at the disappointment in her tone. "I want to make love to you for a very, very long time."

She cocked her head sideways. "And you need a bed for that?"

"I don't plan to be able to move afterward."

She breathed a mock, drawn-out sigh. "If you think I'll wear you out…"

"Is that a challenge?"

She gave a teasing half smile and rapidly blinked her lashes.

In return, he planted a playful swat on her buttocks. "You're on, sweetheart."

Amber stifled a yawn in the bright, midday sunshine, stretching her taut thigh muscles as she leaned on the railing of the ranch house deck. The puppies were below, chasing each other and rolling around on the meadow that sloped toward the river. Off the end of the deck, Amber could see the ranch hands putting up five giant tents in preparation for Saturday's barbecue and barn dance.

She was dividing her time between the Sagittarius Eclipse mystery and the barbecue. She'd never planned an event quite like this before. They'd hired a local band. Hamburgers and hot dogs were making up the main course, while salads, potato chips and condiments seemed to round out the rest. They had plans for a giant cake for dessert, with papers plates, soft drinks and canned beer all around.

Amber wasn't sure how the Ryder International executives would react to the dinner, though she was sure their kids would love the wagon rides, horseshoes and baseball game Stephanie had planned. When she'd broached the possibility of steaks, wine and real china with Sasha, the woman looked at her as though she'd lost her mind.

Okay, so they did corporate entertaining a little differently here in Montana. Amber could conform. And at least the event wasn't likely to damage the Ryder International bottom line.

Tucking her windblown hair behind one ear, she pressed the on button of her cell phone, and dialed Katie's work number.

"Katie Merrick," came the familiar voice.

"It's Amber."

"What? Finally! Have you gone stark raving mad?"

"You've been talking to my mom, haven't you?"

"Of course I've been talking to your mom. And your dad. And Hargrove. You've got him completely confused."

"I thought I cleared up the confusion yesterday."

"By breaking it off over the phone?" The accusation was clear in Katie's tone.

"I'm a little ways away, Katie."

"Where?"

Amber scratched her fingernail over a dried flower petal the rain had stuck to the painted railing, deciding she couldn't keep it a secret forever. "Montana."

Silence.

"Katie?"

"Did you say Montana?"

"Yes. I'm staying with a…well, friend. I need your help with something."

"I'd say you need a whole lot more than *my* help. The dress arrived yesterday."

"What dress?"

"Your *wedding* dress." Katie's voice was incredulous. "The one from Paris. The one with antique alençon lace and a thousand hand-sewn pearls."

"Oh." Right. That dress. Amber supposed they'd have to put it on consignment somewhere. "The thing I wanted to talk to you about at the moment, though, was business."

"What do you mean?"

"I have a problem."

"What problem?" Katie's voice immediately turned professional.

"It's a company called Sagittarius Eclipse. I haven't been able to trace it, but I think it's got to be offshore somewhere, maybe hiding behind a numbered company. It could be connected to embezzlement."

There was another moment's silence. "Where did you say you were?" asked Katie.

Amber drew a sigh. "You remember that thirty dollars I gave you last week?"

"To pay for the dry cleaning on my dress?"

"You're on retainer, Katie. I'm a client."

"*What* is going on?"

"Lawyer-client confidentiality. Say it."

"Lawyer-client confidentiality," Katie parroted with exasperation.

"I think Sagittarius Eclipse is involved in an embezzlement scheme against Ryder International."

"*Montana.*" Katie drew out the word in a triumphant voice, obviously making the connection with Amber's father's business.

Fine by Amber, she'd rather have Katie connecting her to Jared Ryder than to Royce. Even thinking his name brought up an image of last night, and Amber was forced to shake it away in order to concentrate.

"You going into my line of work?" asked Katie.

Creighton Waverley Security was famous in Chicago for specializing in corporate espionage, and they'd investigated plenty of other corporate crimes along the way.

"Just for the week." Though Amber could already see the appeal of the profession. The harder she looked for information, the more involved she became in the hunt.

"You looking for anything specific?"

"A bank account. A name. A guy named McQuestin might be involved."

Although Royce was sure McQuestin was honest, Amber wasn't prepared to rule anything out. She'd looked back as far as she could in the financial records this morning, and Sagittarius Eclipse had received millions over the years. Maybe McQuestin hadn't even broken his leg. Maybe he was on his way to some offshore haven even now.

"I'll see what I can find. And, Amber?"

"Yes?"

"You serious about this breakup?"

Amber didn't hesitate. "Yes."

"Why?"

Good question. Hard to put into words. "He's just not the right guy for me."

Katie's accusing tone was back. "When did he become not the right guy for you?"

"Katie."

"When he made his first million? When he bought you a three-carat diamond? When he received the party nod for the nomination? Or when he planned the honeymoon to Tahiti?"

"Hargrove planned a honeymoon to Tahiti?" It was the first Amber had heard about it.

"Yes! Just last night he was showing me some—"

"You saw Hargrove last night?"

There was a small pause. "He was desperate, Amber. He needed a date for that hospital thing with the Myers."

"You went on a date with Hargrove?"

"Of *course* not." But there was something in Katie's tone. "He couldn't show up stag, and I've met Belinda Myers before, so…"

Amber rolled the image of Katie and Hargrove around in her head. No problem for her. She really didn't care. "Did you have a good time?" she asked.

"That's not the point."

Royce appeared in Amber's peripheral vision, on

horseback, moving along the river trail between the staff cabins and the barbecue setup. Even at this distance, the sight of him took her breath away.

"Gotta go," she said to Katie. "Call me as soon as you find something."

"Uh… Okay, sure."

"Thanks, Katie. I miss you." Amber quickly signed off.

Royce spotted her, and the sizzle of his gaze shot right to her toes. He turned his horse toward the house, and she headed for the deck's staircase.

Glances and brief, public conversations were all Royce had managed to share with Amber throughout the day. So he was disappointed when he finally found her up at the jumping-horse outfit, and she was sitting on the front porch laughing with his sister and another man.

As he exited the pickup truck, Royce's first thought was that Hargrove had found her. The idea tightened his gut and sped up his stride. She certainly seemed happy to see this guy. She was listening to him with rapt attention, smiling, even laughing.

"Royce," Stephanie sang out as his boot hit the bottom stair. Amber glanced up, and the stranger twisted his head.

Royce immediately realized the man was too young to be Hargrove. Plus, he was wearing jumping clothes, not a business suit.

"Wesley, this is my brother, Royce. Wesley is our newest student. He was nationally ranked as a junior."

The young man stood up as Royce trotted up the remaining stairs.

"Good to meet you," Royce said with a hearty

handshake, ignoring how relieved he felt that the guy wasn't Hargrove. Wesley looked to be about twenty-one. Not much younger than Stephanie and Amber, but no immediate competition.

"You, too." Wesley nodded. "I'm honored to be working with Stephanie."

Royce smirked at his sister. "Well, we'll see how honored you feel a month from now."

"Hey," she protested, reaching out to swat his arm.

"Can I grab you a beer?" Wesley offered, nodding to a cooler against the wall. "I picked up a dozen at a microbrewery in San Diego."

"Thanks," Royce agreed, and the younger man headed for the far side of the porch.

"I've got something for you," Amber stage-whispered, and Royce's attention shot immediately to her dancing eyes.

His chest tightened, and he wondered if she was going to proposition him right here in front of Stephanie. Not that it would be a bad thing. They'd seemed to come to a tacit agreement to keep their relationship secret. But there was no real reason to do that. They were both adults. She'd officially broken off her engagement. They were entitled to date each other if they wanted.

"Sagittarius Eclipse," she said, and he realized his brain had gone completely off on the wrong track. "I have a name."

"Yeah?" He pushed an empty deck chair into the circle.

"Norman Stanton."

Royce froze, brain scrambling while Amber kept talking.

"He's an American, originally from the Pacific North—"

"Later," Royce barked.

Amber drew back, squinting at his expression.

He moderated his voice, forcing a smile when he realized Stephanie was staring at him in confusion. "I want to hear how things are coming with the barbecue."

Then he nodded to Wesley as he returned with the beer. "Thanks," he told him. "So, are you training for any competition in particular?"

Out of the corner of his eye, he could see that Amber was confused, probably hurt, but there was nothing he could do about that at the moment. He pretended to listen to Wesley's answer, while his mind reeled.

Stanton. Damn it. A name out of his worst nightmare. After all these years, they were being blackmailed by a Stanton?

How much did the bastard know? How long had he known it? And why the hell hadn't his grandfather or McQuestin told him before now?

Eight

Amber waited until they'd passed the lights of Stephanie's yard and were headed down the dark, ranch driveway before turning to Royce in the pickup truck. "What did I do?"

"Nothing." But his answer was terse, and she could tell he was upset. Their speed was increasing on the bumpy road, and she gripped the armrest to stabilize herself.

"I don't understand. It's good information. I don't know if you realize how hard I had to dig—"

"Where did you get it? Where did you come up with the name Stanton?"

"Katie found a bank account in the Cayman Islands."

Royce hit her with a hard glance, staring a bit too long for safety. "Who's Katie?"

"Watch the road," she admonished as a curve rushed up at them in the headlights.

He glanced back, but only long enough to crank the wheel. "Who is Katie?"

"She's my best friend, my maid of honor."

"I thought you weren't getting married."

"I'm *not* getting married." Amber took a breath. "She would have been my maid of honor. She's a lawyer. Her firm specializes in corporate espionage, but they investigate all kinds of criminal activity."

Royce's voice went dark. "McQuestin is not a criminal."

"I never said he was."

"You had no right to disparage a man's name—"

"I didn't disparage anything. Katie's my friend. She works for Creighton Waverley Security, and she's our lawyer now. Everything she finds out is confidential."

Royce didn't answer, but she could almost hear his teeth gritting above the roar of the engine and the creak of the steel frame as the truck took pothole after pothole.

"Who is Stanton?" she dared.

His hands tightened on the steering wheel, face stony in the dim dashboard lights. "Nobody you need to worry about."

Something inside Amber shriveled tight. She'd felt so close to Royce last night. Between lovemaking, they'd shared whispered stories, opinions, worldviews. She'd thought they were becoming friends.

"I have more," she told him, not above bribery.

"What else?"

She crossed her arms over her chest. "Who's Stanton?"

Royce glared at her. It was the first time she'd had his true anger directed at her. But she stiffened her spine. "Who is Stanton?"

"Forget it."

"*Why?* Why won't you let me help you?"

He geared down for a hill. "There are things you don't understand."

"No kidding."

"No offence, Amber. But I barely know you."

"No offence, Royce. But you've seen me naked."

"And that's relevant how?"

"I'm just saying—"

"That it's not about to happen again unless I talk?"

"You think I'd use sex to bribe you?"

He let go of the steering wheel long enough for a jerking hand gesture of frustration. "Why do you jump to the absolute *worst* interpretation?"

"I'm trying to understand you."

"Well, I'm not having the slightest success understanding you." He sucked in a deep breath.

She let a few beats go by in silence, forcing herself to calm down. In her mind, this argument was completely separate from any future sexual relationship. She moderated her voice. "Maybe if you told me what was going on."

"Maybe if you let me keep my private business private."

Okay, now that crack would probably impact on their future sexual relationship.

"Fine," she huffed. "There's this numbered holding company." She pulled a note from her pocket and checked it in the dim light. "One-four-nine-five-eight, twelve-zero-ninety-three is registered in Liechtenstein with bank accounts in Liechtenstein, Switzerland and Grand Cayman. Its only asset is a company called Eastern Exploration Holdings. Eastern Exploration owns several parcels of property, mostly in the Bahamas. It also owns one company, Sagittarius Eclipse. One-four-nine-five-eight, twelve-zero-ninety-three is solely owned by Norman Stanton."

The truck rocked to a halt in front of the ranch house.

"His last known address was in Boston, Massachusetts," Amber finished.

Royce killed the lights and turned the key, shutting down the engine. "You don't know where he is now?"

"Not yet." She yanked up on the door handle, and the door creaked wide.

"But you're looking?" Royce followed suit.

"We're looking," said Amber, sliding off the high bench seat and onto the dirt driveway. She'd taken to wearing a pair of tattered, flat, canvas runners she'd found in a closet by the back door. They weren't as sturdy as the cowboy boots favored by everyone else, but they beat the heck out of the high heels she'd arrived in.

"How long will it take?" he asked as they headed for the porch.

"I don't know." Her voice was still testy.

Royce frowned at her.

"It'll take as long as it takes. He could be hiding. He might have left the country." She headed up the stairs. "Maybe someone warned him McQuestin was hurt, and he's worried he'll get caught."

"Who would warn him McQuestin was hurt?"

Amber paused at the front door. "Maybe McQuestin."

Royce turned the knob and shoved open the door. "McQuestin wouldn't do that."

She walked inside. "You're putting a lot of faith in a man who's been authorizing secret payments."

"He has his reasons." The door slammed shut, and Royce moved up close.

Amber turned, then drew back from the intensity in his eyes.

He moved closer.

She stepped back again, coming up against the wall in the foyer.

He braced a hand on either side of her, dipping his head.

"Royce?"

"Yeah?" He kissed her, and her protest was muffled against his mouth.

He kissed her again, softer, deeper, and a flame of desire curled to life in the pit of her belly.

His hands cupped her chin, deepening the kiss, pressing his strong body flush against hers, evoking near-blinding memories of the night before.

"What are you doing?" she finally gasped.

"It's not obvious?" There was a thread of laughter deep in his throat, his warm breath puffing against her skin.

"No."

"Makeup sex."

"But I'm still mad at you."

"You are?" He feigned surprise as he kissed her neck, her collarbone, her shoulder. He found the strip of bare skin at the top of her jeans, skimming his knuckles across her navel. "Then let's see what we can do to change that."

* * *

Royce feathered his fingertips across Amber's stomach, the narrowing at her waist, the indentation of her navel and the small curve of her belly. Her skin was pale and supple, a light tan line at bikini level, barely above where the sheet covered her legs.

She was by far the most beautiful woman he'd ever seen. Her blond hair, mussed at the moment, was thick and lustrous, reflecting the pink rays of the rising sun. Her eyes were deep blue, a midsummer sky right now, but they'd been jewel bright last night while they made love. Her lips were full, deep red and tempting.

Even her ears were gorgeous, delicate and small, while her neck was graceful, her shoulders smooth, and her breasts were something out of his deepest fantasy. Add to that her quick wit, her intelligence and her sense of fun, and she was somebody he could keep in his bed for days on end.

He'd had sex with plenty of women over the years, slept with only some of them, ate breakfast with fewer still. And in all that time, he'd never had an urge to bare his soul to a single one.

Now, he did.

Now, he wanted to tell her anything and everything.

He let his fingers trace the curve of her hip bone, made up his mind and took the plunge. "My father killed a man named Stanton."

Amber's head turned sharply on the stark white pillow. "He what?"

"Killed him," Royce repeated, hand stilling, cupping her hip.

"Was it an accident?"

"Nope."

"I don't understand."

"It was on purpose. Frank Stanton was having an affair with my mother."

Amber's eyes widened and she rolled sideways, propping her head on one elbow. "Did they get into a fight?"

"I guess you could say that. My father shot him."

Amber stilled. The sun broke free from the horizon, and the pink rays morphed to white.

"Did your father go to jail?" Her voice was hoarse.

Royce shook his head. "He died that same day."

Amber swallowed. "And your mother?"

"Died with my father. Their truck went off the ranch road in the rain. They both drowned in the river."

"After he shot Stanton."

"I always assumed he panicked." Though Royce had never delved too deeply into his father's possible motivations for speeding down the ranch road with his unfaithful mother. "There was no trial, of course. Everybody chalked the shooting up to a failed robbery, and the accident was ruled just that, an accident. For years, I thought I was the only one who knew the truth."

"How did you know?"

"I found my mother's confession letter."

Amber sighed, eyes going shiny with sympathy. "Oh, Royce."

"I burned the letter, and the secret was safe. But then, on his deathbed, my grandfather Benteen told Jared he'd heard the shot. When my father drove away, Benteen dumped the gun in the river because he didn't want his son tried for murder."

Royce had wished that Jared never found out. But

now it was better that he had. "So, I know, and Gramps knew, and Jared knows." Royce blew out a breath.

"Plus McQuestin," Amber said softly, obviously putting the pieces together. "And somehow Norman Stanton."

"Allowing him to blackmail my family."

She lay back down. "To keep the secret?"

"Our reputation was important to Benteen."

"But, millions of dollars' worth of important?"

Royce had asked himself that same question, and he didn't have a good answer. What the hell were Benteen and McQuestin thinking? His father couldn't be tried. There wasn't a man in the state who'd fault Royce's father for retaliating against Stanton.

That left their mother's reputation. And, as far as Royce was concerned, she'd made her own bed. He couldn't imagine paying millions of dollars protecting a woman who'd betrayed her own family.

Well, from this point on, he and Jared were in charge, and not a single dime of Ryder money was getting into the hands of a Stanton.

"The payments stop now," he vowed to Amber. "And I want to know everything there is to know about Norman Stanton."

She put her hand on Royce's shoulder. "You're not going after revenge, are you?"

He turned his head to look her in the eyes. "I *am* going after my money."

"Royce."

He raised his eyebrows, all but daring her to argue.

She searched his expression. "I don't want you to get yourself in trouble."

His anger switched to resolve, and he couldn't help

but smile. Her sentiment was admirable, but completely unnecessary.

"Darlin'," he told her. "If I was you, I'd be worried about Norman Stanton, not about me."

Six worried Ryder International division heads stared back at Royce around the ranch house dining room table. The doors were closed to the rest of the house, but the windows were open, the happy sounds of an ongoing barbecue and baseball game a jarring counterpoint to the uncomfortable conversation.

If the four men and two women were unsettled by Barry Brewster's firing, they were positively rattled by the potential fallout from the loss of the China deal. Ryder International was a strong company, but it wasn't invincible. They were going to have to take quick and decisive action if they wanted to recover.

Jared was still out of touch, but it didn't take a rocket scientist to figure out the answer. Some of the Ryder companies would need to be sold, perhaps entire divisions, which explained the ashen faces around the table. Nobody wanted to be the sacrificial lamb.

"Construction is the bread and butter of the company," Konrad Klaus opened the conversation. He was out-front and aggressive as always. As the head of the largest and longest-standing division of the corporation, he wielded considerable influence with his counterparts.

"It's pretty shortsighted to mess with high tech," Carmen Volle put in.

Mel Casper threw down his pen. "Oh, sure. Everybody look at sports and culture. It's not always the bottom line, you know. We're carrying the marketing load for everybody else."

Royce cut them all off. "This isn't divide and conquer," he warned. "Jared's not coming back to a war. I've got your reports—"

"We wrote those before we had the facts," said Konrad.

Konrad's respect factor for Royce had never been high. But it was rare that it mattered. It mattered today.

Royce gave him a level look. "Precisely why I asked for them up front. I wanted the facts, not half a dozen individual lobbying efforts."

"So you can pick us off like fattened ducks?" asked Mel.

"*That's* the attitude you want to project?" Royce needed loyalty and teamwork right now. He wasn't looking to get rid of anybody else, but he wasn't looking to babysit any prima donnas, either.

"I say we wait for Jared to get back," said Konrad.

Royce turned to stare the man down. "What part of fifty million dollars didn't you understand?

Konrad glowered but didn't answer.

"We start today," said Royce. He might not be as involved in the operations of Ryder International as Jared, but he was still an owner, and he'd had about enough of people assuming he could be marginalized.

Barry Brewster would never have treated Melissa the way he'd treated Amber. Just because Royce flew a jet didn't mean he was incapable of anything else. Starting here and now, he was taking a stand—both with Norman Stanton, and with the brass at Ryder International.

"I don't see how we do that." Konrad tossed out a direct challenge to Royce's leadership.

"Did this company turn into a democracy when I wasn't looking?" Royce asked softly.

"Our loyalty is to Jared."

"Your loyalty should be to Ryder International."

Konrad compressed his lips. The rest of the division heads looked down at the table. Royce realized it was now or never. He had to firmly pick up the corporate reins.

"I'm hiring an expert to do a review," he announced, having made a split-second decision.

The group exchanged dubious glances, but nobody said anything.

"Creighton Waverley Security."

"You think we're criminals?" Konrad thundered across the table.

"I think they're one hell of a research firm," Royce countered calmly. "We're going to review every company we own, take stock and make our decisions. Anybody who's not on board with it is free to leave."

He looked to each of the people in turn around the table. Nobody was happy, but nobody was walking away, either.

Now that he'd taken the first step on the fly, he supposed the second step had better be to have Amber put him in touch with her best friend's firm.

Amber helped a waiting group of children into the back of the wooden wagon, while a Ryder cowboy double-checked the harnesses on the matched Clydesdale team out front. Sasha was handing out giant chocolate chip cookies while, off to one side, Wesley was teasing Stephanie with his lariat. Amber did a double take of the two. If she wasn't mistaken, Wesley had developed a crush on his riding instructor.

She smiled to herself. Wesley was a very attractive,

fun-loving man. It wouldn't surprise her in the least if the crush was reciprocated.

"I have to talk to you." The mere sound of Royce's voice behind her caused a little thrill to zip through Amber's body. But in contrast to Wesley, Royce sounded tense and serious.

"Something wrong?" She helped the last little boy into the wagon, dusting her hands off on the sides of her jeans.

Royce moved to the corner of the wagon and pushed up the tailgate, sliding the latch to keep everyone safely inside.

Stephanie planted a foot on the wagon wheel and jumped in with the kids. Wesley quickly followed suit, taking a seat next to her on one of the padded benches, and Amber was sure she'd guessed right.

Royce backed out of the way, towing Amber with him as a cowboy unhitched the lead horse and turned the team toward the road.

"I've been meeting with the division heads," said Royce.

"What did you find out?" Amber had realized Royce and the senior managers were missing, and she'd easily guessed they were talking business. She raised her hand to wave to the cheering children as the wagon creaked down the road.

Royce pulled her toward the shadow of the barn, speaking low into her ear, his voice bringing flash memories of their night together. "I was wondering if you could do something for me."

"I don't know, Royce." She glanced around at the crowds. "There's an awful lot of people in the barn right now."

"You have a one-track mind," he admonished.

She grinned at him. She did seem particularly obsessed with making love.

"Not that I'd say no to a more interesting offer," he clarified. "But I was hoping to get in touch with your friend Katie. I need to know the who's who of Creighton Waverley."

The request brought Amber back to reality. "I thought you were going to let *me* investigate Norman Stanton."

"What?"

"I'm doing a good job," she informed him, pursing her lips.

Royce suddenly grinned.

"What?"

"You. Jumping to conclusions."

"Quit laughing at me."

"Then stop being so entertaining."

"Stop being condescending."

"Stop pouting."

"I like investigating. I want to see this through."

Royce's smile turned sly, and he cocked his head meaningfully toward the barn. "Yeah?" he drawled.

"Now who's got a one-track mind?"

"Guilty," he agreed with an easy smile, but at the same time, he backed off.

A cheer went up at the baseball game, while a freshening breeze brought the aroma of hamburgers from the cook tent.

Amber brushed at a lazy fly.

"I'm commissioning a review of all the Ryder companies," said Royce. "We're going to have to make some tough decisions, and I thought Creighton Waverley might be able to help."

"So, I'm keeping my job?"

He brushed the back of his hand along her upper arm and leaned closer again. "Now *that* remains to be seen."

"I'm not bribing you with sex."

He exaggerated an offended tone. "I'd bribe you with sex."

She extracted her cell phone from her jeans pocket. "I'm bribing you with Katie's phone number."

"Fair enough. I'll bribe you for something else later."

Amber couldn't help but smile as she punched in Katie's cell number.

"Amber," came the breathless answer. "I was just about to call you. Are you at a hoedown or something?"

Amber glanced around for the source of a noise that might have made it through the phone. "What makes you ask that?"

"Checked tablecloths, cowboy hats, horses."

Amber glanced down at her phone, then put it back to her ear. "Do you have some kind of monitor on me?"

"No, I have a white Lexus, over in front of the house. At least I think it's the house. The building with the porch and, yep, it's a hitching rail."

Amber whirled around.

Sure enough, Katie was emerging from a low-slung sports car, wearing a short, blue, clingy dress, high-heeled pumps, with her honey-blond hair in a jaunty updo. Her small bag was beaded, and she reminded Amber of how long it had been since she'd had a manicure or a facial.

Amber took a reflexive step away from Royce. "What are you *doing* here?"

"I have to talk to you."

"That's what telephones are for." A sudden fear

gripped Amber. "There's nobody with you, is there?" Like Hargrove or her parents.

"Relax," said Katie as she picked her way along the edge of the baseball field. "Your secret is safe." She grinned and gave Amber a wave.

Several dozen cowboys followed her progress.

"That's Katie," Amber told Royce.

"She does know how to make an entrance," he muttered, watching as raptly as anyone else on the ranch.

Amber felt an unwelcome pinch of jealousy.

"Who's that with you?" asked Katie as she drew ever closer.

"Royce Ryder."

"Nice."

Okay, jealousy was silly. Katie was an attractive woman, and Royce was an attractive man. They'd noticed. So what?

"Do you have any idea how far away this place is?" Katie called across the grass, folding her phone closed now that she was in shouting range.

"It's Chicago that's far away," Royce countered. "Montana is right here."

Katie grinned as she stepped up, holding out her perfect, magenta-tipped hand. "Katie Merrick. Creighton Waverley Security." She shook, then opened her purse, dropped the phone inside and extracted a business card, handing it to Royce.

"I was about to call you," said Royce.

"Well, isn't that perfect," Katie returned, glancing around the ranch yard. "Any chance they're serving margaritas at this shindig?"

It was a slow walk back to the ranch house, where

Sasha whipped up a blender of margaritas while Amber, Royce and Katie settled in on the deck. Gopher immediately jumped into Amber's lap.

"You'll want Alec Creighton's help," said Katie. She'd been all business while Royce had explained his plans for Ryder International.

"Your boss?" asked Royce as he poured the frozen green concoction into tall glasses.

"My boss's son. He's not with Creighton Waverley. He's sort of a lone-wolf troubleshooter. We subcontract to him on occasion. I can give you a list of a hundred satisfied clients if you like." Katie accepted the drink with a nod of thanks.

"How do I get hold of him?" Royce handed Amber a drink. She still couldn't believe Katie had come all the way to Montana. And since they'd done nothing but discuss Ryder International business since she'd arrived, Amber couldn't begin to guess *why* she'd come all the way to Montana.

"I'll get him to call you." Katie took a sip of her drink. "He won't take on a client without a referral."

"Appreciate that," said Royce with a salute of his drink.

Amber couldn't keep quiet any longer, and her voice came out more demanding than she'd intended. "What are you doing here, Katie?"

Katie shrugged. "I missed you."

It didn't ring true. There was something in Katie's eyes—guilt, maybe fear.

Amber was suspicious. "Did you tell my parents I was here?"

"I can't believe you'd even ask me that. Can't a girl visit her best friend?" Katie took another swig, smiling far too brightly. "Okay if I stay over tonight?"

Nine

Wrapped in a fluffy robe, Katie sat cross-legged on the end of Amber's bed while Amber washed her face at the sink inside the en-suite bathroom door.

"Just how long are you planning to stay here?" Katie asked, her voice muffled by the gush of the running water.

"I haven't decided," Amber answered, dipping her face forward to rinse it, then blindly grabbing for a towel.

As the days went by, she thought less and less about going home. Oh, she knew she'd have to, and probably soon. But there simply wasn't anything tugging her in that direction.

"You know the wedding shower's coming up, right?"

Amber peeked out from behind the towel. "Nobody canceled it?"

"Nobody believed you were serious. There are people flying in from all over the country."

Amber tossed the towel over the rack and paced back into the room. "They're still putting on my wedding shower?"

Katie nodded, while Amber dropped down onto the bed.

"The shower cake's gorgeous," Katie offered.

"This is a disaster."

Katie reached out to rub Amber's arm. "You breaking it off with Hargrove was the disaster. The shower, the dress..." Her hand gripped on Amber's shoulder. Then she abruptly stood up and crossed the room.

"I tried on your dress," she blurted out, turning to brace her back against the bureau.

Amber blinked in surprise. "You did? How'd it look?"

"Gorgeous. Absolutely, stunningly gorgeous."

"It's too bad we'll have to sell it," said Amber. "I can't see ever wearing it."

Katie nodded, her eyes staring blankly into space. "Gorgeous. Really gorgeous."

Amber pictured her friend twirling in front of the mirror. Katie always did have a romantic streak.

Suddenly, Katie clenched her fists, and her eyes scrunched shut. "Oooh, you have to promise me you won't get mad."

"Why would I get mad?" Truth was, Amber wondered if Katie had taken pictures while she modeled the dress. It might be interesting to see how it had turned out.

"I...did something," Katie confessed in a harsh whisper.

"To the dress?"

Katie didn't answer, but the color drained from her face.

"Did you spill something on it? Tear it?" Amber waited for an emotional reaction to her wedding dress being ruined, but it didn't come.

Katie emphatically shook her head. "No. The dress is fine."

"Then what are you so worried about?"

Katie picked up a china horse figurine from the top of the bureau, stroking her fingertip across its glossy surface. She looked at Amber then drew a breath.

"Katie?"

"He saw me in it."

"Who saw you in what?"

"Hargrove. He saw me in the wedding dress."

Amber didn't exactly understand why that was a problem.

Katie set down the figurine, her words speeding up, hands clasping together. "After it was delivered, and I had it on and was prancing around my apartment, he knocked on the door. I didn't know it was him. And, well, when I opened it…" She stopped talking.

"That's when Hargrove saw you in the wedding dress?"

Katie nodded miserably.

Amber fought an urge to smile. "I don't think that's bad luck or anything."

"I'm not so sure."

"Seriously, Katie. I can imagine he was annoyed." Hargrove was nothing if not mired in propriety. "But we're selling the damn thing anyway."

Katie drew a deep breath and squared her shoulders. "Thing is, he really, uh, liked the dress."

"Well, at that price, he'd better have liked it."

"I mean, well…" Katie gazed down at her front, picking a dark speck from the terry-cloth pile of the robe. "He really liked *me* in it."

Amber blinked. "So?" It was probably a good fit. She and Katie were pretty close to the same size.

"And—" Katie buried her face in her hands "—turns out, he liked me out of it, too."

Amber was silent for a full ten seconds. "You're going to have to repeat that."

Katie spread her fingers, peeking out as if she was looking at a horror movie. "I am the *worst* friend *ever.*"

Amber gave her head a little shake. "What are you saying?"

Katie just stared at her.

"Are you saying you *slept* with Hargrove?" It wasn't possible. Nothing made less sense than that.

But Katie nodded. "It happened so fast. One minute he was staring at me. Then he was kissing me. Then the dress came off, and well, yeah, there might have been a bit of a tear around the buttonholes—"

Amber shook her head. "You're not making any sense."

"I am *so* sorry," Katie wailed, pressing a fist against her mouth. "You must hate me."

"No. No, it's not that."

"I had to come and tell you in person."

"I'm confused, not mad." Amber tried to make her point. "Hargrove doesn't get overcome with passion and tear off dresses." Not the Hargrove she knew.

Katie blinked like an owl.

"He's staid, proper, *controlled.*"

Katie blinked once more. A flush rose up from the base of her throat, coloring her face. "Actually…"

Amber rose from the bed. "Actually, what?"

"Sexually speaking, I wouldn't call him staid, and I definitely wouldn't call him proper."

"Are you telling me…?"

Katie gave a meaningful nod.

"You had wild, impulsive sex with Hargrove?"

Something deep and warm flared in Katie's eyes, and she nodded.

"And…it was…*good?*" Amber asked in disbelief.

"It was fantastic."

Amber tried to wrap her head around that. "But… What…" She gripped the bedpost to steady herself. "Sorry. We can't get technical about this." She paused. "Can we?"

Katie cocked her head. "I take it it wasn't always good for you?"

"It was, um…" How did she say this? "Kind of boring."

"No way. You mean he didn't—" Katie's blush deepened.

Amber was forced to stifle a laugh. "Whatever it is you're not saying, I'm pretty sure he didn't do it with me."

Katie fought a grin and lost. "So, you're not mad?"

Amber shook her head, sitting back down on the bed. "I broke up with him."

Katie crossed the room to sit beside her, relieved amusement coloring her tone. "You're probably not going to want the wedding dress back."

"Keep it. Maybe you should keep Hargrove, too. Think of them as a set."

"Maybe I will," Katie said softly.

Amber turned to gaze at her friend and saw the glow in Katie's eyes. She raised her brows in a question, and Katie nodded, wiping a single tear with the back of her hand.

Surprised, but not the least bit unhappy, Amber wrapped her arm around Katie's shoulders. "You do realize what this means, don't you?"

"What?"

"I get to wear the maid of honor's dress." Amber paused. "You know, I always liked that one better anyway."

"Take it," said Katie. "It's yours."

Amber drew a deep sigh. "Wow. Does Hargrove know?"

"That I slept with him?" There was a strengthening thread of laughter in Katie's voice.

"That you came here to confess."

Katie shook her head. "He thinks… Wait. I almost forgot." She bounced off the bed to her small suitcase. "I found something for you."

Hunting through her things, she extracted a manila envelope. "Pictures of Norman Stanton. And his brother, Frank. Also a sister and parents—the three of them died quite a few years back."

Amber accepted the envelope, her thoughts going to Royce. Now it was her turn to feel guilty.

"What?" Katie asked, gauging Amber's expression.

"There's something you don't know."

"About the investigation?"

Amber shook her head. "About me." She shut her eyes for a second. "Oh, hell. I'm sleeping with Royce."

Katie drew back. "Whoa. You cheated on Hargrove?"

"No." Amber swatted Katie with the envelope. "I did not cheat on Hargrove. I broke up with Hargrove. Lucky for you."

"True," Katie agreed. Then she sobered. "This cowboy dude? He rocks your world?"

"And how."

"So." Katie cocked her head toward the bedroom door. "What are you waiting for?"

"I didn't want to be rude."

"Unlike me who slept with your fiancé."

"Ex."

"Whatever. Go see your cowboy. I'll catch you at breakfast."

"You sure?"

"Of course I'm sure. *I* don't want to sleep with you."

Amber grinned, came to her feet and headed out the door.

On the way across the hall, she slit the envelope open, sliding out some eight-by-ten photos.

First one was labeled Norman. He had receding hair, dark, beady eyes and a little goatee. Yeah, she could see him as a blackmailer.

The next was Frank, an older picture. This was the guy who'd broken up Royce's family. He wasn't bad-looking, but not fantastic, either. He seemed a little on the thin side. But maybe that was a generational thing.

She flipped to the next picture, raising her hand to rap on Royce's door. But she froze, hand in midair, the picture of Frank and Norman's sister stopping her cold.

The young girl had a trophy in her hand and a broad smile on her face. Amber stared for a long minute, then slowly turned to the next picture. It was the parents, and the next one was a thirty-year-old family portrait. The final picture was another headshot of Norman.

Amber paged back to the picture of the sister for a final look. Then, stomach twisting around nothing, she rapped on Royce's bedroom door.

His voice was muffled and incomprehensible, but she opened the door anyway. He was lying in bed, a hardcover book in his hands, the bedside lamp glowing yellow against his natural wood walls.

"Hey." He smiled, letting the book fall to his lap.

"Hi." She clicked the door shut behind her.

"Something wrong?"

She nodded.

His smile immediately faded. "Katie?"

"Kind of." Amber moved across the room.

His eyes cooled. "News from…home?"

Amber sat down on the bed. "We have a problem."

He tossed the book aside. "You're reconciling with Hargrove."

"What? *No*. How could you say that?"

Royce didn't answer.

"This has nothing to do with Hargrove." She wanted to be annoyed with Royce for even thinking that it might have been Hargrove, but there wasn't time for that. Instead, she covered his hand, trying to prepare him. "I have pictures of the Stantons. And it's not what we think."

"What do we think?"

She slipped the pictures out of the envelope and spread them on the bed. "Look."

Royce clenched his jaw as he leafed through them. "I've seen Frank Stanton before. He lived on the ranch for a while. Worked with the horses. That's how they met."

"Look at the sister," Amber whispered.

Royce shifted his gaze. "She was into horses, too," he surmised. The trophy was obviously equestrian.

"Look at her chin," said Amber. "Her eyes, the hairline."

Royce glanced from the picture to Amber, brows furrowing.

"Stephanie, Royce."

"What about Stephanie?"

"Stephanie is the spitting image of..." Amber flipped the picture over to read the handwriting on the back. "Clara Stanton, Frank and Norman's sister."

"No." He glanced back down. "She doesn't look anything like..." Royce's breathing went deep.

"He's not blackmailing you over murder."

"Son of a bitch."

She didn't want to say it out loud.

"Son of a bitch!"

"Shh."

Royce turned to her with haunted eyes. "This can't be right."

There was nothing she could say to cushion the blow.

"It can't be real."

It was real all right. Stephanie was Frank Stanton's daughter.

"Who else knows?" he demanded.

"No one."

"Katie?"

Amber shook her head. "Not even Katie. I only figured it out in the hallway thirty seconds ago."

He glanced back down at the picture. "We can't tell Stephanie. It'll kill her. She was two years old when they died. She doesn't even know about the affair."

"I won't tell Stephanie." But Amber realized that meant paying off Norman again.

Royce rolled out of bed, pacing across the floor, photo still gripped in his hand. He was stark naked, but the fact didn't seem to register.

He strode past the bay window, raking a hand through his hair. "We…"

Then he turned at the wall, glanced at the picture and threw it down on a dresser. "I…"

He stopped dead, fisted both hands and glared at Amber. "There's got to be a way out."

"I'm sure there is," she agreed in the most soothing voice she could muster.

He crossed back over to the bed, sat down and uttered a crude cuss. "That bastard's got us by the balls."

Amber didn't know how to answer. It was true, but agreeing seemed counterproductive.

"We can't tell Stephanie," he reaffirmed.

Amber nodded.

Royce snagged his phone from the table. He punched a couple of numbers and put it to his ear.

"Who—" Amber stopped herself.

"Jared."

She knew Jared had been out of touch for several days now.

It appeared he still was.

Royce's voice was terse as he left the voice-mail message. "Jared. Royce. Call me now. Right now." He punched the off button then leaned back against the headboard.

She dared to reach out and touch his bare shoulder. It was hot, hard as a rock. "Anything I can do?"

"Short of fixing a deal with the Chinese, finding a sailboat in the middle of the South Pacific or giving Norman Stanton a fatal disease? Not really."

"Right." She slipped across the bed to sit close beside him, curling her arm around his tense back. "Moral support doesn't really cut it at the moment, does it?"

He wrapped one of his arms around her and then the other. Then he bent to kiss the top of her head. "Moral support is better than nothing."

She struggled to find a smile. "That's always been a dream of mine. To be better than nothing."

He gave her a gentle squeeze and whispered above her head. "Will you stay?"

She nodded against his neck, knowing she was falling fast and hard. His troubles were her troubles, and she'd be by his side just as long as he needed her.

In the morning, when Katie asked for a tour of Stephanie's jumping ranch, Royce resisted the temptation to tag along. Much as he'd love to spend the time with Amber, he was afraid he'd end up studying his sister's expressions, movements and mannerisms for traces of the man he'd hated for twenty long years.

She was still his baby sister. He loved her, and he'd move heaven and earth to protect her. But he needed some time to come to terms with the knowledge she was also Frank Stanton's daughter.

What the hell had his mother been thinking?

Had she known which man fathered Stephanie? What

was her plan? Was she going to take Stephanie with her and Stanton? Would she have destroyed that many lives for her own selfish happiness?

The knowledge crept like a cold snake into his belly.

He smacked open the front door, marching onto the porch to take a deep breath of fresh air. He didn't wish anybody dead, not even Frank Stanton. But he wasn't sorry his mother's plan had failed. He couldn't imagine his life without Stephanie.

An engine roared in the distance, dust wafting up at the crest of the drive. Royce squinted against the midmorning sunshine. He knew it was too early for Amber and Katie to return, but he couldn't help hoping.

Amber had been amazing last night. First she'd let him rail in anger. Then she'd offered practical advice. She seemed to have an uncanny knack for knowing when to stay quiet and when to talk. Finally, against all odds, she helped him find a touch of humor in the face of catastrophe.

Afterward, he'd stayed awake for hours, simply holding her in his arms, letting the feel of her body make his troubles seem less daunting.

It was a car that appeared over the rise. A dark sedan, dusty from the long road in, but unmistakably new, and undeniably expensive. The windows were tinted, and the driver moved tentatively around the potholes dotting dirt and sparse gravel.

Not a local, that was for sure.

Royce made his way down the front stairs, wondering if this could be the mysterious Alec Creighton, or perhaps someone from the Ryder Chicago office.

The car eased to a halt. The engine went silent. And the driver's door swung open wide.

Royce didn't recognize the tall man who emerged. He looked to be in his late thirties. He was clean shaven, his hair nearly black. He wore a Savile Row suit and an expensive pair of loafers. His white shirt was pressed, the patterned silk tie classic and understated.

To his credit, he didn't flinch at the dust, simply slammed the car door shut and gave Royce a genuine smile, stepping forward to offer his hand. "Hargrove Alston."

Royce faltered midreach but quickly recovered. "Royce Ryder."

He resisted the urge to grip too hard, though he squared his shoulders and straightened his spine, watching Hargrove's expression closely for signs that there was going to be a fight.

"Good to meet you," Hargrove offered. There wasn't a trace of anger or resentment in the man's eyes. Either he didn't know about Royce and Amber, or the man had one hell of a poker face.

"What brings you to Montana?" Royce opened.

A split second of annoyance narrowed the man's eyes. "For starters, I understand you're harboring my fiancée."

Royce resented the accusation. "It was at her request."

Hargrove's smile flattened. "I'm sure it was. I'd like to speak with her if you don't mind."

"She's not here." The statement was true enough. Amber might be close by, she wasn't specifically on the ranch this very moment.

Hargrove glanced to the house then back to Royce. "You have a reason to lie to me?"

"I have no reason to lie."

Hargrove regarded him with obvious impatience.

"I can try to pass along a message," Royce offered, folding his arms over his chest and planting his feet apart on the dusty drive.

"You do know who I am, right?"

"You said you were Hargrove Alston."

"I'm not accustomed to being stonewalled, Mr. Ryder."

"And I'm not accustomed to uninvited guests on my land, Mr. Alston."

Hargrove's expression went hard. "I know she's here."

"I told you she wasn't."

There was a pause while the entire ranch seemed to hold its breath.

"But you do know where she is."

Royce did. Since he preferred not to lie, he didn't answer.

Hargrove gave a cool, knowing smile. "She does bring out the protective instincts."

The assessment rang true. And it reminded Royce how well Hargrove knew Amber. She had been bringing out Royce's protective instincts from the moment they'd met.

He decided it was time to stop the pretense. "I assume you're here to drag her back to Chicago."

The shot of pain that flitted through Hargrove's eyes was quickly masked by anger. "I'm here to tell her she can't solve her problems by running away from them."

Guilt hit Royce square in the solar plexus. Amber

had, in fact, run away from Hargrove. And Royce had helped her.

His thoughts went to his father, and an unwelcome chill rippled up his spine. His mother had written a letter. Amber had settled for a text.

Not that Royce was anything like Frank Stanton. Looking back to his teenage memories, Frank had deliberately and methodically lured a woman away from her husband and children.

"Do you have any idea why she left?" he found himself asking.

"Only Amber knows the answer to that." Hargrove shook his head in disgust. "Forget that the wedding dress arrived from Paris this week, that the caterer's put the Kobe beef on hold, that the florist has a Holland order in limbo and that the press has been commenting on Amber's absence. We have fifty people arriving for the wedding shower on Saturday. Her mother's frantic with worry."

Royce swallowed, considering for the first time the destruction Amber had left in her wake.

Hargrove's dark eyes glittered. "I can't wait to sit her down and ask a few questions."

"Did you think about canceling everything?" Royce ventured. If it was him, and the bride went AWOL, as Amber had, Royce couldn't see himself waiting around.

"Are you married, Mr. Ryder?"

Royce shook his head.

"Ever been in love?"

"Nope."

"Well, once you get there, you'll find yourself making allowances for the most inappropriate behavior."

"So, you'd take her back?"

"You don't throw this away over some prewedding jitters. Our plans have been in the works for four years. Our relationship is built on mutual goals and respect. And the foundation of my entire campaign has been built around the fresh faces of Mr. and Mrs. Hargrove Alston. If we're lucky, she'll be pregnant by the primaries."

It sounded a little cold-blooded to Royce. But it also sounded as though Amber was fundamentally entwined in Hargrove's life. And he hadn't considered the situation from Hargrove's perspective.

Amber herself had admitted he was a decent guy. He wasn't malicious or abusive. He simply wasn't as exciting as she'd hoped.

Well, hell, honey, it had been four years. When you were in it for the long haul, the thrill of romance eventually turned into the routine of everyday life.

"There's no way you end something like this on a whim," Hargrove finished, and Royce couldn't deny the man's point.

Relationships took work. They took patience and commitment. They didn't need third party interference. An honorable man would have walked away the minute he saw her diamond ring.

And what the hell had Royce expected? Amber wouldn't stick with him any more than she'd stuck with Hargrove. In the end, he would have been left with nothing but a broken heart and the knowledge he'd destroyed another man's life.

Another engine sounded on the driveway. Before the blue pickup even crested the hill, Royce knew exactly who had arrived.

Ten

"**Y**ou *didn't,*" Amber rasped to Katie as the truck rocked to a stop behind Hargrove's car, and the dust cleared around them.

"I really didn't," Katie responded, her face pale.

"Did you talk to him last night?"

"Just about business."

"Did you tell him we were together?" Amber squinted at Hargrove, then at Royce, trying to interpret their posture.

Katie clutched the dashboard. "I hinted we were in Chicago."

"He knew I wasn't in Chicago. He must have tracked you here."

"Damn it," Katie cursed.

"You go talk to him," said Amber.

"No way."

"You're the one who slept with him. Maybe he's here for you."

Katie frantically shook her head. "Neither of us have even mentioned it. He's here for you."

"He doesn't want me."

But Hargrove's accusatory gaze was focused directly on Amber.

"I don't think he knows that," Katie offered.

This time Amber swore between clenched teeth. She grabbed the gearshift, setting up to pull it into Reverse. "I say we run for it."

"I don't think that's an option," Katie ventured, her gaze tracking Royce as he paced toward the truck.

He looked angry.

Had Hargrove been rude?

Royce reached for the handle and swung open her door. "There's somebody here to see you."

"I'm sorry, Royce. I didn't expect—"

"You knew he'd come," said Royce, hand gripping the top of the door frame. "*I* knew he'd come."

Amber had fervently hoped he wouldn't. She glanced at Katie, who sat completely still, eyes front. No help there. Finally, she took a breath and pulled the key from the ignition.

Royce stepped back out of the way, as Hargrove marched up.

"Montana?" Hargrove accused. "Honestly, Amber, could you make things any more difficult?"

Royce backed off farther, and she knew he was leaving.

"Royce, don't—"

But he shook his head, sliding his eyes meaningfully toward Hargrove.

And he was right. They might as well get this conversation over with.

"We need to talk," rasped Hargrove, moving in too close and pushing the truck door closed.

"There's not a lot left to say," she responded, pushing her windblown hair behind her ears and gathering her courage as Royce left.

It was hard for her to imagine what came after *you slept with the bridesmaid, and I fell for someone else.*

"Do you have any idea how much trouble you've caused?" Hargrove growled. "We've got a thousand people working on the wedding. Nobody knows whether to stop, go, or hold."

"I already told you. They can stop."

"You can't just shut this down on a dime, Amber. We had plans. There's the campaign, the press."

"I'm not marrying you to get good press, Hargrove."

He held up his hands in frustration. "This isn't a one-shot article, Amber. We're talking about my entire political career."

"Yours won't be the first high-profile wedding that was canceled."

"And do you *know* what happened to the others?"

"I don't care what happened to the others. I don't love you, Hargrove. And you don't love me."

"That's ridiculous."

"Then why did you sleep with Katie?"

His jaw went taut. "*That* was a mistake."

"Excuse me?" Katie squeaked from beyond the open window, reminding them both of her presence.

Hargrove's nostrils flared.

"A mistake?" Amber scoffed. "What? Did you trip and accidentally tear off the wedding dress?"

"I don't know what she told you."

"I'm right *here*," Katie pointed out, exiting the truck and slamming the passenger door for emphasis.

"She said you were wild with passion."

"That's ridiculous." But a flush rose up his neck.

"You never tore off *my* dress," said Amber.

"That was out of respect."

Amber shook her head at Hargrove. "It was out of disinterest. Admit it."

"I'm not here to fight with you."

"That's good," said Amber as she dared a glance to where Katie was glaring daggers at him. "Because I think I'd have to take a number."

Hargrove glanced at Katie. "Can you give us some privacy."

"No." She stood her ground.

"This isn't about you."

"The hell it isn't."

"*I'm* going to give *you two* some privacy," said Amber.

Hargrove quickly reached for her arm. "Amber—"

"It's over, Hargrove." She backed out of his reach. "I'm truly sorry about the press and the campaign, but I can't marry you."

"Amber!" He looked genuinely fearful. "You don't know what you're doing to me."

She shook her head. "You don't know what you're doing to yourself. Talk to Katie."

"This isn't about Katie."

"It should be." Amber backed up a few more steps. "Don't screw this up, Hargrove," she warned.

Then she turned away, scanning the yard and finding Royce in a round pen, doing groundwork with a black horse.

Heart still pounding, stomach still cramped, she made her way to the rail and leaned over to watch.

Royce shifted his arms, and the horse sped up. Then he slowed it down, turned it and had it trotting in the opposite direction. It was near poetry, and the tension leached out of her body.

Several minutes later, he approached the animal. He stroked its neck, clipping a lead rope to its bridle then tying it to a rail. He walked through the soft dirt toward Amber.

He braced his hands on the opposite side of the fence. "You here to say goodbye?"

She drew back in surprise. "No."

He nodded toward Hargrove. "He came a long way."

"I told you, I'm not marrying him."

"Why not?"

Amber peered at Royce in confusion. "What do you mean why not?" She leaned forward. "I've just spent the last week with you."

He shrugged. "That doesn't mean anything."

She opened her mouth, struggling to form words.

"I'm new, Amber." He stripped off a pair of leather gloves. "I seem interesting and exciting. You're on vacation, having a fling."

Amber's fingertips went to her temple. "A fling?"

He calmly tucked the gloves under his arm and adjusted his Stetson. "Hargrove is willing to take you back. You should seriously consider his offer."

Her frustration was turning to anger. "You said

anybody who told me that was short-sighted and stupid."

"Guess I was wrong."

She shook her head, but he stayed stubbornly silent.

She clenched her jaw, then enunciated her words slowly and carefully. "I do not love Hargrove."

"You don't know that for sure."

"I absolutely know that for sure. Because I love *you,* Royce."

The words went unanswered. But she wasn't sorry. This was no fling. He was falling for her, too. She'd bet her life on it.

No one had ever treated her the way Royce did. He was compassionate, attentive and so very sexy. And she was positive he didn't open up with many other people the way he'd opened up with her. He'd flat out told her nobody else knew about his father. And their lovemaking was off the charts.

He scoffed out a laugh. "You don't love me."

She smacked her hand on the rail in frustration. "What is the matter with you? Are you afraid of Hargrove?"

Royce's eyes glittered. "I'm not afraid of anybody."

"Well, I *know* you feel it, too."

He whipped off his hat, banging it on his thigh to release the dust. "If by *it,* you mean lust, then you're right."

"I don't mean lust."

"People don't fall in love in a week."

"People can fall in love in an hour."

"Not so it lasts." It was his turn to lean in. "It's lust, Amber. It's a fling. What you have with Hargrove is real, and you need to go back to him."

"Hargrove loves Katie."

Royce smacked his hat back on his head. "Then why's he here looking for you?"

"He doesn't know it yet." She realized that sounded lame, but it was completely true. Amber had very high hopes that Hargrove would wake up to the truth about Katie.

"Now you're grasping at straws. Go back to reality, Amber. Get married in that big cathedral and have beautiful babies for the campaign trail."

"Are you *listening* to yourself?" She gripped the rail. "You're willing to throw away everything that's between us?"

A part of her couldn't believe it. A part of her expected to wake up any second. But another brusque, insidious part of her realized she'd made a horrible mistake.

She might have fallen for Royce. But Royce hadn't fallen for her.

"You've spun a nice fantasy, here," he said. Then he nodded toward Hargrove's car. "But your reality is over there."

Her throat closed over, and she swallowed hard. "You're asking me to leave?"

His expression was unreadable. "I'm asking you to leave."

She gave a stiff nod, unable to speak. Royce didn't love her. He didn't want her. And she'd made a complete and total fool of herself.

Two days later, Amber alternated between misery and mortification. Royce might not have loved her, but her heart had fallen hard and fast for him.

It was easy to see what made him such a great pick-up artist. He must make every woman feel loved and cherished—at least temporarily. She wondered about the string of broken hearts he'd left behind.

Then she wondered who he'd be with next. But that thought hurt so much she banished it, blinking back the familiar sting in her eyes as she focused on her mother far across her family's great room.

The replacement-for-the-shower party was in full swing. But Amber didn't feel remotely like celebrating.

Maybe if Royce had simply sweet-talked her into bed, if they'd had fantastic sex, if he'd put her in a cab in the morning, maybe then she could have handled it. But he hadn't simply made love to her. He'd joked and laughed with her, shared his secrets with her, made her feel valuable, important, a part of his world.

"Amber?" Her mother, Reena, approached, concern in her expression.

Amber tried to smile at her mother. Her family had been told that she was the one to break it off with Hargrove. But nobody but Katie knew anything about Royce. Amber planned to keep it that way.

Reena's floor-length chiffon dress rustled to a halt. "Why aren't you visiting, sweetheart?"

"I'm a little tired."

"Are you sure that's all it is?"

"I'm sure." She mustered up a smile.

"That's the best you can do? You look like you're headed for the gallows."

Amber signed. "I'm really not in the mood for a party, Mom."

Reena moved in closer. "But I thought this was what you wanted."

"I didn't want a party."

"Well, you didn't want a shower, either. And the guests were already on their way."

Amber drew a shuddering breath, fighting the tears that were never far from the surface. Emotions alone shouldn't hurt this much. Still, a single teardrop escaped, trailing coolly down her cheek.

"Sweetheart," her mother entreated, drawing Amber close to her side. "Do you miss him so much?"

Amber startled in surprise. How had her mother guessed?

Reena cupped Amber's chin with gentle fingertips, peering deeply into her eyes. "Shall I give Hargrove a call for you? We might be able to talk him into—"

"She's not missing Hargrove," came Katie's voice as she swooped in to join them.

"Of course she is," said Reena. "Just look at her."

"I'm not missing Hargrove," Amber confirmed.

Katie gave Amber a level, challenging look. "She's missing Royce Ryder."

Amber sucked in a gasp.

"Who?" asked her mother, glancing from Amber to Katie and back again.

Katie gave Amber a helpless shrug. "What's the point in hiding it? It's obvious to anyone that you've had your heart broken."

"Who is Royce Ryder?"

"The man she met in Montana."

"I met him at Jared Ryder's wedding," Amber corrected. Where he'd picked her up in the bar for a quick fling. At least that's the way *he* remembered it.

Reena's jaw dropped a notch, and her hand went to her chest. "You were unfaithful to Hargrove?"

"I *wasn't* unfaithful to Hargrove." Frustration finally

gave Amber an emotion to replace despair. "In fact, Hargrove was unfaithful to me." She returned Katie's look. "With *Katie*."

Katie's face went pale, and Reena's jaw dropped another notch.

"They'd already split up," Katie hastened to assure Reena.

"That's true," Amber admitted. "Nobody was unfaithful to anybody."

Katie's voice went soft. "And she did fall in love with Royce."

Amber was too exhausted to deny it.

"Oh, sweetheart." Reena took Amber's hand. Her mother was a romantic to the core. "That terrible man broke your heart?"

"I broke my own heart." As she said the words out loud, Amber admitted to herself they were true. "We barely knew each other. And my expectations were... Well, he's just such an incredible man. You'd love him, Mom. You really would."

Reena's narrow arm curled around her shoulders. "I wouldn't like him at all. He broke my baby's heart."

Jared's familiar voice barked at Royce over the phone. "What the hell did you do?"

"Jared? Finally. Where are—"

"I need an explanation," Jared demanded.

Royce swiveled on the ranch house office chair, assuming Jared had been in contact with the Ryder office in Chicago. "I don't even know where to start."

"Start with how you broke Amber Hutton's heart and infuriated one of our most important clients."

Royce nearly dropped the phone. "Huh?"

"I've only been gone a week, and you screw up this badly."

"She *called* you?" Royce could hardly believe it. What was Amber doing running to Jared?

"David Hutton called me. He's threatening to cancel his lease. You are aware that he's our second-biggest client, right?"

"Don't patronize me."

"Then don't sleep with our clients' daughters."

What could Royce say to that? "It just…happened."

"Right. Well, un-happen it."

"I don't think that's physically possible."

"You know what I mean. Fix it."

"I can't fix it. She's engaged to someone else."

"What?" Jared's voice rose to a roar.

"Hargrove Alston."

"Then why did you sleep with her?"

Royce didn't have an answer for that. There wasn't an excuse in the world for what he'd done.

Jared was silent for a moment. "David thinks she's in love with *you?*"

"I'm not breaking up her engagement."

"Admirable," said Jared.

"Thank you."

"Could've thought of it *before* you slept with her."

Royce grunted.

"So, how're you going to fix it?"

"I'll talk to her."

"What are you going to say?"

"None of your business." Royce didn't have the first clue.

He'd been thinking about it for days, and had come to the conclusion that by bringing Amber to Montana, he'd turned a momentary hesitation into a life-altering event.

Whatever crazy fantasy Amber had spun around Royce wasn't real. She barely knew him. And he barely knew her. If relationships built on years didn't last, there was no hope at all for one that was built on a mere week.

"Make it my business."

"No."

Jared went silent on the other end of the line for a few beats. "You ever think…"

Royce drummed his fingers on the desktop.

"That maybe she's not…"

"Not what?" Did Jared have something intelligent to add here or not?

Jared drew a breath. "I mean, she might really be in love—"

"No!" Royce barked.

"Could happen."

"No, it could not."

"I'm a married man, Royce. And I'm telling you it could happen."

"You've been married a week. Talk to me in twenty years."

"You're going to make a woman wait twenty years?"

Royce felt his frustration level rise. "I'm going to make a woman wait until she's sure."

"How're you going to know that?"

"I'll just know."

"Like you do now?"

"What I know now is that she's taken, and she's

confused, and she has obligations that have nothing to do with me."

"She's not Mom," Jared said softly.

"Don't even go there."

"And you're not Frank Stanton."

"I'm hanging up now."

"Mom and Dad's relationship was demanding and complex. He worked too hard and she had stars in her eyes."

"And you don't think all marriages are demanding and complex?" That was what the long haul was all about. It meant sticking together through the rough times, knowing better times would come again. It didn't mean bailing the second life got a little humdrum.

"Did it ever occur to you that Dad might have shared the blame?"

"He didn't screw around on her," Royce practically shouted.

"Yeah, but he wasn't perfect. He had a temper. Hell, he shot a guy."

"The son of a bitch deserved it. I'd have shot him, too."

"You mean, if he slept with Amber?"

"Hell, yes."

"Gotcha."

Royce went silent, his jaw clamping down.

What had just happened? He was the illicit lover in this triangle, not the betrayed husband.

Jared's voice turned jovial. "Okay, fixing this is going to be way easier than I thought."

"Shut up."

Jared chuckled, and Royce bit down harder on his outrage. His brother could be positively infuriating.

"Let's move on to other problems," he ground out. He wasn't wrong, and Jared wasn't right. And it was definitely time to end this discussion.

His brother's tone changed. "What problems?"

"The China deal fell apart."

"Yeah," Jared sighed. "I was afraid of that."

"We're in a cash crunch because of it. I've got a guy taking a thorough look at our operations. I think we're going to have to streamline."

"He any good?"

"He came highly recommended." Royce drew a breath. "And, Jared. I fired Barry Brewster over China."

"Seriously?"

"He missed the deadline, blew the deal." He'd also insulted Amber, but Royce wasn't going anywhere near that conversation.

"There are a thousand ways to blow a deal with China."

"Yeah, well, he's gone."

"Okay. Your call. You need me to come back early?"

"Let's give it a few more days. There's one more thing…." Royce stopped himself. "You know what? It can wait."

If Jared learned about Norman Stanton and Stephanie, he'd be on the next plane back to the States.

But Royce had already made this month's blackmail payment. Norman Stanton had no idea they were on to him, and there was nothing Jared could do in the short term but worry.

"You sure?" asked Jared.

"I'm sure."

"And fix it with Amber, bro. She's not Mom. You're not Stanton. And everything's a leap of faith."

Amber and Katie stood side by side, gazing into the three-way mirror in Amber's bedroom.

"You don't think it would be too weird?" asked Katie as they admired their reflections in the sleek, sleeveless, pearl-adorned wedding gown and the dramatic oriental silk bridesmaid dress.

"Like I said before," Amber replied. "Think of them as a set. You know I like this one better." She turned and watched the orange, gold and midnight plum shimmer in the sunlight that streamed through her big windows.

"Did I miss something?" came a masculine voice from the doorway.

Amber and Katie whirled simultaneously to see all six foot two of Royce standing in the bedroom doorway. He was wearing a steel-gray business suit, a blue silk tie and a crisp white shirt. His face was freshly shaven, and his blue gaze hungry as he stared at her.

She swallowed the tears that were never far from the surface. His appearance was her dream come true. But she couldn't let herself hope.

"Where did you come from?" asked Katie.

Instead of answering, he strolled into the bedroom, gaze fixed on Amber as he grew closer. "Someone named Rosa said you were trying on your wedding gown."

Amber glanced down at the silk bridesmaid dress. "Something got lost in the translation."

"I was going to rip it from your body." The hunger in his eyes grew more intense.

Amber tipped her head, not sure what to think.

"I flew here at Mach 1," he told her. "All the way

over South Dakota, Iowa and Illinois, I told myself you belonged to Hargrove."

"I don't belong—"

"I told myself I'd reason with you, I'd make you understand you had an obligation to your fiancé, I'd explain again that nobody falls in love in a week, and what you thought you felt for me was an illusion."

He took her hands.

Katie took a few steps toward the door. "Uh, I'm... just going to..." She slipped outside and shut the door behind her.

"At least that's what I told myself," said Royce. "And then Rosa told me you were trying on your wedding dress. And I knew I had to stop you. I knew there was no way I could let you marry someone else."

"I'm not marrying—"

"I still find it impossible to believe a week is any kind of a foundation for a lifelong commitment. I looked up the mathematical odds on marital success. They're not good.

"But I do know I want you. And I know I'll shoot any guy who touches you. And I'm thinking maybe that's a sign that there's something to this."

Amber fought the smile that tightened her lips.

As declarations of love went, this left a whole lot to be desired. But this was Royce, and she knew his demons, and she knew just how difficult it was for him to even contemplate the possibility of happily ever after.

"I love you, Royce."

"You can't know—"

She put her fingertips over his lips. "I do know. And, guess what? I know you love me, too. And I know you're going to figure it out eventually. And if I have to wait a year, or ten or twenty, for you to decide we should stay together, that's fine with me."

His arm snaked around her waist, and he jerked her up tight against him. "I want to start staying together now."

"No problem." She smiled at him, trailing her palms over his chest, wrapping them loosely around his neck. "We'll hang out together while you give this love thing some serious thought."

He settled his other arm around her. "And by hanging out, I hope you mean living together, working together and sleeping together."

"I do," she told him.

"Good." He gave a decisive nod. "Then I'm thinking we'd better be married while we're hanging out. I don't want anyone else to try to steal you. Your father's already a little ticked off at my brother. And there's the whole propriety thing."

"You think it's logical for us to be married while we figure out if we're in love?"

"Completely logical," he said. "Especially if we want a few kids. You're not getting any younger—"

"Hey!" She smacked him on the shoulder.

"And who knows how long it'll take for us to be sure."

"Maybe twenty years?" she asked.

"Maybe even fifty." His expression sobered. His gaze caressed her as he slowly dipped his head. Then his warm, soft lips came down ever so gently onto hers, sealing their bargain.

"What do you say, Amber?" he whispered against her mouth. "Will you spend the next fifty or so years married to me, just in case I love you?"

She nodded, coming up on her bare toes to kiss him again, longer this time, more soundly.

"Yes, I will," she whispered. "Just in case."

His arms engulfed her, and he lifted her completely off the floor. His mouth slanted and his kiss deepened, and she clung to him, heart bursting with joy.

When he finally set her down, slowly sliding her along his body, his grin widened. "Well, what do you know."

"What?"

"I think it might be happening already."

She couldn't help but smile in return. "Imagine that."

He nodded. "And it's really easy. You know, I think I'm going to be very good at this."

"There's not a doubt in my mind."

His blue eyes stared down into hers. "I love you, Amber."

"I know you do, Royce."

"Forever."

"Absolutely."

"Who knew."

"I did."

"You did at that." And he bent to kiss her one more time.

Eleven

Royce couldn't think of a single thing he liked better than the sight of Amber at Hargrove's wedding—wearing the bridesmaid's dress. Katie had been radiant on her walk down the aisle. She'd beamed at Hargrove during the first dance, then laughed with him when they cut the cake. Royce caught the garter again, and this time he knew it was fate.

"She looked spectacular," said Amber as they walked, hand in hand, beneath the lighted tress of the waterfront patio. The reception was in full swing inside the restaurant, notables from both the business and political worlds dancing it up at the black-tie event.

"Your life's not going to be anything like hers," Royce observed, thinking about the reporters hovering in the parking lot.

"No, it's not." Amber grinned, turning to the rail to

stare out across the sparkling water. She took a sip of the bubbly liquid in her champagne flute.

Royce moved up behind her, tracing a fingertip along her bare shoulder. "Any regrets?"

"Yes," she sighed, and he felt a moment's pause.

But she covered his hand with her own, holding his touch against her skin. "I regret saying no to you in the hotel room earlier."

A surge of masculine pride swelled within him, and he leaned down to kiss her shoulder. "I told you so."

"You did."

"Weddings have a way of making women feel all romantic and mushy."

"It's true." She nodded, taking another drink.

"And all those romantic and mushy feelings have a way of turning to—"

"Lust?"

"Which could have been pre-empted," he whispered in her ear. "If you'd only let—"

"There you are, pumpkin," came David Hutton's hearty voice.

Royce immediately stepped back from Amber.

"Seems like I'm always finding you off in a corner with this Ryder fellow at wedding receptions."

"He does have a way of finding me," Amber joked, turning to face her father.

Royce was still a bit jumpy around the man. The two-carat solitaire on Amber's finger had mitigated some of the antagonism, but Royce wasn't sure David had forgiven him for breaking things off with Amber. He also wasn't sure that a jet pilot was an acceptable substitute for a senator as a son-in-law.

"You look amazing," David told his daughter, kissing her gently on the forehead.

"And you look handsome as always," Amber returned.

Royce held out his hand to shake, refusing to let David see anything but confidence. "Good to see you again, sir."

"I trust you'll be making your own wedding plans soon?" David asked him.

"Daddy," Amber admonished.

"Don't want to give the man time to change his mind again."

Royce held the handshake a little longer. "I'm not going to change my mind."

David harrumphed.

"I love your daughter, Mr. Hutton." Royce wrapped an arm around Amber's shoulder and drew her close. "I'm going to marry her and make her happy for the rest of her life."

"I would hope so. What with all the turmoil you caused."

"Daddy, I stopped loving Hargrove before Royce got anywhere near me."

Royce nearly choked on her choice of words. "The wedding will be soon," he assured David.

Amber glanced up at him in surprise. "Royce, we haven't—"

"Very soon." He gave Amber a meaningful squeeze.

David cracked a smile. "You keep my baby girl happy, son. And we'll get along just fine."

"I will," Royce assured the man.

"Call me David."

"Okay."

David winked at Amber and started away. "Don't stay out too late."

"I'm not coming home tonight," she warned him.

David turned his attention to Royce again. "Soon." He waggled a warning finger before he turned away.

"You want to head for Vegas tonight?" Royce asked Amber.

"Vegas is a terrible idea," said Stephanie.

Royce had left the jet under the command of his copilot and dropped into one of the seats in the main passenger cabin.

"Thank you," Amber said to Stephanie from the seat next to him.

They'd picked Stephanie up from a junior jumping show in Denver, and Jared and Melissa were hitching a ride from Chicago to the ranch for the last few days of their honeymoon.

"Well, she'd better come up with something," Royce told his sister. "I don't want her father gunning for me for the next year."

"He likes you," said Amber.

"No, he likes you. He tolerates me because you love me."

"I do love you," she confirmed, giving him a quick kiss on the cheek.

"And I love you," he automatically returned.

"Oh, gag me," Stephanie groaned.

"I thought you were a romantic," Melissa put in, moving up from the back of the cabin where she'd been sitting with Jared.

"I am a romantic. But, yuck, she's kissing my brother."

"Well, I totally get it," said Melissa.

"That's because you kiss my other brother."

Melissa got a gleam in her eyes. "You know what else I do to your other brother?"

Stephanie clapped her hands over her ears. "Pink fuzzy bunnies. Pink fuzzy bunnies."

"What the hell?" asked Royce.

"She's obliterating the image from her brain," Amber informed him.

Royce shook his head at the nonsense. "You," he said to Amber. "Come up with a wedding plan, or we *are* heading for Vegas." Then he exited his seat and moved to the back with his brother.

"Hey." Jared nodded to him, looking up from a table full of reports.

Royce sat down, lowering his voice. "You met with Alec Creighton?"

"I did."

"What did you think?"

Jared glanced to the front of the plane where the three women were chatting. "Seems like a good guy. Smart. On the ball."

"Did you talk to the VPs?"

Jared nodded. "They were shocked about Barry Brewster. It's got them looking over their shoulders. But I think in a good way."

"What about Konrad?"

Jared grinned. "Oh, he really hates you."

"Yeah. I kinda got that."

"He's demanded to deal directly with me from now on. Threatened to quit if you're involved in the construction division."

Royce clamped his jaw, while a burning anger roiled up in his stomach.

"Told him no," Jared said mildly. "Told him you

were taking over the construction division, and if he didn't like it, he should have his letter of resignation on your desk Monday morning."

Royce gaped at his brother. Konrad might be a jerk, but he was an incredibly valuable employee.

"Family is family," said Jared. "It's your company, too, and you did one hell of a job while I was away. Well, except for ticking off David Hutton."

"I'm working on that," said Royce, glancing to Amber, struck as always by how much he adored her.

"That's what counts, bro. Everybody's working hard at head office, looking to streamline, reallocating cash flow. We've survived trouble before."

Royce's attention shifted to his sister, and he lowered his voice. "After that, there's Stephanie."

"Yeah," Jared agreed. "We need to talk about that one."

"Does Melissa know?" asked Royce.

"That Frank Stanton is Stephanie's father?" Jared shook his head. "I'm keeping the club as small as possible for now."

Royce nodded. He was glad Amber already knew; he wouldn't want to have to make the choice to keep a secret from her.

"It was hard enough on me," said Jared. "Finding out what I did the way I did."

Royce nodded his agreement with that, too.

"Stephanie can *never* find out," Jared vowed.

"She won't." Royce had had most of his life to come to terms with his parents' secret, and it had still colored him in ways he hadn't even realized. It had almost cost him the love of his life.

He caught Amber's gaze.

She sobered at the sight of his expression, eyes

narrowing. Then she unobtrusively stood from her seat to move toward him.

He smiled and snagged her wrist, pulling her into his lap to wrap his arms around her.

"What's wrong?" she asked.

"Nothing."

She raised her brows to Jared.

Jared shook his head. "It's all good." His smile was back, and it was easy. "Except *you* can't seem to decide on a wedding."

Royce knew Amber wasn't buying their jovial mood, but she played along. "This is not a decision to take lightly. I'm only getting married once."

"In Vegas," said Royce.

Amber socked him in the arm.

"Tahiti, maybe." Melissa joined in. "On a beach, just family?"

"I vote for Tuscany," Stephanie called out. "Or Paris in the spring."

"She'll be pregnant by spring," said Royce, and Amber gave him a wide-eyed look of surprise.

"And we'd better damned well be married by then," he growled low.

"Babies?" she mused.

"I want babies," he confirmed.

"Good," she whispered and hugged him tightly, pressing her face into the crook of his neck, sighing in contentment, while the rest of his family joked about wedding plans.

HIS CONVENIENT VIRGIN BRIDE

BY
BARBARA DUNLOP

For my husband

One

Stephanie Ryder felt a telltale breeze puff against the skin of her chest. She glanced down to discover a button had popped on her stretch cotton blouse. The lace of her white bra and the curve of her breasts were clearly visible in the gap.

She crossed her arms to block the view, arching a mocking brow at the man silhouetted in the tack shed door. "You, Alec Creighton, are no gentleman."

Wearing a dress shirt, charcoal slacks and black loafers that were at odds with the rustic setting of a working horse stable, his gaze moved indolently from the wall of her forearm back to her eyes. "It took you twenty-four hours to figure that out?"

"Hardly," she scoffed. "But you keep reinforcing the impression."

He took a step forward. "Are you still mad?"

She swiftly redid the button and smoothed her blouse. "I was never mad."

Disappointed, yes. Wesley Harrison had been inches away from kissing her last night when Alec had interrupted them.

Wesley was a great guy. He was good-looking, smart and funny, and only a year younger than Stephanie. He'd been training at Ryder Equestrian Center since June, and he'd been flirting with her since they met.

"He's too young for you," said Alec.

"We're the same age." Practically.

The jut of Alec's brow questioned her honesty, but he didn't call her on it.

With his trim hair, square chin, slate-gray eyes and instructions to go through her equestrian business records with a fine-tooth comb, she should have found his presence intimidating. But Stephanie had spent most of her life handling two older brothers and countless unruly jumping horses. She wasn't about to get rattled by a hired corporate gun.

"Shouldn't you be working?" she asked.

"I need your help."

It was her turn to quirk a brow. Financial management was definitely not her forte. "With what?"

"Tour of the place."

She reached for the cordless phone on the workbench next to Rosie-Jo's tack. "No problem." She pressed speed dial three.

"What are you doing?"

The numbers bleeped swiftly in her ear. "Calling the stable manager."

Alec closed the distance between them. "Why?"

"To arrange for a tour."

He lifted the phone from her hand and pressed the off button. "You can give me a tour."

"I don't have time."

"You are still mad at me."

"No, I'm not."

She wasn't thrilled to have him here. Who would be? He'd be her houseguest for the next few days, and he was under orders from her brothers to streamline the family's corporation, Ryder International. She was a little worried, okay a *lot* worried, that he'd find fault with her management of the Ryder Equestrian Center.

Stephanie didn't skimp on quality, which meant she didn't skimp on cost, either. She was training world-class jumpers. And competing at that level demanded the best in everything; horses, feed, tack, trainers, vets and facilities. She was accustomed to defending her choices to her brothers. She wasn't crazy about defending them to a stranger.

"Are you proud of the place?" he asked.

"Absolutely," she answered without hesitation.

"Then show it to me," he challenged.

She hesitated, searching her mind for a dignified out.

He waited, the barest hint of a smirk twitching his mouth.

Finally she squared her shoulders, straightened to her full five foot five and met his gaze head-on. "You, Alec Creighton," she repeated, "are no gentleman."

The smile broadened, and he eased away, stepping to one side and gesturing to the tack shed door. "After you."

Stephanie waltzed past with her head held high.

It wasn't often a man talked her into a corner. She didn't much like it, but she might as well get this over with. She'd give him his tour, answer his questions, send him back to the ranch house office and get back to her regular routine.

She had an intermediate jumping class to teach this morning, her own training this afternoon and she needed to have the vet examine her Hanoverian mare, Rosie-Jo. Rosie had shied at a jump in practice yesterday, and Stephanie needed to make sure the horse didn't have any hidden injuries.

They headed down the dirt road alongside a hay barn, moving in the direction of the main stable and riding arena. She was tempted to lead him, expensive loafers and all, through the mud and manure around the treadmill pool.

It would serve him right.

"So, what exactly is it that you do?" she asked, resisting temptation.

"I troubleshoot."

She tipped her head to squint at his profile in the bright sunshine. Last night, she'd privately acknowledged that he was an incredibly good-looking man. He also carried himself well, squared shoulders, long stride, confident gait. "And what does that mean?"

"It means, that when people have trouble, they call me." He nodded to the low, white building, off by itself at the edge of Melody Meadow. "What's that?"

"Vet clinic. What kind of trouble?"

"Your kind of trouble. You have your own vet?"

"We do. You mean cash flow and too rapid corporate expansion?" That was the Ryder's corporate issue in a nutshell.

"Sometimes."

"And the other times?"

He didn't answer.

"Are you proud of it?" she goaded.

He gave a rueful smile as he shook his head.

She tilted her head to one side, going for ingenuous and hopeful. It usually worked on her brothers.

"Fine. Mostly I identify market sector expansion opportunities then analyze the financial and political framework of specific overseas economic regions."

She blinked.

"On behalf of privately held companies."

"The vet's name is Dr. Anderson," she offered.

Alec coughed out a chuckle.

"It sounds challenging," she admitted, turning her focus back to the road.

He shrugged. "You need to develop contacts. But once you learn the legislative framework of a given county, it applies to all sorts of situations."

"I suppose it would."

The breeze freshened, while horses whinnied as they passed a row of paddocks.

"Tell me about your job," Alec prompted.

"I teach horses to jump over things," she stated, not even attempting to dress it up.

There was a smile in his voice, but his tone was mild. "That sounds challenging."

"Not at all. You get them galloping really fast, point them at a jump and most of the time they figure it out."

"And if they don't?"

"Then they stop, and you keep going."

"Headfirst?" he asked.

"Headfirst."

"Ouch."

She subconsciously rubbed the tender spot on the outside of her right thigh where she'd landed hard coming off Rosie-Jo yesterday. "Ouch is right."

The road tapered to a trail as they came up to the six-foot, white rail fence that surrounded the main riding arena. Alec paused to watch a group of young jumping students and their trainer on the far side.

Stephanie stopped beside him.

"I didn't mean to sound pretentious," he offered.

"I know." She had no doubt that he was accurately describing his job. Her brothers wouldn't have hired him if he wasn't a skilled and experienced professional.

Alec hooked his hand over the top fence rail and pivoted to face her. "So, are you going to tell me what you really do?"

Stephanie debated another sarcastic answer, but there was a frankness in his slate eyes that stopped her.

"I train horses," she told him. "I buy horses, sell horses, board them, breed them and train them." She shifted her gaze to the activities of the junior class. "And I jump them."

"I hear you're headed for the Olympics." His gaze was intent on her expression.

"The Olympics are a long way off. I'm focused on the Brighton competition for the moment."

As she spoke, Wesley appeared from behind the bleachers, leading Rockfire into the arena for a round of jumps. Even from this distance, she could appreciate his fresh-faced profile, lanky body and sunshine-blond hair.

His lips had been *that* close to hers.

She wondered if he'd try again.

"What about management?"

Stephanie blinked her focus back to Alec. "Hmm?"

"Management. I assume you also manage the stable operations?"

She nodded, her gaze creeping sideways for another

glimpse of Wesley as he mounted his horse. This was his first year on the adult jumping circuit, and he was poised to make a splash. He grinned as he spoke to Tina, the junior class instructor, raking a spread hand through his full, tousled hair before putting on his helmet.

"Your boyfriend?" There was an edge to Alec's voice.

Stephanie turned guiltily, embarrassed that her attention had wandered.

Alec frowned at her, and the contrast between the two men was startling. One light, one dark. One carefree, one intense.

She shook her head. "No."

"Just a crush then?"

"It's nothing."

Alec dropped his hand from the rail as Wesley and Rockfire sailed over the first jump. "It's something."

She glared at him. "It's none of your business, is what it is."

He stared back for a silent minute.

His eyes were dark. His lips were parted. And a fissure of awareness suddenly sizzled through her.

No.

Not Alec.

It was Wesley she wanted.

"You're right," Alec conceded into the long silence. "It is none of my business."

None of his business, Alec reminded himself.

Back inside her house that evening, he found himself staring at Stephanie's likeness in a framed cover of *Equine Earth* magazine that was hanging on the living room wall. The fact that her silver-blue eyes seemed to hide enchanting secrets, that her unruly, auburn hair begged for a man's touch and that the light spray of freckles across her nose lent a sense of vulnerability to an otherwise flawless face, was none of his damn business.

The equestrian trophy in her hand, however, was his business, as was the fact that the Ryder name was sprayed across the cover of a nationally circulated magazine.

"That was at Carlton Shores," came her voice, its resonance sending a buzz of awareness up his spine.

"Two thousand and eight," she finished, coming up beside him.

He immediately caught the scent of fresh brewed coffee, and looked over to see two burgundy, stoneware mugs in her hands.

"You won," he stated unnecessarily.

She handed him one of the mugs. "You seem like a 'black' kind of a guy."

He couldn't help but smile at her accurate assessment. "Straight to the heart of the matter," he agreed.

"I take cream and sugar." She paused. "Dress it up as much as you can, I guess."

"Why does that not surprise me?"

She was in a business that was all pomp, glitz and show. Oh, she worked hard at it. There was no way she would have made it this far if she hadn't. But her division of Ryder International certainly wasn't the bedrock of the company's income stream.

He took a sip of the coffee. It was just the way he liked it, robust, without being sharp on the tongue.

She followed suit, and his gaze took a tour from her damp, freshly washed hair, pulled back in a sensible braid, to her clingy, white tank top and the pair of comfortable navy sweatpants that tapered down to incongruous lime-green socks.

"Nice," he observed.

She grinned, sticking a foot forward to show it off. "Royce brought them back for me from London. Apparently they're all the rage."

"You're making a fashion statement?"

"Everything else was in the laundry," she admitted. "I'm kind of lazy that way."

"Right. Lazy. That was the first thing I thought when I met you." It was nearly nine o'clock in the evening, and she'd only just stopped work to come in and shower for dinner.

"I'm going to assume that was sarcasm."

"The outfit works," he told her sincerely. Quite frankly, with her compact curves and toned muscles, she'd make a sackcloth work just fine.

She rolled her eyes. "Can I trust *anything* you say?"

Alec found himself captivated by the twinkle in her blue irises and the dark lips that contrasted with her creamy skin. She was charming and incredibly kissable, and he had to ruthlessly pull himself back to business.

"Are you aware that Ryder Equine Center has next to no income?" he asked, his blunt tone an admonishment of himself, not her.

When the sparkle vanished from her eyes, he told himself it was for the best.

"We make money," she asserted.

"A drop in the bucket compared to what you spend." Sure, they sold a few horses, boarded a few horses and took in tuition from students. And Stephanie had won some cash prizes in jumping competitions over the years. But the income didn't begin to compare with the massive expenditures necessary to run this kind of operation.

She gestured to the magazine cover. "And there's that."

"Nobody's disputing that you win."

"I mean the marketing value. That's the front cover of *Equine Earth*. It was a four page article. Check out the value of *that* on the open market."

"And how many potential lessees of Chicago office tower space do you suppose read *Equine Earth* magazine?"

"Plenty. Horse jumping is a sport of the rich and famous."

"Have you done an analysis of the demographics of the *Equine Earth* readership?"

Her lips compressed, and she set her coffee mug down on a table.

Alec regretted that she'd stopped smiling, but he forced himself to carry on. "I have no objection to assigning a value to marketing efforts—"

"Well thank you *so* much, oh guru of the framework for overseas economic regions."

"Hey, I'm trying to have a professional—"

The front door cracked sharply as it opened, and Alec instantly clamped his mouth shut. He turned to see Royce appear in the doorway, realizing how loud his and Stephanie's voices had risen.

But Royce's smile was easy, his nod friendly. Obviously they hadn't been overheard.

"Hey, Royce." Stephanie went to her brother, voice tone down, smile back in place.

Royce gave her a quick hug, then he turned his attention to Alec. "Am I interrupting something?"

"We were talking about my career," Stephanie chirped. "The publicity Ryder Equestrian Center brings to the entire corporation." She looked to Alec for confirmation.

He nodded, grateful she seemed willing to keep their spat private.

"Did you show him the video?" Royce asked.

Stephanie looked instantly wary. "He doesn't need to see the video."

Royce set her aside and strode into the room. "Sure he does. What better way to understand your career. Got any popcorn?"

"We haven't had dinner yet. I'm not—"

"Then let's grill some burgers." Royce pushed up the sleeves of his cotton, Western shirt. "I could use a burger. How about you, Alec?"

"Sure. Burgers sound good." So did watching videos of Stephanie, especially since she seemed hesitant. Did she have something to hide?

"Well, I'm not sticking around for this," Stephanie warned.

"Aren't you hungry?" asked Royce.

She stuck her freckled nose in the air. "I'll get something at the cookhouse."

"Suit yourself," said Royce, and Alec caught the faintest glimpse of satisfaction on the man's face.

What was going on here?

Stephanie stuffed her feet into a pair of worn leather boots, shrugged into a chunky gray sweater and stomped out the door.

"I thought she'd never leave," said Royce.

Alec peered at the man. "What's going on?"

Royce turned down the short passage to the kitchen. "We're grilling burgers and watching family videos."

Twenty minutes later, Alec bit into a juicy, flavorful burger. He had to admit, Royce really knew his way around an outdoor grill. Alec was starving, and the burger was fabulous, slathered in fried onions, topped with a thick slice of garden fresh tomato, and encased in what had to be a homemade bun.

Beside him in the opposite armchair, Royce clicked the remote control on the television. "If anyone asks," he said, settling down to his own dinner. "We were simply eating burgers and watching home videos."

Chewing and swallowing, Alec glanced from their plates to the television and back again. "No problem. I've got your back."

Royce nodded.

They made their way through their meals as a young, red-haired Stephanie bounced over foot high jumps on a white pony. Her small hands were tight on the reins, her helmet was slightly askew, and her face was screwed up in determination as she cleared the rails.

Alec couldn't help but smile, and he wondered why Stephanie objected to him watching. She was adorable.

In his short time he'd spent down at the main house on the Ryder Ranch with Royce and his fiancée, Amber, Alec definitely got the sense that both Royce and Stephanie's oldest brother Jared were in the habit of indulging her. Looking at this video, and knowing the age difference between Stephanie and her two brothers, it was easy to see how that had happened.

Turning toward a crisscrossed jump, the pony gathered itself. Stephanie stood in the stirrups, leaning across its neck. The animal's front legs lifted off the ground, back feet kicking out. The pair sailed over the white painted rails, jolting to the dirt on the other side.

The horse came to a halt, but Stephanie kept going, flying over its head, arms flailing as she catapulted forward, thudding into the dirt. Luckily the horse veered to one side, stepping neatly around her little body.

Jared and Royce both ran into the frame. The two teenagers gingerly turned their sister over, talking to her—though Alec couldn't make out the words—brushing the dirt from her little face.

She sat up. Then she nodded, bracing herself on Jared's shoulder and coming to her feet.

Her brothers kept talking, but she shook her head, walking determinedly toward the pony, taking the reins, and circling around to mount. She was too short to put her foot in the stirrup, so Royce gave her a leg up.

Jared kept arguing, looking none too happy. But Stephanie got her way. She turned the horse, heading to the end of the arena. The camera followed her as she restarted the course.

Alec shook his head, his feelings a cross between admiration and amusement.

Suddenly Royce set his plate aside and lifted the remote control, muting the sound.

Alec turned his attention.

"There's something you need to know." Though Royce's tone was even, his expression was narrowed and guarded.

Alec arched a brow.

"This needs to be kept in the strictest confidence," Royce warned.

"Everything you tell me is kept in the strictest confidence." It was a hallmark of Alec's business.

Royce nodded sharply.

Alec waited, his curiosity growing.

"Right," said Royce, fingers drumming against the

leather arm of the chair. He drew a breath. "Here it is then. We're being blackmailed." He paused. "It's Stephanie."

"What did she do?" Dope a horse? Fix a competition?

Royce scowled. "She didn't *do* anything. She's the one in the dark, and we're keeping it that way."

Right. Stupid conclusion. Alec tried another tactic. "Who's blackmailing you?"

"I'd rather not say."

"Okay…" Alec wasn't sure where to go with that.

"It's the biggest drain on the cattle ranch's account."

At least that explained why Amber thought Alec ought to know.

"How much are we talking about?" he asked.

"A hundred thousand a month."

"A *month?*"

Royce's expression was grim as he nodded.

Alec straightened in his armchair. "How long has this been going on?"

"At least a decade."

"*Excuse* me?"

"I know."

"You've spent *twelve million dollars* keeping a secret from Stephanie?"

Royce rocked to his feet, shoulders square, hands balled.

"Must be one hell of a secret."

Royce twisted round to glower at Alec.

"Sorry. None of my business," said Alec.

Still, he couldn't help sifting through the possibilities in his mind. Was there a shady business deal in their past? Did the family fortune originate from an unsavory source? Gambling? Bootlegging?

"You won't figure it out," said Royce.

"I might."

"Not this. And I don't want you snooping around."

"I won't snoop," Alec agreed. He'd respect his client's wishes. "But I might think."

Royce gazed at the silent screen where an elevenish Stephanie was taking yet another spill. "Suppose you can't stop a man from thinking."

"No, you can't."

"Aw, hell." Royce heaved a sigh and sat back down.

Alec gave him a moment. "How bad can it be?"

Royce scoffed out a harsh laugh. "My father was a murderer and my mother was adulterous." He paused. "We're being blackmailed by her lover's brother. The lover was also the murder victim." Another pause, and Royce's voice went lower. "*That's* how bad it can be."

Alec's brain filled in the blank. "And Stephanie is your half sister."

Royce drew back sharply, his expression confirming the truth.

Alec shrugged. "That's the only possibility worth twelve million dollars."

"She's *never* going to know."

"You can't keep paying him forever."

"Oh, yes, we can." Royce grasped the back of his neck. "My grandfather paid until he died. Then McQuestin paid. I took over a couple months ago."

Though it went beyond the bounds of his contract, Alec felt an obligation to be honest. "What are you going to do when he ups his price?"

It was obvious from Royce's expression that he hadn't considered that possibility.

"You'll eventually have to tell her, Royce."

Royce shook his head. "Not if we stop him."

"And how are you planning to accomplish that?"

"I don't know." Royce paused. "Got any ideas?"

Two

Last night's cookhouse burger hadn't measured up to Royce's talents, but it had filled Stephanie's hunger gap. And at least she'd avoided one more screening of *Stephanie Hits the Dirt Across America*.

It was one thing to show that bloopers reel to friends and family, but to strangers? Business associates? She was busy trying to get Alec to take her seriously, and Royce was making her look like a klutz.

Nice guy her brother.

She opened the wooden gate to Rosie-Jo's stall in the center section of the main horse barn and led the mare inside. The vet had given the horse a clean bill of health, and they'd had a great practice session this morning. Rosie had eagerly sailed over every jump.

Stephanie peeled off her leather gloves, removed Rosie's bridle and unclipped the lead rope, reaching through the gate to coil it on the hook outside the stall. She selected a mud brush from the tack box and stroked it over Rosie's withers and barrel, removing the lingering dirt and sweat from the mare's dapple gray coat.

"How'd it go?" Wesley's voice carried through the cavernous barn. His boot heels echoed as he crossed from Rockfire's stall to Rosie-Jo's. He tipped back his Stetson and rested his arms on the top rail of the gate.

"Good," Stephanie answered, continuing the brush strokes.

Though she didn't look up, a shimmer of anticipation tightened her stomach. The barn was mostly empty, the grooms outside with other horses and students. She hadn't talked to Wesley since their aborted kiss two days ago. If he wanted to try again, this would be the opportunity.

"Hesitation's gone," she added. "You tacking up?"

Wesley nodded. "Rockfire's ready to go. Tina has them changing up the jump pattern for us."

Stephanie gave Rosie-Jo's coat a final stroke. Normally she'd do a more thorough job, but she could always come back later. For now, she wanted to give Wesley another chance. Meet him halfway, as it were.

She replaced the brush, dusted her hands off on the back of her blue jeans and started across the stall to where he was leaning over the rail. Suddenly shy, she found she couldn't meet his eyes. Was she being too blatant, too obvious? Should she make it a little harder for him to make his move?

It wasn't like she was experienced at this. Ryder Ranch was a long way off the beaten track. She'd never had a serious romantic relationship, and it had been months—she didn't want to count how many—since she'd even had a date.

She came to a stop, the slated gate a barrier between them. When she dared look at his face, his lips were parted. There was an anticipatory gleam in his blue eyes. And his head began to tilt to one side.

Should she lean in or let him take the lead?

"Am I interrupting anything?" It was Alec's voice all over again, and his footfalls rapped along the corridor floor.

Wesley's hands squeezed down on the gate rail, frustration replacing the anticipation in his eyes.

"Is this some kind of a joke?" he rasped for Stephanie's ears only.

She didn't know what to say. Alec seemed to have a knack for bad timing.

"I'm sorry," she whispered to Wesley.

"Not as sorry as I am."

She turned to face Alec. "Can I *help* you?"

"I hope so." He stopped. After a silent beat, he glanced meaningfully at Wesley.

Wesley glared at him for a moment then smacked his hand down on the rail. "Time for practice," he declared and turned on his heel to lead Rockfire from his stall.

As she watched the pair leave, disappointment clunked like a horseshoe to the bottom of Stephanie's stomach.

"What is it now?" she hissed at Alec, popping the latch and exiting the stall. After securing it behind her, she set off after Wesley.

"Places to go?" asked Alec, falling into step.

"Things to do," she responded, with a toss of her hair. She was going to watch Wesley's practice session. It was part of her job as his coach. Plus, she'd be there when he finished. And by then, Alec should be long gone.

"I'm trying to help you, you know."

"I can tell."

"Is your sex life more important than your company?"

Stephanie increased her pace, stomping forward, ignoring Alec's question.

Sex life.

Ha! She couldn't even get a kiss.

She passed through the open barn doorway, squinting into the bright sunshine, focusing on Wesley who was across the ranch road, mounting Rockfire.

Too late, she heard the roar of the pickup engine, then the sickening grind of tires sliding on gravel.

She had a fleeting glimpse of Amber's horrified face at the wheel before a strong arm clamped around Stephanie's waist and snatched her out of harm's way.

Alec whirled them both, sheltering Stephanie against the barn wall, his body pressed protectively against hers as the truck slid sideways, fishtailing out of control, roaring past to miss them by inches.

"You okay?" his voice rasped through the billowing dust.

She told herself to nod, but her brain was slow in interpreting the signal.

"You okay?" he tried again, louder.

This time, Stephanie managed a nod.

"Stay here," he commanded.

And suddenly, he was gone. Without Alec's physical support, her knees nearly gave way. She grabbed at the wall, mustering her balance, blinking the blur from her eyes while the world moved in slow motion.

As she turned, she took in two ranch hands across the road. Their eyes were wide, mouths gaping. Wesley struggled to control Rockfire, turning the big horse in dust-cloud circles.

Stephanie followed the direction of the hands' attention. A roar filled her ears as Amber's blue truck keeled up on the left wheels.

Alec was rushing toward it

Stephanie tried to scream. She tried to run. But her voice clogged down in her chest, and her legs felt like lead weights.

Then the truck overbalanced, crashing down on the driver's door, spinning in a horrible, grinding circle until it smacked up against an oak tree.

The world zapped back to normal speed. Amongst the cacophony of shouts and motion, Alec skidded to a stop. He peered through the windshield for a split second, then he clambered his way up to the passenger door, high in the air.

He wrenched it open, and Stephanie's body came back to life. She half ran, half staggered down the road, Amber's name pulsing over and over through her brain.

Alec swiftly lowered himself into the truck.

Stephanie grew closer, praying Amber was all right.

Suddenly Alec's sole cracked against the inside of the windshield, popping it out.

"Bring a truck," he shouted, and two of the ranch hands took off running.

Stephanie made it to the scene to see blood dripping down Amber's forehead. The realization that this was all her fault, made her stagger.

Alec met her eyes. "She's okay," he told her, his voice steady and reassuring. "Call Royce. But tell him she's okay."

Stephanie saw that Amber's eyes were open.

She looked dazed, but when Alec spoke to her, Amber answered back.

His hands moved methodically over her body, arms, legs, neck and head.

But then Stephanie saw it.

"Smoke," she tried to shout, but her dry throat wouldn't cooperate.

Alec saw it, too.

People ran for fire extinguishers, while Alec fumbled with Amber's seat belt.

While he worked, he spoke calmly and firmly.

Stephanie couldn't hear the words, but Amber nodded and swallowed. She wrapped her arms around Alec's neck, as the first flames snaked out from under the hood.

He spoke to Amber again, and she closed her eyes, burying her face against Alec's neck. His arms tightened around her, and he slowly, gently eased her through the opening left by the windshield.

Stephanie held her breath, her glance going from the growing flames, to Amber and back again.

Wesley appeared by her side. "You okay?"

The question annoyed her. "I'm fine." It was Amber who was in trouble. And Alec, who might get hurt or worse trying to save her.

The flame leaped higher.

Alec's foot touched the ground outside the truck.

He gripped Amber close to his chest, rising to rush away.

"Get back!" he shouted to the growing crowd, just as the hood blew open, missing the tree trunk and cracking against the roof of the cab.

He staggered forward, but stayed upright and didn't lose his grip on Amber.

Three hands arrived with fire extinguishers, aiming them at the engulfed truck.

Stephanie backed away from the heat. Remembering the cell phone in her hand, she quickly dialed Royce's number.

Another pickup pulled up, and Alec lay Amber carefully across the bench seat.

"Don't try to move," he warned her.

"Hello?" Royce's voice came into Stephanie's phone.

"Royce?" Her voice shook.

"Stephanie?"

She didn't know what to say.

Alec scooped the phone. "Alec here." He took a breath. "There's been an accident. Amber's fine." A pause. "No. No one else was in the truck." He glanced at Stephanie, then down at Amber. "She's conscious."

He moved the phone away from his mouth. "Can you talk to Royce?"

Amber nodded, so Alec handed her the phone. Then he motioned to everyone else to back off. They obeyed, with the exception of Wesley who still hovered next to Stephanie.

When Amber put the phone to her ear and listened, tears welled up in her eyes. Stephanie instinctively moved in to comfort her, but Alec stopped her with his arm.

"Don't touch her," he whispered, keeping his arm braced around Stephanie's waist.

He reached into his pocket, retrieving his own cell phone.

Stephanie looked at him with a question.

"Medical chopper," he said in a low voice, turning away from Amber to speak to emergency services.

Stephanie's attention immediately returned to Amber. Blood was still oozing from the cut on her forehead, and there was a wicked bruise forming on her right shoulder. Her blouse was torn, her knuckles scraped.

Was she really okay? Had Alec lied to Royce? And what did Alec know anyway? He wasn't a doctor.

Okay, so he knew enough to pull Amber from a burning truck.

That was something.

That was huge.

While Stephanie, Stephanie had been stupid enough to march out in front of Amber and cause all this.

Her chest tightened with pain, and a sob escaped from her throat.

Alec turned back. His arm moved from her waist to her shoulders, and he gave her a squeeze. "It's not your fault," he rumbled in her ear.

But his words didn't help.

"Listen to me, Stephanie." He kept his voice low. "Amber is fine. The chopper will be here in fifteen minutes. But it's just a precaution."

"You're not a doctor," she snarled.

"No, I'm not."

"I'm sorry." Stephanie shook her head. "You pulled her out. She could have—"

"Stop."

Amber let the cell phone drop to her chest. "Royce is on his way." Her voice was weak, but just hearing it made Stephanie feel a little better.

"The medical chopper's going to beat him here," Alec told Amber, lifting the phone and gently smoothing her hair away from the wound.

"Want to bet?" Amber smiled, and Stephanie could have wept with joy.

Somebody had located a first aid kit, and Alec gently

cleaned the blood from around Amber's head wound and placed a square of gauze to stop the bleeding.

"Are you okay?" Stephanie dared to ask her.

"Did I hit you?" Amber asked back with a worried frown. "Are you hurt?"

Stephanie quickly shook her head. "No. No. Not at all. I'm perfectly fine. Just worried about you."

"I'm a little stiff," said Amber. She wiggled her fingers and moved her feet. "But everything's still working."

Stephanie mustered a watery smile.

Amber's eyes cut away to focus over Stephanie's shoulder. "I guess that's it for the truck, though."

"It was pretty spectacular," Wesley put in.

Alec frowned at him. "A small fire can do a lot of damage."

Amber looked back at Alec. "Thank you," she told him in a shaky voice.

"I'm just glad you're all right." His smile was so gentle that something warm bloomed to life inside Stephanie.

Amber was going to be okay, and it was because of Alec.

Royce's truck appeared over the rise, tires barely touching down between high spots on the dirt road. A cloud of dust rolled out behind him.

And then he was sliding to a stop at the scene. He burst out of the driver's door, hitting the ground running as the *thump, thump, thump* of the chopper blades sounded in the sky.

Alec watched the towing company employees winch the wrecked pickup onto the flatbed truck. He'd talked to Jared in Chicago, and they agreed to have it removed as quickly as possible. Royce had called to report that Amber would be released from the hospital in a couple of hours. Alec was relieved to learn that Amber's recovery would be short.

She had a few stitches in her forehead, but there were no worries of a concussion. Other than that, she'd only suffered scrapes and bruises. Royce was getting them a hotel room in Missoula, and they were coming home in the morning.

Steel clanked and cables groaned as the half-burned hulk inched its way up the ramps. Several of the ranch employees stood to watch. But it was nearing eight o'clock, and most had returned to their jobs or their homes once they heard the good news about Amber.

Stephanie appeared beside Alec, tucking her cell phone into her pocket and pushing her messy hair back from her forehead. "Amber's making jokes."

Alec was also relieved to see Stephanie getting back to normal. She hadn't been injured, but she'd seemed almost in shock there for a few minutes.

"And how are you doing?" he asked.

"Just a little worn-out." She stilled to gaze at the flatbed that was silhouetted by the final vestiges of a sunset.

"You sure?" he probed.

"I'm sure," she confirmed, voice sounding stronger.

"Good for you."

One of the towing operators was tying down the pickup, while the other started up the engine of the flatbed. Work here was done.

He turned, then waited for Amber to start back to the house with him. Lights had come on in the staff cottages. The scent of freshly cut hay hung in the cooling air. And the diesel truck rumbled away down the ranch road, toward the long hill that wound past the main ranch house to the highway.

"I was looking for a media file," said Alec as the engine faded and the crickets took over.

"A what?"

"That's why I came to find you earlier. Do you have documentation of your jumping career publicity?"

She looked confused.

"I'll need the background information to calculate the dollar value of the exposure," he elaborated.

"I don't understand."

"What's not to understand?"

"You can switch gears that fast?"

It was his turn to draw back in confusion.

"You just risked death to save Amber."

"Risked death?" he chuckled, but then he realized she was serious.

"How did you know how to do that?" she asked.

"It's not exactly rocket science."

She peered at him through the dim glow of the yard lights. "Were you with the fire department or search and rescue?"

"No."

"You pull a woman from a burning truck and carry her to safety only seconds before it explodes. How does that not rattle you?"

"That's the Hollywood version." He steered their course around the corner of the big barn, linking up with the path to her front porch. "I kicked out a windshield. I didn't defuse a nuclear weapon."

"You risked life and limb."

"You know you tend to overdramatize, right?" He did

what needed to be done, and only because he was the closest guy to the wreck.

And, quite frankly, it wasn't fear of the fire and for Amber's safety that had stuck with him. The worst moment had been that split second before he'd pulled Stephanie out of the way of the truck.

"You saved a woman's life, and just like that." She snapped her fingers. "You're working on some mundane report."

"Correction. I'm *trying* to work on a mundane report. Do you maybe have a list or something?"

They'd arrived at the house and mounted the steps, heading in through the door.

Stephanie kicked off her muddy boots, socks and all. "I have a few scrapbooks down at the main house."

"Can we pick them up tomorrow?"

"Sure." She pulled the elastic from her ponytail and ran her fingers through her messy hair. The action highlighted its auburn shimmer, while the pose showed off the compact curves of her body.

It was a struggle not to stare. So, he moved further into the house to where his work was spread out on the dining room table. He dropped into a padded chair, reminding himself of where he'd left off.

"Alec?" she called, coming around the corner.

"Yes?"

When she didn't answer, he couldn't help but turn to look.

She'd stripped off her cotton work shirt and now wore a thin, washed-out T-shirt and a pair of soft blue jeans that hugged her curves. The jeans rode low, revealing a strip of soft, pale skin above the waistband. Her bare feet struck him as incredibly sexy as she padded across the hardwood floor.

"What is it about your past life that led you to rush into a burning vehicle while everybody else stood there and stared in horror?"

"Let it go."

She might look soft and sweet, but the woman had the tenacity of a pit bull.

"I'm curious," she told him.

"And I have work to do."

"It's not a normal thing, you know."

"It's a perfectly normal thing. A dozen guys out there would have done the same."

Stephanie shook her head.

Alec rolled his eyes and turned back to his spreadsheet.

"Let me guess," she carried on. "You were in the marines."

"No."

"The army?"

"Go away."

That surprised a laugh out of her. "It's my house."

"It's my job."

She pondered for a minute. "There's an easy way to get rid of me."

He slid a quizzical gaze her way.

"Answer the question."

He wasn't exactly sure what to say, but if it would get her out of the room and off his wayward mind, he was game to give it a try. "I was in the Boy Scouts."

She frowned. "That's not it."

"Visited dangerous cities?"

A shake of her head.

"Had the occasional bar fight? Never started one," he felt compelled to point out.

She braced her hands on the back of a chair and pinned him with a pointed stare.

"You're not leaving," he noted.

"That's all you've got?" she demanded.

"What more do you want?"

"I don't know. Something out of the ordinary. Something that taught you how to deal with danger."

"I grew up on the south side of Chicago."

"Seriously?"

"No, I'm making that part up."

"Was it in a dangerous part of town?" she asked, leaning forward, looking intrigued.

Alec liked the way her pose tightened her T-shirt against her body.

"Relatively," he told her. Crime had been high. Fights had been frequent. He'd learned how to read people and avoid situations, and how to handle himself when things went bad.

Her voice went low and intimate, as if somebody might overhear them. "Were you like a gang member? In rumbles and things?"

He reflexively leaned closer, lowering his own voice. "No gang. I was raised by a single father, a Chicago cop with very high standards of behavior." Not that Alec had ever been tempted to join a gang. But his father most certainly would have stopped him cold.

"Your father's a police officer?"

Alec sat back. "Not anymore. He's owner and CEO of Creighton Waverley Security."

"So, you work for him?"

Alec shook his head. Work for his old man? Not in

this lifetime. "I do occasional contract work for his company."

"Like this?"

"This is a private arrangement between me and Ryder International."

"There's an edge to your voice."

"That's because you're still asking questions."

"Are you mad at me or your father?"

"Do you ever stop?"

"Do you?"

"I'm paid to ask questions."

"Yeah?" The smile she gave him sent a rush of desire to every pulse point in his body. "I do it recreationally."

They stared at each other in thickening silence, and he could hear the alarm bells warming up deep in the base of his brain. Both Royce and Jared were protective of their sister, and they would not take kindly to Alec making a pass at her.

Not that Alec would ever make a pass at a client.

He never had.

Of course, he'd never wanted to before, either.

So, maybe it wasn't his high ethical standards that kept him on the straight and narrow. Maybe he'd simply never been presented with a client who had creamy skin, deep, cherry lips, perfectly rounded breasts and the wink of a navel that made him want to wrap his arms around her waist, drag her forward and press wet kisses against her stomach until she moaned in surrender.

A sudden rap on the door jolted him back to reality.

It couldn't be Royce. He was still at the hospital. And Jared was in Chicago.

Stephanie hesitated but then turned from Alec and

moved into the alcove off the living room to open the front door.

"I just wanted to make sure you were okay." Wesley's eager voice carried clearly across the room.

Of course.

The soon-to-be boyfriend.

Wasn't that a nice dose of reality.

Three

Brushing her teeth in the en suite bathroom, Stephanie couldn't help but replay Alec's rescue over and over in her mind.

In the moments after the crash, she'd been preoccupied with Amber's safety. And then the helicopter arrived, and the tow truck, and the staff were all anxious and needing to talk. And later she'd been preoccupied with Alec.

But now she knew that Amber was safe. She was alone with her thoughts, and she found herself focusing on those seconds in Alec's arms.

He was surprisingly strong, amazingly fast and obviously agile. His strength had given her a sense of security. Then later, while they'd argued, she'd felt a flare of something that was a whole lot more than security.

She couldn't exactly put a name to it. But it was strong

enough, that when Wesley had showed up, he'd seemed bland by comparison.

She spat the toothpaste into the sink and rinsed her mouth. As she replaced the toothbrush in the charger, she paused, gazing at herself in the mirror.

Attraction, she admitted, glancing at the door that led from the opposite side of the bathroom into the guest room where Alec was sleeping.

She was attracted to him.

She wanted it to be Wesley, but it was Alec.

She gritted her clean teeth, dragged a comb through her curls, braided them tight and snagged an elastic before heading back into her bedroom.

The window was wide, a cool breeze sliding down from the craggy peaks, while the horses blew and snorted in the fields below. Thoughts still on Alec, roving further into forbidden territory, she dropped her robe onto a chair and climbed between the crisp sheets. Her laundry was still behind, and she was prickly warm, so she'd gone with panties and an old tank top, soft as butter against her skin.

She closed her eyes, but nothing happened.

Well, nothing except an image of Alec appearing behind her eyelids.

When he first showed up, he was just a good-looking city guy. There were plenty of those in magazines and on television. And she'd never been particularly attracted to men based on looks alone.

But now she knew his business clothes masked solid muscles. Worse, she'd learned he had a quick mind and a whole lot of courage. And he'd likely saved her life—which was probably a classic aphrodisiac.

Whatever the cause, she could tell she wasn't getting to sleep anytime soon.

She tossed off her comforter, letting the breeze cool her skin, staring out at the three-quarter moon, trying not to think about Alec in the next room. So close.

No. Not so close. So far.

It was fine for her to lay here and fantasize, she told herself. It was perfectly normal and perfectly natural. In real life, it needed to be Wesley, but here in the dark of night…

She flipped onto her stomach. Then she fluffed her pillow and searched for a comfortable position.

She couldn't find one. She flipped back again, reaching for the water glass on her bedside table. It was empty.

Sighing in frustration, she clambered from the bed and crossed the carpet to the bathroom. Opening the door, she flicked on the light.

That exact moment, the door from Alec's room swung open. They both froze under the revealing glare, staring at each other in shock. Her hormones burst to instant attention, and she nearly dropped the glass.

Alec's chest was bare, the top button of his slacks undone. His hair was mussed, and his chin showed the shadow of a beard. As she'd guessed from his embrace, his shoulders were wide, his biceps bulged, and the pecs on his deep chest all but rippled under the light.

His gaze flicked down her body, stopping at her panties, and tension flicked in the corners of his mouth. "Is that from today?"

Her heart pushed hard against her ribs, knowing the skimpy outfit was very revealing.

"Did I *hurt you?*" he demanded.

And then she realized he wasn't salivating over her

bare legs, her skimpy top or the high-cut panties. His gaze had zeroed in on the bruise from where she'd fallen off Rosie-Jo.

She couldn't decide whether to feel relieved or disappointed. "It wasn't you," she assured him. "I fell off my horse."

He took a step forward. "Have you seen a doctor?"

"It's just a bruise."

"It looks deep. Do you need some ice?"

I'm standing here nearly naked. "No."

He moved closer still, and a hitch tightened in a band around her chest, while her hormones raced strategically around her body.

"It'll take the swelling down," he went on. "I can run to the kitchen and—"

"Alec!"

"What?"

"I'm standing here in my underwear."

He blinked. "Right." Then his eyes darkened to charcoal. "Right," he said, his gaze skimming her from head to toe.

She wished she could tell what he was thinking, but his expression gave away nothing. After a long minute, he drew a breath. "Sorry." He took a step back.

"Alec—"

He shook his head, holding up his palms. "Let's just forget this ever happened."

He was right, of course. But she couldn't seem to stop the thick layer of disappointment that slid its way through her stomach. Did he not find her even remotely attractive?

She guessed not, since he hadn't even noticed how she was dressed until she'd pointed it out.

He might have saved her life. He might care about

her physical safety. But apparently it was in a purely platonic way.

"I wasn't—" He took another backward step. "I didn't—" He shook his head. "I'm sorry," he repeated. Then he shot through the doorway to firmly click the door shut behind him.

Stephanie was sorry, too. But she suspected it was for an entirely different reason.

Alec spent the next few days working as fast as humanly possible and avoiding Stephanie as much as he could—which didn't turn out to be difficult, since she was an early riser, and she worked long hours.

Keeping himself from thinking about her proved a considerably tougher challenge. The picture of her in her tank top and panties was permanently seared into his brain stem.

Her face had been scrubbed and shiny, not that she ever seemed to wear makcup. Her shoulders were smooth and lightly tanned, her breasts were perfectly shaped, barely disguised under the thin, white fabric of the well-worn top. Her legs were long and toned, accented by the triangular, flat lace insets of her panties. And her waist was nipped in, stomach flat and smooth.

It had taken all of his willpower not to surge across the tiny bathroom and drag her into his arms.

He drew a shuddering breath, pulled the borrowed ranch truck transmission into fourth gear, and sped up on the final stretch of the road between Stephanie's equestrian stable and the main cattle ranch.

Business Consulting 101, he ruthlessly reminded himself. *Keep your hands off the clients' sister.* His business had been built on integrity. His clients trusted him with sensitive problems that were often high stakes and high risk. If he tossed his principles and made a pass at a client, no one would ever be able to trust him again.

In a self-preservation move, rather than talk to Stephanie face-to-face about her publicity history, he'd mentioned the scrapbooks to Amber. Amber had helpfully offered to hunt them down.

He'd already developed a comprehensive picture of the Ryder Equestrian Center from a business perspective. Not that he was under any illusion that the Ryder brothers wanted to learn the truth about their sister's profitability.

In any event, once he finished with the scrapbooks, he'd head back to the safety of his Chicago office, away from the temptation of Stephanie. The report would stand on its merits. Jared and Royce could use it or ignore it. It was completely up to them.

The main ranch house came into view, and he geared down to control the dust, bringing the truck to a smooth stop on the circular driveway between the house, the barns and the corrals.

Like Stephanie's place, the original ranch house was set on the Windy River. Groves of trees and lush fields stretched out in all directions. There was a row of staff cabins accessed by a small bridge across the river. Working horses were corralled near the house, while clusters of brown and white cattle dotted the nearby hillsides.

Jared Ryder appeared on the porch, coffee cup in hand, and Alec drew a bracing breath as he exited the truck.

He waved a greeting, slammed the door and paced across the driveway. "Didn't know you were in Montana," he said to Jared as he mounted the front steps.

"Just overnight," Jared returned. "Melissa and I wanted to check on Amber."

"How's she doing?"

"She's good. Thanks again, by the way."

"Not a problem."

Despite Stephanie making such a big deal about it, Alec suspected her brothers were both the kind of men who'd rescue anyone in need without a lot of fanfare.

Jared's matter-of-fact nod told Alec he was right.

"I should be done at the Equestrian Center tomorrow," Alec offered. With some hard work, he could wrap things up tonight.

"Glad to hear it. The sooner you get started in Chicago, the better." Then his expression turned serious, voice going lower as he glanced around them. "I hear Royce told you about our little issue."

Alec lowered his own voice in response. "About the blackmail?"

"Yeah."

"He did," Alec confirmed. "And I advised him to come clean with Stephanie."

Jared scoffed out a laugh. "Yeah, that's not going to happen."

"That's exactly what Royce told me."

"He thought you might help?"

"If I can."

Jared gave another considered nod. "Personally, I suggested we hunt him down and—"

"That's not the kind of work I do," Alec quickly put in, on the off chance Jared was serious.

"I wasn't going to suggest we harm him. Though I can't deny the idea has merit. I was thinking more along the lines of explaining to him in excruciating detail what each of us has to gain by ending this, and what each of us has to lose if he keeps it up.

"But it's a moot point anyway. We can't do anything until we find him. And, so far, we haven't been able to find him." Jared gave Alec a significant look.

A moment of silence passed.

"You want me to check into his whereabouts?" asked Alec.

"Amber's friend Katie says you have contacts."

Katie Merrick was a lawyer working for Alec's father's firm, Creighton Waverley Security. Where Creighton Waverley was conservative and by the book outfit, Alec had contacts who could be a little more creative.

"His name is Norman Stanton," Jared offered. "Frank Stanton, Stephanie's biological father, was his brother. The blackmail payments are all tied up in some off-shore company called Sagittarius Eclipse. That's pretty much all we know."

"That's a start." Alec nodded decisively. He'd be more than happy to help track down the man who had targeted Stephanie.

Stephanie needed to purge her wayward fantasies once and for all. And Wesley was the key. Across the arena, he was calling her name, making his way toward her through the soft, deep dirt.

"I've been looking for you," he gasped, as he grew close enough to speak. He ducked through the rails, rising up beside her.

Stephanie was observing Brittany, one of her youngest students, in the starting area of the jumping course.

She smiled briefly at Wesley then nodded to Brittany's trainer, Monica, where she held the bridle of Brittany's horse. Monica stepped back and gave the start signal, and Brittany cantered her horse toward the first two-foot plank.

"How was California?" Stephanie asked Wesley, glancing his way again.

He truly was a fine looking man. His blond hair curled around his ears. He had bright blue eyes and an aristocratic nose. And his quick sense of humor and easy laugh had made him friends throughout the stable.

"It was a long three days," he responded with a warm smile. "My sister has boyfriend trouble. My mother cooked five meals a day. And I missed you."

"I missed you, too." Stephanie told herself it wasn't really a lie, since she wanted so much for it to be true. She rested her elbow on the second rail, tipping her head to look at him.

Truth was she hadn't thought much about him while he was away. Her only excuse was that she'd been busy training. The Brighton competition was coming up in a few short weeks, and it was the unofficial start of qualifying for the Olympic team.

Training was important. It was hard to find time to think about anything else.

Well, except for Alec.

She clamped her jaw down hard, ordering herself to forget about Alec. He'd been skulking around the stable all week, asking questions, printing financial reports, and generally making a nuisance of himself.

Wesley did his part. He took a step closer to her, his shoulder brushing against her elbow.

Brittany turned her horse and headed for jump number four.

Wesley brushed his fingers along Stephanie's bare forearm, easing closer still. He touched the back of her hand, turning it to feather his fingertips across her palm, before cupping her hand and giving her a squeeze.

It was a gentle touch. A pleasant touch. She forced herself to concentrate on enjoying it.

"We need to talk, Stephanie." His blue-eyed gaze went liquid.

"About?"

His smile widened. "About us, of course. I'm dying to kiss you." He moved her hand from the rail and turned her, tugging her toward him, voice going breathy. "I've been thinking about you for three long days."

Stephanie opened her mouth, but the words she wanted to utter wouldn't come out. She hadn't been thinking about Wesley for three long days. And she wasn't dying to kiss him.

Okay, she wasn't exactly opposed to kissing him. But the rush of excitement she'd felt the last two times they'd come close was decidedly absent.

"Tell me how you feel," he breathed.

Brittany cantered past. The clomp of her horse's hooves tossed sprays of dirt, while the *whoosh* of its breathing filled the air. Stephanie used the instant to pull back.

"I really like you, Wesley," she told him.

"That's good." He smiled confidently and moved in again.

"I'm…" Curious? Hopeful? Desperate to have you erase Alec from my thoughts?

"You're what?" he prompted.

"Worried." The word jumped out before she could censor it.

He frowned. "About what?"

"You're my student."

It was a lame excuse, and they both knew it.

Jessica Henderson had been her now husband Carl's student for three years before they announced their engagement. Nobody had been remotely scandalized by the relationship. In fact, half the state horse jumping community had attending their wedding.

"You make me sound like a kid," said Wesley.

"You're younger than me," Stephanie pointed out, feeling suddenly desperate to get out of the kiss she'd been planning for so long.

"Barely," he told her, the hurt obvious in his tone.

"Still—"

"Stephanie, what's going on?"

"Nothing," she lied again.

"I *missed* you."

She tried to come up with something to say.

He stepped into the silence. "You're beautiful, funny, smart—"

"I have a business to run and a competition to train for."

"What are you talking about? What happened while I was gone?"

"Nothing." It was the truth.

His lips puffed out in a pout. "I don't believe you."

Stephanie took a breath and regrouped. "It's just... I need to focus right now, Wesley. And so do you. Brighton is only a few weeks away."

She sped up her words, not giving him a chance to jump back in. "And we both need to nail it. It's your first major, senior event, and I need the ranking."

"I still don't see why we can't—"

"We can't, Wesley."

He reached for her hand once more, squeezing down. "But we're so good together." With the sun slanting across his tousled hair, and the pleading tone in his voice, he suddenly struck her as very young.

"We can be friends," she offered.

His brow furrowed. "I don't want to be friends."

"Yes, you do. We're already friends. We're going to train together and nail Brighton."

"And then what?"

"What do you mean?"

"After Brighton? If we still feel the same way?"

She didn't know what to say. She didn't feel the way she wanted to feel, and she didn't see that changing.

He grinned, obviously taking her silence for agreement. The eager, puppy-dog look was back in his eyes. "I know we have something special."

"We have friendship and mutual respect," she offered carefully.

"There's more than that."

Stephanie took a step back. "Seriously, Wesley, I can't let you—"

"Not right now. I get it." He gave a vigorous nod. "But we both know—"

"No, we don't know—"

Brittany shrieked, and Monica shouted, and Stephanie whirled to see the horse shy to one side. It refused the jump and sent Brittany bouncing into the soft ground.

The girl's breath whooshed out as she landed with a thump on her rear end.

By the time Stephanie was through the fence, Brittany had grabbed two handfuls of dirt and tossed them down in disgust.

She was obviously more angry than injured, but Stephanie rushed to assist just in case.

* * *

Stephanie was angry with herself.

But she was also angry with Alec.

What was he *doing* to her? Why did he have to usurp Wesley? Why couldn't she get the bare-chested image of him out of her head. And *why* hadn't he been interested in her when she was standing half naked in front of him?

All he'd noticed was her stupid bruise.

It was the end of a long, frustrating day, and she marched through the front door. She stripped off her gloves and boots then came around the corner to find the object of her frustration stationed at the dining table, stacks of papers fanned out in front of him. There were magazines, newspaper clippings, financial reports and reference books.

He glanced up, expression unreadable.

She tried to think of a clever greeting, but nothing came to mind. She stood there in silence, her heart beating faster, her hormones revving too high, and her brain tripping up over itself.

"I finished the publicity and promotion calculations," he finally offered. He slid a piece of paper in her direction. "Amber gave me your scrapbooks."

Stephanie ordered her feet to move forward, keeping her attention fixed squarely on the printout as she crossed the hardwood floor. She lifted the paper, scanning to the bottom where each of the past ten years were listed with a corresponding total.

"That can't be right," she found her voice. The numbers were ridiculously low.

"You did get quite a lot of coverage," Alec admitted, setting down his pen and crossing his arms over his chest. "But it's in random placements."

She glanced at him. "Some of those magazines charge tens of thousands of dollars for a single ad. I had the cover. I had the center pages. That's priceless. Ryder International was mentioned over and over again."

"As a targeted placement. Sure, you're going to pay a premium price. But the Ryder International demographic is no more likely to be reading *Equine Earth* as they are to be reading *People* Magazine."

"That's not true."

Alec scraped his chair backward and came to his feet.

"Horse people have money," she repeated her earlier assertion. "They own businesses. They rent real estate."

"Maybe," he agreed. "But maybe not. Now, if Ryder International was in the equestrian equipment business, *Equine Earth*—"

"We're in the equine *breeding* business."

"Revenues from your breeding sales are a tiny fraction of the revenues from the real estate division."

"You're out to get me, aren't you?"

"I'm not—"

She thrust the paper back on the table. "From the minute you walked onto this ranch, you've been out to prove that I'm not a valuable partner in this corporation."

"These numbers aren't my personal opinion—"

"The hell, they're not."

"They're generally recognized calculations for determining—"

"Shut up."

He stiffened. "Excuse me?"

She moved in. "I said shut up. I am so tired—"

"Of what?" he asked incredulously.

"Of you! Of you and your—" She ran out of words. What was she trying to say? That she was tired of being attracted to him? Of knowing that he wasn't attracted to her? Of having his presence at the stable mess with her mind?

He waited, staring hard.

She mustered an explanation. "Of you trying to prove I have no value."

His look turned to confusion. "Is that what you think?"

She gestured to his work with a sweep of her arm. "That's what all this says."

"It says you're a financial drain on the corporation. And you are."

"I'm an asset."

"Not a financial one."

Her throat closed up with emotion, and she hated it.

Why did she care what he thought? Her brothers weren't going to accept this. What could it possibly matter that some opinionated, hired gun of a troubleshooter thought she wasn't pulling her weight?

It shouldn't.

And it didn't.

But then something shifted in his expression, and he cursed under his breath. "I'm trying to be honest, Stephanie."

She didn't trust herself to speak, and she needed him to think it didn't matter, so she waved her hand to tell him to forget about it. She wished he'd back off now and leave her to wallow.

But he took a step closer, then another, and another. His eyes went dark, from pewter to slate to midnight.

She stilled, unable to breathe. Her chest went tight. Her heart worked overtime to pump her thickening blood. And she found herself gazing up at him, feeling the pinpricks of longing flow over her heating skin.

Suddenly he clamped his jaw and his hands curled into fists. "We *can't*."

No, they couldn't.

Wait a minute. Couldn't what? Did he mean what she thought he meant?

"Stephanie. You're my *client*."

Yes, she was.

And that mattered.

At least it should matter.

Shouldn't it?

But a kiss wouldn't hurt. A kiss was nothing. She'd kissed a dozen men, well, boys really. A kiss didn't have to lead anywhere. It didn't have to mean anything.

And then at least she'd know. She'd know his touch, his scent, his taste.

She subconsciously swayed toward him.

"Stephanie." His voice was strangled.

The world seemed to pause for breath.

And then he was reaching, pulling, engulfing her, plastering her body against his, flattening her breasts, surrounding her with his strong arms. His mouth came down on hers, open, hot, all encompassing.

Passion shot through her body, igniting every nerve ending, every fiber from her hair to her toes.

He tipped his head, deepening the kiss. She opened her mouth, shocked that these intense sensations could come from a simple kiss. Her arms stretched around his neck, and her body instinctively arched against him.

His hands slid down her spine, lower, and lower still. She gasped at the sensation, moaning when the heat of his palms cupped her bottom.

She curled her fingertips into his hairline, struggling for an anchor, her knees going weak, as the subsonic vibrations of arousal sapped the strength of her legs. She kissed him harder, her thigh relaxing, allowing his own to press between, sending shock waves through her torso.

"Stephanie," he rasped, and she loved the breathless sound of his voice.

He groaned then, breaking away, reaching backward to unclasp her hands.

But she fought back, shaking free from his grasp, cupping his face and peppering his mouth with quick kisses. She did *not* want this feeling to end.

He gave a guttural groan, enveloping her again, taking over the rhythm, bending her backward and thrusting his tongue deep into her mouth while one hand slid up her rib cage, surrounding her breast.

She kissed him fervently, fists tightening, toes curling, as she struggled to get closer and closer.

Then suddenly, she was lifted from the floor, scooped into his arms. The kisses continued and sensations built as he carried her up the stairs to her bedroom. There, he set her down, and his fingers swiftly scrambled with the buttons on her blouse.

Yes. Skin to skin. They absolutely needed to be skin to skin. She fumbled with the knot in his tie, making little progress. She switched to the buttons on his white shirt.

He chuckled deep in his chest as he swooped off her blouse, removing her bra in one deft motion. "I win," he breathed in triumph.

Then he helped her out, and tore open his shirt, discarding it on the floor.

She sighed in sublime satisfaction as his hot body came

up against hers. Her breasts and belly tingled, and her skin flushed with pleasure.

He lifted her once more, sinking onto the bed full-length. His hand found her bare breast, strumming the nipple to exquisite arousal. His kisses roamed from her mouth to her neck to her shoulder, and finally to the hard beads of her sensitized nipples. She was restless, itchy, and her hands felt empty, but she didn't know what to do with them.

She buried them in his short hair, convulsively tightening her fingertips against her scalp. Her thighs twitched apart, and he settled between them. A burst of desire rocketed through her belly. She reached for the waistband of his slacks, certain they needed less clothing between them and more heated skin.

He helped her out again, rising to strip off the rest of their clothes. He paused then, his gaze sweeping hotly over every single inch of her nakedness.

She loved the way he was looking at her, as if he liked what he saw. She loved that she was naked, loved that she could stare right back at his glorious, hot, sculpted body.

He slowly lowered himself against her, one palm running from her knee to her breasts, then back again. He gently eased her legs apart, watching her expression. Then he kissed her eyelids, took her mouth once more in a deep, lingering, passionate kiss.

His touch became firm, his movements more hurried, and when he tore open a condom, she experienced a moment of fear. But then he was back, and his kisses were magic, and her body took over, spreading and arching and welcoming him.

She expected a pain, but it was minor and fleeting, and the building sparks of desire quickly filled her mind. He adjusted her body, and the sensations intensified. She dragged in labored breaths, hands convulsing against his back, toes curled and hips arching to meet him with every stroke.

They rode a wave that stretched on and on, until his body tensed. His rhythm increased. He cried out her name, while lights and sound exploded in her mind, making her weightless, suspended in time, before she pulsed back to earth and felt the weight of Alec on top of her.

His breathing slowed, and he kissed her temple, her ear, her neck.

Then he dragged in a labored gasp. "Stephanie Ryder, you blow my mind."

She struggled to catch her own breath. "If I could talk," she panted. "I'd tell you exactly the same thing."

He chuckled deep, rolling over to put her on top.

Her limbs felt like jelly. But now that it was over, a soreness crept in between her legs. She shifted to ease it.

"Careful," he warned, reaching his hand between them. He eased out of her body.

But then he frowned, lifting his fingers to peer at them in the bright moonlight. "What the hell?"

He whirled his head, pasting her with an accusing look. "You're a virgin?"

"Not anymore."

He recoiled in what looked like horror. "Why didn't you *say something?*"

"Why would I?" It was her problem, not his. Besides, it wasn't like she was saving herself for some mythical future marriage.

"Because…" he sputtered. "Because…"

"Would you have done something different?" Personally she wouldn't have changed a thing. Virginity wasn't a big deal in this day and age.

"I wouldn't have done *anything at all*."

"Liar," she accused. Half an hour ago, neither of them had been thinking past sex. "Did you tell the first woman you slept with that she was the first?"

He frowned in the starlight. "That's completely diff—"

"Ha! Double standard."

He raked a hand through his mussed hair. "I can't believe we're having this argument."

"Neither can I."

"You'll argue about anything, won't you?"

"Takes two to tango, Alec."

He curled an arm around her shoulders and pulled her tight. "You are impossible."

"And you're inflexible."

"You really should have said something." But his voice was starting to fade as a pleasant lethargy took over her body.

"I didn't," she muttered. "Get over it."

His voice dropped to a whisper next to her ear. "I doubt I'll be doing that for a very, very long time."

Her eyes fluttered closed, and her body relaxed into sleep.

Then, after what seemed like only seconds, there was a loud knock on her bedroom door. She blinked, and the bright sunlight stung her eyes.

"Stephanie?" Royce's voice demanded.

Alec was on his feet, clothes in hand, and through the connecting door to the bathroom in a split second.

"Hang on," she shakily called to her brother.

"Something wrong?"

"Why?" She blinked again, struggling to adjust her eyes.

"It's after nine."

She sat straight up and glanced around, grabbing her discarded clothes and stuffing them under the covers just in case Royce barged in. "I overslept."

"Have you seen Alec?"

"Uh, not since last night." Technically, it was true, since she'd had her eyes closed for the past few hours.

"He's not in his room."

The water came on in the bathroom.

"I hear the shower," she called to her brother. "Meet you downstairs?"

There was a pause. "Sure."

Stephanie flopped back down on her pillow, blowing out a sigh of relief. Not that her sex life was any of her brother's business. But, wow. She'd hate to have to listen to the shouting.

Four

As Alec approached the kitchen, he heard both Royce's and Jared's voices. He adjusted his collar, straightened his cuffs and shoved his guilt as far to the back of his mind as humanly possible.

Then he cringed as he passed the messy dining room table. They all would have seen it on their way to the kitchen, and it was completely unprofessional to leave his work scattered like that.

"We're all heading out there in an hour," Jared was saying.

"Good morning," Alec put into the pause, glancing at the faces around the breakfast bar, first at Jared and Royce, then Melissa and Amber, checking for anger or suspicion.

Nothing he could detect, so he allowed himself a quick glance at Stephanie.

Damn it. She looked like she'd made love all night long. And her gaze on him was intense.

When Amber turned toward her, Alec quickly cleared his throat, moving toward the coffeepot, hoping to keep everyone's attention from Stephanie. The woman had no poker face whatsoever.

"Heading where?" he asked Jared as he poured.

"The airport. We can give you a lift."

Alec didn't dare look, but he could feel Stephanie's shock. It wasn't perfect timing, but he couldn't very well refuse the offer after telling Jared he was leaving today. There was work to do in Chicago, and there was also Norman Stanton to deal with.

Besides, what was he going to do if he stayed? Make love to Stephanie again? If they were alone in the same house, odds were good it would happen. His professional ethics were already teetering on the edge of oblivion.

"Thanks," he forced himself to tell Jared. Then he turned, casually taking a sip from the stoneware mug. "Stephanie? I've got a couple more questions before I pack things up." He nodded toward the dining room, hoping she'd get the hint. It might be their one chance to say goodbye alone.

Standing at the opposite side of the breakfast bar, she was blinking at him like a deer in the headlights.

This time Amber did catch Stephanie's expression, and she frowned.

"Stephanie?" he repeated. If she didn't snap out of it, they were going to have one hell of a lot of explaining to do.

"What?" She gave her head a little shake.

"In the dining room? I had a couple of questions."

"Oh. Right." Now she was looking annoyed with him. That was much better.

She followed him out, but Amber came on her heels, followed by Royce and the rest of the family. Alec was stuck with asking Stephanie some inane business questions, to which he already had answers, as he packed the papers away in his briefcase.

In no time, they were heading out the door to Jared's SUV. Alec hung back, but he only managed the briefest of goodbyes and apologies to Stephanie before he had to leave.

Stephanie spent the next few weeks training hard with Rosie-Jo for the Brighton competition. At first, she'd been angry with Alec for his abrupt departure. Then she'd been grateful. After all, there was no sense in prolonging it.

They'd had a one-night stand, no big deal. She couldn't have asked for a better lover. And, though it was short, it had been wonderful, physically, at least.

But then the gratitude wore off, and she felt inexplicably sad and lonely. She found herself remembering details about him—the sound of his laugh, how his gray eyes twinkled when he teased her, his confident stride, his gentle touch, the heat of his lips and the taste of his skin.

She knew she was pining away for something that couldn't be, for something that had never existed in the first place, except in her own imagination.

She didn't think she felt guilty about making love to him. But maybe she did. Maybe that was why she was pretending their relationship was something more than a fling.

Cold fact was, she'd given her virginity to a man she didn't love, a man who was little more than a stranger.

It was the end of another long training day. She stabled Rosie-Jo and double-checked the feeding schedule. Leading up to Brighton, everything about Rosie's regime had to be perfect, as did Stephanie's.

She pressed her hands against the small of her back, arching as she sighed. Her period was a few days late, and she was getting frustrated with the wait. It was only a small difference, but competing at the most favorable hormonal point in her cycle could be the edge she needed to win. If she didn't get it by the weekend, she could be jumping with PMS.

She pulled her ponytail loose, finger-combed her hair and refastened the rubber band as she made her way to the barn door. She was exhausted, almost dizzy with fatigue today. And she was famished.

She took that as a good sign. It wasn't uncommon for her to polish off a pint of ice cream and a bag of potato chips the day before her period started. Not that she'd indulge in either this close to a competition. She'd have some grilled chicken and a big salad instead.

The thought of the food had her picking up her pace across the yard. But by the time she got to the front porch, she'd changed her mind. Chicken didn't really appeal to her. Maybe she'd do a steak instead.

Then she opened the door and caught the aroma of one of her housekeeper Rosalind's stews. She gripped the door frame for a split second. Okay, definitely not stew. She'd sit out on the back veranda and grill that steak.

The next morning, Stephanie blinked open her eyes, surprised to find it was nine-fifteen. The training schedule was obviously wearing her out. Fair enough. Her body was telling her something. She'd make sure she incorporated an extra hour sleep in her routine for the next two weeks.

She sat up quickly, and a wave of nausea had her dropping right back down on the pillow.

Damn it. She could not get sick.

Not now.

She absolutely refused to let a flu bug ruin the competition.

She gritted her teeth, sitting up more slowly. There. That was better. Wasn't it?

She gripped the brass post of her bed, willing her stomach to calm down.

It wasn't fair. First her period screwup, and now this. She needed to do well at Brighton. She'd trained her entire life for this year of all years. But it was as if the stars were lining up against her.

She started for the en suite, telling herself it was mind over matter. She was young and healthy. And she had a strong immune system. She was confident she'd quickly fight off whatever it was she'd picked up.

She stopped in front of the sink, pushing her messy hair back from her face, groping for her toothbrush and unscrewing the toothpaste cap.

She caught a glimpse of herself in the mirror. Her face was pale. Her eyes looked too big today, and the smell of the toothpaste had her rushing to retch into the toilet.

There was little in her stomach, but she immediately felt better. What the heck was wrong—

She froze.

"No." The hoarse exclamation was torn from her.

Her hand tightened on the counter edge and she shook her head in denial. She could *not* be pregnant.

They'd only done it once. And they'd used a condom.

Okay. She breathed. She had to calm down. She was only scaring herself. How many crazy thoughts had popped into her head since Alec left? This was simply one more in the series.

She drew another deep breath. The nausea had subsided.

It had to be psychosomatic. Her period would start today, maybe tomorrow. Her hormones would get back on track. She'd stick to her training regime, and she'd kick butt in Brighton.

Anything else was unthinkable.

On morning four of the nausea and exhaustion, Stephanie dragged her feet to the bathroom, staring with dread at the home pregnancy test she'd picked up the afternoon before. Even before she followed the directions, she knew what the answer would show.

Sure enough, the two blue stripes were vivid in the center of the viewing window. She was pregnant.

She plunked the plastic stick in the trash bin and moved woodenly to the shower.

As the warm water cascaded over her body, she let a tear escape from her eye. Then another, and another.

What oh *what* had she done? This was her year, first the nationals, then the European championships and finally tryouts for the Olympic team.

The moment she'd trained for, longed for, prayed for her entire life was upon her, and she was going to have a baby instead, without a father. Her brothers would be furious on both counts. They'd be so disappointed in her.

Her mind searched hopelessly for a way to keep it secret.

Maybe she could fake an injury and take herself out of competition. Then she would find an excuse to stay in Europe for six months. And, then… And, then…

She whacked the end of her fist against the shower wall in frustration.

What would she do? Come back to Montana with a baby in tow? Tell them she adopted some poor orphan in Romania?

It was a stupid plan.

Defeated, she slowly slid her way down the wall, water drizzling over her as she came to rest on the bottom of the tub. She wrapped her arms around her knees, staring blankly into space as the water turned from hot to tepid.

"Stephanie?" Amber's voice surprised her. It was followed by a rap on the bathroom door.

"Just a sec," Stephanie called out, rising to her feet, swiftly spinning off the now-cold water.

"You okay?" Amber asked.

"Fine." Stephanie flipped back the curtain and grabbed a towel, scrubbing it over her puffy cheeks and burning eyes.

What was Amber doing in Montana?

"You've been in there forever," Amber called.

"What are you doing here?"

"Royce got restless in Chicago. It was either this or fly to Dubai for the weekend. You want to come down to the main house for a while?"

Stephanie pressed her fingertips into her temples. The last thing in the world she needed was one of her brothers hanging around. She needed to be alone right now.

"I have to train," she called through the door.

"You decent?" asked Amber.

"I'm—"

The door opened, and Stephanie quickly wrapped the big bath towel around her body.

"Morning." Amber grinned.

"You never heard of privacy?"

"We're practically sisters." Then Amber's grin faded. She cocked her head, staring into Stephanie's eyes. "What on earth?"

Stephanie quickly turned away, coming face-to-face with her own reflection in the mirror. Her eyes were bloodshot. Her cheeks had high, bright pink spots, but the rest of her face was unnaturally pale.

"I had a rough night," she tried, but her voice caught on her raw throat.

Amber's arm was instantly around her shoulders. "What's wrong? Did you get bad news? One of the horses?"

"No." Stephanie shook her head.

Then Amber's gaze caught on something. Her eyes went wide, and her jaw dropped open.

Stephanie looked down to see the home pregnancy test box on the counter.

"You can't tell Royce," she croaked.

"You're *pregnant*."

Stephanie couldn't answer. She closed her eyes to block out the terrible truth.

"Is it Wesley?"

Stephanie quickly shook her head.

"Who—"

"It doesn't matter."

There was a silent pause, then Amber touched her shoulder. "Alec."

Stephanie's eyes flew open. "You can't tell Royce."

"Oh, sweetheart." Amber pulled Stephanie into her arms. "It's going to be okay. I promise you, it's going to be okay."

It wasn't often that Alec spent time in his Chicago office. For one thing, his jobs rarely kept him in the city.

He preferred to be on the ground, gathering information from real people in different places around the world.

Consequently his office was stark, almost sterile. In a central location between the river and the pier, it was a single room on the thirty-second floor. The view was spectacular. The desk was smoke glass and metal, with sleek curves and clean lines. Matching chairs were thinly padded with charcoal leather. He used his laptop everywhere he went, and his file cabinets were stainless steel, recessed into the wall.

There was no need for a receptionist, since his phone number wasn't published. He wasn't listed on the building's lobby directory, and he rarely had more than one job on the go at a time.

So, it was a surprise when the office door swung open.

Alec glanced up to see Jared fill the doorway. He walked determinedly inside, followed closely by Royce, their faces grim.

They shut the door and positioned themselves on either side, folding their arms across their chests, as Alec came to his feet. There wasn't a doubt in his mind that they knew he'd taken Stephanie's virginity.

"Stephanie told you," he stated the obvious. He wouldn't lie, and he wouldn't deny it. If they fired him, they fired him.

Jared spoke. "Stephanie doesn't know we're here."

Alec nodded and came out from behind the desk, ready to face them.

Royce stepped in. "Stephanie's pregnant."

The words stopped Alec cold.

Seconds dripped like icicles inside the room.

"I had no idea," he finally said.

"You're not denying you're the father," Jared stated.

"I'm not denying anything. Whatever Stephanie told you, you can take as true."

"Stephanie didn't tell us anything," said Royce.

Then Alec wasn't about to add to their body of knowledge. What happened between him and Stephanie was private.

She was pregnant, and he'd absolutely do the right thing. And her brothers had every right to call him on it. But they didn't have a right to anything more than she was willing to voluntarily share.

Jared took a step forward, and Alec wondered if he was going to take a swing.

"Here's what we're going to do," Jared said.

"I *will* marry her," Alec offered up-front.

"Not good enough," said Royce, squaring his shoulders to form an impenetrable wall next to his brother.

Alec didn't understand. There were limited options at this point.

"We don't want to see Stephanie get hurt," said Jared.

Alec's mental reflex was to make a joke about that being the understatement of the century. But he held his tongue.

"No woman wants a marriage of convenience," said Royce.

Alec still wasn't following.

"She wants a love match."

Alec peered at Royce. "Are you saying you want her to marry someone else?" His thoughts went to Wesley, and he found his anger flaring. Wesley wasn't the father of her child. *Alec* was the father of her child.

His mind wanted to delve into that unfathomable concept, but he forced himself to focus on Jared and Royce.

"We mean a love match with you."

Alec gave his head a little shake.

He'd step up. He'd provide financial and any other support needed, but he and Stephanie barely knew each other. They weren't going to settle down and live happily ever after just because her brothers decreed it.

He would never put any woman in that position. He knew from the catastrophe of his own parents' marriage, exactly what happened when you tried to fake it.

"I hope that was a joke," he intoned.

Jared took yet another step forward. "There is nothing remotely funny about any of this."

Alec looked into the man's eyes. "No, there's not. But you can't control people's emotions. She's no more in love with me than I am with her."

"You can change that," said Royce. "Tell her you love her, and make her fall in love with you."

Alec slid his glance sideways. "No."

Not a chance in hell. There was not a freaking chance in hell he would set Stephanie up for that kind of heartache.

Royce squared his shoulders. "It wasn't a question."

Alec could well imagine that few people said no to the Ryder brothers. They were intellectually and physically powerful men. Add to that their economic wherewithal, and they were pretty much going to get their own way in life.

But Alec didn't intimidate easily, and he had a set of personal principles that stopped well short of duping a woman into falling in love with him.

"I'll marry Stephanie," he told them both. "I'll respect her. I will provide for our child. And I'll lie to the world about it if she wants me to. But I won't lie to her."

He gave a harsh laugh. "You two might think you're protecting her by—"

"We *are* protecting her," said Royce, and Jared's expression backed him up.

"Nevertheless," Alec articulated carefully. "*I'm* going to be honest with her."

Since Alec spent most of his life on the road, a marriage of convenience would be fairly easy to pull off. And after the baby was born, she could decide what she wanted. If it was a quiet divorce, no problem.

Jared and Royce glanced uncertainly at each other. It was obvious the meeting wasn't going the way they'd planned.

"May I assume I'm fired?" Alec put in.

The two men exchanged another glance.

Royce cleared his throat.

"I think we'll leave that up to Stephanie," said Jared.

This time Alec did laugh. "Then you might as well take your files with you when you go. She's pretty ticked off about my valuation of her publicity."

The two men hesitated again.

"It is right?" asked Jared.

"It's right," Alec confirmed.

"Let's maybe leave the business arrangement as is for now," said Royce.

Alec glanced from one man to the other. "You sure?"

They both nodded.

"No point in disrupting everything at once," said Jared. Then he clapped a hand down on Alec's shoulder. "You can come back to the ranch with us."

"You afraid I'm going to try to run off?"

"We don't want Stephanie to be upset any longer than necessary."

"She'll still be upset after I get there." Alec tried to picture their conversation. Then he wondered how Stephanie felt about the baby. Then, finally, he let his mind explore how he felt about the baby.

He'd never planned to have children. The genetics in his family did not lend themselves to quality parenting. His father was incapable of love, and his mother had been unable to put her child's welfare ahead of her own misery.

At least Alec's child would have Stephanie.

For some reason, the thought warmed him. Stephanie might be indulged and impulsive, but she was also sweet and loving. He'd seen her work with both animals and children, and he knew instinctively she'd be a great mother.

And he was going to be a father.

As he exited the office with Jared and Royce, he tried hard to keep the prospect from terrifying him.

At the front of the stall, Stephanie rested her forehead against Rosie-Jo's soft nose. She placed her hand on the horse's neck, feeling it twitch and pulse with strength beneath her fingertips.

"I went to see the doctor today," she told Rosie-Jo, wrapping her hands around the mare's bridle.

Rosie-Jo nickered softly in response, bobbing her head up and down.

Stephanie slowly drew back, gazing into the horse's liquid, brown eyes. Her throat closed over. "I'm definitely pregnant, girl."

Rosie-Jo blinked her lashes.

"And that affects you," Stephanie forced herself to continue. "Because he's afraid I might fall off. He's afraid

I'll hurt the baby." Stephanie closed her eyes and drew a bracing breath. "I'm so sorry, Rosie. I know how you love the crowds. And you've worked so hard. And I've worked so hard. For so long."

Rosie snuffled Stephanie's shoulder.

Stephanie opened her eyes to the blur of gray horse hair, her voice catching. "So, he doesn't want me to jump anymore."

"That sounds like good advice to me," someone rumbled behind her.

Rosie snorted, while Stephanie startled. She turned and came face-to-face with the man who'd haunted her dreams.

"Alec?" She struggled to make sense of his presence in the barn. "What are you doing here?"

"Your brothers picked me up in Chicago." His gaze scanned her thin cotton shirt, blue jeans and worn boots.

The implication of his arrival, and the meaning of his opening words penetrated Stephanie's brain.

He knew she was pregnant.

And her brothers must know, too.

She felt the walls close in. She hadn't prepared for this moment, hadn't had any time to even think about it. She'd assumed it would be weeks, even months before her pregnancy was general knowledge.

"I believe Amber gave you up," Alec offered.

Stephanie didn't respond, her mind still grappling with the fact that he knew, that he was here, that the secret was out.

"When were you planning to tell me?" he asked, face impassive, tone guarding his mood.

The word *never* sprang to mind. Though she knew she wouldn't have kept it from him.

"I don't know," she managed, answering him honestly. "I hadn't thought about it." It was enough of a challenge coming to terms with the situation herself.

He shook his head and gave a scoff of disbelief. "You hadn't *thought about it?* You're unexpectedly pregnant, and it's not on your mind twenty-four seven?"

"I just found out."

"You told Amber a week ago."

"And I saw the doctor this morning. I hadn't even decided—"

"Decided *what?*" His voice went deadly low, and his gray eyes turned to black.

"What to do." She had her riding career, her students, her business. Not to mention a baby, then a child. She'd never even known her own mother, how would she handle it all?

He wrapped his hand firmly around her upper arm. "Stephanie, if you even think about—"

She blinked up at him.

"—harming our baby."

Harming? What was he talking…

Then her eyes went wide, and she jerked her arm from his grip. "What is the *matter* with you?"

"Me? You're the one who hasn't made up her mind—"

"How to *raise* the baby." She smacked him on the front of his shoulder. "Not whether to keep the baby."

He didn't even react to the blow. "You can't be happy about this."

"Of course I'm not happy about this. I'm not ready to be a mother. I have a business to run. My jumping career is ruined. And my brothers know I slept with you."

"Your brothers will get over it."

Her brothers. She groaned inwardly.

Royce and Jared knew Alec had made her pregnant.

Wait a minute. She looked him up and down. "You're still standing."

"I am."

She cocked her head. "How come you're still standing?"

"You thought your brothers would kill me for sleeping with you?"

"I never thought my brothers would find out."

"Yeah." He glanced away. "I was kind of counting on the same thing."

Then the fog lifted, and a picture came clear in her mind. Of *course* her brothers hadn't harmed him. They needed him alive.

She didn't know whether to be furious or mortified. "You're here for a shotgun wedding."

"Something like that," he admitted.

She felt guilty on a whole new front now. Alec was a decent guy. He didn't deserve this.

She shook her head. "Don't worry about it."

"Do I look worried?"

"You definitely look worried."

"It doesn't have to be a big deal."

"It doesn't have to be anything at all." Making up her mind, she turned decisively and started down the corridor.

Alec settled in beside her.

She finger-combed her hair and refastened her ponytail at the base of her neck. "Thanks for stopping by, Alec. You're an honorable man. But your baby is safe in my hands. I'll drop you a line once it's born."

He coughed out a laugh. "Yeah, right."

"Your life is in Chicago. Leave this to me." In this day and age, a reluctant husband was a complication not a benefit. What had her brothers been thinking?

"Not quite the way things are going to happen," he said.

"They can't make you marry me."

"Now that part's debatable."

"Okay. Maybe they can make you. But they can't make me." She spotted a length of binder twine on the floor and reflexively stooped to pick it up.

"They want what's best for you, Stephanie."

She wrapped the orange twine neatly around her hand. "No, Alec. They want you to pay for your sins."

"They want to protect you."

She gave a dry chuckle. "From what? A scarlet letter?"

He didn't respond.

"I'm a big girl, Alec. I made a mistake, and I'm going to pay. But it doesn't mean you have to get dragged along for the ride." She peeled the loop of twine from her hand and reached for the door latch.

His hand shot out, blocking the door shut. He stared down at her with an intense singularity of purpose. "Get this straight in your mind, Stephanie. You *are* marrying me."

She squinted at him in the dim light. "That was a joke, right?"

"Am I laughing?"

"I don't know what they threatened you with."

"Nobody threatened me with anything."

"Then why are you talking crazy?"

"I'm talking logic. It doesn't have to be forever."

"And what girl doesn't want to hear *that* in a marriage proposal?"

"Stephanie."

His words shouldn't have the power to hurt her. She barely knew the man. And she needed to keep it that way.

She stuffed the twine in her pocket and crossed her arms over her chest. "Marriage would make a bad situation worse."

He imitated her posture, crossing his own arms. "Marriage would make things right."

Suddenly the entire conversation seemed absurd, and a cold laugh burst out of her. "How do you figure?"

His jaw clenched. "I'm the baby's father."

"Yes?"

"I have a responsibility."

"To do what?"

"I don't know," he practically shouted. "Provide for it."

"You can write a check without having a marriage license."

"Is that what you want?"

"Yes."

"And I have no say?"

"Not really."

He glared at her for a long moment. Then he smacked the door open and marched out of the barn.

As she watched his retreating back, Stephanie realized she had won.

She tried to feel glad about that, but somehow the emotion wouldn't come.

Five

"Well, what was I *supposed* to say?" Stephanie challenged. Sitting on a submerged ledge, water to her waist in the ranch swimming hole, she stared at Amber over the rippled surface of the water.

"Yes?" Amber suggested as she pulled the last couple of strokes across the small, cliff bordered pool and settled on the ledge next to Stephanie. Her forehead was completely healed, and the cut from the accident would barely leave a scar.

The swimming hole was a favorite place for Stephanie. Water from a small tributary to the Windy River trickled down a waterfall and gathered in a deep pool, hollowed out over millennia. The semicircle cliffs were open to the east, so the morning sun soaked into the granite, heating the water, keeping it comfortable all summer long.

It was near noon, and the sun streamed down on Amber's wet, blond hair, reflecting in her jewel-blue eyes.

"And actually *marry* him?" Stephanie swiped her own wet hair back from her forehead, tucking it behind her ears.

"You are having his baby."

"And, we're practically strangers."

"Not completely." Amber's eyes took on a meaningful gleam.

Stephanie glared in return. "Nobody gets married because of a baby anymore."

Amber didn't answer, but an opposing opinion all but oozed from her pores.

"What?" Stephanie prompted.

"You're pregnant, Steph."

"I know that." Stephanie had tried hard to push it from her mind. But the reality wasn't going anywhere.

"A husband might not be such a bad thing."

"I thought you'd be on my side."

"I *am* on your side."

Stephanie snorted her disbelief.

"We're only suggesting you give it a try."

"And if I fail?" Which was a foregone conclusion in Stephanie's mind. And therefore the entire exercise was a waste of time.

"Then you fail. Nothing ventured—"

"We're talking *marriage,* Amber." Stephanie couldn't believe her future sister-in-law could be so cavalier about something so serious. Maybe Stephanie was a hopeless romantic, but she didn't want to stand up in front of God and her family and take vows she didn't mean.

"It doesn't have to be a traditional marriage."

"Maybe that's what I want."

Amber cocked her head, silent for a few moments. "Are you saying you have feelings for Alec?"

"No!" Stephanie's denial was quick. Her emotions caught up a split second later. She didn't have feelings for Alec. She wouldn't allow herself to have feelings for Alec. "I just want…"

"What?"

"Normal. I want something about this entire mess to be normal."

"Define normal." Now Amber was being deliberately obtuse.

"A date? A candlelight dinner? Maybe a movie? Something, anything even a little bit romantic."

Amber snorted out a laugh. "What's romantic? Melissa went undercover and spied on Jared, and Royce picked me up in a bar." She snapped off a twig and tossed it into the pond. "I was a one-night stand that never went home."

Despite herself, Stephanie's interest was piqued. "You and Royce had a one-night stand?"

"Not the first night."

"Which night?"

"None of your business."

"Did you know you loved him?"

"Not at the time."

"Were you a virgin?"

"No."

"But you loved him later. So, somewhere, deep down inside, you must have known."

"Don't do this, Stephanie."

Stephanie clamped her jaw. Amber was right. Comparing herself to Melissa and Amber was futile. They were with men that they loved, men who would stick around, share their lives forever.

Leaves crackled on the trail behind them, and Stephanie turned to see Alec emerge from the trees.

His attention was fixed on Stephanie. "Royce told me I'd find you here."

Amber made to stand up, but Stephanie grabbed at her arm. "Don't go."

"You two have a lot to talk about."

"We've already talked." Stephanie had no desire for a repeat argument. She didn't have the energy.

Amber glanced up, obviously assessing Alec's expression. "I don't think you're done yet." She came to her feet, stepping her way out of the pool where she snagged a towel from a rock. Then she stuffed her feet into a pair of bright blue thongs.

Stephanie braced herself as Alec crouched down beside her. He was wearing a pair of lightweight khakis and plain, white dress shirt. His shoes were too formal, but at least he'd forgone the tie.

"Swimming?" he asked conversationally.

"No. Riding a bike."

"You think sarcasm's going to help?"

"I don't think anything's going to help."

"Right." He shifted. "So, your long-term plan is to wallow in self-pity?"

Stephanie refused to answer. Instead she swung her legs back and forth in the water.

She heard a rustle, then he stepped onto the ledge to sit. He'd stripped down to a pair of black boxers, and she quickly shifted her gaze to the other direction.

"You've seen me naked," he rumbled, amusement clear in his tone.

She might have seen him that way once, but she didn't

intend to see him that way again. She scrambled to put her feet under her.

His hand came down on her shoulder. "Oh, no you're not."

"You're going to hold me prisoner?"

"If I have to." The hand remained firmly in place.

Stephanie gave an angry sigh.

"I was thinking a garden wedding would be nice."

"What part of no didn't you—"

"We could do it here, if you like. Or in Chicago."

"Alec, we can't—"

"There's a ring in my pocket. Simple, but a couple of carats. It should impress your friends." He glanced across the shiny surface of the pool. "Probably not a good idea to give it to you here."

Despite herself, she turned to look at him. "You bought me a diamond?"

"Of course I bought you a diamond. We're getting married."

"You can't bribe me with jewelry, Alec."

"I'm bribing you with a name for our baby."

"I'm hardly a fallen woman."

"This isn't about you, Stephanie."

"Of course it's about—" She almost said me, but she clamped down her jaw instead. Her jumping career was ruined, and that was that. The baby was her priority now.

He smiled. "Ah. A glimmer of responsibility."

"Of course I'll do what's best for the baby." Beneath the water, her hand moved subconsciously to her abdomen.

"Marrying me is best for the baby."

She didn't answer.

"I'm under no illusions that we can 'make it work,'" Alec continued.

"Ah. A glimmer of reality," she mocked.

He frowned at her. "We barely know each other."

"You got that right."

"This isn't my first choice, either."

She stifled a cold laugh, but he ignored her silent sarcasm.

"I'll be honest with you, Stephanie. When it comes to women, I'm not a long-term kind of guy. And I don't see that changing."

Wow. This proposal just kept getting better and better.

Did he mean he'd continue dating? She supposed there was nothing to stop him from doing just that. He had an apartment in Chicago, and he traveled on business most of the time.

She shouldn't care. She had no right to care. Though it would be embarrassing if he was seen in public by someone she knew.

"Will you be discreet?" she asked him.

"Excuse me?"

"With the other women. Will you be discreet?"

His brows knit together. "What other women?"

"You just said your lifestyle wouldn't change."

"I didn't—"

"I assume that means I'm free to see other men," she added defiantly. "Although it would be more complicated for me to—"

"Whoa," he roared. "You are *not* going to be seeing other men."

"Isn't that a double standard?"

"Double *standard?*"

"I'm trying to understand how this will work."

Perhaps refusing Alec had been the wrong strategy. Maybe agreeing to marry him and pressing on the details would be more effective. She'd bet it wouldn't take him long to back out.

"Well, one way it will work, is that my pregnant wife won't be sleeping with other men."

"So, I'll be celibate then?"

"Damn straight."

"For how long?"

"For as long as it takes. It worked just fine for the first twenty-two years of your life."

"That was before."

"Before what?"

Frustration goaded her. "Before I knew how much fun it was to have sex."

Alec's eyes frosted to pewter. His mouth opened then closed again in a grim line.

She didn't care. Let him think she was embarking on a spree of debauchery. So long as it changed his mind about the wedding.

"You're lying," he finally said.

"That sex is fun?" she deliberately misunderstood, crossing her arms beneath her breasts. "You were there, Alec. Do you think I'm lying?"

"You are impossible." But his gaze dipped to her cleavage and the clingy one-piece bathing suit.

The heated look brought a rush of memories, and she realized that talking about their sex life might not be the brightest move. It had been far better than mere fun. And the experience was still fresh in her mind. And, given different circumstances, she'd definitely be in favor of repeating it.

"I'm merely pointing out some of the impracticalities of your master plan," she told him.

"Stephanie, in five or six years, you are going to have a

child in your life asking about their family. Do you want
to tell them Daddy was a one-night stand, or do you want
to tell them Mommy and Daddy had a fight and don't live
together anymore."

Stephanie's brain stumbled on the picture of a five-year-
old. There *would* be a five-year-old. And she'd be solely
responsible for raising him or her.

Panic rose inside her. How would she manage? Her only
role models were a grandfather and two teenage boys.

"I can't—" She came to her feet, water rushing down
her legs and dripping from her suit.

Alec rose. "Don't you dare—" But then her expression
seemed to register. "Stephanie?"

She was going to have a baby. She was honest to God,
going to have a baby.

She felt the blood drain from her face.

She'd never fed a baby, burped a baby, changed a diaper.
What if she did something wrong? What if she forgot
something important? What if she inadvertently harmed
the poor, little thing?

"Stephanie," he sighed in obvious exasperation. He
reached for her, pulling her to his body. His bare chest
was warm from the sun, and his arms were strong around
her. She had a sudden urge to bury her face and hide there
forever. His deep voice vibrated reassuringly in her ear.

"Marry me, Stephanie. It won't be perfect. It won't be
romantic. But we'll at least be honest with each other."

His sincerity touched her and, miraculously, she didn't
feel so completely alone. She let herself sink into Alec's
strength. Then she gave in and nodded against his chest.

Stephanie had preferred to hold the wedding at the
ranch, and that was fine with Alec. He'd done his duty

and informed his father, omitting the fact that Stephanie was pregnant. History might be repeating itself on one level, but the unplanned pregnancy was the only thing his marriage would have in common with his parents'.

Jared and Melissa had flown to the ranch. Then Melissa and Amber had joined forces to convince Stephanie to put on at least a cursory show for the ceremony. It would only be the six of them and a preacher, but they couldn't completely hide the event from the ranch workers, nor should they. It was better if it looked natural.

In the end, they'd chosen a quiet spot by the river. It was a couple of miles up a rutted, grassy road from Stephanie's house, out of sight from the working areas. A field of oats rippled behind them, while horses grazed on the hillside, and the river burbled against a backdrop of cottonwood trees.

Alec and the preacher arrived first, but within minutes, Jared's SUV pulled up with the rest of the party. The men all wore suits, while Amber and Melissa chose knee-length dresses, Amber in bronze, and Melissa in burgundy.

Stephanie was the last to emerge from the backseat. But when she did, Alec couldn't stop staring.

Her white dress was simple, strapless with a high waist and a sparkling belt below her breasts. The skirt fell softly to her knees, showing the curves of her slim, tanned calves. Her shoes were pretty, white satin ballet slippers against the long green grass.

Her hair was upswept, brilliant auburn under the deep, blue sky. She wore diamond earrings and a delicate, matching necklace, and subtle makeup had toned her freckles to nothing. His gaze was drawn to her graceful neck and smooth, bare shoulders.

Alec was far from a romantic man, but he was forced

to fight the urge to sweep her up in his arms and carry her off on a honeymoon.

She took a tentative step forward, and then another.

It was no traditional march down the aisle, and she seemed uncertain of what to do.

Alec moved forward, meeting her halfway, taking her hand so that they approached the preacher together. Her fingertips trembled ever so slightly against his skin, and he fought a thickness in his chest and the desire to pull her tight against him and reassure her. His reaction was ridiculous. The ceremony was as simple as they could make it. They were here to get the job done, nothing more.

The preacher began speaking, and everyone went still.

Stephanie stared determinedly at Alec's chin while she spoke her vows.

Alec by contrast watched her straight on, continuing to marvel at how stunning she looked. He realized that he'd never seen her in a dress, never seen her in jewelry, or with her hair in such a feminine style.

He'd known she was beautiful. He'd been physically attracted to her from minute one. But this incredible creature standing in front of him surpassed any dream or expectation he'd ever had. Once again, he found his imagination moving to a wedding night and honeymoon.

He ruthlessly shut that thought down. He had to keep a distance between them. Royce and Jared's plan to make her fall in love was both foolish and dangerous. Alec's mother had loved his father, and his father's indifference had destroyed her.

Then the preacher was finishing, inviting Alec to kiss the bride.

It seemed silly to do it, but churlish to skip.

So Alec bent his head. He struggled for emotional

distance as he rested a hand on her perfect shoulder, slid the other arm around her slim waist and touched his lips to hers.

It was a tender kiss, nothing like the ones they'd shared when they made love. But sensations ricocheted through him, nearly sending him to his knees.

He held it too long.

He kissed her too hard.

He just barely forced himself to pull back.

When he did, she finally looked at him. Her cheeks were flushed, her mouth bright red, and her silver-blue eyes were wide and vulnerable. Something smacked him square in the solar plexus, and he knew he was in very big trouble.

Even in the midst of her stressful wedding day, Stephanie's heart lifted when she saw McQuestin sitting on the front porch of the main ranch house. The old man was like a second grandfather to her, and she'd missed him while he'd been in Texas recovering from his broken leg.

She rushed out of Jared's SUV, leaving Alec in the backseat.

"You're home," she called, picking her way carefully along the pathway in her thin, impractical shoes.

The old man's smile was a slash across his weather-beaten face. His moustache and thick eyebrows were gray, and his hair, barely a fringe, was cut close to his head. His battered Stetson sat on his blue jean covered knee, while a pair of crutches were leaned against the wall next to his deck chair.

"Married?" he asked gruffly.

"I am," she admitted, giving him a hug and a kiss on his leathery cheek. She hoped her brothers hadn't told McQuestin about her pregnancy.

"How's the leg?" she asked, brushing past the subject of the wedding.

"Be right as rain in no time. This your gentleman?" He nodded past Stephanie.

Her hand still resting on McQuestin's shoulder, she turned to see Alec mount the stairs a few feet in front of Jared and Melissa. Royce's truck came to a halt behind the SUV.

"That's him," said Stephanie.

McQuestin looked Alec up and down. "She's too young to get married." An accusation and a challenge were both clear in his tone.

Alec stepped forward and wrapped an arm around Stephanie's bare shoulders. His hand was warm, strong and slightly callused, and her skin all but jumped under the touch.

"Sometimes a man has to move fast," he responded easily. "Couldn't take a chance on somebody else snapping her up."

McQuestin's faded blue eyes narrowed. "You're not stupid. I'll give you that."

"I told you you'd like him," Jared put in.

"Never said I liked him. Said he wasn't stupid. Now this one, I like." He nodded to Amber as she joined the group. "Got a good head on her shoulders."

"That she does," Royce agreed, and Stephanie realized McQuestin would only have met Amber today. Melissa on the other hand had been engaged to Jared before McQuestin's accident.

McQuestin glanced around at the circle of six. "You go away for a couple of months, and look what happens?"

The comparison of the three relationships made Stephanie uncomfortable. She shrugged out of Alec's embrace and backed toward the door. "I'll go see how Sasha's doing."

"She's got that table all decked out in delicates," said McQuestin. "I'm afraid to touch it."

"We're celebrating," said Melissa, giving him a hug on the way past. "It's good to have you back."

McQuestin winked at her. "A poker game with you later, young lady."

"You bet." Melissa fell into step behind Stephanie, passing through the doorway. "I think he lets me win," she confessed in a whisper.

"If you're winning, he's letting you," Stephanie confirmed.

"Who is he?" asked Amber as the door closed behind the three women. "We only had time for 'hi, how are you,' before we left for the ceremony."

"He's been the ranch manager forever," said Stephanie, slowing her steps as she approached the dining room table.

It was set with her mother's china, the best crystal wineglasses, an ornate, silver candelabra and low bouquets of wildflowers. Sheer curtains muted the lighting, and Sasha had baked a stunning, three tiered wedding cake. It was pure white, decorated with a cascade of mixed berries and was sitting on the sideboard with an ornate silver knife and a stack of china plates.

Stephanie gripped the back of a chair. "I feel like such a fraud."

"You're not a fraud," said Melissa, coming up on one side.

Amber came up on the other, flanking Stephanie with support. "And it looks delicious."

The unexpected observation made Stephanie smile. "Are we looking at the bright side?"

"No point in doing anything else."

"I suppose that's true," Stephanie allowed as she wandered over to the cake.

It did look delicious. She reached around the back, and swiped her fingertip through the icing then licked the sweetness off with her tongue.

"I can't believe you did that," Melissa laughed.

But Amber followed suit, tasting the icing herself. "Yum. Butter cream."

"It's good," Stephanie agreed.

"I love cake," Amber snickered.

Stephanie lifted the knife. "Let's cut it now."

"Oh, no, you don't." Melissa trapped her wrist.

Stephanie struggled to escape. "What? You worried it's bad luck."

"I don't believe in wedding luck," said Amber, swiping another finger full of icing. "My fiancé saw the wedding dress before the ceremony *and* slept with the bridesmaid. And that turned out to be good luck."

Stephanie and Melissa both blinked, round-eyed at Amber.

"Royce slept with a bridesmaid?" Stephanie asked in astonishment.

"Not Royce. My old fiancé, Hargrove. He slept with my best friend Katie. So I say to hell with luck. Let's eat the cake."

"Hello?" came Alec's censorious voice from the doorway.

Stephanie and Melissa both dropped the knife, and Amber guiltily jerked her finger away from the bottom layer.

"Amber has a thing for cake." Royce's tone was dry next to Alec, but there was a twinkle in his eyes exclusively for Amber.

"That's true," Amber admitted, grinning right back at him, making a show of licking the tip of her finger.

Something about their easy intimacy tightened Stephanie's chest. She didn't dare look at Alec, knowing his expression would be guarded. There was no intimacy between them. They were barely acquaintances.

A few words, no matter how official, couldn't make this a real marriage.

She knew she'd repeated the vows, and so had Alec, because the preacher had pronounced them husband and wife. But there'd been a ringing in her ears, and she'd had trouble focusing her eyes. She couldn't honestly say she recalled any of it.

Except the kiss. She remembered the kiss all too well. And she remembered her body's reaction to it—the arousal, the yearning, the fleeting fantasy that he'd scoop her into his arms and carry her off on a honeymoon.

"Stephanie?" Alec interrupted her thoughts.

Before she could stop herself, she glanced his way and caught his neutral expression, no twinkle, no teasing, no private message.

"The cake," he prompted. "It's up to the bride."

Amber playfully elbowed her in the ribs. "Let's do it."

Stephanie forced a carefree laugh, turning away from Alec. "I don't care if we cut it before dinner."

"Not without a picture," said Melissa.

Stephanie kept the smile determinedly pasted on her face. "Sure."

Alec dutifully moved up next to her and the ornate cake, draping an arm around Stephanie's shoulders.

Despite her vow to remain detached, she flinched under his touch.

"It'll all be over soon," he promised in a whisper.

"Maybe for you," she snapped. "You go right back to your regular life."

He stiffened. "You want me to stay?"

"Of course not." But she realized it was a lie.

She desperately wanted him to stay.

Six

It had been two weeks since Alec had seen or heard from Stephanie. Back in his compact, Chicago office, he'd filled every spare second with reviews of the various Ryder International divisions and queries to the possible whereabouts of Norman Stanton. He'd called in every outstanding favor and, quite literally, had feelers out all over the globe.

But no matter how hard he concentrated, he couldn't get Stephanie off his mind. He knew he had to stay well away from her for both their sakes, but he couldn't help wondering what she was doing. Was she still battling morning sickness? Was she picking out baby clothes? A crib? Thinking about a nursery? Had she been to the doctor again?

He was tempted to call, but he had to be strong. He'd seen the loneliness in her eyes and caught her fleeting glances his way after the wedding ceremony. She was vulnerable right now, and Alec couldn't risk having her look to him for emotional support.

His instinct to care for his wife and unborn child might be strong, but if he gave in, it would be Stephanie who got hurt in the end.

A news update droned in the corner on his small television set, while the cordless phone on his desktop sharply chimed.

It was an unfamiliar area code, and he snapped up the receiver. "Creighton here."

"Alec. It's Damien."

Anticipation tightened Alec's gut. "What've you got?"

"We found him."

Alec rocked forward in his chair, senses instantly alert. "Where?"

"Morocco."

Alec closed his eyes for a brief second of thankfulness. "Good. Great. What now?"

Damien Burke was a decorated, former military man. He'd done tours in both special forces and army intelligence, and there was nobody Alec trusted more.

"The U.S. doesn't have an extradition treaty with Morocco. Not that I'm suggesting we involve the Moroccan authorities. But Stanton will know that. You can bet that's why he's here. And that limits our bargaining power."

"It's not like we didn't expect this," said Alec. The man was smart enough to illegally drain millions of dollars from the Ryders then hide out in a foreign country. It stood to reason he'd done his research on extradition laws.

"I may be able to get him to Spain," Damien offered.

Alec was cautious. "How?" Kidnapping was not something he was prepared to authorize.

Damien chuckled, obviously guessing the direction of Alec's thoughts. "Margarita Castillo, Alec. Trust me, I'm not about to break the law and get myself thrown in a Moroccan jail."

"Who is she?"

"An associate who, I promise you, will have Norman Stanton on an airplane within twenty-four hours."

"And then?"

"And then a friend from Interpol will lay out the man's options."

Alec battled a moment's hesitation. "You won't do anything… You know…"

Damien scoffed. "'You know' won't be even remotely necessary. I've watched the man all day. He's soft as a tourist. We're shootin' fish in a barrel here."

"Good." A tentative satisfaction bloomed to life inside Alec. He might not be able to be with Stephanie in Montana, but he could do this for her.

Not that she'd ever find out.

"Touch base again tomorrow?" asked Damien.

"Thanks," said Alec, signing off and sliding the phone back into the charger.

"—arrived at Brighton earlier this morning," said the female, television news announcer, "and seen here heading for the barn area with her mare Rosie-Jo."

At the sound of the familiar name, Alec's gaze flicked to the television set.

"Anyone who follows the national circuit will remember this pair from Caldona where Stephanie Ryder and Rosie-Jo took first place."

Alec reflexively came to his feet, drinking in the sight of Stephanie's smiling face. She was dressed in faded jeans and a white cotton blouse. Her auburn hair was braided tight, and her amazing clear blue eyes sparkled in the Kentucky sunshine.

"She's had an extraordinary year," the male co-anchor put in.

"And an extraordinary career," said the female. "If they take the blue ribbon this weekend, you have to expect the pair to be a shoe-in for the Olympic team."

If they *what?*

"People are calling Rosie-Jo a cross between Big Ben and Miss Budweiser," the announcer continued.

Alec gave his head a startled shake.

This was Brighton.

It was live.

Stephanie wasn't allowed to jump. It was too dangerous for the baby.

"High praise, indeed," the other answered.

Alec knew she was unhappy about the pregnancy, and he knew how desperately she wanted to compete. But she wouldn't... She couldn't...

She stepped past a cluster of reporters, Wesley beside her, leading Rosie-Jo.

"What would it mean to you to win at Brighton?" one reporter asked her.

"I'm sorry?" she cocked her head to better hear above the noise.

"What makes Rosie-Jo so special?" asked another, drawing Stephanie's attention.

"Ambition." She smiled. "She's a powerful jumper, and she loves her job, so she's always totally enthusiastic. But she's still very careful."

Stephanie took a step back, giving a friendly wave but ignoring the rest of the questions.

Alec flipped open his cell phone, dialing hers as he

powered down his computer. He got her voice mail, left a terse message to call him then tried Royce.

By the time Royce's voice mail kicked in, Alec was out the door on his way to the airport. He didn't know what the hell she was thinking. Forget about who was vulnerable and who might get hurt, his job was to protect his unborn child.

The reporter's question had startled Stephanie, so she'd pretended not to hear it. Word that she'd scratched from the competition had obviously not yet leaked out. But it would be common knowledge by Friday at the latest, and there would be questions, although she had no idea how she was going to answer them.

Wesley turned Rosie-Jo into her appointed stall at the Brighton grounds. His shoulders were tense, and he'd barely said a word since they boarded the plane in Montana.

She'd been waiting since the wedding for his sullen mood to lift. She kept thinking another day, another week, and he'd stop acting like she'd kicked his dog.

He unclipped Rosie's lead rope, and the horse startled.

"Wesley," Stephanie sighed, knowing time was up. He needed to focus completely on jumping, and that meant she had to confront the situation head-on.

"Yeah?" He concentrated on coiling the lead rope in his callused hands.

"You can't ride like this."

He didn't look up. "Ride like what?"

"You know what I'm talking about."

He crossed to the stall gate and slipped the catch. "I'm fine."

"You're not fine."

He set his lips in a thin line, opening the gate.

She followed him out. "We need to talk—"

"It's none of your business."

"I'm your *coach*."

He glared at her, obviously struggling to mask the hurt with anger. "And I guess that's all you ever were."

Guilt tightened her chest. "Wesley, I never—"

"Never what? Never said we had a future? Never said you liked me? Never rushed off to marry that—"

"Wesley," she warned.

"Why did you lie?" The pain was naked in his eyes now. "All that stuff about us talking about it later. Why didn't you just tell me up-front it was him?"

Wesley was in worse shape than she'd realized, and she knew she had to talk him down. Riding Rosie-Jo at Brighton was a once in a lifetime chance for him to make a splash in front of a huge, national class audience.

"I didn't lie," she told him sincerely. "I do like you."

His lips thinned, and he turned to walk away.

She rushed after him, pushing her hesitation to a far corner of her mind. It was time to be completely honest. "I married Alec because I'm pregnant."

Wesley's head jerked back.

"We got married because of the baby."

He stopped and blinked at her in stunned silence.

"I don't know where it's going, or what will happen in the long-term. But I didn't lie to you, Wesley."

He glanced reflexively at her stomach. "That's why you're not riding."

"Yes."

"You mean…" His brain was obviously ticking through the math, going back to Alec's first visit to the ranch.

"Don't even go there," Stephanie warned, already

regretting her impulse. Her behavior was none of Wesley's business.

"Right." He squared his shoulders. "So it's a marriage of convenience. You're not in love with him."

She didn't answer.

After a beat of silence, the pain and anger cleared from Wesley's eyes. Then he smiled. "So, afterward…"

In an instant, Stephanie realized her error. His hopes were up all over again.

It took Alec the rest of the afternoon to get from Chicago to Lexington and take the short hop to Cedarvale and the Brighton facility.

He tried Stephanie's cell phone again, then tracked down her hotel and had the front desk try her room. In the end, he was forced to talk his way into the restricted area of the grounds and walk methodically through the horse barns looking for her.

He finally spotted her in the distance, outside, next to a white rail fence line decorated with sponsor bulletin boards.

Even at this distance, she took his breath away. The late day sunshine glinted off her hair. She was silhouetted against a dark background, her jeans and white blouse accentuating the body that he adored. He swore he could hear her voice, her laughter, her gasps when he drew her against him and kissed her.

It was all in his mind, of course. He was deluding himself if he thought she'd ever laugh with him again after this.

He wished he didn't have to be mad at her. He didn't want to fight. He wanted to hold her in his arms, caress her and kiss her, tell her everything was going to be okay. Then he wanted to figure out a way to make it okay.

For a moment he wondered if he'd played it wrong at their wedding. She'd asked him to leave, but if he'd stuck around, maybe she wouldn't be here. Their baby would be safe. And he wouldn't be headed for a confrontation that was sure to hurt them both.

As he drew closer still, he saw she was talking to a couple of reporters. Despite his simmering anger, he had to give her kudos for that.

But then he saw who was standing beside her. Wesley again. And the kid was way too close. They were practically touching. While Alec marched forward, Wesley reached up and cupped his hand over her shoulder, giving it a squeeze.

Alec quickened his pace.

The sun was setting, but the barn area was still alive with activity. Grooms walked horses, stable hands moved feed and manure, while technicians worked in the broadcast tents, setting up sound and video equipment for the weekend.

Alec halted beside Stephanie, and in one swift motion wrapped his arm around her shoulder, dislodging Wesley's hand.

Stephanie turned to stare at him. While Wesley's head whipped around. Both reporters immediately stopped talking. And the television camera swung to Alec.

"Alec Creighton," he introduced himself with a nod. "Stephanie's husband."

Stephanie froze beneath his embrace, while the two female reporters' jaws dropped open.

"Sorry to interrupt, darling," he put in easily.

One reporter recovered more quickly and stuffed her microphone in Alec's face. "You're married to Stephanie Ryder."

"Stephanie Creighton," Alec corrected, though they'd never actually discussed her changing her name.

"When did you get married?"

"Tell us about the wedding."

"We were married in Montana. At the Ryder Ranch." Alec made a show of smiling down at Stephanie. "It was a simple ceremony, just the family."

The reporters switched their attention to Stephanie.

"This is big news. Were you planning a formal announcement?"

Alec didn't give Stephanie a chance to speak. Not that she seemed particularly capable of joining the conversation.

"You can take this as a formal announcement," he told them. "You can also take this as notification that Stephanie won't be competing this weekend."

Both microphones went to Stephanie. "You're not competing?"

"Thank you," said Alec. "That's all we have to say for the moment." He swiftly turned her away and started back across the yard.

"You *did not* just do that," Stephanie rasped as they angled across the lawn to the nearest building.

Wesley seemed to have found his feet and was struggling to catch up with them.

"What are you doing here?" Alec demanded of Stephanie.

"What do you mean?"

Wesley caught them at a trot, and Alec pasted him with a warning glare.

Was the kid suicidal?

Stephanie was Alec's wife. Wesley had absolutely no right to be touching her.

"This is a private conversation," Alec announced.

Wesley looked to Stephanie for confirmation, and it was all Alec could do not to send the man sprawling.

"It's okay, Wesley," said Stephanie. "I don't know what he's doing here, but—"

"Goodbye, Wesley," Alec interrupted.

Wesley hesitated a second longer in a transparent and hopeless attempt to pretend he had a choice. Then he shot Alec a hostile look and peeled off to one side, tracking for one of the technical tents.

Stephanie stopped dead. "What is the *matter* with you?"

"Not here," Alec growled, scanning the grounds, looking for a place that offered privacy. It didn't seem promising.

"We'll go back to the hotel." He switched their direction.

"Those were reporters," she hissed under her breath.

"No kidding."

"An hour from now, everybody's going to know we're married."

"Were you planning to keep it a secret?"

"No. I don't know. I hadn't really thought about it."

"What about the baby? Were you planning to keep that a secret, too?"

"Yes. For now anyway."

He grunted, struggling to hold his temper.

She didn't seem to feel guilty. She didn't seem contrite. Had she somehow convinced herself it was okay to fly eight feet in the air and come crashing down on the back of a eighteen-hundred-pound animal? He'd seen her last bruise. The sport was bloody dangerous.

They took a stone pathway to the main hotel tower, crossed the lobby and entered an elevator.

As the elevator filled up, Alec nabbed her hand and

tugged her close beside him. She pressed the button for the twenty-sixth floor.

It was a short walk down the hallway to her room. She inserted the key. He opened the door. Then he shut it behind them.

She immediately turned on him, back to the picture window that looked over the arena. "Are you out of your mind?"

He ignored the question. "Do your brothers know you're here?"

"Of course they know I'm here. Why are you acting like I've done something wrong?"

He advanced on her. "Because you're *pregnant*."

"I know I'm pregnant. That doesn't mean my life stops."

"*This* part of your life stops."

She paused. Her eyes darkened. Then she waggled her finger at him, stepping three paces backward as she shook her head. "Oh, no, no, no. I am not going to sit home in Montana twiddling my thumbs for the next seven months."

He stepped forward once again. "Well you're sure as *hell* not sitting on the back of a horse jumping six-foot oxers."

She blinked. "What?"

"I know you can be reckless. I've heard you're irresponsible. But honest-to-God, Stephanie—"

"What?" she shouted.

"You are *not* going to compete in show jumping while you're pregnant with my baby."

She stared at him like he'd grown two heads. "What makes you think I'm competing?"

He gestured out the picture window. "You're here."

"I'm coaching Wesley."

Nice try. "With Rosie-Jo?"

"Wesley's riding her."

"No, he's not." The woman was caught. She might as well own up to it.

"Yes, he is."

"Rosie-Jo is your horse."

"She's also a once-in-a-lifetime jumper. She's not taking a year off just because I'm forced to."

Alec stopped. A chill of unease spread through him. "You're not jumping?"

"Of course I'm not jumping, you idiot. It's dangerous."

"I *know.* That's why I'm here."

Her shoulders relaxed. "To stop me from jumping?"

"Yes."

"I don't understand, Alec." She gave her head a little shake. "Where did you get the idea…?"

He raked a hand through his hair. "I saw you on television this afternoon. You were here. You had Rosie-Jo. The reporters—"

"And you jumped to a conclusion."

"Apparently."

Her eyes narrowed. "Where were you?"

"Chicago."

"And you flew all the way to Cedarvale?"

"What was I supposed to do?"

"Phone me?"

"I tried."

"Trust me?"

Alec didn't have an answer for that. How could he trust her? He barely knew her.

"It's my baby, too, Alec."

"I know."

"I'm not going to hurt our baby."

Alec drew a breath. He supposed he knew that now. But he had no way of knowing that back in Chicago when the evidence had stacked up against her.

The hotel room telephone jangled.

Stephanie kept him in her sights with a censorious expression as she crossed to answer it.

"Hello?"

She paused. "Yes."

She nodded. "Okay… I know… Thank you."

She hung up the phone then turned to Alec.

"What is it?"

"Word's getting around. You've just been included on a VIP reception invitation for tomorrow night."

She waited, and Alec wasn't sure what to say.

"What are you going to do?" she finally asked.

He knew what he should say, knew he should get his butt back on that plane and leave her the heck alone. But now that he was here, he couldn't bring himself to leave. He found his emotions making deals with his conscience.

He promised himself it would only be for a day or two. He'd get them a suite, so they both had privacy. He wouldn't let her get close, wouldn't let her depend on him. He wouldn't do anything to mislead her.

But when he spoke, his voice came out soft and deliberate. "I guess I'll stick around and be your husband."

"This way," Stephanie said to Alec, pointing to an aisle that stretched between two racks of clothes in the exhibition hall in the basement of the hotel. For the first time in weeks, she felt lighter, almost happy. She'd always enjoyed the social events around major jumping competitions, and she woke up this morning vowing to enjoy them this weekend.

It would be odd hanging out with Alec, odder still that people would know they were married. But at least she'd have a dancing partner.

She supposed there was always a silver lining.

"You have got to be kidding me." Alec stopped dead in his tracks in the middle of the exhibition hall entrance, staring in obvious disbelief at the racks of costumes, hats, shoes and accessories.

"Our party's a 1920s theme," she offered, halting beside him.

He gazed deliberately around the barnlike costume rental setup. "They bring all this in for horse jumping?"

"Tonight isn't the only theme event. And with this many wealthy people in one place, it's a prime opportunity for fund-raising."

People were starting to pile up behind them, so she snagged his arm and tugged him forward.

"You mean I have to dress up in a costume *and* give away my money?" he asked.

"You really don't get out much, do you?" she couldn't help teasing him.

"Not like this," he told her, gazing around the jumble of merchandise taking up about a quarter of the cavernous room. "I'm more a dinner at Palazzo Antinori or a cruise on the Seine kind of guy."

"A closet romantic," she reflexively observed, then cringed at the unfortunate choice of words.

His expression turned serious. "No, Stephanie. I'm not a romantic of any kind."

She sensed some kind of a warning in his words.

"Over there." She cheerfully pointed, changing the subject as they made their way past a suit of medieval armor and a shelf of colored wigs and sparkling Mardi Gras masks.

Alec leaned in close, his tone still dire. "I don't want you to…" He obviously struggled for words.

She refused to prompt him. She really didn't want to pursue this line of conversation.

"To get caught up—"

"In the 1920s?" she wedged in.

"In our marriage," he corrected.

She let sarcasm color her tone. "You afraid I'll mistake a dance for a declaration of undying passion and devotion?"

He backed off a little. "You seem…"

"What?" she demanded.

He shrugged. "Happy. Animated."

"And you attribute that to *you?* Wow. That's some ego you've got going there Alec."

"It's not my ego."

"Right."

He clenched his jaw. "Forget I said anything."

"I will."

"Good."

"You're faking, Alec. I get that. I'm faking it, too." She might have let her emotional guard down for a moment, but she wouldn't make the mistake of enjoying herself again.

He searched her expression. "Fine."

"Fine." She nodded in return. Just flipping fine. Bad enough she had to fake a marriage. Now she wasn't allowed to smile while she did it.

She put her attention on the costume racks again, now simply wanting to get this over with. "You might as well pick something?"

He glanced around. "I'm not a fan of costumes."

"Yeah? Too bad."

He shot her a look of annoyance.

What? She was supposed to get happy again? "Be a man about it," she challenged. "Put on some pinstripes and spats. Be grateful it's not superhero night."

His look of horror almost made her smile.

"You'd look good in red tights."

"Not in this lifetime."

"Check those out." She gestured to a rack of suit jackets.

For herself, she moved further down the aisle, finding a selection of flapper dresses.

She started through them one by one. After a few minutes, she came across a sexy, silky black sheath, dripping with shimmering silver ribbons that flowed from the low-cut neckline, past the short hem of the underdress to knee-length.

With a spurt of mischievousness, she held it against her body. "What do you think?"

His gaze traveled the length of the garment, eyes glittering with what looked suspiciously like humor. "You show up in that, doll-face, and I'd better be packin' heat."

This time, she did crack a smile.

She pulled the dress away from her body, turning it and making a show of taking a critical look. "Too much?"

"Not nearly enough."

She could have sworn there was a sensual edge to his tone. But his cell phone chimed, cutting it off.

She hung the dress back on the rack, battling a wave of prickly heat that slowly throbbed its way through her system. Faking, she reminded herself ruthlessly. Faking, faking, faking.

"Alec Creighton," he said into the phone.

His glance darted to her for a split second, then he turned away, lowering his voice.

She told herself to focus on the costumes and give him his privacy. He had his own life, and she had hers. As he'd so clearly just pointed out, this intersection between them was completely temporary.

Still, she couldn't help catching snatches of the conversation. She heard him say tomorrow, then airport, then Cedarvale.

It sounded like he was leaving, and a wave of disappointment surprised and worried her. It was good that he was leaving.

But then she heard him say her brothers' names. She blinked at his back, listening unabashedly to the final snatches of the conversation.

As he signed off, she quickly grabbed another dress, pretending to be absorbed by it.

"This one?" she asked.

It was a soft, champagne silk, with a low V-neck, spaghetti straps and covered in sparkling, criss-cross beading. The silk came to midthigh, while a wide, sheer, metallic lace hemline, slashed to points, rustled around her knees.

"They don't have anything with sleeves?" he frowned.

"It's the roaring twenties," she told him, trying not to wonder about his phone call. "I'm supposed to look like your moll. What do you think? A wide choker and a long string of pearls?"

"I think you'll be the death of me."

"What about the red one?" she lifted another from the rack. "It comes with satin gloves and a feather boa.

Alec's nostrils flared. "Better stick with the gold."

"It's champagne."

"Not the red, and definitely not the black."

"Fine." She put the red one back, wishing she was brave enough to ask about the phone call. Was he leaving? And why had he mentioned her brothers? "What about a long cigarette holder?" she asked instead.

"Absolutely not. You're pregnant."

"Shhhh." She glanced quickly around, worried someone would overhear.

He moved closer, leaning down to whisper. "You're pregnant."

"I wouldn't really smoke anything."

"Don't even joke about it."

"Who was on the phone?" she blurted out.

"A friend."

"Does he know my brothers?"

Alec's brow furrowed. "No. Why?"

"No reason," she lied, glancing away. "I thought it might be about the Ryder International review. Are you leaving tomorrow?"

"You trying to get rid of me?"

She looked back up at him again, puzzling over why he'd hold back the truth about the phone call. If the friend didn't know her brothers, Alec wouldn't have mentioned their names. "I need to get Wesley prepared," she told him.

Alec's jaw tightened, eyes squinting further. "I'm staying."

"Okay," she agreed.

He gave a sharp nod of acknowledgment.

Moving away from yet another uncomfortable moment, she gestured to the rack of suits. "Did you find something to wear?"

"I'm not wearing pinstripes."

"How about a hat?" She selected one with a center dent and a wide, satin band and tried to place it on his head.

He jerked sideways, out of the way. "How about a suit jacket and a pair of slacks, and I write a check big enough that nobody cares?"

Seven

Chandeliers dangled from the ballroom ceiling, while massive ice sculptures and floral arrangements decorated white linen tables. The waiters wore period tuxedoes, and a big band played a jazz tune on a low stage in one corner of the room.

On Alec's arm, Stephanie glittered. Her rich, auburn hair bounced in a halo of tight curls to her bare shoulders. It was pulled back on one side by an elaborate, rhinestone clip, which matched her ornate necklace and dangling earrings. Her makeup had been done in a bright twenties-style, and the shimmering, champagne dress clung to her lithe body.

Alec couldn't help a surge of pride as people turned to stare. His marriage might be a sham, but he was the envy of every man in the room.

He leaned down to whisper. "You should dress up like a girl more often."

"They're not looking at me," she whispered back, smiling politely at the onlookers.

"Yes, they are." More people turned to stare.

Up to now, it hadn't occurred to Alec to wonder how Stephanie had made it to twenty-two as a virgin. But now it sure did. He also realized men would be lining up to take his place the minute he was out of the picture.

It was not a pleasant thought.

"They've heard," she told him in an undertone.

"Heard what?"

"About us. That we got married."

He disagreed. "It's you." Still, at the mention of his temporary position, he couldn't stop himself from curling his arm around the small of her back.

"Oh, sure," she mocked. "Really give them something to talk about."

"I could give you a kiss."

"You're incorrigible."

"Just playing my part."

"Play it from over there." She quickly sidestepped out of his embrace.

He followed, snagging her around the waist once more. "And how will that be convincing?"

"Give it your best effort."

"Oh, I intend to," he drawled.

"Stephanie," purred a woman in a floor-length, peacock-blue, sequined gown. She swept in front of them with a flourish, looking to be about sixty-five, though very well preserved. Her streaked blond hair was decorated with blue feathers, and she brandished a matching fan like a weapon.

"Mrs. Cleary," Stephanie greeted with a smile, and the woman's gaze immediately jumped to Alec. She raised her sculpted brows.

"This is my husband, Alec Creighton," Stephanie supplied smoothly.

Alec liked the sound of that. He let his hand slip to hers, and he stroked the pad of his thumb across her diamond ring and the matching wedding band.

Stephanie jolted her hand away. "Mrs. Cleary is the president of the Brighton Fund-raising Committee." The tone told him he ought to be impressed.

"A pleasure, Mrs. Cleary." He gave her a warm smile and used his newly freed hand to shake with her.

She checked him over carefully. "Please, call me Bridget."

"Bridget," he obliged.

"I hear congratulations are in order." The words were more an accusation than a tribute.

"Indeed, they are." Alec drew Stephanie firmly to his side, feeling her soft curves beneath the sexy dress. There was no law telling him he couldn't enjoy his acting role. "We're looking forward to starting a family."

He felt her stiffen, but how could she complain? He was simply smoothing the pathway for the inevitable announcement of her pregnancy.

"Stephanie?" came a second voice, a younger woman this time. "Are you going to introduce me?" She offered Alec a gleaming white, perfectly straight orthodontic smile.

She looked to be in her late twenties and wore a bright purple, beaded dress, and a matching headband. She held a long cigarette holder, and her blond hair was upswept in a riot of curls. Her lashes were dark with heavy makeup, and she wore fishnet stockings with high-heeled, black shoes accented by an oversize silver buckle on the sexy ankle strap.

In another time and another place, he would have smiled right back at the undeniably beautiful woman. She was the stuff of erotic dreams. But Alec found he preferred Stephanie's more understated look. And it wasn't just the fake husband in him speaking. Interesting.

"Rene," Stephanie greeted, her voice slightly tight, features carefully neutral. "This is my husband, Alec."

There was a proprietary inflection on the word husband. Nice.

"Pleasure to meet you, Alec the husband," Rene giggled as she extended the back of her hand, wiggling her fingers in an obvious invitation.

He ignored the hint, and shook her hand instead of kissing the back.

She gave a mock pout with her jewel-red lips.

A tall, thin man appeared. He wore an outrageous purple velvet coat with leopard-print trim and matching slacks.

"Rene," he admonished, from beneath a broad brimmed hat. Then he glared a warning at Alec.

Alec had to bite down hard to keep from laughing. It was tough to take a man seriously when he was dressed like a sitcom pimp.

"Alec Creighton," he said instead and extended his hand. "I believe our wives know each other."

The man's eyes went round.

"Wife?" Rene cackled. "That'll be the day."

"My apologies," said Alec. Then he smiled warmly down at Stephanie. "But I highly recommend it." He glanced back at the man. "You should think about asking her."

The man looked like a deer in the headlights.

Alec could feel Stephanie's body vibrate with repressed laughter.

"What do you think, sweetheart?" Alec asked her.

"Dance," she sputtered, grabbing Alec's arm and turning him away from Rene.

Alec quickly took the lead as they wove their way through the crowd.

"You are *bad*," Stephanie accused.

"They deserved it. So, who is she?"

"She's the princess of the circuit. Her father owns a stable of jumping horses."

"Big deal. So do you."

Stephanie snorted out a laugh. "Not like he does."

Alec drew her into his arms and swung her into the latest song in a Duke Ellington tribute. "You're not intimidated are you?"

"By Rene?" Stephanie easily followed his lead.

"Yes." He waited. He'd learned to recognize it when she was stalling.

She paused. "Maybe once. She's been glamorous since she was twelve."

"You're glamorous now."

Stephanie coughed out a laugh. "Not like her."

Alec let his hand trail along the smooth silk of Stephanie's dress, letting the tactile memory remind him of exactly how gorgeous she'd looked walking out of her hotel bedroom earlier. She'd positively taken his breath away.

Now, his voice went husky. "Better than her."

She didn't answer, but she seemed to mold slightly closer against him. He gathered her tight, ignoring the warning that was sounding in his brain.

"Besides," he forced himself to joke. "She's obviously jealous of your husband."

"Ego, Alec?"

"A man can tell these things."

"Because she was flirting with you?"

"Exactly."

Stephanie chuckled. "She flirts with everyone."

"I'm quite a catch," he protested, telling himself to put a little distance between their bodies.

He ignored himself.

"You have quite the ego."

"Part of my charm."

"You have charm?"

He didn't answer. Instead he savored the feel of her in his arms, inhaling the scent of her hair, letting the haunting strains of a saxophone solo carry them away.

"I suppose you do," she said softly.

"What?"

"Have charm."

He drew back. "You're conceding a point?"

"You also have looks," she continued. "But you already know that. Every woman in the room is envious of me right now."

"You mean every man is envious of me." He drew a breath. "How is it," he struggled to frame the question that had been nagging at him for weeks. "That you stayed a virgin all those years?"

"I don't get out much."

"I'm serious."

"So am I."

"Stephanie?"

She shrugged against him. "I honestly never had any offers."

Now that was ridiculous. He chuckled low. "Maybe there weren't any verbal offers. But, trust me, there were offers. You've had at least two dozen since you walked into this room."

She pulled back. "Where?"

"Never mind."

"You're crazy."

"I'm just smarter than you."

She rolled her eyes.

"More observant," he amended.

"You have a vivid imagination."

"And you have a sexy rear end."

"You keep your mind off my— *Hey,* there's Royce. What's he doing here?"

Alec didn't know whether to resent the interruption or be grateful Royce had arrived so promptly.

Before he could make up his mind, Stephanie was out of his arms and heading off the dance floor.

Alec followed closely behind.

She glanced from her brother to Amber. "Where did you guys come from?"

Amber grinned, but her quick glance at Alec told him she knew they were here about Stanton.

"We were in Chicago," she told Stephanie. "But you know your brother. I mentioned you might need moral support, and the next thing I knew we were taxiing down the tarmac."

Stephanie's brows knit together. "But I'm not even riding."

"Exactly," said Amber, drawing Stephanie a small distance away from Alec and Royce.

Royce gave him a nod. "I got your voice mail."

"Damien has news," Alec returned. "Amber knows?"

Royce stepped closer and kept his voice low. "Amber's the brains of the outfit. She was the one that noticed the resemblance between Frank's sister and Stephanie."

Alec nodded. "You have an intelligent fiancée."

"I have an amazing fiancée."

Alec's gaze strayed to Amber's black and red costume. The women were drawing more than their share of appreciative male glances. "You might want to hurry up and marry her."

Royce looked around, clearly making the same observation as Alec. "She's having trouble deciding on the wedding location." His shoulders squared. "But we might have to make a detour through Nevada on the way home."

Alec gave a chopped chuckle, while Royce took a half step toward Stephanie and Amber to stare a man down.

The man moved on, and Royce drew back. "What time's the meeting?"

"Wesley has a warm-up scheduled at three. Stephanie has to be there. I told Damien I'd call when the coast was clear."

"He's here?"

"On his way." It would be good news. Alec might not have heard the details yet, but if Damien was finished in Spain, Norman Stanton was no longer going to be a threat to the Ryders.

"How do we know Stanton won't go back on his word?" Royce asked Damien.

Alec had waited until Stephanie was occupied in the arena with Wesley and Rosie-Jo, then he'd given the all clear signal to Damien, Jared, Royce, Melissa and Amber. The group had assembled in the hotel suite's living room.

Jared nodded to back up his brother's question. "The man's a blackmailer and a thief."

Damien cast a fleeting glance to Alec. He wasn't used to having his situational assessment questioned. But he was also a consummate professional, so he wouldn't make an issue.

"Norman knows we can reach out and touch him in Morocco," he answered simply.

Alec straightened from where he'd propped his shoulder against the arched entryway to the dining area. "There aren't a lot of places left for him to hide."

"He must be pretty ticked off," Melissa put in. "What's to stop him from calling a tabloid and exposing it to the world?"

"Arrest and incarceration," said Alec.

Jared elaborated. "Stanton must have thought he was safe in Morocco. Yet Damien tracked him down and lured him to Spain. He knows we're tenacious, and he has to be feeling like there aren't a lot of places left to hide."

"Could the police really extradite him from Spain?" asked Royce.

Damien gave a little half smile. "Technically, yes. Practically… It's hard to say. But if you're Norman Stanton, do you take that chance?"

"We've got him trapped in a standoff," Alec clarified. "He talks to Stephanie, we press charges."

"A smart man takes the money and runs." Jared nodded.

"Any chance we can get the money back?" asked Amber. Then she glanced around at the blank faces. "We're talking about twelve million dollars here."

"I can look into it," said Damien. "But he'll have spent a lot of it already."

Royce shook his head. "I'm done. Stephanie's the important thing. I say if he walks away, we walk away."

Melissa's eyes went wide. "Excuse me? Twelve million dollars?" She glanced to Jared, and it was obvious the sum was news to her.

"Paid out over at least ten years," Jared told his wife.

"It was Grandpa Benteen and McQuestin," Amber elaborated. "They didn't know how else to—" She stopped, suddenly casting a guilty glance to Jared, obviously realizing Melissa might not know about Stephanie's illegitimacy.

"We have another problem," Alec told the gathering.

Everyone went silent.

He snagged one of the dining room chairs, straddling it backward in the archway and propping his elbows on the back.

Damien backed off a few steps, positioning himself near the glass patio door.

"Your mother was six months older than your father," Alec explained to Jared and Royce, trying to keep it as straightforward as possible. "Since they died together, she was deemed to have predeceased him."

Both men watched him, expressions growing wary.

"In his will, should his wife predecease him, your father asked that his estate 'be divided among my children, then alive.'"

There was a split second before the words sank in.

"Stephanie's not his child," said Jared.

"Frank Stanton." Melissa shook her head.

"But we can fix it?" Royce asked.

"I talked to Katie Merrick. It'll take a few lawyers, and a stack of contracts, but it's doable. Trick is, you'll have to get Stephanie to sign them without reading them."

"Too late for that." Stephanie's terse voice intruded.

Alec jerked his head toward her.

Stephanie stood in the foyer doorway. Her face was pale, but her eyes glittered with anger.

"Oh, no," Amber rasped.

Alec came to his feet.

Stephanie stared at her bothers. "I'm…" That was as far as she made it.

Both of them stood, but she held up a hand to stop them. "And nobody was going to *tell* me?" She turned her accusing stare on Alec.

"What did you hear?" he asked, his mind scrambling for a damage control plan.

"Is this a conspiracy?" She glanced around the room. Her gaze stopped on Damien. "Who's this?"

Damien glanced to Alec.

"He's yours," Stephanie scoffed at Alec. "Of course he's yours. Is this why they hired you?"

Alec took a step forward. "Stephanie."

"Wow." She gave a shaky laugh. "Is that what you're doing for us? Is Ryder International even *in* financial trouble?"

"Stephanie," Jared began.

"You should sit down," Royce put in.

Stephanie rounded on him. "*You* should start talking."

The two stared at each other for a moment.

"We were being blackmailed," said Royce.

"By Alec?"

"*No*," Alec jumped in, unable to remain silent any longer. "By Norman Stanton. I *was* looking into your finances." He wasn't about to hit Royce and Jared with an *I told you so,* but it was darn tempting.

"So you claim." Stephanie glared at him. "But we both know you can fake pretty much anything."

"Alec's not the bad guy," said Amber.

"Then who's the bad guy?"

"Frank Stanton," said Royce.

"And he's my father?"

"Can we talk about this later?" asked Royce, his gaze going pointedly to Damien.

"Sure." Stephanie shrugged. "Don't mind me." She crossed to a desk and picked up some papers. "I just dropped by for the insurance forms. Let me know how this all turns out. I'll sign anything you want."

"Don't start sulking," warned Jared.

Alec felt a flash of anger. He moved to position himself between the two. "I think she's got a right to be a little upset," he told Jared.

Jared's eyes narrowed down. "Stay out of it."

"I don't believe I will." Alec folded his arms across his chest. They were the ones that hired him. They insisted he marry Stephanie. Convenience or not, she was his wife.

Royce stepped up beside his brother. "It's a family matter."

"I'm family."

"Not really."

"I have a piece of paper that says so."

Stephanie stepped back in. "And they have a piece of paper that says *I'm* not. Procured by *you,* if I overheard correctly."

"You're still our sister," Jared hastily put in.

"Half sister. Out of the will."

"There you go again," Royce all but shouted. "The most dramatic possible—"

"I think you'd better leave," Alec said to the brothers.

"Us leave?" Jared's voice was incredulous. "*You* leave."

"It's my hotel room. And she's my wife—"

"Give me a break!" Stephanie threw up her hands. "*I'll* leave."

"No." Alec's hand shot out to stop her. "We need to talk." Past today, they were still having a baby, and they still had to make that work.

"Let go of Stephanie," Royce growled.

Amber came to her feet, voice commanding. "Stop this. All of you. I mean it."

She placed herself between Alec and Royce. "Alec wants to talk to Stephanie."

Royce clamped his jaw in silent protest, but everyone filed out. Alec was left alone with Stephanie. "For the record," he told her, "I advised them to tell you the truth."

She didn't turn around. "Why didn't you tell me the truth?"

"I promised I wouldn't."

She was silent for a moment. "So a business contract is more important to you than your wedding vows?"

Alec drew a breath.

"Never mind," she continued. "Don't answer that."

He moved a few steps toward her. "It was complicated. I had no right—"

She turned. "No right to be honest with your wife?"

"Don't twist things to score points."

The woman had enough on her side of this argument without doing that.

She dropped into one of the French provincial chairs. "So, I guess I'm a bastard."

He pulled out another chair and angled it toward hers, sitting down. "So am I. It's not so bad."

"I meant literally, not metaphorically."

"So did I."

Her expression softened ever so slightly. "Really?"

"My father eventually married my mother." Though that had turned out to be more a curse than a blessing.

Stephanie slumped back in the chair. "My mother had an affair."

"So it would seem."

"I've had her up on a pretty high pedestal all these years."

Alec leaned forward, covering Stephanie's hands where they rested in her lap. "She was human."

"You accept infidelity?"

"I understand weakness and imperfection."

"Are you imperfect, Alec?"

"I took your virginity and made you pregnant while I was working for your brothers. Then I lied to you. Well, held back the truth anyway."

"And you'll eventually be unfaithful."

He drew back. "What? No. Why would I—"

"Can you really stay celibate for months on end?"

"I don't know," he admitted. He'd never tried.

It had only been a couple of weeks since the wedding, but so far he hadn't had any overwhelming desire to sleep with other women. Ironically the only person he wanted to make love to was Stephanie.

"You'll eventually give into temptation," she determined.

"Where is this coming from?"

"My mother did. Your parents did. We did."

"You've really wandered off on a tangent here." He wanted to talk about her family, to make sure she was coping okay with the truth.

"I'm merely pointing out that we both have the infidelity gene."

He coughed out a surprised laugh. "It comes down to principles and personal choice."

"*We* slept together."

The reminder made him aware of their joined hands, her sweet scent and those cherry-red lips that were slightly parted with her breath.

"Yes, we did," he agreed.

"When we shouldn't have."

"That's debatable. We didn't betray anyone."

"Except maybe ourselves."

Alec shifted his chair closer and raised their joined hands. "Do you feel guilty, Stephanie?"

She gazed into his eyes. "Do you?"

He shook his head. "I don't have a single regret about making love to you. And I don't hate Frank Stanton. And I'm glad your mother gave into temptation. If not for that, you wouldn't be here."

"So, I should be grateful?"

"You should be sensible. Don't rail against things you can't change. Just make the best of what you have."

She seemed to think about that for a minute. Then her lips softened, and her voice went low. "I miss you, Alec."

Desire instantly overran his brain. "I'm right here."

"That's not what I meant."

"I know." He steeled himself against the urge to drag her into his arms. "But you're upset and vulnerable, and I still have a few principles left."

Silver sparkled to life deep in her eyes. "How can I get rid of them?"

Simply by breathing. His hands convulsed around hers. "You can't."

A sharp rap sounded on the suite door, and Stephanie frowned.

Alec felt like he'd been saved from himself. They were only going to stay away so long.

Eight

"You know Stephanie's going to see him," Amber warned Royce in an undertone.

Alec slowed his steps, not wanting to intrude on what was obviously a private conversation, but wanting to know about anything that involved Stephanie.

She and her brothers had talked late into the night. Then Alec had seen her briefly at breakfast. But Wesley was in final preparation for competing tomorrow, so Stephanie's entire day was being spent at the arena. It annoyed Alec that Wesley was still flirting with her.

Royce gave Alec a nod of welcome. "I'm half tempted to buy it for her," Royce said to Amber.

"You know you can't do that," Amber returned. "The price tag's up over a million dollars."

"Hey, Alec," Royce greeted, and Amber turned around to face him.

Alec wished he could ask what they were debating. He hoped there weren't any more family secrets being kept from Stephanie.

He settled for, "What's up?"

"Blanchard's Run is here," said Amber.

Alec nodded, hoping to bluff his way through the conversation.

"Stephanie's still upset," said Royce.

"You can't buy her a million dollar horse to make her feel better," warned Amber, jabbing Royce with her elbow. "Tell him, Alec."

"She's right," Alec agreed. Stephanie didn't need monetary bribes from her brothers. She needed them to respect her enough to be honest with her.

"She's had her eye on him for months," said Royce.

"Here she is now," Alec warned them, as Stephanie approached from the opposite end of the barn. Her smooth, sexy stride carried swiftly along in her tooled cowboy boots.

Amber and Royce both turned.

"Uh-oh," Amber breathed.

Stephanie's attention had been caught by one of the stalls. She stopped and drew back in obvious surprise. Then she turned to walk to the gate.

She stood there for a few moments staring at the horse inside. Then she squared her shoulders and resumed walking toward them.

Nobody said a word as she approached.

"You knew, didn't you?" she asked her brother.

"We just found out," Amber quickly put in.

Stephanie cocked her head as she gazed steadily at Royce.

"We just saw him," he backed Amber up.

"But you weren't going to tell me."

They didn't deny it.

"Was that for my own good, too?"

When nobody immediately answered, she shook her head in disgust then paced off down the center aisle of the barn toward the hotel and the main offices.

Alec went quickly after her. "What was that about?"

She didn't break her stride. "Blanchard's Run."

"He's a horse, right?"

"He is."

"And you want to buy him?"

"I do."

"But he's expensive." Alec had the full picture now.

"He's a bargain."

"A million dollars?"

"You're just like the rest of them."

"Hold up there for a second." He snagged her arm, tugged her to a stop before she could exit the barn and join the crowds outside.

She stopped, but turned on him, eyes blazing.

"Is this important?" he asked.

"Not at all," she denied.

"Stephanie?"

She drew in an impatient sigh and crossed her arms beneath her breasts. "Why do you want to know?"

"Because I do. Because you're not mad at me, you're mad at them." He jabbed his thumb back in Royce's direction. "And because I hate it when you act like a spoiled kid."

Her eyes narrowed.

"You're not, you know. You're an intelligent woman who knows what she wants and how to work for it. You want this horse, and I'm curious to know why."

"Fine." She drew a breath. "I've been interested in

Blanchard's Run for nearly a year. I've studied his blood-lines and the conformation of his offspring, along with their competition records. And I think the combination of Blanchard's Run and my retired mare, Pinnacle, would produce fast, smart, high jumpers. If science and genetics has anything to say about it, the EBVs of their offspring would be off the charts."

"EBVs?"

"Estimated Breeding Value."

"Oh."

"In technical terms, they would be worth a whole lot of money."

"Really?"

"Yes, really. I can also breed him to three other mares I've bought this year, partly in anticipation of a future acquisition of Blanchard's Run. Then, three, maybe five years from now, if his existing offspring prove out the way I expect them to, and if the Ryder foals show promise, we'll be able to get top dollar for the animals."

Alec was impressed. "So, why don't your brothers want you to buy the horse?"

"Because they've never listened long enough to know my plan is based on concrete science. They assume I'm operating on emotion instead of intelligence."

"They're wrong," said Alec.

"Yeah? Well, since I'm out of the will, I don't have much of a leg to stand on anymore."

"There is that." Even as Alec was agreeing with her, he was coming to a decision.

It had nothing to do with guilt. And it had nothing to do with his feelings for Stephanie. And it wasn't to help her feel better after yesterday's revelations. It was a good business decision, plain and simple.

* * *

Stephanie blinked in disbelief at Blanchard's Run's ownership papers. They'd been delivered to the hotel suite five minutes ago, with her name on the envelope.

She squeezed her eyes shut and shook her head against what had to be an illusion. But, no, she wasn't crazy. That was her name, and Ryder Equestrian Center, and Blanchard's Run's pedigree.

The suite door opened.

Alec strode in and glanced at the papers. A grin spread across his face.

"You?" she asked in amazement.

"I thought you made a convincing case."

She stared up at him, her brain grappling with the situation. "You bought Blanchard's Run?"

He tossed his key card on the table near the foyer. "Was it all true? The EBV thing?"

"Of course it was."

"Good. 'Cause if it's not, I just made a very big mistake."

"It's all true," she assured him with a nod, emotion stinging the backs of her eyes. Nobody had ever trusted her like this before.

"I'll expect him to make money," Alec warned.

She nodded. "He will."

"Are you hungry?"

Suddenly she was. "Starved."

"You want to go out or stay in?"

"Could we eat out on the balcony?" she asked, warm feelings for Alec blossoming inside her. It was a gorgeous night, and she loved the view across the grounds to the arena. She felt like celebrating. And she felt like being alone with Alec.

"I'll call room service," he offered.

"I'm going to shower." She hugged the ownership papers to her chest, smiling all the way to her bedroom.

Alec had made a business investment in her. He trusted her to make good decisions, to make money.

She set the papers carefully on the bedroom desk, smoothing them out. Then she stripped off her work-worn clothes and headed for the shower.

She scrubbed her hair and rinsed it with conditioner. Then she shaved her legs and used some of the rose scented shower gel and body lotion provided by the hotel. After blow-drying, she wrapped herself in a fluffy robe and wandered back into her bedroom.

The windows were open, letting in the fresh night air.

She felt light and happy, optimistic about the future for the first time in weeks. Blanchard's Run would kick Ryder Equestrian Center to a whole new level.

She pulled open the dresser drawers. Her choices were limited, but she was in a mood to dress up.

She found a matching set of underwear, white lace panties and a low-cut bra. She pushed a pair of pearl earrings into her ears, fastened the matching necklace and bracelet, then crossed to the closet for the single dress she'd brought along on the trip.

A soft, clingy knit, it had narrow straps, a low square-cut neck and crisscrossed ties decorating a tapered V back. The skirt flared over her hips, cascading softly toward her knees. She quickly realized the bra wouldn't work and tossed it back in the drawer.

In the bathroom, she put on a little makeup. She tied her hair up, then brushed it back down, then twisted it in a messy knot at the back of her head, letting wisps curl across her forehead and along her temples.

She heard a knock on the suite's outer door. Alec's footfalls told her he was answering, and she gave the waiter a few minutes to finish setting up. Then she slipped her feet into little black sandals and left the bedroom.

Alec wasn't in sight, but the glow of candlelight flickered through the glass, balcony door.

She wandered outside to find hurricane lamps decorating the patterned, white, wrought-iron tables. Linen and silverware was set out, and plump, peach colored cushions softened the chairs. Salad had been served, while a low wreath of flowers surrounded the glass chimney candle at the center of the table.

"Madame?" came a low voice as a tuxedoed waiter appeared.

He pulled out her chair as Alec arrived in the doorway.

He'd also showered and shaved. He wore charcoal slacks and an open collared, white, dress shirt.

His gaze took in her outfit. "You look very nice." The words were reserved, but there was a burn in his eyes that warmed her from head to toe.

She sat down, and Alec took the chair opposite.

The waiter poured them each a glass of ice water to go with their salads, then melted away, closing the glass door behind him as a chorus of crickets ebbed and flowed from the shrubs and grass far below.

"Do my brothers know you bought Blanchard's Run?" She tried a bite of the fresh greens, avocado and raspberry vinaigrette salad.

Alec shook his head, tasting the salad himself. "You can surprise them."

"They'll be very surprised."

Alec shrugged. "It's your horse, your stable."

She took a few more bites, then dared a personal question. "How did you afford him?" She loved the horse, but she didn't want Alec going out on a limb financially.

He stared levelly at her.

"I'm sorry," she quickly apologized. "Was that too personal?"

"No. It just hadn't occurred to me that you didn't know."

"Know what?"

"Anything about my financial status."

"Or your family. Well, except for that little bit about your parents."

"Where I know pretty much everything about you."

She set down her fork. "More than me, as it turns out."

He gave a rueful smile.

The waiter reappeared, removing their salad plates and replacing them with chicken and pasta before disappearing once again.

"Financially I'm perfectly comfortable," said Alec.

Stephanie wasn't sure what that meant.

"I didn't have to borrow money to buy Blanchard's Run," he elaborated.

"So, you didn't marry me for my money?"

He smiled at her. "I didn't marry you for your money."

She cut into the tender chicken. "You know, we never signed a prenup."

"Are you worried?"

"Not anymore," she deadpanned.

"You could come out ahead on this," he speculated.

"Good to know. Since I have very expensive taste in horses."

Alec coughed out a laugh, and she smiled along with

him. His slate eyes reflected the glint of the candlelight, and the flicker of the flame bounced off the planes and angles of his face. He was a spectacularly handsome man.

Her gaze was drawn to his open collar, pushing her thoughts to his muscled chest and impressive shoulders. She couldn't help but remember him naked, in the pale light of her bedroom, his touch, his scent, his taste.

She moved on to his hands, stilled now on the silverware that rested against his plate. The things those hands had done to her.

"Is Madame finished?" The waiter's voice startled her.

"Yes, please." She drew a ragged breath, shifting in her chair as she became aware of the prickled heat chafing her skin.

"We'll skip dessert," Alec told the man. "Thank you for your time."

"Very good, sir." Once more, he disappeared, this time leaving the suite. They were alone.

A full minute of silence ticked by while the breeze freshened, and candlelight flicked across the planes and angles of Alec's face.

"You bought me a horse," she sighed, still not quite believing it could be true.

He shrugged. "I know most guys go with flowers."

"But you're not most guys."

"I guess not."

"*Definitely* not."

He bunched his napkin and tossed it on the table. "So, what did you get me?"

"I was supposed to buy a gift?" She feigned alarm.

He nodded. "It *is* our anniversary."

"What anniversary is that?"

"Fifteen days."

"Ahh," she nodded. "The little known fifteen-day horse-themed anniversary."

"Celebrated from Iceland to Estonia."

"We're in Kentucky."

"So, no present for me?"

She tucked her hair behind her ears. "I saw a ten-gallon hat in the gift shop downstairs."

He grinned. "Not my style."

"A silver, long-horn steer belt buckle?"

He rose from his chair. "Try again."

"I've got a nice riding crop in the trailer."

"Did you mean that to be sexy?"

"Noooo," she chuckled as she shook her head.

"Thank goodness." He made his way around the table. "I mean, *ouch*."

"You'd prefer sexy underwear to leather?"

He held out his hand. "Sexy underwear would definitely be my first choice for a gift."

She placed her hand in his, taking a deep breath and screwing up her courage. "Had to go without a bra tonight," she confessed.

His gaze dipped down. "Guess that saves me some unwrapping."

She rose to her feet, heart pounding, perspiration beginning to glow on her skin. "Yes, it does."

"I've missed you," he said.

"I'm right here," she parroted.

He smiled at the joke. "That's not what I meant." And his gaze did a tour of her body. His eyes darkened to pewter, going molten with desire.

"It's not what I meant, either," she whispered, zeroing in

on his lips, coming up on her toes, while his hand wrapped around to the small of her back and drew her close.

She stroked her palms up the length of his chest, reveling in the play of muscles beneath the thin cotton. She curved over his shoulders, to the back of his neck, into the rough texture of his hairline, while his mouth slowly descended to hers.

She parted her lips, her entire body softening in reaction to her nearness, his touch.

He stopped, lips a fraction of an inch from hers. "Tell me this isn't gratitude."

"Would it matter?" she couldn't resist asking.

"I know I should say yes." He sucked in a breath. "But, honestly. Maybe."

"It's quid pro quo," she teased.

"Sex with you is worth a million dollars?"

She drew back. "Sex? I thought we were talking about a kiss."

"We can stop at a kiss," he assured her, settling his arms more comfortably around her waist.

"I think we should do that," she responded.

"You're lying."

"Absolutely." She inched back, pasting a sultry smile on her face and sliding one of her straps off her shoulder. Then she pushed down the other. The slinky fabric caught on her hardened nipples, clinging there in the candlelight.

Alec glanced around, obviously confirming they had privacy. Then he drew her into the shadow of the overhang.

"For a million dollars," he whispered, as his lips finally came down on hers in an explosion of taste and texture. He kissed her deeply and thoroughly, and her body nearly melted when his fingers found her zipper and pushed it down.

Her dress fell away, the breeze of the night caressing her skin. He surrounded her near naked body with his strong arms, hands roaming everywhere as he pressed her against the smooth, warm concrete wall.

She squirmed against him.

And his breathing rasped. "For a million dollars, I think we're going to have to do it twice."

Twice turned out to be essential for Alec. Because the first time was over far too fast. And he was convinced he could make love to Stephanie all night long.

In his bedroom now, he kissed the damp skin at the back of her neck, drawing her heated body more solidly into the cradle of his own. She fit perfectly. Everything about her fit perfectly, and he was beginning to wonder if he'd ever grow tired of holding her in his arms.

"Tell me about your family," she said softly, toying with the sheet he'd drawn over them both. The comforter had long since hit the floor, and most of the pillows were scattered around the room.

"Not a good time," he breathed. He wanted to focus on here and now, not on the past, and not on the future.

She eased onto her back. "Why not?"

He gazed down at her incredibly gorgeous face. There were two freckles nearly merged together on the cheekbone below her right eye. He kissed them, loving that he was close enough to observe that and so many other intimate and delightful things about her.

"Alec?" she prompted as his hand slid over her hipbone, wandering down her thigh.

"What?"

"Why not?"

He drew back a few inches. "Let me see... Maybe because I've got a beautiful, naked woman in my arms?"

"We already made love."

"We're doing it twice, remember? You insisted."

"I need a rest."

"Liar."

She grinned but didn't give in. "You have to tell me something about your family."

"I was an only child, and my father was a hard-ass."

"How so?"

"He was harsh and demanding, with expectations that nobody could ever hope to meet." Alec kissed her ear, letting his fingertips flutter over her flat stomach.

It blew him away to think of his baby in there. It also blew him away to have her in his bed again. He'd slept with plenty of women, but he'd never felt this close to any of them. And he'd never felt so protective and so completely privileged.

"Did he hurt you?" she asked in a small voice.

Alec drew back again. "You mean physically?"

She nodded.

"Of course he did. But I was a teenager by then, and I could take it."

Her eyes widened in sympathy, and she wrapped her arms around his neck, squeezing tight.

"I love the effect," he told her, hugging her back. "But I'm not crazy about the motivation."

"Oh, Alec."

"Don't do this, Stephanie. It was a long time ago. It wasn't that bad, certainly nothing to turn into a movie of the week."

"Nobody ever hit me," she told him.

His hug tightened reflexively. "They'd better not have."

"It's not fair."

"Nothing's fair. But I got the girl in the end, so I win."

It was her turn to draw back. "You mean me?"

"Who *else* would I mean? How bad do you think I am at this?"

That coaxed a smile out of her. "You mean pillow talk?"

"Like I'm going to lay in bed with you and talk about some other woman."

She shrugged. "How should I know?"

Her question brought a warm glow to his chest. "I love it that I was the first."

"You didn't seem that thrilled at the time."

"I was feeling freaking guilty at the time."

The sympathy was gone from her eyes, and the teasing light was back. "For taking advantage of my innocence?"

"For not having properly appreciated the privilege of being your first lover."

"What about your mother?" she asked.

"You're not going to let this go, are you?"

"No."

He hesitated for a long moment. But Stephanie deserved to know the truth. "She died when I was ten."

Her eyes clouded. "Oh, no. What happened?"

This time, Alec's hesitation was even longer. "She swallowed a bottle of sleeping pills."

Stephanie's eyes went wide. "She killed herself?"

He nodded. "Very few people know that."

Stephanie shook her head to assure him she'd keep the secret. "Do you know why?"

"My father was a hard-ass," Alec repeated.

She closed her eyes and drew him close. "Oh, Alec."

"It was a long time ago." It truly was. "I don't even know why I told you."

"Quid pro quo," she whispered against his shoulder, kissing him softly. "You know all my secrets."

"I do." He skimmed his hand over her belly, along her thighs and around to cup her bottom, feeling so incredibly lucky to be so close to her. "Have I ever told you how grateful I am that you'll be my baby's mother?"

She drew back, giving him an astonished gaze. "Seriously?"

"Seriously." He hesitated.

"Why?" she finally whispered.

He gave in to complete honesty. "Because you're everything I'm not."

Her eyes went round, and he bent to kiss her smooth stomach.

"You hear that, kid?" His voice unexpectedly thickened. "You're going to have the best mother in the world."

She stroked her fingers through his hair, and he kissed her again, softly and leisurely. Then he pecked and suckled his way over her stomach to her breasts. She gasped as he took one pebbled nipple into his mouth, and his body instantly reacted to her taste and texture. Stephanie arched her back, and a small groan came from her lips.

He slipped an arm beneath the small of her back, moving to the other breast, while his hand went on an exploration of its own. After long minutes, he kissed his way to her mouth. She tasted sweet, hauntingly familiar, and he battled a dread of letting her go.

He thrust his tongue into her mouth, feeling a desperation

to brand her as his own, wanting the memory of tonight to be seared indelibly into both of their brains.

She kissed him back, deeply and thoroughly, her palms sliding down his back, over his buttocks, along his thighs. He didn't want to rush her, but the urge to push inside grew stronger and stronger.

Then he felt her thighs twitch. They eased apart, welcoming him. It was all he could do to fight the freight train of desire as instinct took over, and his hips automatically flexed forward.

She bent her knees and rose to meet him, the heat of their bodies searing against each other. He drew his head back, watching her wide eyes as he slowly eased inside. Her cheeks were flushed, her dark lips parted in small gasps, and her pupils dilated as she stared deep into his soul.

He stilled, his voice a rasp. "I could do this forever."

"Please do."

"Oh, yeah."

He watched her intently, while his need built, and the tension in his muscles coiled to painful. Still, he refused to move. A single movement would be the beginning of the end. And he didn't want this to end. He quite literally wanted to stay right here for the rest of his life.

"Oh, Alec," she moaned, and a lightning flash of lust shot through him.

"I know." He held fast.

But her eyes fluttered shut, and her hips flexed forward, and her legs wrapped around him, catapulting his subconscious into action. There was nothing he could do to stop the long strokes of pleasure propelling them forward.

Her nails dug into his back. Her gasps were music to his ears. He inhaled her scent, reveled in her hot, moist core, guiding them both as long and as high as he could manage. Then her cries rocked his world, and her body convulsed against him, and his name on her lips sent him over the edge into rhythmic paradise.

Nine

The scattered showers of the new day made the jump course heavy and less than ideal. But Rosie-Joe had excelled in worse conditions than this.

"Make sure you give her time to get her footing before the triple combination," Stephanie told Wesley.

He was dressed, pressed, trimmed and ready to go, his round coming up in only minutes.

"The rain won't spook her," Stephanie continued. "Keep her balanced, and she should run clean. Just keep your head in the game."

Wesley nodded, his gaze suddenly focusing on something in the distance. A smile grew on his face that seemed just a little too confident.

"Are you listening to me?" she asked, as horses, grooms and competitors shifted around them. The announcer's voice was clear on the PA. The crowd applauded as Bill Roauge and Zepher made it cleanly over the water jump.

"You worry too much."

"Wesley—"

He leaned in close, brushing her arm. "Just wish me luck," he whispered. Then he brushed something from her cheek and tucked her hair behind one ear.

Suddenly a blur of movement crossed her vision. Alec's big hand wrapped around Wesley's arm. Wesley staggered backward, as Alec propelled him ten feet to stop abruptly against the wall.

Stephanie was too stunned to move.

Had Alec lost his mind?

She couldn't see his face, and she couldn't hear his words. But she could see the set of his shoulders, and the width of his stance, and his hand was clamped tight around Wesley's arm. Wesley's cockiness turned to shock, while most of the blood seemed to drain from his face.

The groom holding Rosie-Jo stared in stupefaction, while Stephanie finally spurred herself to action, marching across the floor.

"Do you understand?" Alec ground out in a harsh voice she'd never heard before.

Wesley gave a rapid nod, and before Stephanie could say anything, he broke away from Alec and brushed past her.

She turned, torn between going after him and demanding answers from Alec. But Wesley was already mounting Rosie-Jo, and she couldn't think of a single thing to say to him that might help. So, she rounded on Alec.

"What is the matter with you?" she hissed, moving close to face him.

"Not a single thing."

She gestured to Wesley. "He's about to ride."

"So what?"

"You've completely blown his concentration."

Alec pasted her with a hard stare. "He should have thought of that before coming on to another man's wife."

"What?" she sputtered. What on earth was Alec's problem? After last night, how could he possibly think she had any interest in Wesley?

"You going to watch him?" Alec grimly nodded to where Wesley was entering the ring.

She had to watch.

Of course she had to watch.

"We are not through here," she warned Alec.

"We never are," he sighed as she turned for the fence.

Alec fell into step beside her.

"What are you doing?" she asked.

"I'm coming with you."

"It's probably better if you—"

"This isn't negotiable, Stephanie."

"Then at least stop scowling."

They stopped at the fence as Rosie-Jo cleared the first jump.

"He wasn't coming onto me," she muttered in an undertone.

"I agree," said Alec.

And she turned to him with frank astonishment.

"He was testing *me*," said Alec.

The crowd cheered as Rosie-Joe cleared the next jump.

"Testing you for *what?* You were there last night, Alec. You already won." She reflexively scrutinized Wesley's lineup for the vertical.

"To see what I'd do if he made a move on you. He saw

me coming, Stephanie. He looked me straight in the eyes, launched that smug grin and moved in on you."

Stephanie clearly remembered Wesley's touch and his whisper. "I had dirt on my cheek," she defended.

"No, you didn't. You had a husband within eyeshot and a young pup looking to test the waters."

The crowd cheered again.

"You're paranoid." But she had to admit, something had seemed off about Wesley's gesture. And there was no denying he'd been pushing the boundaries with her since she'd told him about being pregnant.

"I'm not paranoid. I'm realistic."

"He knows it's a marriage of convenience," she felt compelled to defend Wesley. It was probably her own fault for not being clear with him three days ago.

"It doesn't matter."

"It does to him."

Butterflies formed in Stephanie's stomach as Rosie-Jo lined up for the triple. She held her breath.

Oxer, vertical, vertical.

He'd done it. Stephanie let out a breath and applauded along with the rest of the crowd.

But on the next jump, Rosie-Jo rubbed a rail.

Stephanie swore under her breath as the announcer acknowledged the fault.

They made the last three jumps clean, their time putting then in eighth place. A respectable showing.

As the pair approached the exit gate, Stephanie and Alec stepped to one side. Alec tossed an arm over her shoulder.

She knew what he was doing, but she also knew it was what she'd signed up for. And, while she wasn't sure Wesley had deliberately taunted Alec, it was probably better if he understood the boundaries up front, particularly while they were working together.

Wesley scrutinized Stephanie. Then his gaze shifted to Alec. It immediately dropped to the ground. She smiled and congratulated him as he passed, but he didn't look up again.

"What did you say to him?" she couldn't help asking Alec.

"That another man would have taken his head off. And he would have."

"I can't believe this has got blown so far out of proportion." She needed to talk to Wesley. The sooner, the better.

"He's a punk kid," said Alec, drawing her further back from the gate, out of the way of the horse and groom traffic, turning to face her. "It's past time for him to learn right from wrong."

"It's partly my fault," she acknowledged. "For telling him we were getting married because of the baby."

Alec's steel gaze burned into hers. "That doesn't change our vows."

"It gave him expectations."

"Are they valid, Stephanie?" The noise of the crowd and loudspeaker disappeared under Alec's intensity.

The question annoyed her. "What do you think?"

"Then tell him."

"I did. I tried. He refuses to understand."

Alec's jaw went hard. "He understands now."

She couldn't help but worry about Wesley. "Did you scare him?"

"Absolutely. And I wasn't bluffing. If he comes near you again—"

"I'm still his coach."

"You know what I mean. And he knows what I mean."

The crowd applauded, and Stephanie glanced behind herself to the board, seeing a new leader. Wesley was bumped to ninth.

She turned back to Alec and heaved a sigh. "This is going to be very complicated."

"No, it's going to be very simple. You'll be professional. He'll be professional. And nobody will get hurt."

"Sometimes you sound like my brothers."

Alec unexpectedly twitched a grin. "That's definitely not what I was going for."

And suddenly last night was between them, as vividly as if they'd had videotape. She remembered his body, the feel, the taste, the sound of his voice and the intimate things they'd said.

It was a crazy situation, a confusing situation. They had one last night before they separated and went back to their individual lives. She hadn't the vaguest idea what would happen to them then. The only thing she knew for sure was that she'd spend this last night with Alec.

In the morning, Alec watched Stephanie preparing to load the Ryder stables trailers on the Brighton grounds. It was overcast, with rain threatening again. He'd pretty much blown his flight out of the Cedarvale Airport, but he didn't care. He was staying right here until she was on the road.

Stephanie had flown in last week, but she was traveling home with the horses, a couple of grooms and Wesley. Alec wasn't crazy about the arrangement, but he was the one who'd bought Blanchard's Run. And now she insisted on accompanying the stallion back to Montana.

She was dressed in blue jeans, scuffed boots and a navy

T-shirt, and he couldn't help but contrast it to the way she'd looked last night. She'd worn a sexy, white nightie—for a short time, anyway. Then they'd made love and retired to the deep whirlpool tub. Afterward, they'd wrapped themselves in the plush robes provided by the hotel.

They'd sat up late on the balcony, talking about family, music, even politics. Anything to avoid the real topic, which was what happened next in their relationship. Afterward, she'd slept in his arms, while he let his imagination explore risky and unlikely scenarios, involving him and Stephanie, and their baby.

He was playing with fire here, and he knew full well somebody could get hurt. He only hoped it was him and not Stephanie.

Rosie-Jo's hooves clanked on the ramp up to the cavernous trailer, while Royce appeared at Alec's side.

"Any updates on the money?" asked Royce.

Alec nodded. "Damien called last night. Since Stephanie knows the truth, our negotiating position has changed, He thinks he can get back a million or two."

"That's it?"

"He thinks Norman Stanton liked women, ponies and high living. There's a house in Miami, a sports car and an astonishingly small bank account."

Royce crossed his arms over his chest. "Not enough to impact the corporation's bottom line."

"Nowhere near," Alec agreed. "But I'll have some final numbers on that for you in my formal report next week."

Royce nodded, glancing at his watch. "You flying out of Cedarvale?"

"I am."

"The Lexington flight leaves from there in forty minutes."

"I'll catch the next one."

"The next one's tomorrow."

Alec shrugged. "I'll get there."

"I've got the jet. You need me to drop you off somewhere?"

There was something odd in Royce's tone, and Alec searched the man's expression.

Was there something he wanted to talk about in private?

Did he have more secrets?

If he did, Alec wished he'd do them both a favor and keep them the hell to himself. The last thing he wanted was to get embroiled in Ryder family politics again.

"I hear you put Wesley into a wall yesterday," said Royce.

"That's an exaggeration."

"Not from what I heard."

"Who'd you hear it from?"

"It wasn't Stephanie."

Alec hadn't thought it was, particularly since he hadn't left her side for nearly twenty-four hours. He did wonder if it was Wesley himself.

"He was out of line," he told Royce.

Royce gave a thoughtful nod. "I know how that goes."

Alec wasn't sure what Royce was getting at. Was he annoyed because Alec had gone after one of their stable clients?

"What did he do?" asked Royce.

He touched her cheek? He touched her hair? Both of those things sounded lame when they were out of context. "None of your business," said Alec.

"Then, tell me something." Royce turned away to watch the Ryder crew, prepping the trailer, widening his stance, stuffing his hands into the front pockets of his blue jeans.

Alec followed his line of vision to where Stephanie was coiling a lead rope. Wesley was packing up the ramps in preparation to leave.

"About my sister." Royce continued, tone thoughtful. "Would you shoot any guy who touched her?"

"In a heartbeat," said Alec.

Royce clicked his cheek. "That's how it starts."

It wasn't exactly a trick question. "Name one guy who wouldn't?"

Royce turned back to Alec. "So, I take it you're going with Plan A."

"Plan A?"

"The one where you make her fall in love with you."

"I'm not going with Plan A." Plan A was fraught with peril.

Then again, he wasn't going with Plan B, either—the one where he disappeared from her life for months at a time.

He hadn't come up with any plan that seemed workable under the circumstance.

"I'm going to say goodbye," he told Royce. Then he left him behind, crossing the small chunk of parking lot that brought him to Stephanie.

"We're about ready to take off," she informed him as he approached, smiling openly, her face scrubbed fresh, her auburn hair flowing in the wind.

"Are you sure you wouldn't rather fly?"

She cocked her head. "Didn't we already have this debate?"

"I wasn't happy with the outcome."

"I'm staying with Blanchard's Run. I'm going to protect your investment."

But his investment wasn't the most valuable thing involved in this package. "You hired his personal groom to take care of him."

"I'm driving to Montana, Alec." Her expression sobered, and her clear blue eyes reflected the gathering clouds. "What about you?"

"Back to Chicago."

She nodded, and her smile came back. It looked a little forced to him, but he couldn't be sure.

"For a week," he elaborated, watching her closely. "Then I'm coming to Montana."

She sobered then swallowed.

"My report will be ready."

"Oh. Right." She gave a little laugh. "Of course."

He wanted to say more. He wanted to tell her he was coming for *her,* not for the damn report. He wanted to tell her they would work this out, that he was falling fast and hard for her, and he was having trouble picturing his life without her.

But it was too soon. And he couldn't risk hurting her. He had no idea how she felt. And half a dozen people were watching them.

He should have asked her last night. But, the truth was, he was afraid of her answer. She'd told Wesley it was a marriage of convenience. And it was. And it might never be anything else.

"See you in Montana?" he asked.

She nodded. See you in Montana.

Ten

Stephanie wished she'd had at least five minutes alone with Alec before the meeting convened around the dining room table at the main ranch house. She's been on the road for days, arriving home last night with Blanchard's Run. Her cell phone conversations with Alec had been sporadic and brief during the long stretches of isolated highway. And there'd been little privacy for evening conversations, since she was sharing motel rooms with the female groom.

She missed him. And she was beginning to doubt her memories. She'd tried to cling to the intimacy they'd shared in Kentucky, but as the days rolled by, she began to fear she'd imagined it.

She'd wanted to talk to him alone before the meeting, but his plane had been late. It was raining hard. And her truck got stuck in the mud on the way down the hill from her place in a pocket where there was no cell signal.

She was the last to arrive. She was wet through to her underwear. Her hair was stringy, and mud caked her boots. Her shower had been a waste of time, and the makeup she'd applied after lunch was long gone. So much for hoping Alec might find her attractive.

"There you are," said Royce as she kicked off her boots in the front hallway.

"Got stuck on Moss Hill," she explained, swiping her hands over her riotous hair, hoping against hope she didn't have mascara running down her cheeks.

"Just got here myself," McQuestin put in, in an obvious attempt to make her feel better.

Stephanie's gaze skipped around the long, rectangular table, Jared, Melissa, Royce, Amber, McQuestin, ah, finally, Alec at one end. The last time she'd seen him here was their wedding. And she couldn't quite contain her smile. He looked so good, immaculate suit, fresh shave, trimmed hair.

He smiled back and gave her a nod, but something about him seemed reserved.

She quickly schooled her features, taking an empty chair halfway down one side.

"Are we ready?" asked Jared where he was positioned at the other end of the table.

There were several nods.

"Then let me start by thanking Alec for his hard work. We know this won't be easy. And we understand we're not going to like everything you have to recommend. But I'd like to say on behalf of my family, that we'll take a serious look at all of your suggestions."

Alec nodded his head in acknowledgment. "I appreciate that, Jared." He shuffled a stack of papers in front of him. "Perhaps I'll start with the ranch." He looked to McQuestin.

"The cattle operation has lost money for several years in a row."

McQuestin screwed up his weathered face, narrowing his eyes.

"However," Alec continued. "Beef prices are on the rise. While land values are at a low. So selling doesn't make sense—"

"'Course it doesn't," said McQuestin.

"With some streamlining to management," Alec continued, "the ranch ought to be able to break even."

"Streamlining?" McQuestin challenged.

"You've stopped paying the blackmail, for starters," said Alec. "And best practices have come a long way in the past thirty years. I'd suggest hiring an agricultural studies grad and—"

"An academic?" McQuestin spat.

"McQuestin," Jared warned. "We said we'd listen."

But Alec was smiling. "Unless you'd like to enroll in college yourself."

McQuestin's bushy brows went up, while everyone else tittered with laughter.

"The details are in my report." Alec flipped a page. "On to the real estate division. As I'm sure you're all aware, it's had the highest profitability for the past few years. But that's about to be challenged. Rental rates are on a downward trend in Chicago, and vacancies are expected to rise."

Stephanie glanced at Jared, but his expression gave away nothing.

"You have a couple of choices there," said Alec. "Ride it out, or sell off either or both of the Maple Street and industrial properties. I'd absolutely recommend keeping everything you've got in the downtown core. When the market recovers, that will go up first."

Jared nodded, but didn't venture an opinion.

"*Windy City Bizz* magazine," said Alec. "Sell that puppy just as fast as you can."

Royce sat up straight. "No. That's Amber's—"

"No, Royce." Amber put her hand on his shoulder. "You should sell it."

"There's no saving print publications," said Alec. "Particularly periodicals."

Stephanie drew a sigh, gauging Amber's expression. She looked sad, but not hugely upset. Stephanie, on the other hand, was getting more uncomfortable by the minute.

Ryder International had been a strong and growing company for as long as she could remember. Jared was an amazing entrepreneur, and Royce seemed to excel at acquisitions. She couldn't quite believe they were in this much trouble.

"What about the jet?" asked Royce, tension evident around his mouth.

"You're going to need it," said Alec. "I know it feels like an indulgence, but you've got interests in half a dozen states. You need to be mobile."

Amber gave Royce's arm a squeeze.

"On the legal issues with your father's will." Alec's gaze flicked to Stephanie for a split second. "I'd recommend vesting Stephanie with nonvoting shares."

Stephanie was sure she couldn't have heard right.

"She doesn't have time to pay attention to the corporate issues—"

"Wait a minute," Stephanie blurted out. She glanced from Jared to Royce, and then to Alec. "You don't want me to vote?"

"I don't want you to *have* to vote. There are a myriad of things that you—"

"How is that different?" What was the matter with him? How could he have blindsided her like that?

He directed his next words to Jared. "You and Royce should have an equal partnership. Frame up a dispute resolution process if necessary, but don't make Stephanie the swing vote."

"Wait a minute," Stephanie shouted.

Jared shot her a look. "We'll give it some thought."

"How can you—"

"Stephanie," Jared warned. "We can discuss it later."

She compressed her lips then turned her cold glare from Jared to Alec. "It's a stupid idea."

"Steph," Royce put in kindly. "You can convince us of that later."

"Fine," she huffed. Her brothers would never go for it anyway. She might only be a half sister, but they loved her. They wouldn't strip away her power for no reason.

What was *wrong* with Alec? What could have changed between the time he bought her Blanchard's Run and now?

"High tech is the future," said Alec. "I wouldn't recommend selling, but you might want to look at some international licensing deals. You can maximize your sales without growing the division to an unwieldy size."

Nobody answered to that.

"On sports and culture." Alec flipped a page in front of him. "I'd suggest standing pat."

Stephanie blew out a sigh. It wasn't relief. It was, well, okay, it was relief.

"Except for the jumping stable."

She stilled, feeling all gazes land on her.

"It's a cash drain, and there's no end in sight." He looked up, taking Stephanie in along with everyone else, pausing no longer, no shorter on her stunned expression than on any of the others. "You need to sell off the entire operation. The sooner the better."

Stephanie found her voice. "Wait just a—"

"May I please finish?" he cut in.

"No, you may not finish. You've just recommended selling something that I spent half my life—"

"Stephanie—"

"—building!" She came to her feet.

"I don't expect you to—"

"How could you *do* this?"

"Will you have a little faith?"

"No. I will not." She rapped her knuckles down on the polished tabletop. "Is there any part of my life you're *not* planning to destroy?"

Alec's lips compressed, eyes darkening to pinpoints.

Stephanie turned on Jared. "Since I have no voting privileges, I guess you two can do whatever you want. But I'm not going to sit around and listen to this guy pick over our family like a vulture."

"Stephanie," Royce tried.

"No!" She turned on her second brother, backing up, scraping her chair legs against the wood floor as she pushed it out of the way. Then she pivoted on her stocking feet and stalked for the door, grabbing her muddy boots on the way out.

"Excuse me," Alec's voice intoned to the group behind her as she slammed the door.

She quickly stuffed her foot into the first boot. Then hopped in place on the porch as she struggled with the other.

The door opened and Alec stepped out. "What the hell is the matter with you?"

"With me? With *me?*" She rammed her foot down to the sole, straightening and flipping her hair over her shoulder. "You're the one out to destroy my life."

He folded his arms over his chest. "You are rushing to preposterous conclusions."

She leaned in. "Tell me one thing, Alec. Why did you buy me Blanchard's Run?"

"Why do you think I bought you Blanchard's Run?"

She gave the only plausible answer she'd come up with. "Because you felt guilty."

"It was not guilt."

"Why then?" she rattled on. "So I'd sleep with you?"

He sputtered out a cold laugh. "Yeah, right."

She forced a note of contempt into her voice. "Well, congratulations, Alec. It worked. I slept with you because you bought me a horse."

"No, you didn't."

"Oh, yes, I did." She glared straight at him, and his eyes flickered with uncertainty.

"What?" she asked sarcastically. "Did you think I'd fallen for your good looks, wit and charm? Think again, Alec. I wanted the horse. You got me the horse. I figured I owed you. And since we'd done it once already—"

"Stop it."

"Truth hurts?"

"Lies hurt, Stephanie."

"Yeah. They do. And we've been a lie from minute one. I'm sorry I forgot about that."

She nodded toward the door behind Alec. "Better get back to your job. My brothers can let me know what they decide." Then she turned, searching for every scrap of dignity she could muster as she paced down the stairs.

As Alec reentered the house, the faces staring at him from the dining room table alternated between condemnation and frank curiosity.

"We stopped them from going after her," Amber informed him.

"I'm sure you did." Alec could well have imagined Jared and Royce's first reaction was to rush outside and save their sister from him. "Thank you," he finished, including both Amber and Melissa in his gratitude.

"We're not selling the jumping stable," Royce informed him, clearly ticked off.

Alec shook his head in disgust. When he'd planned his little speech, he'd planned it all the way to the end, where he revealed his master plan and became Stephanie's hero. He hadn't counted on her being so dogged in her interruptions. And he sure hadn't counted on hearing such a painful truth about her feelings for him.

He'd been looking forward to getting back to Montana from the minute he left Stephanie at Brighton. Now all he wanted to was get the hell out of the state.

He dropped back into his chair. "I want you to sell the jumping stable to *me*."

They all blinked at him in silence.

He threw up his hands, spelling it out in detail. "I'm married to Stephanie. It'll be half hers. This way, Ryder International won't be stuck with the financial liability, but she'll still—"

"Did you tell that to Stephanie?" Amber asked.

He glared at her but didn't answer the question. "I can afford the cash drain. I'll be a silent partner."

Jared snorted. "That's why you don't want her to have voting shares in Ryder International."

"She's going to be a little busy with other interests," said Alec. That, and he'd selfishly assumed she might want a little time left over for him.

"You need to tell her," said Melissa.

"So she'll be grateful?" His voice was sharper than he intended, and Jared frowned at him.

"Sorry," Alec apologized. "You all know my marriage to Stephanie is a sham—"

"Say what?" McQuestin seemed to come back to life.

"She's pregnant," said Alec, not willing to keep any more secrets.

"And you did the right thing?" asked McQuestin, lined face screwing up as he narrowed his eyes, sizing up Alec as if he was debating getting his shotgun. A little late for that.

"I did the right thing," Alec confirmed. "I'll live up to my responsibility, including providing for her and my child by buying and financing the Ryder Equestrian Center. But there's nothing more than that between us."

"Are you sure?" asked Amber.

"Positive," said Alec.

Royce looked to Jared. "Yeah. Except that he'll shoot any man who touches her."

Jared's eyebrows shot up, and he turned his attention to Alec. "You poor bastard."

"What?" asked Melissa.

"It's a joke," said Royce. "A bad joke."

"Explain," demanded Amber.

Alec gathered his paperwork. Jared and Royce's pity was the final straw. If a man had to have his heart broken, he could at least do it in private. "I'll leave a copy of my recommendations for your review. You are, of course, welcome to use or discard anything."

"Explain," Melissa echoed.

Jared gave in. "You know, when Dad murdered Frank Stanton—"

McQuestin rocked forward. *"What?"*

Royce jumped in. "It's a barometer of how much you love your wife."

"Alec's in love with Stephanie?" asked Melissa.

"Alec is saying goodbye," said Alec, turning for the door.

McQuestin jumped into the fray. "Your father didn't murder Frank Stanton."

Everybody went silent and stared at McQuestin. Even Alec froze then turned back.

"It was self-defense," said the old man. "Your mother had changed her mind. She refused to leave with Stanton. Stanton got mad and shot at your dad. He hit your mother by accident in the shoulder, and your father shot back. Your father was rushing her to the hospital when the truck went into the river."

"Then why did Gramps hide the gun?" asked Jared.

"Make it look like a robbery." McQuestin gave him a stern look. "Trials are unpredictable."

And the affair would have been public knowledge. Alec didn't agree with the action, but he thought he understood the motivation. Still, it didn't change anything for him. His hope of a future with Stephanie was over. The sooner he got back to Chicago, the better.

The room went silent as everyone digested the revelation.

"I've got a plane to catch," Alec put in. He didn't exactly

have a ticket, since he'd been hoping to stay here with Stephanie. But nobody needed to know that.

"If you leave," Amber ventured, cocking her head sideways. "How are you going to shoot any man who touches her?"

"Nobody's shooting anyone," he returned. And Stephanie didn't want or need his protection.

Royce came to his feet. "You're just going to abandon her?"

"What part of marriage of convenience don't you understand?"

"The part where you fell in love with my sister."

Alec opened his mouth to deny it, but he found he couldn't lie. There was no point in even attempting to salvage his pride. "She doesn't love me."

"Are you sure?" asked Amber.

Alec gave a sharp nod.

"Then change her mind," Jared put in mildly. "Melissa didn't start off loving me."

Royce grinned. "And Amber took some convincing."

Amber socked him in the arm. "I loved you, dummy. I just didn't tell you about it."

It was painful for Alec to watch the interplay. "It's better if I just leave."

"You sure?" McQuestin put in gruffly, his pale gaze boring into Alec. "Because if you're wrong, and you break that little girl's heart. *I'm* the one who'll be shooting at *you*."

Two miles from the main ranch, Stephanie jerked her car to the side of the muddy road and brought it to an abrupt halt.

Her hands were shaking. Her stomach ached. And she

couldn't seem to muster up enough strength in her leg to push the clutch and gear down for the hill.

What was she going to do?

She'd come home with such high hopes. But the days and nights at Brighton now seemed like a cruel dream. She'd fallen fast and hard for her husband, and it had seemed like he was falling for her. She'd even dared to hope it was love.

But he didn't love her. He didn't even like or respect her. Why else would he have stripped away her business?

There had to have been other options.

Why was it *her* who had to sacrifice everything?

She gripped the steering wheel, her anger reviving, blocking out her heartache.

But then she remembered *Windy City Bizz*. Amber loved that magazine. Yet, she'd quickly agreed to sell it. And Royce had offered up the jet. And Jared had spent years building up their Chicago property inventory. He had huge plans for construction in the next decade, yet he was looking at selling.

Stephanie swallowed, a horrible thought creeping into her mind. Had she just let her brothers down? Was this why they kept secrets from her? Did they think she couldn't handle the hard truths?

She sat back, shoulders drooping, considering for the first time in her life that she might have some responsibility to turn a financial profit, not just to provide theoretical PR and goodwill. She had an obligation to her family. And she had an obligation to Alec.

Another ranch truck rocked to a halt beside her. But she didn't even look up.

Moments later, Amber banged on the window.

"Stephanie!"

Stephanie blinked blankly at Amber. Her pride was in tatters and her heart was broken to bits.

She loved Alec.

She realized he wasn't trying to hurt her. He was trying to treat her like an adult, a functioning partner. He'd done her the courtesy of telling her the hard truth about her stable, instead of trying to sugarcoat it so she wouldn't get hurt.

She loved him, and he respected her. And she'd just destroyed any chance they might have had at building a future together.

"Will you open—" Amber grabbed the door handle and yanked the driver's door wide. "You have to come back."

Stephanie shook her head. She couldn't go back. She was mortified by her behavior, and she needed to go home and bury her head.

"He's leaving," Amber rushed on. "He's leaving now. McQuestin threatened to shoot him, but he's still leaving."

"What?" Stephanie managed to say, completely confused by Amber's agitation.

"Stephanie." Amber took a breath. "Listen to me. Alec wanted to sell the stable—"

"He was right," Stephanie nodded, swallowing her pain.

"—to *himself.*"

Stephanie struggled to make sense of the words.

"*He* was going to buy it. *You* were going to run it. Hell, you were going to own half of it, since you're his wife."

Stephanie felt the blood drain from her face, while the roar of a hurricane pounded in her ears.

Amber grabbed her hand, tugging on it. "You have to come back. *Now.*"

Stephanie fumbled with her seat belt catch. "I don't understand."

"He loves you."

"Who loves me?" Stephanie pushed off the seat, landing on the muddy road.

"Alec. He loves you."

Stephanie didn't believe that for a minute. And even if he had, he didn't anymore. Still a little part of her heart couldn't help holding out hope. "He said that?" she dared ask as Amber bundled her into the passenger seat of the other truck.

"He said he'd shoot any man who touched you." Amber swung into the driver's side and put the truck in gear.

"That's not exactly the same thing," Stephanie pointed out.

"It's some kind of a joke. But Royce says it means he loves you. But he's convinced you don't love him. And he's heading for the airport. From there, with his job, who knows where he'll end up." Amber glanced across the seat, voice lowering. "So, if you love him, Stephanie…"

Stephanie stared back. She slowly nodded.

"You need to tell him. And you need to do it right now."

"I'm sorry," Stephanie mumbled. "I wasn't thinking. You gave up the magazine. Royce offered the jet. Of course I'll give up the stable. I didn't mean to sound so spoiled and selfish back there."

Amber unexpectedly smiled. "Me giving up the magazine is nothing compared to you giving up the stable. Your brothers were never going to let that happen. Of course, as it turns out, that wasn't what Alec meant anyway."

"He wants to *buy* the stable?" Stephanie turned the revelation over in her mind.

"And he made it clear you'd be half owner. And he'd be a silent partner. And he was doing it to provide for his wife and his child."

"Oh, no." Acute regret slid through Stephanie's stomach.

"But it's good news."

Stephanie blew out a sigh. "I said some things. To Alec. When I thought he was out to get me."

"What things?"

Stephanie groaned. "He must hate me."

"What things?"

"That I only slept with him the second time—"

"You slept with him a second time?"

"And a third and a fourth and a fifth. Maybe more. I kind of lost count."

Amber laughed. "Well, that sounds promising."

"No." Stephanie shook her head. "I just finished telling him I'd only done it because he bought Blanchard's Run. It was gratitude sex, and I didn't find him either handsome, funny or charming. I may have said I didn't like him. I definitely implied he should get lost."

"Do you think he believed you?"

"I was pretty convincing."

"But you're in love with him?"

Stephanie moaned, bending forward around her stomachache. "Yes."

"Maybe try telling him that." The truck rocked to a halt. Stephanie looked up to see Jared, Melissa, Royce and McQuestin standing in the front driveway.

She glanced frantically around for Alec, opening the door, stepping out.

"He's gone," said Jared.

"How long?" asked Amber.

"Twenty minutes, at least." Royce shook his head.

"I'm going after him," Stephanie decided. Amber was right. While Stephanie had been dead wrong. She owed him an apology, and she was going to suck up her pride and tell him she loved him.

She was sure it would be nothing but a lesson in abject humiliation, because no man was going to love a woman who'd behaved the way she did. And despite his joke to Royce, she was sure Alec would be happy to put as much distance as possible between himself and her.

She looked to Amber. "Give me the keys."

"You'll never catch him," said Melissa. "And it's dangerous to try."

"Take the Cessna," McQuestin put in.

Royce looked at the old man, then grinned. "We'll take the Cessna." He grabbed the keys from Amber and headed to the truck at a trot. "Come on," he called to Stephanie.

She sprinted after him.

It was a five-minute drive to the ranch airstrip. Royce sped through his pre-flight checklist. Stephanie slapped on the earphones and strapped into the seat and braced herself for takeoff.

In no time, they were skimming a thousand feet above the ranch road. The road met the main road, and they banked east. There'd be little traffic before the Interstate, so Alec's black car should be easy to spot.

After they found him? Well, things were definitely going to get tough. She tried to come up with a speech in her mind, something, *anything* that might help him forgive her. But she was drawing a blank.

"Painful, isn't it?" asked Royce through the radio.

"I was so stupid."

He laughed. "We all are. I told Amber she should marry her former fiancé. I could have lost her right then and there."

"But you didn't."

"No, I didn't."

Stephanie peered out the small windshield, scanning the length of road in front of them. Range land whizzed by, with the occasional barn or stream. "We don't know how this one's going to turn out."

"He loves you, Steph."

"I may have killed that."

"You can't kill it. Believe me, you can't kill it."

Stephanie drew a breath, desperately trying to convince herself that Royce knew what he was talking about. But the fact was, he didn't. His and Amber's relationship was unique and special. It wasn't representative of every other relationship in the world.

"There he is," said Royce, pointing to the road. And Stephanie's heart went into overdrive.

Royce overflew the car, checked for traffic, then turned the Cessna in a tight circle, bringing it down on the pavement of the road. They coasted to a stop, and he shut off the engine.

Stephanie removed her headphones, unclipped the harness then clambered out of the small seat, stepping on the wing strut before dropping down to the pavement.

"Go get 'em, tiger," Royce called with an encouraging grin.

Stephanie couldn't muster up a smile in return. Her palms were sweating and her knees were weak. She took a few trembling steps along the centerline, watching for Alec's car to come into view. She didn't have long to wait.

The black car coasted to a stop, but Alec didn't get out.

Squinting, at the tinted windshield, Stephanie forced herself to walk toward it.

Finally the door opened, and Alec stepped out, frowning. "What the hell?"

"I'm sorry, Alec."

He looked at the plane, then back to her. "What the *hell?*"

"It's Royce. We were afraid you'd beat us to the airport and get on a plane, and I wouldn't be able to find you."

"So you landed on the *highway?* Have you lost your mind?"

"I came to apologize."

He was still frowning. His eyes were squinted down in anger. "It never occurred to me in a million years that I'd have to make this rule. But don't you ever, *ever* take my baby up in an airplane and land on a public roadway."

"It's perfectly safe. We checked for traffic."

"Stephanie."

"Okay. Okay. I won't." She paused. "But don't you want to know why I'm here?"

"To say you're sorry?"

She screwed up her courage. "To say I love you."

His expression never flinched. "They told you about me buying the stable?"

She nodded.

"And you're grateful for that?"

"It's not about gratitude."

His look turned skeptical. "Really?"

"It was never about gratitude for Blanchard's Run."

"That's not what you said an hour ago."

"I lied an hour ago."

"But you're not lying now?"

"No."

He took a step forward, jaw clenched, expression grim. "Explain to me, Stephanie. How exactly am I supposed to tell the difference?"

It was a fair question. She moved closer to him. "I guess you can't."

His expression softened ever so slightly. "So, when you tell me that you love me? Which, by the way, I desperately want to believe—"

"But you need proof?" she ventured.

"And it can't be sex."

"Too bad." Her voice dropped low. "I've been thinking about sex all week."

Something twitched in his expression.

"I missed you so much," she told him. "I thought about you all morning. I imagined you pulling me back into your arms, holding me tight, and telling me everything was going to work out for us."

"And instead I threatened to sell your home out from under you."

"I should have listened longer. And it shouldn't have mattered. I should have been able to handle the hard truth."

"I should have started with the punch line."

"I love you, Alec. I don't know how to prove that to you, but I'm willing to do anything you say."

A grin twitched the corners of his mouth. "Marry me?"

"I already did."

He reached out and took her hands in his. "Have my baby? No. Wait. You're already doing that."

She couldn't help but smile.

"And since we're already having amazing sex…" He drew her in closer. "I can't come up with a single thing that would definitely prove you love me."

"I could shoot somebody," Stephanie ventured.

His hand slipped to the back of her neck, fingers burrowing into her hairline. "What are you talking about?"

"Amber said it was some kind of a joke. It meant you loved me."

"I do love you," he admitted, and a heavy weight lifted from Stephanie's chest. "But there'll be no shooting involved."

"Okay by me. Hey, I have an idea."

"Shoot."

She rolled her eyes. "What if we live happily ever after? We pull that off, you can be sure that I love you."

Alec smiled as he leaned in. "Deal." Then his lips came down on hers, and he drew her tightly into the circle of his strong arms.

She pressed her body against him, clinging to him, loving him with ever fiber of her being.

Epilogue

After considering nearly every wedding location on the planet, Amber had finally decided on a casual wedding at the ranch. She and Royce were married in the meadow overlooking Evergreen Falls.

She'd confided in Stephanie that it was as far removed as she could get from a cathedral and a ballroom in Chicago—the plan she'd had in place with her former fiancé, the one who was now married to Katie, her best friend and maid of honor.

It was full on summer, a year since Stephanie had met Alec. Their baby girl was now three months old, and little Heidi had slept the ceremony away in her father's arms. Now she was resting her head on his shoulder, staring wide-eyed at the lively country band that had taken over the deck of the ranch house.

The patio had turned into a dance floor, with the overflow spilling onto the lawn.

"You going to start riding again?" Royce asked Stephanie as he twirled her in his arms to the sweeping strains of a breakup song.

"I just got the okay from the doctor."

"But did you get the okay from Alec?"

Stephanie laughed. "Did you get the okay from Amber to keep flying?"

Her brother frowned.

"Same thing," she pointed out.

"Not exactly."

"Yes, exactly."

"How many times have you fallen off a horse?"

"Dozens," she responded. "Hundreds."

"I rest my case. I've never once fallen out of my airplane."

Stephanie caught the warm gaze of her husband, and he playfully waved Heidi's hand in her direction.

"Alec wants me to ride," she informed her brother.

"Alec wants you to smile. Trust me, he doesn't want you to ride."

"He can't stop me."

"He can get you pregnant again."

"He would nev—" Stephanie frowned. Wait a minute. Was that why he was being so cavalier about birth control?

Royce started to laugh.

Stephanie stopped dancing and drew back from his arms. She turned, eyes narrowing in Alec's direction.

Alec shot back a look of confusion.

"Melissa," Royce sang, drawing his six months pregnant sister-in-law into his arms.

"What did you say to her?" Melissa's laughing voice followed Stephanie to the edge of the patio.

Alec's brows narrowed in confusion, while Heidi gurgled and waved her arms toward Stephanie.

"How many kids do you want?" she asked Alec, retrieving her daughter and settling Heidi against her shoulder.

"As many as I can get," he answered with a grin.

"I'm not giving up riding."

"Huh?"

"You can't keep me pregnant all the time."

"Who says I'm trying to keep you pregnant?"

"Royce."

Alec's gaze shot past her. "Well, what the hell does Royce know?"

She leaned in. "You didn't want to use a condom last night."

Alec lowered his voice. "You're still breast-feeding."

"It's not foolproof."

"Nothing's foolproof."

"I'm jumping Rosie-Jo tomorrow," she warned.

"Go for it. I'll baby-sit."

"Really?"

"Yes, really. And stop listening to your brother. He's trying to stir up trouble."

Stephanie glanced to where her brother had switched dance partners once more. He now held his bride, Amber, in his arms, her gauzy white dress flowing around the satin slippers on her feet. He whispered something in her ear, and she smacked him in the shoulder. He just grinned and winked.

That was her brother Royce, all right, stirring up trouble.

"I think our princess is tuckered out," said Alec,

smoothing his hand over Heidi's silky hair as her mouth stretched in a wide yawn.

Stephanie smiled. "Home?"

"Home." He nodded.

She turned and caught Amber's gaze, giving her a little wave.

Amber mouthed, "thank you," keeping her head tucked against Royce's shoulder. They'd see each other for a proper goodbye in the morning before the couple left on their honeymoon.

"Want me to take her?" asked Alec as they made their way toward the stairs to the deck. Through the house was the fastest way to the driveway and their truck.

"I'm fine," Stephanie answered, starting up the short staircase while Alec kept close behind.

Heidi's warm little body relaxed into sleep, even as they passed the drummer.

"Keys in the truck?" asked Alec as they crossed the living room.

"Should be." Stephanie snagged a final cheese puff from the buffet on the dining room table.

"You're *still* hungry?" Alec teased.

"You try feeding a baby." She took two steps back and washed the cheese puff down with a strawberry.

Alec pulled open the front door and stood aside to let her pass.

"Thank you, sir," she mocked as she sashayed through.

"I just like the view from—" Alec nearly barreled into the back of her where she'd frozen still on the top step.

"Hello, Alec." Damien gave him a nod.

But Stephanie's gaze was fixed on the man standing next

to Damien. He was older, clean shaven, his jawline softer, face wrinkled and shoulders stooped.

The front door banged open to Royce's jovial voice. "You trying to sneak—" Royce stopped, too. Then a lighter set of footsteps came to a halt on the porch.

"Stanton," Royce growled.

Alec stepped around Stephanie and Heidi, putting his body between her and Norman Stanton.

"We'd hoped the party would be over," Damien apologized.

"What the hell are you doing?" Alec demanded of his friend.

Royce took a step forward, coming parallel with Alec, while Jared appeared out of nowhere.

Norman Stanton cleared his throat. "I'm sorry—"

"You're *sorry?*" Royce roared.

Norman swallowed convulsively, and Stephanie found herself pitying the man.

"I didn't mean to intrude."

"This is my *wedding.*"

"I knew you were leaving tomorrow," said Damien, stepping forward to hand Royce an envelope.

Alec stepped up to Damien, voice low. "Start talking."

Norman spoke up. "I never meant to hurt any of you."

Jared stepped forward. "If you're not hightailing it off Ryder land in about thirty seconds, you're the one who's getting hurt."

"It was Clifton," said Norman.

"Don't you *dare* speak my father's name."

"Damien?" Alec warned in another undertone.

"I thought he murdered Frank!" Norman all but wailed.

Everyone stilled, and Stephanie found herself mesmerized by the pain in the older man's eyes.

"He was my brother. And he was murdered. And I went after revenge."

Stephanie glanced at her brothers to see them exchange a look.

"I told him the truth," said Damien.

"I know now that it was self-defense," Norman clarified. He peered between Alec and Royce, seeking out Stephanie's gaze. "He loved your mother."

Alec stepped sideways, blocking Norman's view.

"And he loved you."

"Don't you speak to my wife," said Alec.

Stephanie touched Alec's arm. "It's okay."

Alec didn't move. "No, it's not."

Royce's incredulous voice rang out. "This is *ten million dollars.*"

Stephanie turned to see the envelope flutter to the ground.

"I wanted to pay you back," said Norman.

"I helped him liquidate," Damien put in.

"I'm sorry," Norman repeated. "I wanted to make him pay. But I never meant to hurt any of you."

His gaze once again sought out Stephanie. "Frank was my brother, and you were my niece. He talked about you all the time. I couldn't wait to meet you. He said he was bringing you home." The man's voice caught. "Instead I claimed his body."

Tears gleamed in Norman's eyes, and something tugged at Stephanie's heart.

The man looked old and broken, nothing like his picture, nothing like the villain she'd expected.

"I'll get you the rest of the money," Norman told Royce and Jared.

"How?" Royce demanded.

"I gave him a job," said Damien.

"You *what?*" asked Alec.

"I was wrong." Damien shrugged. "He didn't blow the money on women and ponies."

Stephanie moved her attention to her husband.

"No?" Alec asked, watching Damien closely.

Damien gave him a meaningful smile and shook his head. "Let's just say my organization can use his talents."

"Did you steal it from someone else?" Jared demanded.

"It's your money," said Stanton. "I've been holding it for you."

"We'll be looking for interest," Royce put in.

Alec transmitted a silent question to Damien, and Damien's smiled broadened.

Norman's hungry gaze was glued to Stephanie.

She could feel his loneliness and sorrow pierce straight to her soul.

He was her uncle, the brother of a father she didn't remember. She found herself wondering what Royce would do if he thought someone had killed Jared, or the other way around, or what both of them would do if they thought someone had harmed her.

She shifted around Alec, gazing into Norman's lined face in the pool of lamplight.

His eyes went wide, darting to Heidi as she drew closer.

Royce shot forward, but Alec's arm reached out to block him.

Stephanie smiled gently at Norman. "Would you like to meet your grandniece?"

Twin tears slipped out of his blue eyes, trailing swiftly down his pale, sagging cheeks.

Stephanie eased Heidi away from her body, exposing her little pink face. "This is Heidi Rae Creighton. Heidi, this is your uncle Norman."

She felt Alec's gentle hands close around her shoulders.

Norman stood frozen for a full minute.

Then he lifted a shaking finger, gently stroking the back of Heidi's tiny hand. "Heidi Rae." His voice was strangled with emotion.

Stephanie's chest tightened, and tears stung the backs of her eyes.

Royce appeared in Stephanie's peripheral vision. She braced herself, but Royce's body language was no longer hostile.

"This check good?" he asked gruffly.

Norman didn't take his eyes off Heidi. "It's good," he affirmed.

Royce gave a sharp nod as Jared joined them.

Alec's hands squeezed Stephanie's shoulders, and he leaned down to whisper. "You are an amazing woman. And I love you *so* much."

* * * * *